A journalist by profession, **Douglas Jackson** _____ rmed a lifelong fascination for R_____ _____ his first two highly prais_____ _____ _gula_ and _Claudius_. His thi_____ _____ _____ ced readers to his new seri_____ _____ Six more novels recounting _____ _____ _____ ned and dedicated servant _____ _____owed, earning critical acclaim and confirming Douglas as one of the UK's foremost historical novelists. Writing as James Douglas, he is also the author of four successful adventure thrillers. An active member of the Historical Writers' Association and the Historical Novel Society, Douglas Jackson lives near Stirling. To find out more, visit www.douglas-jackson.net

Praise for the Gaius Valerius Verrens novels:

'As exciting as an action movie . . . if you have not read this series then please do so, start at book one and enjoy the ride'
PARMENION BOOKS

'Douglas Jackson brings history to life in a compelling way'
DAILY EXPRESS

'_Saviour of Rome_ is such a fine addition to the series . . . Jackson writes beautifully and this is on full show here . . . this is one of my very favourite series of novels, regardless of genre'
FOR WINTER NIGHTS

'Splendid . . . a vivid recreation of a long-dead world'
ALLAN MASSIE

'Brings a visceral realism to Rome'
DAILY MAIL

Also by Douglas Jackson

CALIGULA
CLAUDIUS
HERO OF ROME
DEFENDER OF ROME
AVENGER OF ROME
SWORD OF ROME
ENEMY OF ROME
SCOURGE OF ROME

and published by Corgi Books

SAVIOUR OF ROME

Douglas Jackson

CORGI BOOKS

TRANSWORLD PUBLISHERS
61–63 Uxbridge Road, London W5 5SA
www.penguin.co.uk

Transworld is part of the Penguin Random House group of companies
whose addresses can be found at global.penguinrandomhouse.com

Penguin
Random House
UK

First published in Great Britain in 2016 by Bantam Press
an imprint of Transworld Publishers
Corgi edition published 2017

A CIP catalogue record for this book
is available from the British Library.

ISBN
9780552172288

Typeset in 11/13pt Sabon by Falcon Oast Graphic Art Ltd.
Printed and bound by Clays Ltd, Bungay, Suffolk.

Penguin Random House is committed to a sustainable
future for our business, our readers and our planet. This book
is made from Forest Stewardship Council® certified paper.

MIX
Paper from
responsible sources
FSC® C018179

1 3 5 7 9 10 8 6 4 2

For my friends Elaine and John, the driving forces behind The Daily Mile, which is helping transform the health of Britain's schoolchildren

HISPANIA – ROMAN SPAIN
1ST CENTURY AD

Mare Cantabricum

Pyrenaei Montes

Lucus Augusta

Legio

Red Hill Mines

Asturica Augusta

Iberus

Emporiae

Caesaraugusta

Durius

Barcino

Tarraco

Tagus

Toletum

Saguntum

Mare Balearicum

Anas

Olisipo

Emerita Augusta

Corduba

Carthago Nova

Hispalis

Mare Hibericum

Fretum Gaditunum

N

0 — miles — 200

0 — km — 200

Some are of the opinion that he was driven to his rapacious proceedings by the extreme poverty of the treasury and exchequer.

Gaius Suetonius on Vespasian
(*Lives of the Twelve Caesars*)

I

Northern Hispania, AD72

He lay in a shallow depression overlooking the dusty valley. The relentless Iberian sun beat down fit to melt the jagged rocks beneath him and the top of his skull burned like glowing coals despite the cloth scarf covering his face and head. Only the pitiless predator's eyes remained visible to strike fear in anyone who looked upon them. He'd been stalking the convoy all this long, hot day, but it was only in the last few minutes that he finalized his plan of attack. He went over it once more in his mind before squirming backwards to where the others crouched, invisible behind the brow of the hill.

'They have to cross the river at the old ford below Vulture Cliff.' He drew a rough map in the sand with the point of his dagger and the ten men leaned close to catch his whispered words. 'That's where you'll stop them.'

'How?' A throaty growl from a heavily bearded man with brick red features and eyes turned to mere slits by years of squinting into the Asturian sun. 'There are thirty of the hook-noses guarding the wagons.'

1

The leader produced a grunt of irritation behind the cloth mask. Always it must be Buntalos with the unnecessary question. The hook-noses were a mixed squadron of Parthian auxiliaries from the wing based at Legio, and Buntalos was right, there were too many of them for a direct attack. One or two of the others darted a nervous glance at their comrade. They'd learned early it was unwise to risk the anger of the man who led them.

'You do what we discussed last night.' He let them hear his irritation. 'Show yourselves among the rocks. Change positions to make them think your numbers are greater. They'll be keen to reach the fort before nightfall, but the ford is rocky and the escort won't risk an all-out charge against a well-positioned enemy. If they probe you, show them how good you are with a sling shot. That should hold them for long enough.'

'And you, Nathair?' This time it was young Sigilo and the leader allowed himself a hidden smile. It still sounded odd to hear the name in his own tongue rather than Latin.

Serpentius.

The Snake.

'If you hold their attention I will do what must be done.'

His companions nodded solemnly, even Buntalos, who, for all his truculence, was a steady hand with a blade and a deadly slinger. A potter by trade, a bandit when it suited him. Serpentius had saved his life when the village where they'd wintered had turned out to fend off marauding wolves during a blizzard. Buntalos had followed him like a sheepdog ever since. The others were experienced night raiders who'd lifted sheep and goats from the villages in the lower valleys or snatched sacks of grain from a storehouse serving one of the Roman mines. Such raids were a rite of passage among the hill tribes and a link to the old ways. In the years before Serpentius returned to his homeland they'd become ever bolder as Hispania's garrison troops were sucked into the civil war that had come close to tearing the Empire apart. Thankfully, the days of great retaliatory sweeps by thousands of merciless legionaries were long past, though the district procurator might send out a squadron or two of auxiliaries on a training exercise that doubled as a punitive expedition.

This raid would be different.

Serpentius watched his men trot off down a gully that would lead them to the river crossing. They wore home-spun tunics and head cloths that matched the dusty mountain terrain and within moments they'd merged into the landscape. Buntalos and the others knew these hills as well as they knew the rocky fields and scrubby gardens of their home villages. They'd reach their destin-ation well ahead of the heavy wagons and their mixed escort of auxiliary cavalry and infantry. The escort commander might send a small patrol to check the cross-ing, but Serpentius had faith in his men's ability to stay out of sight. Any Asturian who retained a semblance of independence had years of experience avoiding patrols sent to comb the mountains for labour to work endless hours in the mines or smelting workshops.

He crawled back to the lip of the bowl and squeezed into a narrow gap between two large boulders. From this vantage point he could watch the road with-out exposing his silhouette on the skyline. Below, ten covered wagons lumbered into sight, each pulled by a team of four bullocks and guided by a driver walk-ing at the shoulder of the lead beast. Serpentius turned his attention to the mounted escort, a dozen cavalry troopers from the wing at Legio. They rode with shoulders slumped and heads down, evidence of the boredom and frustration at having to match the slow pace of the carts. Ten of the Parthian cavalry rode in front of the wagons, with two acting as a rearguard. He counted another eighteen infantry trudging nine to each side of the line of carts and no doubt sick of eating the dust kicked up by the horses and the iron-shod wagon wheels. They'd be tired after the long march from the Red Hills mines, but they looked alert enough.

He felt an instant, visceral loathing for the men in the pot helmets and chain-mail vests. Hired killers whose first thought was for plunder and rapine, they served Rome in return for a pension and a brass diploma that listed their service. On that final day the diploma would proclaim them a citizen of an Empire that placed a tax on anything born of nature, and much that wasn't. A soldier would have applauded their dispositions: flexible enough to react to attack from any quarter, infantry providing close protection and cavalry able to respond quickly to the slightest threat. Serpentius would have preferred something a little more inviting, but given the importance of the cargo the precautions hardly came as a surprise. In fact, security was a little lighter than he'd expected, which raised certain possibilities. He scrutinized the line of wagons again because those possibilities were both positive and negative, but they could only be tested by close inspection.

When the rearguard disappeared from sight he counted to a hundred before slipping over the crest and down the boulder-strewn slope. He moved with animal stealth by long-honed instinct from one piece of cover to the next. In the past he wouldn't have noticed

4

the exertions of the day, but a pounding head and the dull ache in his lower back were a reminder of the wounds he'd suffered in Rome and Jerusalem. The *medicus* said the injuries would never fully heal, but they'd affected Serpentius more than he'd expected. His feet were less sure than of old and his breathing more ragged, causing an occasional dagger of pain in his chest. Some of the edge that had made him one of the most feared men in Rome was lost for ever. He could only pray that was all he'd lost.

He smiled. Despite the doubts, Serpentius understood the aura of threat he carried with him. Loss, suffering and the scars of war had given him a face that promised pain and death. Fifteen years a slave and a gladiator had honed his wiry frame into a lightning quick, whip-thin weapon of muscle and sinew. His speed and endurance, and the skills he'd acquired to keep him alive in the most dangerous place on earth, turned him into a killing machine. He'd lost count of the opponents who'd died beneath his sword. The men he led believed him an invincible combination of the stealthy mountain lynx that threatened their flocks and the savage desert leopard, of which they'd only heard fireside tales. The gladiator tricks he'd taught these slow farm boys and pot makers gave them the swagger of warriors among their tribes and clans. They were proud men, brave and eager for the fight. Yet courage couldn't hide the reality that in combat with the auxiliaries they'd last only as long as it took their enemy to decide between the throat and the heart.

That vulnerability was the reason he'd ordered them to stay on the far side of the river and avoid contact. Their presence was a ruse designed to provide Serpentius with an opportunity, nothing more. He didn't want anyone killed, on either side. In truth he'd been reluctant to use them at all. But his friend needed his help and there was no other way.

Serpentius reached the plain, but deliberately kept well back from the convoy, ready to drop into the skimpy cover of the dried grass and scrubby bushes that carpeted the valley bottom. Concealment became more difficult as he advanced and the valley narrowed. He slowed as the ford came into sight in the distance. The river here suited his purposes almost perfectly: not too shallow, fast flowing even in summer, fed by a thousand cool streams that tumbled from the rugged, cloud-wreathed mountains to the north.

With the convoy in view he had no choice but to go to ground. He dropped to his belly and crawled forward until he could see two clearly agitated horsemen peering past the last wagon in the direction of the river. The faint sound of shouted orders reached him, but there was no evidence yet of panic. It made sense for the infantry to remain in position while the cavalry vanguard assessed the strength of the force contesting their river crossing.

He knew what would be going through the escort commander's mind. Was the threat only to his front, or was there a greater force ready to fall from the heights on to his flanks and rear? Until he was certain of the answer the infantry would stay by the wagons searching the ground around them for signs of bandits. Serpentius created a shallow nest in the dry earth and waited with tiny black ants crawling over his body and the scent of thyme in his nostrils. He pulled a scrap of stale bread from the pouch at his belt and chewed at it to extract what nourishment he could. When the sun had moved a certain distance across the great blue bowl above he risked another glance through the bushes. One of the cavalry rearguard had ridden off towards the head of the column, accompanied by half the infantry. Gambling that their advance would attract the focus of their comrades, he slithered towards the rearmost wagon in a smooth, undulating crawl that would have graced his serpentine namesake.

A whiff of rank sweat from one of the bullocks told him he was close enough for now. He burrowed into the prickly depths of a thick patch of gorse and waited. His plan, such as it was, could hardly be described as detailed. First, they had to stop the convoy at a moment and in a location where the escort commander would have no choice but to form a defensive perimeter for the night. Naturally, the man would send a messenger for reinforcements, and Serpentius heard a shouted conversation and a clatter of hooves on the road that confirmed he'd just done so. Had he been inclined, the Spaniard could very easily have ambushed the courier further up the trail, but why take the risk when the closest available troops were several hours away? Now it was just a matter of waiting for an opportunity.

A few hundred paces distant his Asturians would be making occasional appearances among the rocks and keeping the auxiliaries' attention with insults and threats. The first attempts would already have been made to shift them, but the threat of a lead slingshot hurled with enough force to take out an eye and pierce the brain would make even the bravest man pause. More infantry, advancing behind their painted oval shields, would soon have swept the bandits clear, but Serpentius guessed the auxiliary commander wouldn't risk leaving the convoy entirely undefended. It meant he'd be unable to put together a sufficient force to make a decisive sortie into the jumble of boulders and gorse guarding the far

7

side of the ford. Like Serpentius he would wait, hoping the bandits would see the futility of their position and withdraw. In the meantime the Spaniard could only pray the remaining guards would relax their vigilance long enough to give him his chance. This type of thing would have been much easier in the night, which was his natural element. But he couldn't do what must be done in the dark.

The faintest of movements drew his gaze to the left and he froze. What he'd seen was a flickering tongue hidden in the shadows at the base of the gorse bush. Behind it dangerous bronze eyes with elliptical pupils gazed from a triangular head attached to a sinuous body the length of a *gladius* blade. The upturned snub nose and striped pattern on its scales told him it was an asp, the most venomous of all Hispania's vipers, and the coiled defensive posture that it didn't appreciate sharing its shady resting place. With infinite care Serpentius drew his right hand across his body, extended his forefinger and moved it right to left in a gentle arc. The motion attracted the snake and its head followed the waving finger, retreating as it prepared to strike. Serpentius's left hand whipped round to take it behind the head before it had the chance. As the twisting body coiled round his wrist and the snake fought to sink its fangs into his flesh he rolled on his back, drew his dagger with his right hand and sliced the head from the body.

Hardly had he thrown the decapitated snake aside before a clamour of activity broke out somewhere close to the head of the convoy. He peered between the gorse stems in time to see the remaining rearguard mount his horse and ride towards the ford. At the same time, the two Parthian footsoldiers within his arc of vision looked at each other, scanned their surroundings one last time and jogged off in the wake of the trooper.

The driver of the rear cart watched them go, all his attention on what was happening further ahead. With a silent curse Serpentius realized his men had somehow overstepped themselves. Perhaps Buntalos, always keen to prove his courage, had made a feint charge too far into the ford and his comrades had been drawn after him. All it would take was the slightest miscalculation and the cavalrymen would be on them like hawks, with the infantry quick to join the bloodletting. A piercing scream confirmed his suspicions. No time for pity, even if he'd felt any. Their stupidity and their sacrifice had given him his opportunity. He slid through the scrub towards the rear wagon, one eye always on the back of the driver, who'd moved away from his charges to find a better view of the slaughter. A moment later he was hidden from potential discovery by the leather awning of the cart. He swung himself nimbly over the gate and into the bed of the wagon.

Serpentius had never been a man to show his emotions, but he felt a thrill of excitement as he recognized the vehicle's contents. Four heavily built wooden chests stacked in the centre of the floor exactly as he'd been told, each fastened with an iron lock. The locks were sealed by red wax imprinted with the mark of the procurator. The Spaniard had no time for finesse. He knew that whoever his friend sought would quickly work out the purpose of the ambush.

A sweep of the blade sliced away the seal of the nearest chest to reveal the keyhole. From the pouch on his belt he retrieved a pointed piece of iron the length of his forefinger and narrow enough to fit into the lock. The fastening was sturdily made, but crude; familiar from the many hours he'd spent working on an identical

9

model supplied by his friend in Asturica. He forced the iron rod into the keyhole and began to exert pressure in a certain way that would spring the mechanism. In practice he'd taken mere moments, but now his fingers felt uncharacteristically leaden. He was conscious of every passing second. His ears strained for evidence of the escort's return. By now they'd have dealt with the ambushers and soon their suspicions would be aroused by the pitiful numbers who'd faced them. He took a deep breath and steadied himself. With a loud snap the lock opened. He lifted the lid and pulled back the linen cloth covering the contents.

'You were right,' he whispered to himself. He picked up one of the dull grey metal bars stacked inside and weighed it in his hand before returning it to its place. It took only moments to open a second chest, with similar results. Satisfied with what he'd discovered, he crawled across the remaining chests and looked past the edge of the leather wagon cover. He'd been informed the second to last wagon was also suspect and he'd planned to inspect the contents if he could. One look told him it was impossible. The driver was back at the head of his bullock with his stick raised ready to encourage the beast into movement.

Enough. Serpentius crept to the rear of the cart, slipped over the sill and wriggled through the grass towards the nearest patch of scrub.

He was halfway when he heard the shout and the thunder of hooves in the distance. The trooper had been returning to his rearguard position when he thought he'd caught a fleeting glimpse of something moving amongst the tussocks. Now the something became a man who rose to his feet and sprinted for the much-too-distant slope. The cavalryman, a bearded veteran, grinned and hefted the seven-foot spear in his right hand, already anticipating the kill. He'd been denied the opportunity of skewering one of the bandits who'd ventured too far into the river to taunt his comrades, but this one was as good as dead. He directed the leaf-shaped iron point at the centre of the cloth-covered back and kicked his mount into an easy canter.

Serpentius glanced over his shoulder and gauged his lead over the approaching trooper. He knew he had no chance of reaching the slope, but he wanted to put as much distance between himself and the man's comrades as possible. The Spaniard felt no fear, quite the opposite. In combat he'd always found an icy calm that channelled what other men called fear into a potent mix of speed and agility. The attribute had kept him alive against men who thought they were quicker and better. He'd already noted the way the auxiliary handled his spear and the fact he was in no hurry, which spoke of an expert cavalryman. He could almost read the man's mind: an easy kill, simpler by far than spearing a hare on the run or a wild boar. But Serpentius had faced mounted killers many times and the trooper's experience only made him predictable. Certain elements of the strike would be ingrained on his soul. Without warning the Spaniard changed his angle so he appeared to be running diagonally for the safety of the slope. He heard a triumphant shout as the cavalryman altered course to follow him.

The more opponents Serpentius faced in the arena, the clearer it became to him that survival was more than a combination of physical attributes and mental awareness. He couldn't fully explain it, but the most successful gladiators were those who found a way to block the emotions dictating their actions. Fear, anger or enthusiasm had no place on the bloody sands of an amphitheatre. More dangerous by far was an ice-cold detachment that took a man beyond emotion and handed control to some inner sense. He remembered the superstitious awe in the eyes of the Thracian who tried to describe it. 'It takes a special kind of courage to give yourself up to something so ethereal and allow a power beyond understanding to rule heart and mind and body, but if you can find it you may live. You have everything else, but if you don't take that final step you'll eventually meet a man who has.' His finger had sliced across his throat in a gesture that had sent a shiver of dread through the young Serpentius. A few months later the Thracian won his *rudis*, the wooden sword that proclaimed his freedom, but he was dead within a year, stabbed in the back over some trivial gambling debt.

Now Serpentius drew back the scarf covering his face and sought the inner tranquillity that was the prelude to the cold place. His mind tuned itself to the rhythm of his feet across the dusty earth, the thunder of hooves in his ears, and the warmth of the air across his cheeks. Gradually all disappeared and he became nothing but a shadow, aware, but not part, of the world around him. In his mind he saw the horseman closing, felt the excitement building as fingers tightened on the ash shaft of the spear. Closer still. He maintained his pace, choosing not to speed up even though it would have delayed the moment. A slight adjustment in the spearhead and he knew the exact place where it would strike. The horse's snorted breath was almost on his neck. Hardened muscles tensed for the thrust. The spear arm stiffened to take the impact. The shadow was falling. No, not falling, diving. Into a tight forward roll that took Serpentius below the spear point. A somersault that brought him back to his feet so that within two strides he was at the astonished cavalry trooper's side. Two hands reached out, one high, one low, to grasp the spear shaft. The rider's grip instinctively tightened. Serpentius allowed himself to fall, his weight plunging the spearhead into the earth so the rider's own momentum catapulted him from the saddle to land on his shoulder with bone-crunching force. As the Parthian auxiliary lifted his head, gritting his teeth against the fiery pain in his left arm, the last thing he saw was the lanky whip-thin figure striding out by the cantering horse's flank before vaulting effortlessly into the saddle.

Serpentius abandoned his mount near a hill village west of Asturica Augusta and took to rocky mountain paths where he would leave no tracks for any pursuer. He reached the city long after nightfall, but he knew the man he sought would still be at work. The town watch had barred the great double gates and he didn't choose to draw the attention of the guards in the twin towers. Instead, he kept to the shadows beyond the city walls until he found the quadrant he was looking for. Asturica's walls had originally been built for defence, but now their main function was to control the passing of those doing business in the district capital. Yet for a man with friends there were always ways to circum- vent such obstacles. The small iron gate at the base of the stonework had once been used to access a well in the gully that ran below. The well had long dried up and the gate went out of use. Tonight, it would be open.

When Serpentius pulled at the heavy iron door he tensed for the scream of rusted metal, but he had nothing to fear. Meticulous to the last detail, someone had oiled the ancient hinges. He waited until a cloud obscured the full moon and slipped through the feet-thick wall into

13

an unlit street. A momentary hesitation to search his surroundings for any patrolling *vigiles* and he was on the move again.

The house was on the north side of the city, part of an impressive block in a wealthy area frequented by lawyers who did the majority of their business at the nearby basilica. Serpentius became ever more watchful as he reached the street. Two lamps marked the entrance and he studied it for a count of a hundred to make sure it wasn't under surveillance by anyone else. When he was certain he retraced his steps and darted into a stygian alley that flanked the side wall of the house. Without pausing he slipped across the wall with the help of a few handily positioned cracks in the masonry. His old friend had laughed at this excessive caution, but Serpentius reflected that it was obsession to detail that had kept him alive for so long. He crouched in the shadow of the wall for a few moments, noting that the shutters of one room were open a few inches allowing the dull glow of a small oil lamp to show. It was the signal that the man was alone and waiting to see him.

The Spaniard crossed the garden in a dozen strides and walked confidently through an open door and along the familiar painted corridor. He paused on the threshold. It was a big room, part bureaucratic headquarters and part dining room, with a half partition across the centre to divide the two functions. To his left the dining area lay in darkness, but shadows flickered on the walls of the office with its wooden niches filled with scrolls. It was only when he stepped inside and his nostrils picked up the familiar metallic tang that he knew he'd made a terrible mistake. He should have run, but his feet carried him forward of their own volition. The slumped figure lay across the broad table and he might have been asleep if it hadn't been for the great dark stain spread across the documents he'd been reading. Knowing it was pointless, Serpentius stepped forward and reached out for the shoulder of the man who'd been his friend.

A bulky figure in the uniform of a senior Roman officer stepped from the shadows accompanied by two soldiers. Serpentius could hear others pouring into the room behind him, but he didn't resist as rough hands gripped his arms.

'You are under arrest for the murder of a consular official and treason against the state.'

II

Rome

This was worse than the hour before battle. Gaius Valerius Verrens clenched his left fist to keep his hand from shaking as he waited for his bride to appear. A lavish cloth pavilion had been created for the ceremony at the villa his sister Olivia shared with the father of her child on the family estate at Fidenae. His own neighbouring villa, on land Valerius had been granted by the Emperor Vespasian for his heroics during the campaign to take Jerusalem, lay unfinished despite the efforts of dozens of tradesmen he'd hired to complete the work in time for the ceremony. He looked up to the unblemished eggshell blue of a perfect summer sky. The movement must have been accompanied by a soft groan, because the man behind him laughed.

'Patience,' counselled Titus Flavius Vespasian, resplendent in his consular robes. The son of the Emperor and heir to the purple would be one of ten guests to twitness the wedding rites. 'Anyone would think you were waiting to climb a siege ladder with the arrows whistling round your ears.'

'Perhaps I'd rather be?' Valerius answered wryly.

'Don't be a fool, Valerius,' Titus hissed. 'Thank Fortuna for the day you met Tabitha.' The words were accompanied by a smile, but a certain edge to his voice told Valerius he had picked at an old wound. Clearly he'd reminded his friend of his former lover Berenice of Cilicia – Queen Berenice. The Emperor had insisted Titus relinquish the beautiful Cilician ruler as part of the agreement to make him heir. Berenice, acutely attuned to the ways of great courts, had taken the decision with dignity, but it had left Titus scarred, and the quarrel with his father was still fresh in his memory.

'I . . .' Before he could apologize, Valerius's attention was drawn by the gasps of the servants and slaves who craned their necks from every vantage point.

He followed their gaze as a slim, veiled figure took her place on the villa steps with his sister at her side. A princess of the Syrian state of Emesa, Tabitha had been on a clandestine mission for Queen Berenice when Valerius saved her from a band of Judaean assassins. Together they'd fought their way into Jerusalem as Titus's soldiers took their bloody revenge for the long and frustrating siege of the city. They'd also become lovers, and when Valerius returned to Rome it only seemed natural Tabitha should accompany him.

She should have been dressed by her mother, but since that lady had died years before, the task was undertaken by Olivia. The *tunica recta* Tabitha had worn the previous night was fastened in place with a band of silken wool tied in the Knot of Hercules that only her new husband was privileged to unpick. Tabitha's long dark hair had been divided into six strands and plaited with bright ribbons. Over it was placed the flame-coloured veil, the *flammeum*, that masked her beauty and identified her as a bride. Valerius sensed Tabitha's eyes on him through the thin cloth of the veil and he shivered in anticipation. A fine fat sheep with brightly coloured ribbons tied in its wool was led, bleating piteously, to an adjacent part of the precinct where the priest waited. They watched as the *victimarius* cut its throat and opened it so the priest could study the entrails. A worried murmur went up from the slaves as he consulted the glistening coils and steaming organs for what seemed an inordinately long time. Valerius caught Olivia's eye and saw a hint of amusement on her lips. She knew her brother well enough to be sure he'd arranged the proper outcome.

The priest rose from his inspection shaking his head in amazement at what he'd discovered. 'I have never seen such an auspicious day,' he announced to an enormous cheer. 'The name Verrens will live long in the annals of the Empire.'

Valerius felt a nudge and Titus whispered, 'Nicely done, brother, I couldn't have arranged it better myself. By the way, my father asks you to attend an audience. Noon in three days.'

Valerius stiffened. It could be anything. Vespasian had let it be known he valued his opinion, but in Valerius's experience any visit to the Palatine, where the Emperor had taken up residence in preference to Nero's more ostentatious Golden House, contained an element of risk.

But he couldn't think about that now. This was the moment. He took a deep breath and tried to swallow, but his throat was as dry as a Parthian salt pan. He should be blissfully happy; instead his mind was a turmoil of contradictions. Apart from occasional fleeting relationships he'd been alone for so long he wasn't quite certain how to feel. What kind of husband would he make? Oh, he knew the ideal of the Roman husband. Stern and unyielding, the master of his house and all who dwelt in it. By marrying him, Tabitha became his property, to be taken or discarded at will. But he didn't feel like that. Most Roman men married for position, or power or wealth, not love. But Valerius and Tabitha's love had been forged in the heat of the Syrian desert and the flames of the Great Temple of Jerusalem. Just the sight of her made his heart swell to fill his chest. He felt sure it was a real love. A lasting love. And Tabitha was not the usual subservient Roman bride. She was a princess of Emesa. A follower of the Judaean faith who had agreed to accept her husband's because her children would grow up, not just as Roman citizens, but of the patrician class.

Lupergos, Olivia's partner, had decorated the pavilion as a woodland bower with tree branches, blossoms and colourful tapestries. Now Olivia led Tabitha to Valerius's left side and he felt slim fingers entwine with his. There was a current fashion for longer ceremonies with various innovations, but together they'd decided they would marry in the old style, in a way Valerius's father would have approved. They spoke only the traditional words, and Valerius felt his heart thunder in his ears as Tabitha's nervous, husky voice whispered: '*Quando tu Gaius, ego Gaia.*' In as much as you are Gaius I am Gaia.

Valerius lifted the veil of the *flammeum* and, for the first time that day, looked into the enormous, sapphire blue eyes that had captivated him since the first moment they'd met.

'I love you,' he whispered. She smiled and her honeyed flesh seemed to glow, but a small tear rolled down her cheek. He lifted his fingers to brush it away, but before he could reach it Olivia took them both by the hand and led them to a fleece-covered stool to make the sacrifice to Jupiter. The traditional spelt cake tasted like ashes in Valerius's mouth and suddenly all he wanted was for the ceremony to be over. To be alone with Tabitha.

But first they must endure the feast, a lavish affair because it was expected and Valerius was now a rich man. The cellars of the Great Temple of Jerusalem had proved to be filled with gold, and even a Judaean merchant's most innovative hiding place was no proof against a legionary with the scent of treasure in his nostrils and a crowbar in his hand. The line of wagons carrying plunder from the city had stretched to the far horizon. Thanks to Titus, Valerius's service merited a senior tribune's share, enough, and more, to allow him to take his seat in the Senate. Vespasian's gift of half the neighbouring estate that had previously belonged to the philosopher Seneca doubled the family holdings. Only two years earlier Valerius had been a penniless exile wandering in the desert. Now he sat at a table set with gold, an Imperial favourite and a valued counsellor with the resources to live a life of ease if he chose.

Tabitha sat demurely by his side as a stream of richly clad men approached to offer their congratulations, but he knew that, like him, she was thinking of what was to come. They'd lived together in a town house on the Esquiline since returning from Jerusalem, but Olivia insisted they spend the last month apart and to his surprise Tabitha had readily agreed. She moved in with his sister at Fidenae while Valerius spent the longest month of his life poring over the estate accounts or working on the occasional legal case to keep him from dying of boredom. The men who stooped to whisper their regards were Valerius's clients: merchants, lawyers and ambitious minor politicians. Valerius was their patron, just as he was client to Titus. They expected him to use his influence to help them advance, and they in turn were obliged to provide support when he requested it. As the familiar faces passed by, Valerius sipped his wine and ate a little of the sumptuous food, always conscious of Tabitha's presence.

After the dinner came the ordeal of the wedding procession through the dusk to Valerius's new villa, two miles to the north, where rooms had been prepared. They were accompanied by a small army of slaves and servants who shouted ribald and often lewd comments about the groom's romantic prowess and the bride's fertility. The singing was loud, out of tune and boisterous, and more than one guest or couple went missing in the dark on the way. Still, the proper rites were performed: the placing of one of three coins with the god of the crossroads, the next handed to the groom by Titus as a token of Tabitha's dowry, and the third retained for the god of the house. At one point Olivia appeared from the darkness at Valerius's side.

'You are fortunate among men, brother, to have made such a match,' she whispered. 'I was not certain at first when you returned from the east with your exotic mistress. If I had thought you would listen I would have advised you to keep her that way and find yourself a Roman maiden of status.'

'And now?' He kept his voice equally low with Tabitha on his opposite side talking with a servant's awestruck daughter about her faraway homeland.

'Now I have come to know Tabitha and see her true worth.' Olivia locked eyes with her brother. 'In many ways she is a remarkable woman, clever, well read and insightful. Without fear, or she would not have given up everything she knows to follow you to what, for her, is an alien place. She loves you, but does not worship you. She is strong where it matters, in her heart, which you will discover if you ever stray from the path of right and justice. She will bring you joy and she will test you. She is the right woman for you, Gaius Valerius Verrens. We have become friends.'

He smiled at his sister. 'I hoped you would.'

Valerius felt Tabitha's touch on his arm and Olivia faded back into the crowd. And then they were alone. The rituals complete. The sound of the guests quietly fading, but for the occasional cry of passion or protest. The servants silent. It seemed unnatural at first. They had spent so much time at the centre of a whirlpool of ceremonies and celebrations it was difficult to believe they were together at last.

Tabitha looked slowly around the room, the walls lit by a dozen flickering oil lamps. They'd discussed the decoration together, but this was the first time Tabitha had seen the results. The painter had turned the wall plaster into a series of framed panoramas so it appeared the occupants were looking out from a window across open country. One of them showed a desert scene, so Tabitha would always have a connection to her homeland. Another, a mountain vista that reminded Valerius of a journey he'd once made with Serpentius through the high Alps. There were fields and forests and beaches so lifelike you wondered why the birds and animals didn't move.

She came to him and laid her head on his shoulder. When they were close it always amazed him how someone who could dominate a room with her beauty and the force of her personality could be so small and vulnerable. The warmth of her body seemed to seep into

22

him and he allowed himself to relax for the first time since the ceremony.

'Come,' he said, leading her towards the bed in the centre of the room.

She took her place on the coverlet and studied him with a look of enquiry that transformed into a smile of pure mischief. 'Is this when I am supposed to struggle and squeal as if I am afraid of the terrible thing that is about to happen to me?'

Valerius laughed. 'Is that what Olivia told you?'

'She said that is what a virtuous Roman maiden would do, even if she was not so virtuous.'

'But you are not a Roman maiden.'

'Or virtuous. So . . .' she looked significantly at the Knot of Hercules at her waist.

The silken loops seemed to fall away beneath his fingers. When it was undone he moved to join her on the bed, but she slipped over the edge and stood facing him with her head at the height of his chin. When she looked up, the reflection of the oil lamps in her eyes made them seem as if they were filled with fire.

'An Emesan maiden would dance for you, and her dress would be made up of veils which she would remove one by one, revealing a little more of herself each time.' Her voice was husky with passion and Valerius felt as if there was a stone in his throat. 'But since I am a Roman wife I am at my husband's command. Ask what you will of me.'

Valerius felt a sudden wave of desire and he had to resist the urge to carry her back to the bed and . . . 'Remove your *stola*.'

She did as he ordered, but very slowly, her fingers plucking nervously at the cotton as she unwound it from her body.

'Now your dress.'

Tabitha unfastened the brooches at her shoulders and allowed the dress to fall away, her eyes never leaving his. Beneath she wore a translucent white shift that clung to her body and hinted at the tantalizing swellings and hollows beneath.

'All.' He almost choked on the word. 'I want to see it all.'

Her hands reached for the bottom of the shift.

Everything they did and everything they felt was as new and fresh as the first time, but with an intensity neither had experienced before. A lifetime on earth is but an hour in Elysium. Valerius had no idea how long they spent there, only that when he woke it was daylight and the world seemed a brighter, better place and a new Gaius Valerius Verrens had taken his place in it. He had never felt so alive. It wouldn't have surprised him to pull back the sheet and find he had a right hand.

He smiled and lay back and a beautiful nymph's face appeared above his. 'You look very pleased with yourself?'

'A certain lady gave me reason to believe I have every right.'

She slipped on top of him, so he could feel the firmness of her breasts against his chest, and something interesting was happening lower down.

'I wish it could be like this for ever.'

He was about to say it could be, then he remembered the summons from the Emperor.

'He will take you away from me,' Tabitha sighed when he told her.

'It could be anything. Perhaps he wants to give me a position at court?'

'No.' She seemed certain. 'I saw it in Emesa and with

Queen Berenice. To the Emperor a man like you is a weapon, one to be used sparingly and only in time of dire need, but a weapon all the same. Any new honour would come through Titus. If the Emperor has sent for you it is to send you into danger.' She raised her head and kissed him full on the lips. 'We must make use of what time we have.'

Much later he heard a whisper.

'Promise me one thing, Valerius.'

'If it is in my power.'

'Come back to me.'

III

Valerius felt dwarfed by the enormous marble-clad buildings that towered over him like cliffs as he climbed the gentle slope of the Victory Road on the north flank of the Palatine Hill. His mood was wary, but approaching the seat of the Empire's most powerful man held no terrors for him. He'd first walked this path almost ten years before, at the Emperor Nero's bidding, resigned to what seemed certain death. In the years since, he'd gained honourable scars and grey hairs in three wars, been duped, betrayed and dishonoured, lost friends and lovers, but finally, he hoped, found peace.

He'd changed and so had his city.

When he looked out over the Forum towards the Esquiline Hill, the sea of red-tiled roofs was pocked with gaping blackened holes, the ongoing legacy of the great fire of eight years earlier. The owners of the burned-out buildings were either dead or didn't have the resources to rebuild their holdings. To his right lay the great Golden House villa complex Nero had built on the charred remains of an entire district, and the lake where he had staged grandiose naval engagements in which ship-borne gladiators fought to the death. To his left, the Capitoline and the reborn Temple of Jupiter, greatest and best, the vast structure at last close to completion after two years of work. Valerius had played his own, unwitting, part in the destruction of the temple and he had an irrational sense that its resurrection went hand in hand with his own recovery after the horrors of Jerusalem. The project had been the first act of Vespasian's reign, funded by the *fiscus judaicus*, a tax on Jewish males across the Empire who were continuing to pay for the failed rebellion in their homeland.

He announced himself to the black-clad gate guards. Once they'd satisfied themselves he was on the list of visitors, they passed him through into the gardens of what had originally been the palace of Tiberius. Here he was met by the Emperor's secretary, Junius Mauricus, an ambitious young man who greeted him with the coolness of one who resented Valerius's ease of access to his master. Valerius responded amiably enough. No point in making an enemy of an official whose freedman predecessor was now a member of the Senate. Mauricus led him along the familiar marble corridors with their alcoves filled with busts of Vespasian's predecessors. Nero was there, and Claudius, alongside Augustus, Tiberius and Caligula, but Valerius noted that neither Galba nor Otho nor Vitellius had been given space. Their absence puzzled him, because Vespasian had never struck him as a vengeful or vindictive man. The Emperor had offered Vitellius his life if he laid down the purple, even though the former governor of Germania was as responsible as any man for the civil war that had come so close to bringing down the Empire. The memory of the corpulent emperor who had been his friend reminded Valerius of the probability that Vespasian had summoned him to be ordered on some clandestine mission that would take him into danger again.

He knew he could refuse. Titus had hinted as much when they'd inspected the part-built villa north of Fidenae. 'You deserve all this and more, Valerius, for the service you have done the Empire and my family, never forget that.'

But without Vespasian's support would the Senate have endorsed Valerius's senior military tribune's share of the vast spoils of Jerusalem where he had served Titus in an entirely unofficial capacity? Neither could Valerius forget it had been the Emperor who had reinstated his award of the Gold Crown of Valour, the honour bestowed by Nero. Valerius had always thought of the Corona Aurea as a gaudy bauble, but he'd been strangely moved when Domitian, Vespasian's younger son, had ordered it taken from him. Domitian had been jealous of Valerius's relationship with Domitia Longina Corbulo and falsely accused him of charges of treason that had left him facing a death sentence. Only Domitia's intervention had saved his life, but that intervention had lost her to him for ever.

Would it be Syria, Parthia or the Danuvius frontier, all areas where he had previously fought and survived? Germania was another festering sore, still volatile in the aftermath of the Batavian revolt that had seen two legions wiped out and another four humiliated. Sporadic outbursts of rebellion meant eight legions had to be stationed there that could have been of greater use elsewhere.

'This way.' Mauricus led him through double doors into the familiar receiving room, with its raised golden throne and the great marble statue of Laocoon and his sons. The last time Valerius had been in this room, the then Emperor Galba had ordered him on a mission to negotiate peace with Aulus Vitellius. Before he could set out, the Praetorian Guard had butchered Galba and it was in his successor Marcus Salvius Otho's name that Valerius eventually rode north.

Vespasian could have no illusions about how precarious his seat on that golden throne might be. Yes, he had the support of the eastern legions, and the army Vitellius had led from Germania had been vanquished, but he still had to win over the vast majority. The Emperor had appointed Titus prefect of the Praetorian Guard, and replaced its cohorts of legionaries from Germania loyal to Vitellius with his own men. Yet there were many in the Senate with long memories and fine bloodlines who resented the rise of a man they called the Muleteer: Vespasian having been forced to sell those animals in a period of financial distress.

'Gaius Valerius Verrens, Caesar.' Mauricus announced him in a strong voice that echoed from the bare walls.

The throne was empty and it took a moment before Valerius realized the Emperor was standing over a table close to the balcony that overlooked the Forum. A wooden model of central Rome covered the table top. Valerius had seen it once before, when Nero had outlined his plan to build his great Golden House on the ashes of thousands of houses in the Third and Fourth districts. The normal, unadorned toga Vespasian wore and his lack of regalia told Valerius this was to be an informal audience.

'Ah, Verrens. A welcome face in a day that has not been filled with them.'

'Caesar,' Valerius bowed. Vespasian would be in his sixty-third year; stout, balding and more careworn than Valerius remembered, but still outwardly unaffected by his lofty status. He could be hard on those he considered fools, but he had been the same as a general. He could also be generous and forgiving to those he liked.

'Come,' the older man smiled. 'We do not stand on ceremony among friends. Mauricus? Send for my son.' The blue eyes twinkled. 'My *elder* son.' Vespasian was perfectly aware of the enmity between Valerius and his son Domitian. 'While we are waiting perhaps you would like to see this.' He beckoned Valerius over to the table. 'You recognize it?'

'Of course, Caesar.'

'Cities develop.' The Emperor nodded absently. 'Sometimes naturally, sometimes steered by the hand of man. My predecessor Nero, for instance, before the great fire, gave orders for any street requiring rebuilding to be created around an open square to combat just such a cataclysm. In that respect, at least, he left Rome the better for his reign. The Domus Aurea, however,' he picked up a substantial building in the centre of the model, 'I view differently. Some would say the scale matches its creator's vanity. It is not in my nature to criticize my predecessors. I will only say that, from an architectural point of view I find it out of proportion with its neighbours and I have plans for it, but first . . .' He replaced the building and picked up a sunken oblong that represented Nero's lake. He looked around with a puzzled frown. 'Now, what did I do with it? Yes, here it is.' Sitting on the balcony was what looked like a small upturned barrel on a similar oblong of wood, which he placed in the position previously occupied by the lake. 'There.' He studied Valerius with a smile. 'My gift to Rome.'

Valerius blinked. On closer inspection it was a model of an arena. An enormous amphitheatre that dwarfed everything in the city except the even vaster Circus Maximus.

'You think me a hypocrite, Verrens?'

'No, Caesar.' Valerius almost choked on the words. 'It's magnificent.'

'It will seat up to eighty thousand spectators. I fear there will be no great military advances during my reign, so I must give my people spectacle instead of victory. Of course, I may be dead by the time it's complete. Titus! I've just been showing Verrens how we're going to fill in Nero's boating lake.'

'Consul,' Valerius bowed as Titus entered the room by a hidden doorway.

'Have you told him how you're going to pay for it, Father?'

'I was just coming to that. Come, we will sit in the sunshine on the balcony. Bring wine,' he called to a slave hovering nearby. 'I find the sun eases my old bones.' He eased himself on to a padded couch beyond the window and Valerius and Titus joined him. 'How will we pay for it? I expect we will borrow. I've squeezed the Jews once to rebuild the Temple of Jupiter; I doubt even they can afford twice—'

Titus saw Valerius frown and interrupted his father's flow of words. 'You're wondering why we don't use the treasures of Jerusalem?'

'It would seem a possible solution,' Valerius agreed.

Titus grimaced as he remembered the aftermath of the siege: the great temple a tower of flame, the bittersweet scent of roasting flesh and the long lines of wagons filled with plunder. 'All that gold. I thought it limitless at the time. A thousand kings' ransoms . . .'

'But we've discovered that even a king's ransom doesn't go very far when it comes to running an empire,'

Vespasian resumed. 'I will be candid with you, Verrens: it turns out that this empire I have inherited is on the very brink of financial disaster. The treasury empty, officials white-faced and trembling with fear when I approach, and the mints tell us that the silver denarii issued by Nero during his tenure are considerably less silver than they should be. It means every denarius we do have is worth twenty per cent less than its face value.' He sipped his wine and sent a meaningful glance in the direction of the treasury in the Temple of Saturn on the far side of the Forum. 'Eventually I will be forced to raise taxes and squeeze the provinces, but that will make me unpopular. An emperor cannot afford to be unpopular so early in his reign, particularly a New Man whose father was a tax farmer. But the problem is not silver—'

'It's gold,' Titus intervened for a second time. 'And that is why we have asked you here. I'm afraid your Empire must ask one last service of you, Valerius.'

'Your Emperor,' his father corrected. 'The problem lies in the goldfields of Hispania Tarraconensis. During the late war, particularly after the death of Servius Sulpicius Galba, the legions of the province were riven by division over their loyalties, firstly between Vitellius and Otho, and later between Vitellius and myself.' The shrewd blue eyes held Valerius. 'I attach no blame. When Vitellius marched from Germania in such overwhelming force every man was forced to make a choice. At that time there was no certain outcome and no certain legitimacy.'

As a lawyer Valerius could have argued that this was semantics. Otho had been hailed Emperor by the Senate and people of Rome, but since Vespasian had been in the same position as Vitellius when his own legions marched on Italia it didn't seem politic to make the point.

32

'Even individual cohorts of the same legion were split over who to support,' the Emperor continued. 'With no guidance from Rome, and little more from Tarraco, individual unit commanders were forced to act on their own authority, with varying degrees of success. In the north, around Asturica Augusta, local tribespeople, who had long been thought to be fully Romanized, sensed this weakness and attacked our convoys and supply depots. The supply of gold dropped to a trickle, most of it from the mines around Carthago Nova in the south.'

'Naturally, the treasury officials were concerned,' Titus said. 'But they assumed the mines were operating as normal and storing the gold until it could be safely dispatched. They have been proved wrong. Although the supply has increased, it is still much less than it was before Galba left Spain, and much of the backlog is unaccounted for. We have had various excuses about lower yields, labour problems and continuing trouble from bandits.'

'With respect, sir,' Valerius addressed Vespasian. 'You have been Emperor for two years. Surely the legions are no longer divided? A proconsul with five thousand legionaries at his back should be able to get the mines working again and teach the natives a lesson.'

'That may well be true, young man, but there are no five thousand legionaries. At the end of the civil war the Batavian revolt was at its height and threatening to ignite the entire Empire. I was forced to assign the First Adiutrix and most of the Tenth and Sixth legions to join Petilius Cerialis on the Rhenus. I cannot release them until we are certain the entire area is pacified and the threat from east of the river extinguished. Our entire presence in Hispania consists of a few auxiliary units, a vexillation of the Sixth based at Legio in the north and another from the Tenth at Carthago Nova, and they are scattered across the country providing security.'

'My father replaced the proconsul with a man he trusts: Gaius Plinius Secundus.'

'Pliny?' Valerius frowned at the mention of the familiar name. Pliny was an old friend and fellow lawyer who had spoken for him at his trial for treason.

'Plinius Secundus must deal with his own problems in the south before he can venture to the northern goldfields,' Titus continued. 'In the meantime he has asked us to send him a special agent he can dispatch to Asturica Augusta. A man with a nose for trouble, subtle and versed in the ways of the law, but capable of wielding a sword at need. A lawyer and a soldier. In short, Valerius, you.'

'The Empire cannot function without gold,' the Emperor continued relentlessly, 'and our most prolific source is the goldfields of Hispania. I am appointing you *legatus iuridicus metallorum*, with a warrant giving you full powers to inspect all aspects of metalworking in northern Hispania. The decision will be yours, in discussion with the proconsul, of course, whether you use these powers overtly or covertly. Is something troubling you, Verrens?'

'My apologies, Caesar,' Valerius bowed; he'd barely been listening. 'I've just recalled that I have an old friend who had connections with Asturica.'

Titus laughed. 'Your Spanish wolf. The man I told you about, Father, the one who rescued me from the Judaean skinning knives.'

Vespasian gave him the look of a commander who believed generals should never allow themselves to end up within range of skinning knives, Judaean or otherwise.

34

'We left Serpentius with the *medicus* of the Twelfth,' Valerius said. 'When he recovered from his wounds he intended to take ship direct to Hispania. The generous bounty you provided would have purchased him a small estate. He talked of planting vines and olive trees, but it is difficult to imagine a wolf pushing a plough.'

'You have heard nothing from him?'

Valerius shook his head. 'For all I know he could be dead.'

IV

Serpentius clawed his way up through a dark pit of insensibility like a swimmer struggling towards the surface of a pitch black sea. Gradually it returned to him. The room with the scrolls. The spreading pool of darkness beneath his friend's bowed head. The triumphant, malignant faces. And finally the explosion of light he thought had ended it all. He opened his eyes and a soft whimper escaped him at the terrible finality of eternal night. He was blind.

'Quiet,' a voice hissed at his side. 'If they hear a sound they'll beat us all.'

The Spaniard drew in a ragged breath, the air thick as sludge and warm as blood. A wave of fear washed over him and he had to dig deep into his soul to rediscover the courage that had sustained him through the long years of slavery. *Remember who you are and who you have been. You are a man and a warrior. Whatever it requires you will endure. Whatever you must endure you will survive.* Gradually the panic faded. He turned in the direction of the voice and felt a familiar weight on his arms and legs. Heard the faint chink of metal on metal that sent a new chill of terror through him.

'Where am I?' he whispered to the blackness.

'In a deep mine under the mountain somewhere south of Baeduniense.'

'Mine?' Serpentius's reeling mind struggled with the reality even as he tested the iron chains that bound his wrists and ankles.

'Yes,' the voice choked on a sob. 'And you'd best get used to it, friend, because you're never going to see the light of day again. We are the Lost and they don't call us the Lost for nothing. Condemned to be worked to death in a place that is worse than Hades.'

'How can I work when I'm blind?'

'You're not blind.' A soft snort of bitter laughter. 'Though it would make no difference to them if you were. A blind man can carry his weight in ore the same as a sighted one. They douse the oil lamps at the end of the shift and don't light them again until they serve the slops at the start of the next one.'

Careful not to make any noise with the chains, Serpentius raised his hands and rubbed his eyes. He could see? Yes, there was definition in the blackness. In places less dense, and in others more so, as with the deep shadow that identified his unseen companion. Suddenly he understood exactly where he was. Trapped in a tiny wormhole in the earth with an entire mountain pressing down on him. He felt a moment of sheer, irrational panic, returned for a heartbeat to the slimy depths of the Conduit of Hezekiah beneath Jerusalem and the terror which had unmanned him in front of his friend Valerius. The scarred face of the one-handed Roman swam into his mind and he clung to the image like a drowning man until the new panic faded.

He took a deep breath. What would Valerius do? Valerius would bide his time. He'd watch and he'd wait, and once he'd watched long enough he'd make his plan. Then, when the time was right, he'd fight. And he'd win.

'Tell me everything,' he hissed to the man chained to him.

He was ready when the first oil lamp flared, burning its image into his eyes. The jailer passed down the line throwing each man a small chunk of stale bread and hesitating just long enough before each prisoner for him to dip it into the foul broth in the bucket he carried. Serpentius had forgotten how hungry he was, but even so his stomach rebelled at the bitter liquid.

When his eyes adjusted to the glare he was able to see his companions for the first time and the sight quailed his heart. The men crammed the sopping bread into their mouths with an animal ferocity as if it was the last they'd ever see. His closest companion was a skeleton in a ragged tunic, eyes sunk deep in a face filthy with dust and his flesh pocked with untreated sores. His bush of hair and unkempt beard were caked with grey dust, making it impossible to tell his age. Most of the others – there must have been twenty of them – were in a similar condition, but Serpentius recognized a few newcomers by the muscle on their bones. Not a man met his eye. Each was lost in the depths of his own suffering. Six months, his companion had said, was the most anyone lasted.

From his position in their midst Serpentius guessed they were in a side chamber of the main mine, entered by a narrow entrance at the head of the sloping floor. The two guards who accompanied the jailer were armed with spears cut down for ease of use in the confined space and they wore short swords at their belts.

A single chain connected the ankle shackles of the cowed prisoners and when the jailer reached the end of the line he unbolted it from a ring on the wall and hauled it clear. No order was given, but every man struggled painfully to his feet. One of the guards hovered close, ready for any sign of hesitation or rebellion in the new prisoner, but Serpentius was prepared thanks to his companion's warning. A few of the men were slowed by weakness or injury and the guard showed what Serpentius had avoided, lashing out mercilessly with the butt of his spear until the prisoners were formed in a ragged line. The guard pushed the man at the head of the line hard in the back so he staggered towards the entrance, followed by the man behind. The ankle shackles had just enough give for a man to take a full step, but they chafed with every movement. After three steps on the rough ground Serpentius felt the sting of the edge cutting into the skin on his ankle bone, and the warmth of blood trickling over his feet.

They filed through the entrance past a pile of picks and shovels heaped against the wall. Beyond lay a stack of waist-high cane baskets. Once again Serpentius silently thanked his anonymous informer as he hefted a short pick in his right fist. Those at the head of the line took a pick or shovel and once they were gone the others picked up the baskets. It was entirely arbitrary and depended on your place in the line at the end of the previous shift.

Someone thrust a lit oil lamp at Serpentius and he coughed as the noxious smoke swirled in front of his face. A brutal push in the back propelled him forward in the wake of the man ahead and he struggled to retain his balance. The tunnel was perhaps three paces wide and two high and a tall man like Serpentius had to walk at a crouch. They must have been in one of the upper parts of the mine because the floor sloped relentlessly downward. The atmosphere became steadily more breathless and the cloyingly thick air tasted of rotten egg. To one side a sealed leather pipe two handspans in breadth twitched every few seconds and Serpentius realized it must be some kind of ventilation system. No point in suffocating your slaves before you worked them to death.

But not everyone down here was a slave or a jailer. As they struggled along in their chains the prisoners were passed by a group of broad-shouldered men carrying heavy hammers. One of the hammer wielders barged into Serpentius as he passed, slamming him into the rock so the impact removed a patch of skin from his bare shoulder. The man glared at him with his single eye, the other a weeping pit of red. Serpentius ignored the challenge and concentrated on the next treacherous step. The flickering oil lamp revealed the tunnel had been carved from the solid rock; water seeped from the walls to form a slimy stream beneath his feet. Down and down they went until the air quality became so poor that the lamps began to sputter and threatened to go out.

At last they reached what must be the ore-bearing level. An overseer carrying a short whip examined each prisoner in turn and ordered them into side chambers in teams of three.

'You, new man,' he pointed to Serpentius. 'Down there.'

Down there was the lowest level. As Serpentius worked his way past the overseer the thongs of the whip lashed out to catch him on the shoulder and a lightning bolt of pain made him cry out. Every instinct urged him to retaliate. It would be so easy to twist the wrist chain around the overseer's neck and snap it. But that would get him killed and Serpentius wasn't ready to die yet. He looked round and met the man's gaze.

'That was just a taste of what's to come,' the overseer sneered. 'I've been told to pay special attention to you—' But the arrogance faded from his voice when he recognized the message in Serpentius's eyes. 'Get on with it.'

Down there meant a cramped chamber where the tepid, filthy water had pooled a foot deep. Their only consolation was that this was where one arm of the ventilation pipe ended and faint puffs of air made the torrid atmosphere just bearable. Serpentius shared the chamber with a hammer man, another pick wielder and a sickly looking prisoner carrying one of the cane baskets. The man with the pick placed his lamp in a notch in one of the walls and Serpentius followed suit. The hammer man rolled his shoulders and hefted the hammer in two hands, bringing the iron head around to smash into the solid rock. Once, twice, thrice, the clang of each strike echoing round the chamber.

He staggered back, allowing Serpentius and the other pick man to attack the fissures with their picks, chipping tiny pieces of stone that fell into the water at their feet, where the fourth man used a short iron shovel to transfer them to his basket. After only a few minutes sweat was pouring from Serpentius. He realized with a thrill of fear that within weeks, or even days, all the spare flesh would melt from him, and his strength with it. His throat was parched and he reached down to scoop up a handful of water, only for the hammer man to dash it from his hand.

'Fool.' He glanced towards the entrance. 'Whatever

you've done you don't deserve to die like that. It's deadly poison. Wait for the water carrier to come round.'

Serpentius nodded his thanks. After an hour the man with the shovel had filled his basket. He made a huge effort to get it on to his back and the leather straps over his shoulder, but eventually the big hammer man had to help him.

'He won't last the day,' he predicted after the man had struggled from the chamber, his knees threatening to buckle under the weight. They continued working hour after hour and eventually the hammer man was proved right. The man with the basket left, but when the basket returned another prisoner carried it. Serpentius was a former gladiator, a superbly fit man who exercised with the sword every day, but his shoulder muscles shook with the strain of bringing the pick up to strike time after time. His head reeled and his lower back ached where Josephus's sword blade had penetrated his flesh and scraped across his hip. He winced as he remembered the lightning bolt of agony, the disbelief and the sense of betrayal as the Judaean traitor stabbed him in the back outside the Great Temple of Jerusalem. On and on. Someone must have refilled or replaced the lamps, but Serpentius never noticed. It was only when a hand touched his shoulder and turned him towards the entrance that he realized everyone else had stopped working.

He could barely put one foot in front of the other as they staggered wordlessly up the slope towards the sleeping chamber, the strong supporting the weak.

Survive? Endure? After two weeks of backbreaking labour, lying exhausted in his own filth and living on a diet a pig would have turned its nose up at? Serpentius knew that was fantasy. He had to escape soon, or he would undoubtedly die here.

Still, he had been able to gauge the relative strengths and weaknesses of his jailers, and, perhaps more importantly, of his companions.

V

Valerius sailed from the port at Ostia on a glittering sun-drenched morning that turned the gently undulating Mare Tyrrhenum into a vast mirror. Neptune, most capricious of all the gods, showed his kinder face and the gentle breeze drove them west across the ocean at a rate that would have put a smile on the face of the most gloomy of captains. On the third day they docked at Pallas on the island of Corsica to deliver a cargo of oil and replace it with timber, one of the few things the place had in abundance. The other was fierce and merciless bandits, and, though they were said to keep to the mountains, Valerius and his fellow passenger, a jolly merchant by the name of Tiberius Petro, stayed on board throughout the loading and unloading. Petro, a short, fat Ligurian, with the face of a mischievous cupid and a cap of dark, curly hair, had a wealth of stories from his travels. Valerius discovered the merchant was one of the few civilians who'd visited Cepha on the Armenian-Parthian border and Petro kept his companions entertained during the four days it took to reach Tarraco, capital of Hispania Tarraconensis.

The voyage gave Valerius time to ponder the task

Vespasian had set him. At first he'd found it surprising that Pliny had made his request for assistance through the Palatine. Over the years, they'd been allies and opponents fighting cases in the law courts at the basilica, and Pliny, who hoarded obscure pieces of knowledge the way others hoarded silver, was one of the few men Valerius could call friend. He'd been a cavalry prefect under Vespasian in Germania and would have had his province long ago had he not fallen foul of Nero and been forced into retirement and obscurity during his chaotic reign. Pliny had been the only man who spoke for Valerius at his trumped-up trial for treason and loaned him money to escape Rome when Domitian's death sentence had been commuted to exile. He must know that Valerius wouldn't have refused him if the approach had been made direct? Yet there was a logic in taking the official route. Vespasian's endorsement and the appointment as *legatus iuridicus* gave Valerius a power that would open doors and overcome obstacles. The only problem was that the fact Pliny believed he might need that power made it likely this mission would prove more complicated and dangerous than it appeared.

Still, all that was to come. Tabitha's face swam into his head. It might have been a difficult parting from his bride of three weeks, but his wife – diminutive and Hellenistically beautiful, but with a core of well-tempered iron – had been philosophical as she'd kissed him goodbye on the steps of their new home. 'The quicker you are gone the quicker I will have you back,' she had said. There were no tears, only an assurance that with Lupergos's help she would see the villa completed by the time of his return.

'I have a potion guaranteed to cure the worst ship

45

sickness, lord.' Valerius looked up to find Petro watching him. 'Squid ink, chopped toad bladder and *allec*.' Valerius grimaced. *Allec* was the sludge residue left from the fish guts used to make *garum*. 'It tastes revolting,' Petro grinned, 'but I suspect that is part of its virtue.'

Valerius swallowed. 'It sounds more likely to kill than cure. But it is not ship sickness that ails me.' He hesitated, but . . . why not? He told the merchant about his wedding and the recent, reluctant parting from Tabitha, though not the reason for it.

Petro's plump features took on a solemn air and he sighed. 'A new wife is like an unbroken filly. Give her all your attention and she will lick honey from your fingers and come at your call. Ignore her too long and she is apt to bite them off and run wild.' The impish grin returned. 'Not that I am suggesting . . .'

Valerius had passed through the port of Tarraco once before. During an earlier mission for Vespasian, then a mere legate, he'd come to offer support for Servius Sulpicius Galba's bid to take the purple. Only three years ago, but the trials Valerius had experienced since made it seem a lifetime – a lifetime that had seen the deaths of four emperors and hundreds of thousands of their subjects. So it was a familiar sight that greeted him as the creaking merchant ship slid between the twin headlands beneath a sky that glowed with all the splendour of a peacock's breast feathers. Red-tiled roofs of cavernous warehouses on either hand, a harbour bustling with water craft of all shapes and sizes and a quayside that resembled a disturbed ants' nest.

He stepped on to the dock on legs unused to a stable platform, to be greeted by the overwhelming, familiar scent of *garum*. Hundreds of amphorae of the pungent fish sauce were stacked high waiting to be loaded into the ship for the return journey to Ostia, next to bales of the pale yellow wool for which Tarraco was famous. A customs inspector, a centurion accompanied by two legionaries, appeared to check the ship's cargo while Valerius's baggage was being unloaded. One of the legionaries demanded to see his travel papers and he was forced, against his better judgement, to show the Imperial warrant Vespasian had provided to ease his passage. The man's eyes widened and Valerius knew that within a few hours the whole town would be aware an envoy from Vespasian had arrived on the ship.

'I wish you a safe onward journey, lord.' Petro smiled gravely as they said their farewells at the foot of the gangway.

'I will miss your stories as much as your company,' Valerius replied. 'Who knows, perhaps we will meet again if Fortuna wills it.'

A merchant pointed him in the direction of a trustworthy slave who would carry the small chest containing his belongings to the governor's palace. The slave led the way through the steep, narrow streets behind the harbour. Valerius had climbed these same streets with Serpentius and he felt a pang of something very close to grief as he remembered looking down at his friend in the medical tent outside Jerusalem. Serpentius had lain on his side with a bloody bandage covering the terrible wound in his back inflicted by the Judaean turncoat Josephus. The feral, vicious sneer that made the former gladiator appear so fearsome had been replaced by a haggard, grey mask. His eyes were closed and his sunken cheeks bristled with a week's growth of white stubble. Once he'd been the most dangerous fighter to grace the arenas of Rome. Now he looked like an old man.

They had been as close as brothers, and with the same instinctive understanding. Valerius felt more vulnerable without Serpentius by his side than he did without the right hand he'd left in the burned-out ruin of a villa in Britannia.

Tarraco sprawled over a series of ridges overlooking the sea. Valerius followed the slave to a broad square at the top of the largest hill. On the far side lay a single enormous building with white stucco walls and an ochre-tiled roof that shimmered in the midday heat. A pair of legionaries guarded the pillared entrance and they stiffened to attention as Valerius approached and announced he had an appointment with the governor.

'Your name?' The men eyed Valerius's travel-stained cloak with suspicion.

'Gaius Valerius Verrens. I'm an old friend of governor Secundus.'

One of the soldiers gave him a look that said 'we'll see about that'. 'Wait here.' He disappeared inside leaving Valerius under the gaze of the remaining guard, returning a few minutes later with a look of consternation on his stolid, peasant face.

'He said to ask you to show your right hand.' Valerius flicked back his cloak to reveal the carved wooden fist that replaced the hand he'd lost at Colonia. The soldier slammed his fist into his chest in salute. 'Please follow me. The governor apologizes for not greeting you personally, but he is indisposed at present.'

Just how indisposed became clear when the guard led Valerius into a shaded courtyard with a garden at its centre. Gaius Plinius Secundus sat on a couch in the portico with one foot raised. He had put on weight since Valerius had last seen him and heavy jowls gave him a

48

mournful air quite at odds with his normally cheerful disposition. The couch was surrounded by low tables, most filled with scrolls, but one left clear for his writing tools. Pliny had a voracious appetite for knowledge, always reading or investigating, collecting specimens, testing out new theories and disproving old ones.

He looked up as Valerius came into view and managed a pained smile. 'You have never been more welcome, Gaius Valerius Verrens. Pallas?' A young man stepped from a doorway behind him. 'Have the main guest room prepared for my friend and tell the cook there will be two for dinner,' Pliny ordered. 'I did not expect you for another week at the earliest, or I would have had you met at the harbour. Not personally, of course, as you can see. You'll have a cup of wine?'

'I will, Pliny, but I'm sorry to see you like this.'

'I'm suffering from a touch of gout. It won't kill me but it makes movement difficult. Hippocrates suggests it is caused by an overindulgence in drink, food and sex.' He produced a wry smile. 'While I plead guilty to the first and second, I'm afraid the third is long behind me these days. You had an uneventful journey, I hope?'

Valerius nodded. 'It gave me time to read the reports you sent to Rome.'

'Yes.' Pliny sounded doleful. 'Would that they had been more optimistic. But I prefer not to talk on an empty stomach. After dinner I will give you a more up-to-date view of the current situation. Now,' he picked up his stylus, 'Pallas will see to your baggage and get you settled in. I must finish this chapter of my *Historia Naturalis*. The subject is medicines we can obtain from plants. Did you know that *Colchicum autumnale*, the common meadow crocus, can be turned into an infusion which is a specific for gout? Unfortunately, taken in excess it is also a deadly poison and I choose not to test the theory.'

'Then I will leave you to your work,' Valerius bowed.

They dined on succulent steaks of tunny fish and squid cooked in its own ink, followed by a pair of roasted fowl and slices of apple and pear coated in honey. The food was served on silver platters and Valerius smiled at a memory. 'The last time we ate together, it was on chipped fireclay in your kitchen,' he said. 'Who would have believed our fortunes could have altered so radically?'

'That's true.' Pliny washed his fingers in a bowl brought by one of several slaves who attended them. 'We have much to be thankful for, you and I. For instance, it is sometimes difficult to believe that I once watched the friend sharing my table kneel beneath an executioner's sword. There are few alive who can claim such an experience. It still puzzles me that Domitian saw fit to commute the death sentence to exile.'

The observation contained a certain measure of query, and if anyone deserved the truth it was Pliny, who had risked his reputation by speaking for Valerius at his trial. But Valerius had learned to be wary. Only two other people knew of Domitia Longina Corbulo's intervention, and the reason for it. Better it stayed that way.

'There's nothing he would have liked better than to see my head rolling in the dust,' he admitted. 'But the letter Mucianus brought from Vespasian rescinded my original death sentence and he couldn't go against his father's express wish.'

'An emperor's favour is not to be underestimated, nor

disdained.' Pliny's features took on a troubled air. 'For instance, I honour him for this appointment, but there are times when I wish I was alone with my books back in Rome. Any proconsulship would be a burden for an honest man with the Empire's interests at heart, but this is doubly so. When Vespasian summoned me to the Palatine he told me the man who solved the conundrum of the missing gold of Hispania Tarraconensis would be the man who saved the Empire. Even able-bodied I'm not certain I would have lived up to his expectations. There is so much to do here. The answer lies in the north, and with this leg I doubt I would survive the journey. That is why I asked him to send you. He has outlined the general situation?'

'Since the late war the yields from the northern mines have dropped dramatically.' Valerius repeated what Vespasian had told him. 'Bandits are blamed, perhaps the richest seams have been worked out, and there are said to be manpower problems. What I don't understand is why you haven't sent a mining expert to investigate?'

'But we have,' Pliny cried. 'An experienced engineer, Marcus Florus Petronius. Does the name mean anything to you?'

'Should it?'

'He said he served with you in Armenia. You traversed some mountain track together. The longest night of his life, he told me.'

Now a face swam into view. Petronius had been the man who'd guided the night march to outflank Vologases, the Parthian King of Kings, before his defeat by Gnaeus Domitius Corbulo.

'A good choice,' he complimented Pliny. 'I remember Petronius as clever, enterprising and courageous.'

'And with substantial experience of the mining

industry.' Pliny's face turned grim. 'His latest report hinted at a great revelation. What was happening at Asturica Augusta was of even greater significance than we originally believed. But he would not make direct accusations until he had proof. Since then, nothing.'

'Is it possible his reports are being intercepted?'

'I doubt it. We had alternative procedures in place. It seems he has simply disappeared. I tell you this so you will not underestimate how dangerous this could be, Valerius. The goldfields are in barely accessible mountain areas and the mine workers were once Rome's most implacable enemies. It took Augustus ten years and seven legions to conquer the Astures and the Cantabri.'

'But that was ninety years ago,' Valerius pointed out. 'They've been living under Roman law ever since. Galba raised an entire legion from Hispania.'

'Roman citizens,' Pliny agreed. 'The sons of families who prosper under Rome's rule, but many – some would say most – have not. You must not underrate the level of resentment you will find in Asturica and I believe there may be ample reason for it. The mines are owned by the state, but much of the workforce and supplies are provided by Asturian aristocrats. Little more than bandit chiefs with a head for business and an eye for a profit. Originally the men who worked the mines would have been slaves – captives from the Cantabrian Wars – but Augustus soon realized he needed a more stable workforce. He ordered hundreds of villages uprooted entire and moved to where they could provide a workforce for the mines.' He paused in his narrative while a slave cleared away the last of the plates and poured another cup of wine from the jug. 'Tens of thousands of people,' he continued eventually, 'torn from their ancestral farmlands and hunting grounds, deprived of a living and forced into the service of the state. The men from the communities around the mines provide their labour to offset the taxes imposed on them by Rome. And it is not just the mines. Many of the processes use substantial amounts of water, sometimes enormous amounts, to clean the ore or, in some cases, to flush it from the mines. This requires the diversion of hundreds of native streams, the building of miles of canals and aqueducts, and all in terrain that can scarcely be traversed by man. The miners who work for the leaseholders are poorly paid and, according to Petronius, the food is fit only for pigs. They work by the light of oil lamps in a perpetual cloud of smoke, never seeing daylight for sometimes months on end.' Pliny's face darkened at the image he was creating and Valerius realized he must have inspected one of the southern mines and was speaking from experience. 'The mining process also creates a fine dust that can turn a man's lungs to stone if breathed for long enough. There are frequent collapses which can bury dozens, sometimes hundreds of men. They chip at the face of the rock with picks, or power massive crushing machines before the ore is carried to the surface on the backs of the miners, encouraged, shall we say, by overseers armed with whips. So you see, Valerius, any benefits provided by Roman rule only accrue to a few rich men and those who support them, not those who actually create the wealth.'

Valerius hesitated before he replied, considering the impact of the mining operations on the people and the land. He wondered what he would have done if it had been his people and his land. 'I am surprised they bear it,' he said eventually.

'They do so only with reluctance, I can assure you,' Pliny acknowledged. 'And because they have little choice. We have deprived them of their traditional live-lihoods of hunting and farming. Their hills have been stripped of timber to supply charcoal for the smelters. For generations they have known no other life. The populace is composed of large confederations, such as the Cantabri, the Astures, the Vaccaei and the like. These in turn are divided into individual tribes. I have charted them all, but those that interest us are the Cigurri, the Lancienses and the Zoelae. If indeed raiders are disrupting the gold trains they are the most likely tribes to supply them, but . . .' he raised a hand to suppress the question he knew was coming, 'they are also divided into smaller clans, any of which could be responsible. Security for the goldfields is provided by a few cohorts of the Sixth legion at Legio. The commander there has sent a request to take his troops into the hills and carry out a sweep intended to wipe out any bandits in the area. I understand his frustration, but I have ordered him to hold his hand. Such a move would be like thrusting a stick in a hornets' nest and I cannot act without proof. Before the late wars the proconsul of Hispania Tarraconensis could call on the power of three full legions, but now . . .'

'The present proconsul has the leavings of two . . .'

'And those scattered across the entire province,' Pliny confirmed.

'You don't paint a very pretty picture, Pliny,' Valerius said drily.

'Best you should know exactly what you are getting into, Valerius. The Emperor has promised to give me more soldiers – either the First Adiutrix, or more likely the Seventh –' he smiled at Valerius's reaction '– you have fought with both, I know. But the situation on the Rhenus is such that he can't afford to move them quite yet. He is also committed to improving the lot of the ordinary people of Hispania. I have drawn up plans to widen the allocation of Roman citizenship and grant new powers to local communities. But to make these changes requires gold. Somehow, we must provide it and end the corruption which is endemic to these people.' He let out a soft belch and laid aside his cup. 'I always find a bath eases the digestion. Will you join me and we can continue our discussion?'

'Of course.'

VI

'The hand is so much part of you it seems wrong when you remove it like that,' Pliny said. Undressing in the *apodyterium*, Valerius had pulled off the stock and laid the wooden fist of his right hand aside. 'Does it affect you at all?'

From anyone else such an enquiry would have been bad manners, but Valerius was perfectly accustomed to Pliny's habit of questioning everything. Any experience that could broaden his knowledge would be of interest.

'It was odd when I first had it fitted,' Valerius admitted. 'Each time I removed it I experienced the pain of the day it was taken from me. But use makes master. These days I take it off every night and replace it each morning almost without thinking.'

Pliny limped past the *tepidarium* to the *caldarium* and slipped into the steaming pool of clear water with a groan of ecstasy. 'I also find a bath eases the pain of the gout. Now, where was I?'

'You were talking about corruption in the goldfields.' Valerius dropped into the pool beside his friend.

'Ah, yes. Corruption. Bureaucracy is essential to the successful flow of gold, silver and lead from the mines of

Hispania to the vaults of Rome. Yet in a system of supply and demand there is always room for a venal official to make a profit. Leases are auctioned to the highest bidder, but that bidder will undoubtedly also be the one who pays the largest bribe to the official in charge. Most of the mines are state-operated, but miners have to be fed. How simple for a mine operator to claim he paid out x sesterces a day to feed his workers when in fact he is paying out y and pocketing the difference? Fortunately, or unfortunately, the flow of gold was so immense that as long as the people responsible maintained it those in charge were happy for them to take their cut. Corruption became part of the system, therefore whatever else you discover you will find corruption.'

'Then how will I know if I've discovered something significant?'

'I'm afraid I cannot answer that,' Pliny admitted. 'But I'm confident you will know it when you see it, Valerius. What Petronius uncovered plainly went beyond mere corruption – gold production is two-thirds the level before the civil war. Perhaps if you can find out what has happened to him you will have taken the first step to discovering what it was?'

Valerius frowned. It was like being asked to find a single turd in a cesspit. Whatever the outcome, he had a feeling his hands were going to get very dirty. 'Do you have any suggestion how I go about this?'

'I have an old comrade who lives in Asturica Augusta.' Pliny's voice dropped and his eyes flickered towards the doorway. Valerius suppressed a wry smile. If his friend believed his secrets weren't safe in the very heart of his headquarters they were in deep trouble indeed. 'His name is Marcus Atilius Melanius. He is one of the city's leading citizens, but a man who lives quietly in retirement and has no links to the mining industry. Petronius was to contact him in time of need, but I don't know if he ever did. At least he will be able to show you how the land lies. Do you intend to use the title Vespasian conferred upon you?'

'I don't know yet,' Valerius admitted. 'On the one hand high rank conveys a certain level of power; on the other it makes me conspicuous and could prevent people from speaking. Better, I think, to enter the city as a simple traveller, perhaps with a letter of introduction to your old comrade. Whatever Petronius discovered is likely to be buried deep, but someone somewhere has knowledge of it.' He paused for a moment, staring at a wall painting of a sea monster devouring a bireme galley, but his mind was already in the north. 'The key is to find that person and put pressure on them. That might be the time to bring out the Emperor's warrant.'

Pliny nodded thoughtfully. 'You may be right. Perhaps we can discuss it further in the morning? I intend to stay immersed for another hour. I doubt you will want to stay that long . . .'

Valerius thanked him and pulled himself out of the pool. Normally an attendant would have been waiting to dry the governor and his guest, but the slave was nowhere in sight. Valerius had to search through cupboards to find oil for the stump of his arm. When he'd dressed he pulled the cowhide stock of the artificial hand over the mottled purple surface of his wrist and tightened the leather thongs with the ease of long practice. He was preparing to leave when an odd sound drew his attention: a soft gurgling as if someone had decided to empty the main bath.

He slipped to the curtained doorway. Yes, it was

definitely coming from the *caldarium*. He drew the thick curtain slowly to the side. At first his eyes struggled to interpret the scene in front of him. Two fully clothed men, stocky and bearded, were apparently working on something in the bath. A thrill of fear paralysed him for a moment, during which the anonymous something heaved up and thrashed, before the combined strength of the two men submerged it again. Pliny!

Valerius crossed the marble floor in four strides, his left thumb automatically seeking the little button on the back of his wooden fist. The man holding Pliny's lower half must have noticed movement because he looked up with a cry that alerted his fellow assassin. Too late. The second man rose and half turned to meet the threat, but Valerius had already launched into a scything punch that took him on the upper cheek.

A blow from the wooden fist would stun any man. This blow was designed to kill. The button on the back of the fist released a four-inch blade that sprang from the centre knuckle. Now the needle point entered the assassin's right eye and pierced his brain. Valerius hauled the knife clear with a twist and the dying man dropped into the pool, his life blood turning the waters red. The second assassin gaped at his companion and released Pliny's legs, backing away across the pool. Valerius had a choice of going after him or helping his drowning friend. There could only be one decision. He plunged into the water and felt for the submerged Pliny. The groping fingers of his left hand quickly found a hank of thinning hair and he pulled the governor's head to the surface. The killer continued to glare from the far side of the pool, caught between an urge to finish the job and the greater call of survival.

'Guards!' Valerius roared. 'Guards to me.'

The surviving assassin spat an insult at Valerius before sprinting for the doorway. Pliny lay back with his eyes closed and his flabby chest chillingly still. Valerius hauled the inert body from the water on to the marble floor beside the pool. Drowning was nothing new to Valerius, but, by Fortuna's favour, in his case it had never been permanent. He remembered looking up through a clear blue sea at the hull of a Roman merchant ship. How had they brought him back? Yes, that was it. His ribs had ached for a week. He heaved Pliny up, with the governor's back against his chest, put both arms around him and squeezed with all his strength. Once, twice. Thrice. Jupiter's wrinkled scrotum, was he too late? Finally, a long, rasping groan from Pliny's throat followed by an enormous gout of water and the contents of his stomach. For a moment he lay in Valerius's arms, his body shaking. His features were as pale as fresh milk and his eyes twitched open to peer up at his saviour. He was smiling.

'Why, I do believe I was dead.'

By the time Valerius supported Pliny from the bath house, the failed assassin had been pinned to the packed earth of the courtyard by four snarling guards. The governor shrugged himself free and straightened to his full height. His face was a mask of fury and the guard commander turned pale before his wrath.

'We will discuss how he came to be here later. For now prepare him for the question.' The guards dragged the man up and Pliny studied the swarthy bearded face. 'You would do well to tell me what you know now, or it will be the worse for you.' The assassin's only reply was to spit at his feet. Pliny nodded slowly, as if the gesture was what he'd expected. 'Take him away.'

* * *

A new Pliny this, the grim, unyielding interrogator, watching in silence as his subordinates prepared the familiar instruments: the hot coals, the pincers and pliers, the shears, the hooks and the assorted glittering blades. The assassin watched too, from a position on the far wall of the stables where they'd strung him up by the arms from a pair of manacles. Stripped naked, his body gleamed with perspiration in the glow from the brazier, his manhood already shrivelled up seeking sanctuary in the hairy bush of his crotch. The building had been cleared for the occasion, but it still stank of horse shit, mouldy hay and the rank sweat of generations of its equine occupants.

Pliny, dressed in a formal toga, sat on a padded couch with his gouty foot raised, far enough away from his subject to avoid any spilled bodily fluids. A secretary appeared and stood by with a stylus and wax block to record the questions and the replies.

'You do not have to stay, Valerius,' Pliny said without taking his eyes off the man who'd tried to kill him.

'Better if I do.'

'Very well. What is your name?'

It took time and persuasion. While the knives were being heated to a fierce glowing crimson, the torturers removed the large toe of his left foot with a cold chisel, a mere foretaste of what was to come. The almost casual amputation, carried out with brutal indifference, brought a gasp of agony and the man's face turned pale beneath his deep tan.

'Who sent you?'

The assassin closed his eyes and blood ran down his chin where he'd bitten through his lip.

'The right ear, I think.'

The horrible prolonged shriek that followed the

suggestion sent a shiver down Valerius's spine. A red-hot blade had the benefit of cauterizing the wound as it was created. One of the torturers held the wilted scrap of flesh before the assassin's eyes then tossed it on to the brazier. It sizzled and cooked, filling the stable with the mouth-watering scent of frying meat, before curling up into an unrecognizable blackened crisp and disappearing in a flicker of blue flame.

And so it went. They took him apart one piece at a time. No mindless pummelling brutality this, just a cold, clinical professionalism that told the victim the only way to save what was left was to tell everything he knew. When it came, it was like a dam bursting. The names tumbled out one after the other in a guttural dog Latin Valerius could barely decipher. First the man's own. Brutus, a mere bandit, he pleaded, from west of Carthago Nova. He and his companion Venico had been recruited by ... a mumbled name that clearly meant nothing to Pliny.

'Ask him again. How did he gain entry to the palace? How did he know where to find me?'

Brutus hesitated, which was a mistake. There went one eye, the right, courtesy of a glowing spike accompanied by a horrible bubbling scream that seemed to go on for ever.

When they resumed, his voice was hoarse from the screaming. They'd been ordered to meet a man at an inn down by the port. The man informed them that the governor was a creature of habit. He would enter the bath at the seventh hour. Their informant would ensure a certain door was left open, the guards would be elsewhere. The attendant would be dealt with. An unfortunate accident would then occur.

'Who?' Pliny's voice shook with emotion. 'Who betrayed me?'

The assassin could give no name, but he provided a description that made the governor go still.

'Find him,' he hissed to the guard. 'Find him if you have to scour the whole province.'

It wasn't enough, of course. They had to be sure. When the assassin thought he'd given them everything, it turned out he was wrong.

'I regret the necessity,' Pliny explained later. 'But if it is going to be done it must be done properly or there is no point.'

'What will happen to him?'

Pliny frowned. 'A personal attack on the governor of a Roman province? He will be crucified, what is left of him.'

'Who was it?'

'A clerk.' Pliny looked weary and old. 'Acondus, who worked very closely with my secretary. Whoever paid him would know my intentions the moment they were written down. Of course, with the assassins discovered – and I have yet to thank you and your ingenious little knife for your services – his usefulness was at an end. The *vigiles* found him in an alley with his throat cut. He is no help to us now.'

Valerius considered for a moment. 'Could the attempt on your life have anything to do with my mission?'

Pliny winced at the possibility, but shook his head. 'Not directly, I think.' He met Valerius's eyes. 'I believe I may have suspected something of this nature, deep down, because I ensured all correspondence involving you was directly between myself and the Emperor or Titus. Asturica Augusta? Yes, it is possible, but why now?'

'Because they fear you are getting too close.'

'Poor Petronius,' Pliny sighed. 'I sent him to his doom.

Perhaps you should reconsider, Valerius? The Emperor would not want you to share his fate.'

'No.' There was iron in Valerius's voice. 'I gave him my vow and too much is at stake to turn back now.'

Pliny smiled and laid a gentle hand on his shoulder. 'I thought as much. Then, given the change in circumstances, I believe you should follow your original instinct and make a low-key entry to Asturica Augusta. A soldier on his way to visit old comrades. I could send you with a supply convoy – they come and go all the time – but they take an age. Better I think to accompany the courier who leaves tomorrow carrying my reply to the officer in charge of the fort at Legio. He's to have an escort of troopers from my guard squadron, so you should be safe enough on the journey. The courier is based at the fort so it's possible you may find out how things lie there.'

Pliny had called Asturica a hornets' nest, but from where Valerius sat it seemed more like a den of vipers. He had a feeling the only way to get the information Vespasian sought would be to place himself amongst them.

VII

The five men sat deep in the shadows of a shabby, dilapidated room illuminated solely by moonlight that filtered through the open shutters. Their faces were mere pools of darkness marked by the icy glint of eyes that reflected either inquisitive anticipation of what was to come or fearful apprehension. Each had his own thoughts about the current situation, but only one man's views mattered. This house was one of several that man owned in Asturica Augusta: a dusty, half-derelict building on a back street where their comings and goings would go unnoticed. For more than three years, since Servius Sulpicius Galba had marched in triumph from Tarraco's gates escorted by the Seventh legion, they'd profited from the chaos of the civil war. Now their world was changing.

'Our lives will be forfeit if Vespasian discovers what has been happening here.' The man they had come to hear, a grim presence in the corner, announced the painful truth of which they were all aware in a soothing voice designed to steady fraying nerves.

Each could have pointed out that he would not be here but for this man's encouragement and the temptation of the gold he had quite literally poured before their eyes. One of them wanted to say it, but he knew that in the end it would make no difference. He had taken his share along with the rest. Nothing could change that.

It was another man who spoke. 'Then we must stop. Now.'

'Do you really believe that will solve anything?' The leader laughed. The man had always been weak. 'All it will do is harden their suspicions when the gold yields suddenly rise again after three years. On the contrary, we should continue what we're doing. In fact, we must increase it.'

'What?' Four mouths gaped.

'Why do you think I always insisted we should build up such a large reserve? Not because you were already rich beyond other men's wildest imaginings. No,' he shook his head, 'I did so because gold is power.'

'You said Asturica deserved to be the richest place in Hispania,' another man dared to speak out. The leader recognized the voice of the sceptic, always questioning, but kept loyal by his greed. 'This should be its greatest city, because this is where the greatest natural resources are. Strong men make strong decisions, you said. We would use the gold to create a new Rome in the west that would be the equal of the capital.'

'That was before the old fool Galba got himself killed. Before a *new man* like Vespasian could take the throne against all the traditions of the Empire. A former muleteer and the son of a tax farmer, with not an ounce of true patrician blood in his veins.'

'He won the war,' the weakling pointed out. 'He has been hailed Emperor by the Senate and people of Rome.'

'And the Senate is already plotting against the muleteer and his brood.' The leader's gravelly voice was dismissive now. 'They saw what happened to Vitellius and they panicked because they believed they would be served the same way after Vespasian's brother Sabinus was butchered on the Gemonian Stairs. Now they see what an enormous mistake they have made. A man like Vespasian does not have the bloodline to rule the Empire. Why does he keep so many legions on the Rhenus?'

'To keep the Batavians honest.'

'No, because he still does not trust the German legions who originally supported Vitellius. And without Spanish gold he cannot buy that trust.'

'What are you suggesting?' The latest interruption came from the facilitator, without whose connections and access none of this would be possible. He did not understand his position of strength, but of them all he was the man of whom the leader was most wary and he was careful to treat him with respect.

'The governor, Gaius Plinius Secundus, came within a heartbeat of uncovering our scheme.'

The room seemed to freeze as they sensed the enormity of what was to come. 'You told us you had stopped the flow of information. Stopped it dead.'

'That is true, but Plinius Secundus is not a man to give up so easily. He is like a hunting dog on the trail of a boar; once he scents blood there will be no stopping him. That is why I have acted on your behalf to ensure he is not in a position to continue.'

They all registered the 'on your behalf' which ensured their heads would roll alongside his if the knowledge ever left this room.

'You sent assassins to kill the governor?'

'Hopefully he is already dead.'

'You're mad.' The weakling sounded genuinely shocked. Did he even realize his timidity put him next on the leader's list?

'Not mad,' the leader corrected. 'Pragmatic. Think on it, my friends. It was him or us. Did you want to feel the cold blade of the executioner's sword kiss the nape of your neck before the blow? Or have your arms torn from their sockets as you hung on the cross for hour after hour in the terrible heat with the scourged wounds on your back salted? That was the end that awaited you if I had not had the courage to act. Now you must have the courage to follow me. The only way to stop Vespasian killing us all is to topple Vespasian.'

'No!'

'You're talking treason.'

The leader stood, his presence seeming to fill the room, and now he did not hide his contempt. 'Do you really think it makes any difference if the blood that spurts from your neck is the blood of a thief or a traitor? I can assure you that the thief's head will certainly roll, but a man with the courage to stand up for Rome gives himself a chance of not just life, but prosperity. This is not treason. It is natural justice. Titus Flavius Vespasian has no right to the purple.'

'Then who has? You?' The weakling almost laughed and the leader decided he really would have to deal with this problem before long.

'No.' He raised his voice. 'You may come in.' A moment later a tall, slim figure appeared from a side room where he'd been listening. 'A man with the blood of Caesars in his veins. Servius Sulpicius Galba named an heir before he died, but that heir was killed before he could don the purple. His descendants are the true Imperial family.'

'Vespasian is a usurper and a commoner.' A young voice and a strong one. 'Rome needs strength and a steady hand that was born to rule. I believe what you have done in Asturica has been directed by the guiding hand of Jupiter. Not one of the men who took the throne during those three years deserved to rule. Why then would you send them the gold that would have allowed them to continue? You bided your time until a worthy candidate came forward. When I am Emperor, far from being punished, the men in this room will be raised to the highest offices of the Empire.'

He could feel their continued scepticism and he faltered for a moment, but the leader came to his aid.

'And how is this to be achieved?'

'I already have the support of my comrades in Hispania.' His tone had regained its authority. 'The Seventh is Galba's legacy and will follow his heirs. The German legions can be bought with the gold in your coffers. That same gold will keep the units on the Danuvius frontier where they should be, holding the barbarians at bay. One of our allies is already prepared to march. When he arrives with his men we will form a second Hispanic legion and march on Rome, with the Rhenus legions on our flank.'

'Can we truly succeed?' the sceptic demanded.

'We must succeed.' The weakling had found his courage. 'Or we are all dead.'

'There is one thing.' A new voice, one that had been quiet for too long. The enforcer.

'Yes?'

'It is my understanding the man Petronius had an Asturian ally.'

'That's true,' the leader said thoughtfully. 'But there is no return from where he is.'

'Why take a chance?'

'Why indeed.'

VIII

In the perma-heated darkness, Serpentius worked away silently at the short length of wood he'd secreted all day beneath his tunic. It was from the broken handle of a shovel and had cost him a day on the baskets and a beating from the overseer to obtain. The four-inch iron nail he used to gouge minute splinters from the centre of the ash shaft had come from the hammer man who'd urged him not to drink the water on that first day. Vegeto was a free man from Baeduniense who risked losing his wages for even the suspicion of any contact with the Lost. He was as slow of mind as he was large of form, but Serpentius had sensed a goodness in the man that belied his habitual fierce scowl. It had encouraged him to cultivate the Asturian until he felt confident enough to ask for the sliver of metal. From the way Vegeto looked at him, Serpentius knew the other man expected him to use it to kill himself.

If he couldn't escape soon, it might come to that.

Still, he'd come up with a plan and chosen the men to help him carry it out, even if they didn't know it yet. But first he had to hollow out the length of wood. At this rate it would take another three or four days. In the darkness he could hear the soft groans and whimpers of his fellow prisoners. A faint muttering in the distance marked the location of the guards who shared a room carved out of the rock a little further up the main passage. Six guards alternating through the night, with two on duty at any one time while the others slept alongside the jailer.

Once every seven days, as Serpentius reckoned it, the jailer and his guards would arrive an hour earlier than normal. This was the day they ran a water pipe down from the surface to flush out the accumulated filth of the twenty prisoners, and wash down the men themselves, ragged tunics and all. Despite every attempt to squeeze out the water they lived in a permanent damp that covered their tattered clothing with green mould.

The thought of sleep reminded him how exhausted he was in mind and body. Every day he spent in this fetid pit of Hades cost him strength he couldn't afford to lose. He closed his eyes and tried to rediscover the ability to find oblivion he'd learned during the long campaigns with Valerius. He must not give up hope. Valerius would never give up hope. He thought of the times they'd risked life and limb together, always just one step ahead of the axe man, sharing a bond, a brotherhood so powerful it might even be called love. Where are you now, my brother? With that dangerous little Judaean beauty in the villa at Fidenae you always planned to return to?

He tried to remember her name but it escaped him. It had been like this ever since some Flavian trooper put a dent in his skull during the sack of Rome three years earlier. His memory of things long past was as good as ever, but he would forget where he'd left objects or sometimes even whether he'd eaten. When he'd allowed his hair to grow in the Asturian fashion a woman had pointed out the white circle in the centre of the steely grey that turned him, quite literally, into a marked man. So, he'd shaved his head once more and reverted to Serpentius the scarred former gladiator. He ran his fingers across the half inch of stubble on his scalp. It had grown again now, but that was no reason for celebration down here, where the lice bred in their teeming thousands and seemed to favour any tuft of hair or fold in a tunic.

At some point he must have slept because he woke automatically moments before the jailer appeared in the prisoners' side tunnel and lit the first lamp. In the glaring flare of light Serpentius watched intently as the man entered a few paces ahead of the guards. They were still half asleep, but wary. This pair were just brutes in uniform, but the Spaniard had identified two former soldiers among the rest who would be more of a threat to his plan.

'Don't you want your bread?' the jailer snarled.

'Yes, sir. Thank you, sir.' The Spaniard snatched the mouldy fragment and dashed it in the swill bucket.

By the time they'd crammed the bread into their mouths the main chain had been removed and the guards kicked them into line to pick up their tools. Serpentius always ensured he slept close to the doorway so he didn't have to carry a basket and none of the other prisoners had the will to challenge him. The free miners streamed past as he selected his pick. By now the tool was as familiar in his hands as a sword had once been, but before he could accept his oil lamp, someone smashed into him with enough force to knock him to the floor.

A huge figure loomed over him. 'I've told you before not to get in my way.'

Serpentius stared up at his tormentor. No point in apologizing. An unmistakable message in the single eye told Serpentius this man meant to kill him. The only wonder was that it had taken this long. He remained the only link to the information Petronius had possessed. The big hammer twitched threateningly in the man's hands and a little half smile flitted across his coarse features. They called him Cyclops.

Serpentius pushed himself wearily to his feet and turned away. He sensed the moment the hammer came up to shoulder height in the big, meaty hands. Heard the gasps as it began the plunge towards his unprotected back. With a blur of movement he spun out of range as the iron head smashed with an enormous clang to raise a shower of sparks from the quartzite floor. Cyclops grunted with frustration and raised the hammer for a new attempt.

It would have been so easy. For Serpentius the falling hammer was as sluggish as a gently turning water wheel. Even in his chains he could step inside it to left or right. A flick of the wrist would allow him to bring the pick head round to pierce the giant's exposed belly and rip it clear to leave his guts spilling on to the ground. Or a pirouette – granted, not as simple with the iron around his ankles, but still possible – would plunge the point into Cyclops' kidneys and condemn him to a well-deserved, painful, and lingering death as his piss turned black.

The thought made him smile, but it couldn't be. Making the kill look easy would show the guards just how dangerous Serpentius could be, and the mining overseers knew exactly how to deal with dangerous men. They would weigh him down with chains until he could barely move and his chance of escape would be gone.

So Cyclops must live – for now.

That meant Serpentius would have to take risks.

Cyclops might be slow, but he was strong as a bull and the Spaniard's strength had been sapped by the weeks underground. Serpentius's speed, his greatest asset alongside his skill at arms, would inevitably be slowed by the chains and his movement restricted by the tight confines of the shaft. All these calculations went through his head in the time it took to dance out of range, forcing the crowd of watchers who penned in the two men to back away. A push in the back told him Cyclops might not be working alone, but that would have to wait for now.

They circled each other warily and he studied the man who faced him with increased concentration. The hammer wielder was plainly bemused at his lack of immediate success, but there was no hint of fear in his eyes. Cyclops truly was enormous, and hard with it. Iron-muscled and not an ounce of surplus flesh on that huge frame. Serpentius noticed the iron rings that decorated the other man's knuckles and the shine that showed where they'd been deliberately roughened to do more damage.

Serpentius had killed more opponents in the arena than he could count, but he wasn't just a killer. Uniquely among warriors, gladiators were encouraged to entertain as they dispensed death. Serpentius killed with a style that had made him the crowd's favourite. He could make an opponent look a fool or, if he happened to respect him, a worthy fighter who would be allowed to come within a hair's breadth of disembowelling the champion right up to the moment his head rolled in the bloody sand. The hammer, clumsy as it was, presented the greatest danger. One tap on the ankle or knee and he'd be disabled and at the mercy of a killing blow. So.

As Cyclops raised the hammer in a two-handed grip,

Serpentius dropped the pick and swung his chains with all his strength so the heavy links wrapped around his enemy's wrists. Had it been a lesser man, the brittle bones would have snapped, but Cyclops was made of stronger stuff. All the blow achieved was to numb his hands and forearms so the hammer dropped from nerveless fingers.

Cyclops roared with frustration. 'You will pay for that a hundredfold, little mouse.'

The big man darted in with a flailing punch that would have near taken Serpentius's head off had it landed, but Serpentius swayed back out of range. By now his mind operated on a level that was almost beyond what he would call 'self', allowing instinct to take over from consciousness. It took courage to give up command to something he didn't truly understand, but that instinct had seen him to victory in countless arena contests.

Now it had pinpointed a tiny scar, the legacy of an old injury or wound. Nothing was certain and Serpentius would have to get dangerously close, but it offered a definite opportunity. For the moment, though, he must stay clear of the shovel hands that could crush his ribs, tear his arms from their sockets or break his neck with a single twist of the wrist. His keen eyes ranged over the scarred arms and upper torso. He was so drawn to what he saw there that he almost fell to Cyclops' latest rush, and only just managed to scramble away. The giant grunted in frustration, but the feral grin grew wider.

'Run if you want, little mouse, but you can't run for ever.'

For the moment, Serpentius concentrated on staying alive. Yes, he was sure now. But it would have to wait. Patience. This was not the time to attack. Instead, he feinted left, drawing a strike from Cyclops that surprised him with its speed and connected with his upper arm with enough force to numb it.

A ragged cheer went up from the shadows surrounding them and Serpentius was left in no doubt who the majority of the miners wanted to survive this contest. If that was the product of a glancing blow, just how much damage could Cyclops cause him? Yet something told him the other man wasn't interested in punching his way to victory. No, his favoured method was to get close, accepting what punishment was required to smother his opponent with his sheer bulk, crushing ribs and spine with arms that were capable of snapping a man in half. Nothing would please Cyclops more than the sound of snapping bone.

Without warning, Cyclops rushed forward, his right hand reaching for Serpentius's shoulder, but the leathery skin of his fingers slipped on the Spaniard's flesh, made slimy by a combination of oil and sweat. Cyclops expected his opponent to dance clear; instead Serpentius darted forward and smashed a closed fist into his chest with enough force to make him grunt. The blow made the bigger man pause and Serpentius moved away. Cyclops rubbed at the skin where the blow had struck, a bare patch in the thick pelt of hair that covered his body. A look of puzzlement formed on the broad peasant face.

Serpentius allowed himself a smile. Cyclops might be a miner now, but he was undoubtedly a former soldier. The punch had been aimed at a white pockmark the width of a man's thumb just to the right of the giant's left nipple. To a warrior who knew what he was looking for, the rubbery skin and the position hinted at a certain type of wound.

Each time Serpentius danced away from the grasping fingers the howls of frustration from Cyclops' supporters grew louder. But Cyclops could be patient too, and gradually he forced the Spaniard back against the crowd.

This time when Serpentius darted for safety a foot stuck out from amongst the spectators and left him sprawling on the hard rock. He sprang upright into the path of a scything right hook and even a former gladiator's lightning reactions couldn't save Serpentius from a glancing blow to the side of the head. His vision went red and he felt the skin ripping as the iron-clad knuckles skidded across his scalp, drawing blood that poured down his face in a crimson rush. The force of the punch threw him into the crowd where eager hands immediately pushed him back towards the grinning giant. At last Cyclops managed to get his huge arms around Serpentius and no matter how he wriggled and twisted in the giant's grip the Spaniard couldn't break free. He'd never experienced such strength. Cyclops held him tight to his chest and slowly increased his power. Serpentius cried out as his ribs ground together and his back felt as if it were about to snap. The only thing that saved him was Cyclops' decision to deny him a quick end. Cyclops grinned and nodded to the crowd. He relaxed his grip just enough to allow Serpentius to breathe. Serpentius's head slumped against Cyclops' shoulder and his cheek rasped against the other man's coarse stubble. His brain still spun from the blow he'd taken, but he knew that unless he could free himself he would soon be dead.

The massive arms resumed their pressure and Serpentius cried out to the ancient gods of the Astures for aid. He screamed and his mouth touched the other man's cheek. In desperation he clamped his teeth on the bunched flesh, simultaneously shaking his head like a dog and working his jaw. The skin tore and blood flooded his mouth, but still he worked at the big man's savaged flesh. Now it was Cyclops who shrieked as Serpentius growled and chewed until he came away with a mouthful of dripping meat that left a gaping gore-filled crater in the hammer man's face. The Spaniard spat the obscene gobbet into the giant's single eye. Yet still the great arms maintained their pressure. In desperation, Serpentius butted the exposed cheekbone making the bigger man mew like a suffering child. Cyclops turned his face away from the assault, but all he did was expose his right ear. Again the Spaniard closed his teeth over the rubbery flesh, drawing a howl from the other man. At last the hammer man released his grip and Serpentius fell free, still with the big Roman's ear clamped between his teeth. Cyclops backed away, attempting to stem the blood pouring from his wounds.

Choking back the urge to vomit, Serpentius staggered after him, knowing he only had one chance. With all the power he could generate he smashed his skull into the big man's chest, making him stumble back. The blow seemed to paralyse Cyclops. He clutched at his breast in bewilderment and his eyes flicked from side to side seeking escape. But there was no escape from Serpentius's lightning attacks. Again and again the Spaniard hammered his fist against the giant's left breast where the arrow had struck the gods only knew how many years before. Struck in such a place and at such an angle that Serpentius knew the surgeons had been forced to leave it for fear of killing their patient. Instead, they had cut the shaft as short as they could and allowed the wound to grow over it, leaving it to the gods to decide whether Cyclops would live or die.

Well, the gods would not save him now.

Every blow forced the iron closer to Cyclops' heart

and the agony of it robbed him of his strength and forced him to one knee. Serpentius saw his chance. With one final leap that had all his remaining strength behind it, he landed a flying kick on the precise spot where the arrow had penetrated. Cyclops gave an awful cry and straightened for one last time as the iron ruptured his heart. The single eye widened in disbelief and his hands scrabbled desperately at his chest until, with a final choked groan, he pitched forward on to his face.

Serpentius turned to glare at the men surrounding him. His eyes glittered in the light of the oil lamps and the blood streaming down his forehead and cheeks made him look like a demon from the underworld. Not one would meet his challenge, but he saw a look of bemusement on the overseer's face that told him it hadn't been meant to end like this. He saw Vegeto among the watching men. The miner gave him a brief nod of acknowledgement and the Spaniard bent and retrieved the pick. Without a word he set off for the gold face.

When their voices couldn't be heard above the crash of hammers, Serpentius held a whispered conversation with Vegeto. At first the Asturian was astonished by the Spaniard's request, but what he'd seen in the tunnel was proof enough that this was a man whose powers were to be respected. In his stolid way he outlined what he already knew and added: 'There will be more. I will find out the rest tonight.'

'Do not take any risks, Vegeto. I do not want your life on my conscience.'

The big man snorted as if the suggestion was an insult. 'I am of the Paesici, stranger, I can move like a wolf in the night.'

Serpentius smiled at this unlikely claim, but Vegeto only nodded grimly, and he knew he would do his best.

On the way back to the sleeping place, Serpentius managed to pull a startled Clitus into a side chamber. A tall, saturnine man whose wasted frame must once have been powerful, Clitus was one of the prisoners Serpentius had identified as having the strength of body and will to be part of what he planned. Now he named the others and asked Clitus to do what he could to have them lie in a group that night.

'We have to escape or we die here,' he said in a voice so low as to be inaudible beyond the man it was aimed at.

'Escape is impossible,' Clitus hissed. 'The chains. The guards. And even then what?'

'You saw me fight today. Nothing is impossible. You must explain that to the others. If we work together we can escape. Anyone who is willing and able. If we stay here we die.'

'How?' Suddenly Clitus's voice held a faint edge of hope.

'When do they wash us down again?'

The other man thought for a moment, counting the days in his head. 'Four days,' he said.

'Good. For now bide your time and keep your strength. I will give you more information closer to the time.' Serpentius kept his tone flat and emotionless, but inside his spirits soared. What Vegeto had told him had confirmed it could be done. Now it was up to him.

IX

There had been times in his life when Valerius felt the saddle was his only home. He'd travelled from one edge of the Empire to the other: endured avalanches crossing the Alps, traversed the length of Germania pursued by crazed Batavian auxiliaries, marched over the parched plains of southern Armenia on the way to a victory that never was, and ridden the length of Roman Syria in the company of the woman who would become his wife. Now the mountains of northern Hispania awaited him.

It helped that his escort consisted of a good-natured group of auxiliary horse soldiers from the First cohort of the Faithful Vardulli. The men were on detachment to Pliny, but the main element of their unit remained in Britannia. Their cheerful demeanour told him they were pleased to be back in their native land carrying out ceremonial duties for the new governor rather than playing hide and seek in the mountain mists with the Ordovices or the Deceangli.

'But it's good to be in the saddle,' said Abilio, the escort's *decurio*. A twenty-year veteran, he had keen dark eyes and moustaches that drooped to his chin, a style favoured by most of his men. 'You soon tire of spending hours polishing parade helmets and it's not good for a cavalryman to let his backside get soft.'

Valerius returned his grin. 'A Thracian archer of my acquaintance once told me a proper cavalryman should have a backside like leather . . .'

'And thighs that could crack a nut,' Abilio confirmed with a bark of laughter. A distinctive brass helmet fitted with ornate cheekpieces hung by a strap from his shoulder and he wore a vest of light chain armour. Like his men's his legs were encased to the knee in striped *braccae*; a heavy cavalry *spatha* hung from his belt and he carried a seven-foot spear. 'I like the Thracians,' he said. 'Born in the saddle and prepared to follow orders. Not like those mad Pannonian bastards. They'd start a fight in an empty room and charge through a stone wall just to show how hard they were.'

On the second day, they emerged from the coastal mountains that guarded Tarraco on to a great open plain, skirting round the city of Ilerda, where Divine Caesar had famously defeated Pompey the Great. The weather stayed fine and they bypassed the doubtful pleasures of the Imperial guest houses that dotted their route. Instead, they camped in the open, only visiting towns when they needed to change their mounts and the pack horses carrying their supplies. Valerius gained his companions' respect by volunteering to share their duties despite his unusual status as a more-or-less guest. Soon the saw-toothed rampart of the Pyrenees mountains dominated their eastern horizon, while to the west a thick haze shimmered over the fertile, cultivated plain.

Pliny's courier Marius, a legionary cavalryman, was, like most of his kind, young, intelligent and reticent to the point of secretive. He kept to himself and passed his time scratching at pieces of bark with the end of a burned twig, much to the amusement of the Vardulli. Still, it was difficult to be part of such a small company and not converse in some way. By the time they reached Esca he was comfortable enough to join the desultory conversation around the campfire. Valerius was curious about what he'd been doing with the twig and the bark. After some persuasion, Marius shyly showed him a series of remarkably lifelike drawings he'd made of the auxiliaries. There was even one of Valerius.

'Do I really look like that?' The man staring back at him had a hard, almost hawkish expression only softened by the sardonic twist to his lip, courtesy of the old knife wound that scored his cheek. Implacable obsidian eyes stared out from below unruly dark hair. He thought of himself as young, but in the drawing he looked what he was, a worn-out veteran of a dozen wars.

'It's probably not very good.' Marius offered him another version, full length from a distance.

Valerius smiled. 'Better, but,' he laughed, 'you seem to have forgotten this.' He raised the wooden fist.

Marius gaped. 'I didn't know, sir.'

Young soldiers, though they feigned disinterest, were always curious to know what had happened to Valerius's hand. Normally, he would only say that he'd lost it in battle. Tonight he wanted to win Marius's confidence, so he treated his companions to the defence of Colonia, and the last stand in the Temple of Claudius in all its horror and heroism.

'Suetonius Paulinus awarded me the Corona Aurea.' All the men not on guard lay by the fire listening and Valerius let his eyes drift around the circle of attentive faces until they fell on Marius. 'And the Emperor Nero himself placed it upon my brow.'

'What glory,' the young man cried. 'To have the Emperor's favour.'

'An emperor's favour can be a fickle thing,' Valerius shrugged. 'And I would give back that golden bauble and all the glory and the honour to see the faces of my comrades and hear their voices one last time.'

The veteran soldiers murmured agreement, but the eyes of the young men still glowed with visions of fame and valour.

'And Boudicca? Is it true what they say of her?'

'Ah, Boudicca.' Valerius allowed his voice to quicken and his imagination to run free. 'As tall as a rowan tree, with hair of burnished copper and breasts like the sweetest melons all painted gold . . .'

They grinned at each other. This was the kind of story a soldier could appreciate, even if he didn't believe a word of it.

When the flames of the campfire died to a dull flicker, Valerius unrolled his blanket beside Marius.

The young cavalryman turned to face him. 'What was Boudicca really like?'

'A handsome woman consumed by hate,' Valerius admitted. 'But we had given her reason to hate. Tell me, Marius, if you are willing, how things stand in Asturica? I heard different tales in every tavern in Tarraco.'

Marius hesitated only a moment to marshal his thoughts and knowledge into a coherent form. 'I'm not surprised, sir, because the situation is confused which-ever way you look at it. On the one hand there are whispers that the gold is running out and we'll soon all be going home to Italia. Yet speak to a common miner and he'll tell you of great nuggets gleaming in the lamplight just waiting to be plucked. It depends, of course,' his voice took on a scholarly tone, 'what kind of mine you are speaking of. There are several different methods, producing ore, dust or, more rarely, the sought-after nuggets.'

'You are an expert, I find, young Marius?'

Marius gave him an embarrassed glance. 'If I have given that impression I apologize, sir,' he laughed. 'I only know what I have heard in passing. The locals are stubborn folk, tight-lipped and secretive, but treat them with courtesy and show an interest in the natural philosophy of their land and one or two will show a different side. Even those, though, have become more distant lately.'

'Why would that be?'

Marius's voice dropped to a whisper. 'The ghosts of the past are stirring.'

Valerius wondered if he'd misheard. 'What?'

'That's what they say, sir. I believe it means that some among them see an opportunity to return to the old ways, before the mine workings flattened their mountains, filled in their valleys and poisoned their rivers.'

'Can it really be so bad?'

'Oh, yes,' came the matter-of-fact reply. 'You only have to look at the Red Hills to understand how destructive it can be. Like your Boudicca, sir, they have reason to dislike us, and now that we have been weak for so long – I mean relatively speaking, of course – it may be that some of them believe they have an opportunity to do something about it.'

'A rebellion? Do they understand what that would mean?'

'I couldn't say, sir.' Marius's voice had turned defensive, as if he felt he'd said too much. 'It is difficult to tell with them. All I can say is that were I in their place I would not be satisfied. And then there are the bandits.'

'I was told they had become more active and daring?'
Valerius invited a more detailed explanation, but the
younger man only shrugged.

'That may be the case, sir, but I haven't witnessed it.'

'You think I was misled?'

'All I can say, sir, is that we – that is my commander
– responds to every bandit attack with all the speed and
force he can muster. Inevitably, by the time we reach the
site the bandits have been fought off or have fled. They
are never strong enough to take a full convoy, but one or
two wagons will be missing, with perhaps a casualty
or two among the wagon drivers or muleteers. The thing
is, apart from the usual signs of disturbance around
the camp or ambush site, any tracks fade and then
vanish within a few hundred paces. It is as if the
raiders suddenly take to the air. That's why we – I mean
the more superstitious among the men – talk about The
Ghost.'

'The Ghost?'

'Laugh at me if you wish, sir,' the courier said
defensively, 'but the men have a pure dread of ever meeting him.'

'I would not laugh at you, Marius,' Valerius said
gently. 'Tell me, does this Ghost have a name?'

'In the Asturian tongue he is called "Nathair". A man
of almost supernatural powers, newly returned from
only the gods know where. He can pin a butterfly to a
tree with his knife point and is so fast with a sword that
anyone who faces him is dead before they even realize
he has unsheathed it. They say he cannot be killed.'

Valerius experienced a chill at the familiar list of
accomplishments. 'Does he have a face, this Ghost?'

'He keeps it masked. Only the shades of his victims
have ever seen it.'

'*Nathair*?' He knew the answer to his question before it left his lips.

'It means Snake, sir.'

Serpentius?

X

Serpentius brushed away one of the big rats that sniffed about the sleeping prisoners every night. Large as cats, they lived mostly off dropped food and what had passed through men's bodies, but they weren't averse to human flesh. One bite from their foul teeth would be the prelude to a lingering, painful end.

He willed himself to be strong. Experience had taught him how agonizing this would be, but when the alternative was certain death a man must be prepared to suffer pain. He had no idea how long it would take, or even if he'd succeed. But he had to try. He pulled the short section of shovel handle from his loin cloth, praying the balled piece of linen that passed as a stopper had held. Would it be enough? He'd used Vegeto's nail to hollow out a cavity in the centre of the ash, but didn't dare make it too large for fear the frail container collapsed.

Holding the shaft upright, he removed the linen ball and raised his body so he could pour the contents over his lower legs. Frugal with the first: he must share it equally. Mars save him, but there wasn't much. He rubbed the pitiful dribble of oil he'd stolen from the lamp over his ankles and feet beneath the iron rings of the shackles.

Now for the difficult part.

It was a trick he'd learned in his earliest days as a gladiator. Men destined to kill each other in the arena shared a special bond. As they'd been lying in their irons in the barracks of the *ludus* one night he'd been astonished when one of his companions stood up and walked to the door.

'What's happening?' he'd whispered to the man next to him.

'Nestor the *retiarius* has what you might call an assignation with a certain lady.'

'You mean he's escaping?'

'Not escaping,' the gladiator assured him. 'You're new here. Believe me, there's no escape. Out there in the city you'd be picked up before the cock crowed three times and then what? I'll tell you. The cross and a long, lonely death. It's not a bad life here. Fed and watered, and the occasional woman. If you're good enough you might even be handed the *rudis* and your freedom. If not, we're all going to die anyway. With Fortuna's favour it'll be quick. A sword in your hand and a friend by your side, right?'

'Right,' Serpentius said uncertainly. 'But how does Nestor do it?' He shook his shackled ankle.

The answer was that Nestor was one of the smaller gladiators, with correspondingly small feet. With the help of a little oil and the loss of a few inches of skin he could work his feet through the shackles. Serpentius had been born lean, and his calling had transformed him into a lethal blade of bone, sinew and muscle, but he had normal-sized feet. In time, he could do what Nestor did, but at greater cost.

Now, in the mine, he began working at the ring on

his left ankle, twisting and pushing at the same time.

What seemed a lifetime later sweat was running down his body and his heel and the front of his foot were a ball of agony and rubbed raw. Blood caked his hands, but he was nowhere near freeing the ring. Twist and push. Twist and push. How many times had he done it? Two hundred? Four? Twist and push. Ignore the pain.

As he worked he whispered instructions to Clitus.

'Your job, and the job of the others, is to look after the jailer. He must not make a sound. You'll have one chance. Don't worry about the guards. I'll take care of them.'

'But your chains, you can't—'

'Trust me.' Serpentius gritted his teeth to stifle his groans. Twist and push. Twist and push. Flesh is only flesh. Iron is iron. If he'd had a knife, he'd have cut the solid pad of his heel away. Could a man walk without a heel? But he didn't have a knife. Twist and push. Mars and Jupiter, would it never end? Twist and—' He slumped back, resisting the urge to cry out as the bloody ring slipped over his foot to free his left leg. It could be done. But how long had it taken?

He reached for his right ankle.

According to Vegeto, the free workers made their way to the mine at dawn. That meant, on this day, flushing-out day, the jailer and the guards with the water pipe should appear an hour before dawn. Dawn. Serpentius raised his eyes to the invisible ceiling of the sleeping chamber. He'd lost count of how long he'd been here. How many days was it since he'd seen a dawn. Forty? Fifty?

One way or the other he vowed this would be the last.

He crouched in the darkness to one side of the entrance, his agonized feet deep in the filthy ooze. Surprise was the key. If the jailer noticed a gap in the bodies on the floor he'd alert the guards. To ensure he didn't, Clitus and the others had shifted together to mask the space where Serpentius usually lay. Could they take the jailer? That couldn't be his concern. He had enough to think about. His heart thundered in his chest and he willed it to slow. If ever he'd needed calm it was now. He ran through what was about to happen in his mind, trying to establish the rhythm that would govern his actions and reactions. To identify the imponderable that would imperil his plans and what he must do to negate it. His fingers shifted their grip on the nail.

Voices echoing in the main shaft. A man complaining about the weight of the pipe. The jailer would enter first to light the oil lamps. The guards would follow close behind carrying the pipe, their spears laid aside just this once.

A soft glow of light in the entrance. Serpentius pressed himself back, trying to make himself one with the wall. Still. Be invisible.

First, the jailer, muttering to himself, his starved rat's face illuminated by the oil lamp he held in front of him, eyes only for the first lamp in its niche in the wall. One, two, three steps. The first guard appeared hauling at the leather pipe and grunting. The jailer reaching up to light the lamp with the one in his right hand, the bucket of slops in his left. The second guard giving the pipe one last heave and stepping into the chamber.

Now.

There is a lump on a man's throat that is uniquely vulnerable to attack and also part of the apparatus that allows him to communicate. Serpentius was a keen student of the myriad ways of dealing death. A punch directly on the lump, with the knuckle protruding, would have done the job, but the rusty, four-inch iron nail did it better. The first the guard knew of his impending doom was a choking sensation. He couldn't scream, he couldn't breathe and some-one had lit a fire in his throat. By now Serpentius was already turning away, the wrist chains whirling towards the second guard alerted too late by the sound of his comrade's last indrawn breath. As he pivoted to meet the threat Serpentius's chains settled round his neck and instantly tightened, choking off any shout for help. The Spaniard hauled with all his strength, twisting the links so the loop tightened like a strangling rope until, with a crack like a snapping twig, the guard's neck broke. He laid the twitching body to the ground, taking in the welcome sight of the jailer being drowned in his slop bucket before turning back to the first man.

Shock had pinned him in place, his hands clawing at the terrible spike in his throat and the blood running down his neck, but now he realized his error and turned to stagger towards the guardroom. Serpentius was on him in two bounds, his hand twisting in the man's hair. Somehow he'd found a heartbeat to retrieve the dead guard's *gladius*. Now he sawed the nicked blade across the man's neck in a single stroke that released a fountain of blood.

He hauled the body back into the chamber. The jailer's legs gave one last jerk and a large bubble burst in the slops with a 'plop' that broke the stunned silence. Clitus and another man – Thaumasto, wasn't it? – stared at him with gaping eyes as if they couldn't believe what they'd done. Serpentius held out his arms with the chain hanging between. Clitus was the first to recover. He searched the jailer's clothing until he found the crude key to unlock Serpentius's shackles.

'Now do the rest,' the Spaniard growled softly. He stood over the remaining prisoners. 'Any who are able should come with us,' he whispered. 'There is only pain and death if you stay.'

'Pain and death if we come,' one man, more feeble than the rest, muttered. 'They'll catch you before you get out of the valley.'

'So be it.' Serpentius nodded. 'But all are welcome.' To Clitus: 'Take the guards' uniforms. Give them to whoever fits best.' Clitus picked up the second guard's sword and held it awkwardly, but his eyes were filled with determination.

'No.' Serpentius managed a rictus of a smile. 'I'll do this alone.'

He stalked silently up the ill-lit passage until he came to the curtained guard chamber. The sound of soft breathing and one rasping snorer greeted him. From what he'd learned there should be four. He twitched the curtain aside and in the dull light of the oil lamps in the main passage he made out their sleeping forms. It was the work of moments. The fourth guard came awake as Serpentius stood over him.

'What's happening?' He rubbed his eyes.

'Go back to sleep, friend.' Serpentius placed the point of the sword beneath the man's breastbone and put his weight behind it.

Six men in uniform, escorting eight prisoners to the entrance of the mine shaft. Fortuna had favoured them so far, but Serpentius knew it wouldn't last. Some of these men were going to die. He'd given them their chance. The strong would survive and at least the weak would slow and divide the pursuit. And, he vowed, the strong would have their revenge. But to do that they had to get out of the mine before the main workforce arrived.

Thanks to Vegeto he had the layout of the outer mine in his head. Two guards at the entrance, but a half century within call. The legionaries were divided between the smelting house, where the gold was extracted from the crushed rock and turned into ingots, and the fortress-like storehouse where the ingots were held before being transported to Tarraco. The air turned cool and fresh and the oil lamps flickered in the draught and Serpentius knew they were approaching the entrance. He whispered to the others to wait and summoned Clitus and Thaumasto to follow him.

'They will be tired, bored and desperate for their relief,' he assured them. 'Their attention will be on the east and the first hint of the rising sun. They stand one to each side of the entrance. You will take the guard on the right. The right,' he gestured with his sword to that side of the tunnel, 'you understand?' Clitus nodded and Thaumasto's eyebrows knotted in concentration. 'It will be like the jailer. One to silence him and the other to kill him. I will take the one on the left. Wait for my signal. We must act together.'

They crept up to the entrance. Serpentius seemed to flow over the ground, but his companions agonized over every step. The Spaniard waited till he could hear the sound of a man breathing and raised his left hand. Two more strides and they could see the blue-black of the night sky and the first faint trace of dawn on the skyline. The outline of a Roman helmet pinpointed the guard on the right. Serpentius dropped his hand and stepped out into the open.

The guard on the left was more asleep than awake. The first he knew of his coming death was a hand clapped over his mouth before the sting as the *gladius* was dragged across his throat. Serpentius held him till he died, feeling the last frantic beats of the heart in the shuddering body, and with the familiar metallic scent of blood in his nostrils.

From behind came groans and thrashing, muttered curses and the sound of metal upon metal. He dropped the dead man and turned to find Clitus and Thaumasto still struggling with the second guard. Thaumasto had his hands over the man's face and Clitus was lunging with the sword at his chest. Serpentius bent to ram his own sword into the guard's throat. He pulled back the cloak.

'Chain mail,' he whispered. 'Always go for the throat. Quicker and quieter. You can let go now, Thaumasto. Dead men don't shout for help. Fetch the others.'

By the time Serpentius and Clitus had dragged the dead men into the mine they'd been joined by the other prisoners. Serpentius stripped one of the corpses of his sandals and cut a piece from the guard's tunic to wrap his bleeding feet. He stepped into the open and studied the skyline. The faint line had turned into a splash of orange and pink and against it he could see the silhouette of a straggling column of men. He turned to the prisoners. 'Follow me and stay below the crest of the hillside. We go west, then north. If you become separated, just follow the course of the river into the mountains. We will find you.'

He set a fast pace he knew his companions couldn't maintain for long, but there was no help for it. They had to get to the river before their former captors loosed the dogs.

When they were clear of the mine he took a last look back. Whatever happened he would die before he entered that den of Hades again.

XI

Rome

'Tiberius likened ruling the Empire to having hold of a wolf by the ears. I do believe he understated the complexity. It is much more like trying to control an entire pack.'

Vespasian's tone was cheerful enough as he made the pronouncement, but Titus could see that the cares of high office were already taking their toll of his father. Worry lines furrowed his brow and his mouth had assumed a habitual downturned look of grim contemplation. Sometimes it seemed that only in the arms of his lover, Antonia, did his father find peace. Not that the knowledge brought Titus any consolation. He still couldn't wholly forgive Vespasian for ordering him to set aside Berenice, whom he'd loved with just as much devotion and passion. But that was in the past. Now they held the wolf by the ears and the first priority was to keep hold of it.

'You would rather we had left all this to Vitellius?' Titus waved a hand at the raised platform where Vespasian's predecessor's golden throne had sat until it was carried away to be melted down. The receiving room was in the heart of the great Golden House constructed by Nero. Vespasian was never comfortable in the grandiose palace complex, but had yet to find a use for it.

'Thirty steps,' the Emperor marvelled. 'Perhaps he believed the closer to the gods he sat the more like them he would become. Poor man.' Vespasian inspected the rear of the platform and the curious contraption there. 'It's rather like the lifts that take the beasts to the main level of the arena.'

'He was so fat by the end he couldn't climb the stairs.' Titus didn't hide his scorn.

'Then he was no fool,' his father said, a mild rebuke in his tone. Usurper or no, Vitellius had been Emperor. The legionaries of Marcus Antonius Primus claimed the Golden House had been stripped bare by the time they took the place. Vespasian's younger son Domitian had not been inclined to believe them, but a few months earlier a building crew clearing the site of Vitellius's burned-out villa had uncovered a fortune in gold coins and statuary buried in the garden. The Emperor bent and picked up something from the floor behind the platform. 'A horse on wheels. A child's toy.' He shook his head. 'I never intended for him to die, or the boy. In fact I ordered otherwise. He could have passed away his remaining years in relative comfort on Sicilia and I would have encouraged Lucius through the *cursus honorum*.'

'Then the men who killed them did you a service,' Titus said brutally. 'It's much tidier this way.'

'True.' A wry smile flitted across Vespasian's puffy features and he replaced the toy. Titus returned the smile. His father could be kind-hearted and was seldom vindictive, but he could also be ruthless when he needed. He'd duped thousands of civilians to surrender at Tarrichaeae in Judaea with a promise of freedom, only to slaughter the elderly and infirm as a signal of the price for defying Rome's rule. It had worked. All but three Galilaean fortress cities surrendered as soon as the legions appeared at their gates.

'Ah, Domitian, you are here at last.' Vespasian turned as a slight figure appeared in the doorway.

'Father.' The young man bowed. 'Brother. I hope I see you well?'

'All the better for seeing you, brother,' Titus replied with an equal lack of sincerity.

'I wanted to show you what we intend,' Vespasian smiled, 'before it is announced in the Senate.'

The smile on Domitian's face froze at the word 'we'. That 'we' meant the two men who jointly ruled Rome. A 'we' that excluded the third, and in Domitian's view just as capable, member of the Flavian dynasty. They seemed to forget – or deliberately forgot – that in his father's absence Domitian had taken control of Rome after the death of Vitellius. Reigned as Emperor in all but name for more than six months. He'd begun the rebuilding of the Temple of Jupiter Capitolinus and the Castra Praetoria, both destroyed in the fighting. Since then he'd been reduced to minor roles. Even his consulship had been a mere suffect appointment, both temporary and honorary. Titus on the other hand was feted wherever he went, everyone's favourite. Always at his father's right hand and given command of the Praetorian Guard, a position of immense power. Domitian had been forced to ride with the generals in the wake of the chariot carrying Vespasian and Titus at the triumph to celebrate their victory in the Judaean Wars. Hundreds of thousands of Romans had hailed Titus *Imperator* as he rode with his father at the head of five legions and countless carriages piled high with the spoils of Jerusalem. Gold and silver wrought in every way imaginable, gems of extraordinary colour and lustre, loose or worked into crowns or diadems, bolts of silk in purple and gold. Had Domitian not fought too, in the final battle that defeated the Batavian rebels of Julius Civilis? And what was his reward? Nothing. Not even a word of thanks from his father, while Petilius Cerialis was appointed governor of Britannia.

'You look out of countenance, my son. Is something wrong?'

'A bad piece of fish,' Domitian lied.

'You should whip your cook,' Titus said solemnly. He'd noticed his brother's reaction and was perfectly aware of the reason. Perhaps if Domitian hadn't styled himself Caesar and placed himself on the throne the moment Marcus Antonius Primus had retaken the city he might have fared better. It hadn't helped that he'd married without his father's permission before the Emperor returned to the capital. And there was something odd about that union. Titus was acquainted with Domitia Longina Corbulo. Clever, beautiful if you liked your women slight and delicate, and with a strong personality that mirrored her soldier father. Too strong, he thought, to be attracted to someone like Domitian. But then, who knew with women? He studied his brother. Unlike Titus, Domitian had failed to inherit his father's strong features or physical presence. He had a weak chin and a curiously feminine mouth. Where Vespasian was straightforward, loyal to his friends and trustworthy, Titus knew Domitian could be cruel, capricious and downright treacherous. And then there was the matter of Valerius. 'Come, brother, some fresh air will dispel the ill humours.'

As Vespasian led the way through the corridors to Nero's man-made lake, the two younger Flavians held slightly back.

'A rumour reached me that a certain member of your household has been in touch with members of the Society,' Titus said quietly.

'You should know better than to believe everything you hear at the baths, brother.' Domitian's tight smile told his brother he'd been correct. The Society was a guild of criminals: gangsters, thieves and killers for hire. They had their stronghold in the Subura, a pestilential slum in the centre of the city, but their tentacles stretched across the Empire.

'And you should know that Gaius Valerius Verrens is under my protection – and my father's.'

'Why should a crippled upstart with ideas above his station concern me?' Domitian sneered.

'You understand exactly what I mean, brother.' Titus allowed his voice to harden. 'Verrens is on a mission vital to all our interests. If he is not allowed to complete it you and I may end up in pieces on the Gemonian Stairs like uncle Sabinus.'

'If he does not complete this *vital* mission it will not be because of anything I do, it will be because you selected a dangerous fool for the task.'

They glared at each other for a moment. Vespasian tutted. 'You must never fight, my sons. Our unity is our greatest strength. We three are the future of Rome. Come, Domitian.'

They followed their father out on to the balcony overlooking the lake. 'This is where I will build our legacy. We will drain the lake and build the greatest arena the world has ever seen' – he turned to his sons with a smile – 'and a hundred generations of Romans will give thanks to the Flavians. I will place Nero's colossus at the gates . . . with a few alterations, of course. It would be a pity to waste it.'

But Domitian's thoughts were elsewhere. Rome's future? His father was in robust health and might live another twenty years. Titus could last another forty and there was no reason he should not yet beget an heir. Only by a happy accident would Titus Flavius Domitianus ever wear the purple. And then there was Verrens. Had his brother been telling the truth about the urgency of this mission?

In a way it didn't matter. An arrow loosed could not be returned to the bow no matter the good intentions of the archer. He had loosed the arrow and the arrow would take its course. But he had seen what was left of his uncle Sabinus on the Gemonian Stairs and he had no intention of ending up there. It would bear thinking about.

XII

They reached Legio on the afternoon of the twelfth day. A Roman fortification had existed here since the time of Augustus and the Cantabrian wars, and Valerius could see why. The fort stood in a perfect defensive position on a raised plateau cushioned in the junction of two rivers. The stone walls and wooden palisade dominated everything around and it could only be attacked directly from the north. Valerius's little column was approaching from the south, travel-weary: even the seasoned cavalrymen of the Faithful Vardulli admitted to being saddle-sore after close to two weeks on horseback.

Now their minds were focused on a cool bath to wash away the all-encompassing dust of the journey, a cup of sour wine in a local tavern and the ministrations of a comely whore. In truth, it wasn't much of a place. Valerius could see the red-tiled roofs of stucco-walled barrack blocks and administration buildings. A civilian settlement lined the road from the *porta praetoria* and sprawled on to the south bank of the smaller of the two rivers. They passed wooden shops and workshops, a forge where a smith's apprentice was turning out iron hob-nails for a nearby cobbler, and a stinking tannery where the women scraping hides didn't even raise their heads as they passed.

Two men stood guard at the bridge, but they called out when they recognized Marius.

'You'll get it hot,' one of them predicted with a grin. 'Proculus was expecting you days ago. Everyone reckoned the Ghost had taken you.'

Mention of the Ghost took Valerius back to his conversation with the young courier a week and more earlier. Nathair. The snake. At first he'd been certain this Ghost must be his old Spanish comrade. The name and the description of his fighting qualities were too much of a coincidence. But the more he considered it, the more unlikely it seemed. More than two years had passed since he'd left Serpentius in Judaea being treated for a terrible sword wound that would have killed him if it had been more expertly placed. The Spaniard also suffered spasmodic fits after a legionary had smashed his skull during the fall of Rome. If he survived, Titus had provided the former gladiator with enough gold to buy a small estate where he could settle down and perhaps take a wife. Why would such a man turn bandit?

Yes, Serpentius had never hidden his bitterness against the Romans who burned his home and killed his family, but that had been twenty-odd years ago. The Spaniard was no fool and in all the time Valerius had known him he'd never talked of revenge. Yet the bandit raids were one of the factors the authorities in Asturica Augusta claimed were responsible for the lack of gold reaching Rome. Perhaps discovering more about this Ghost should be one of his lines of investigation.

'I am afraid you may find our commander a little distracted.' Young Marius didn't seem put out by his welcome. 'He has many conflicting responsibilities and few resources to fulfil them.'

'You said he is the legion's *praefectus castrorum*?'

'Yes, sir,' the courier confirmed. 'Tiberius Claudius Proculus. The legate is with the main detachment of the legion at Moguntiacum on the Rhenus.'

The main gate of the fortress, the *porta principalis*, was on the east side and guarded by twin towers. To the north a squadron of auxiliary cavalry exercised their horses on a flat area of ground between the arms of the two rivers. Valerius was immediately struck by the style of their armour. Abilio, the escort commander, reined in beside him and studied the riders with professional interest as they wheeled and galloped across the iron-hard earth, forming line and square as if by instinct.

'They're good,' he said. 'Not as good as us, but still good.'

Valerius smiled at the grudging respect of one horse warrior for another. 'Their equipment is unusual.' Something about the tall, plumed helmets and fish scale armour appeared chillingly familiar.

'Not Thracians, that's for certain. Moesian?'

'They're from the First ala Parthorum,' Marius informed them. 'One of the few auxiliary regiments they left us. Four hundred cavalry and six hundred light infantry.'

'Parthians?' Valerius had never heard of a Parthian auxiliary unit.

'Yes, the ala has been in Hispania since the Cantabrian war. Some minor Parthian lord decided he owed tribute to Augustus and they've been supplying recruits ever since.'

Valerius detected something in the way he spoke about the easterners.

'You don't approve, Marius?'

'It's not for me to approve or disapprove, sir,' Marius said defensively. 'All I will say is that my commander is very short of mounted soldiers and they are given a latitude not allowed some other units.'

Valerius would have probed deeper, but he saw they were being watched by the officer supervising the auxiliaries. The man considered the newcomers for a few moments before guiding his horse towards them. Valerius kept his wooden fist beneath his cloak, but he needn't have concerned himself. The officer, a dark-eyed, bearded hawk of a man in a green tunic and polished chain armour, ignored the mere civilian and addressed his auxiliary counterpart.

'Claudius Harpocration, prefect First ala Parthorum, and you are?'

'Abilio Sabinus, *decurio*, First Faithful Vardulli.'

'So not the reinforcements I asked for?'

'I'm afraid not, sir. Attached to the governor's household, and currently on escort duty.' He nodded to the courier. 'Nursemaids, you might say.'

Harpocration didn't smile. 'And how long will you be in Legio?'

'We're to accompany the next gold shipment back to Tarraco. We were told we might be here for a week.'

Harpocration stared at him, then nodded slowly. His eyes passed over Valerius as he hauled his horse's head round and rode back to his men. The one-handed Roman studied the retreating horseman. The last time he'd seen that look was from a Parthian Invincible on the field at Cepha who'd promised to take his head and use it as a drinking bowl.

'A strange character, and very interested in your comings and goings,' Valerius said to Abilio.

'They are a proud people, and arrogant with it,' Marius answered.

'Just running an eye over us,' Abilio said. 'Not that we're much to look at, only the ten of us. Now, Marius, which way to the bath house? We'll want to get cleaned up before we pay our respects to your commander.'

The bath house lay in the south-eastern corner of the fort. Once they'd washed and changed into fresh clothes they made their way through the barrack blocks.

By the time they reached the headquarters Marius had already reported to Tiberius Claudius Proculus. The camp prefect's secretary announced that he would receive the others individually. Valerius waited in an anteroom while Abilio, the serving officer, had his audience. The legate's administrative offices formed three sides of a large parade square perhaps a hundred paces in width. The complex stood at the very heart of the camp, at the junction of the Via Praetoria and the Via Principalis. As well as offices it housed a basilica where the commander could address his troops under cover, and the *sacellum*, where the Sixth's standards, including its eagle, would normally be stored in suitable dignity. In this case, Valerius suspected, the eagle would be with the legion's legate at Moguntiacum and the *sacellum* would contain only a few cohort and century banners. Close to the *principia* stood the *praetorium*, the legate's living quarters.

Eventually, Abilio was ushered out. He flashed Valerius a wry look as he passed. The secretary stood by the door and Valerius walked past him into the inner office. He'd dressed in a fine toga for the meeting and the man behind the desk looked up in surprise.

'You asked to see me?' The voice was brittle with suppressed irritation and Proculus's expression matched it. He had the tormented features of a man condemned to spend life chewing pebbles and broken glass and wondered when the next portion was about to arrive. An unhealthy grey shadow tinged his sunken cheeks.

'It seemed a courtesy to present my credentials and a letter of introduction from the governor.' Valerius ignored the coolness of his welcome and handed over a leather scroll case.

Proculus's frown deepened as he read the letter. 'My apologies, sir. Had I known you'd held high military office and are a holder of the Corona Aurea I would have seen you immediately. Be sure I will have my clerk whipped for his trouble.'

'There is no need for that, prefect,' Valerius assured him. 'It is not something I wished widely known. A man's fortunes and good name have a way of ebbing and flowing with each change of emperor.' Proculus gave him a suspicious look. Was he being provoked? It took either a brave man or a foolish one to speak so freely of emperors. Valerius smiled. 'I mean only that I am a man for whom status is not important.'

Proculus coiled the scroll and rapped it against his desk. 'This letter from Governor Secundus asks me to provide you every help and support in some quest he does not specify?'

'An old comrade who saved my life in Armenia asked for my help,' Valerius explained. 'But I was travelling. By the time I finally managed to answer his letter he didn't reply.'

'And you think he is in Legio?'

'His letter mentioned Asturica Augusta.' Valerius and Pliny had concocted the scheme before he'd left Tarraco. Better a man of some status for access, official or otherwise, than a nobody. And what was more natural than to seek out an old comrade who had saved your life. It gave Valerius a reason to ask questions about Petronius, but didn't link him directly to the investigation into the missing gold.

'I have no authority in Asturica,' Proculus complained. 'It is governed by a civilian administration. More to the point I do not have the resources to offer you any support. Every man is needed for duty.' He waved at a parchment map pinned to a frame near the doorway. 'I have a quarter of the men I need to properly defend this fort, but I am told my priority is to provide security for the mines, guards for the gold trains, engineers to keep the aqueducts flowing. The entire area is plagued by bandits. I asked Governor Secundus to send me a reinforcement of two cohorts to allow me to make a clean sweep of the mountains and remove at least this threat, but no, I am instructed to stay in camp and somehow turn one man into four.'

'I heard mention of some Ghost who leaves no tracks.'

Proculus gave a bark of disgust. 'There is no Ghost, as I keep telling these fools. Only a man who is cleverer than the idiots I am able to send against him. He has time to make his raids, carry off the gold and cover his tracks before they come close to him. But we will have him soon enough. If you had been a week earlier you would have seen the heads of a dozen of his accomplices on display outside the fortress.'

'Did they betray his whereabouts before they died?'

'No,' Proculus admitted. 'But it is only a matter of time.'

'Then I pray Fortuna favours you.' Valerius bowed. 'Clearly Governor Secundus was unaware of the difficulties you face. Be sure I will see he is given the full story when I return. In the meantime all I ask is your leave to travel in your area of responsibility.'

'At your own risk?'

'Of course.'

'Then you have it.' Proculus rubbed the back of his hand across his eyes. 'I will also tell my clerk to give you a letter of introduction to the head of Asturica's *ordo*. Hopefully he will be able to help you find your friend. Now, if you please . . .'

'Thank you for your time, prefect.' By the time Valerius reached the door Proculus was already peering at a new list of demands.

Next morning Valerius said his farewells to Abilio and the rest of the escort. The Vardulli commander couldn't hide his concern when Valerius revealed that Proculus wasn't able to provide him with an escort or guide while he was in Asturica.

Abilio rubbed a gnarled hand across his stubbled chin. 'The governor didn't give me any details, but when he briefed us to bring you north with the courier he hinted there was more to your visit than mere courtesy. Had he known this would happen, I think he might have wanted us to stay with you. As it is, I've pledged my troop to reinforce the Parthians when they guard the next gold train south.'

'Do not trouble yourself, Abilio,' Valerius assured him with a smile. 'I'm well versed in the ways of staying out of trouble. I'm just another traveller seeking out an old friend to visit, to drink too much wine and tell lies about how much better it was when we were young.'

'Then I wish you a safe journey onward, and may Fortuna be with you, sir.'

Marius approached with some advice as Valerius readied his horse. 'If you push hard and change your mount at Palantia you should be able to make Asturica Augusta before sundown and avoid a cold night in the open. I thought this might save you some trouble if you are travelling in the area.' He handed over a long leather tube containing a rolled-up scroll. Valerius made to open it, but the young man laid a hand on his arm. 'Not yet, I think, but at need. It is as accurate as I can make it and I'd be glad of its return when you have finished with it.'

'Thank you for your mysterious gift, Marius.' Valerius was genuinely touched. 'I will certainly treasure it and return it before I go back to Rome. And also for your entertaining company on the way north.'

Marius grinned at the compliment. 'It was my pleasure on what could have been a long, dull ride. I gained the impression that you are a man who takes an interest in his surroundings?'

Valerius hid his unease behind his smile. 'As much as the next man.'

'You will find much to interest you in Asturica.' The courier patted the neck of Valerius's bay mare. 'But don't be too trusting of those you meet until they prove worthy of it.'

'You said the tribesfolk could be distant.'

'I don't mean the tribesfolk,' Marius said softly. 'I'm talking about the men who run the place. The *ordo*. They're all Roman citizens now and put on fashionable airs and graces, but not long ago their families were thieves and bandits. They have been cheating people for so long they believe anything else is abnormal. Anyone honest is regarded as gullible and an opportunity for profit.'

'Thank you for your advice.'

'There is one other thing. When I left Tarraco Governor Secundus's secretary gave me a letter to be opened only when I reached Legio. It instructs me that should a certain person – identified by a distinctive physical feature – need to get an urgent message to the governor I am ordered to make myself available to carry it.' Valerius stared at him, but Marius only grinned. 'Such things are not so unusual for men who serve the governor. There is a tavern by the bridge – the innkeeper's daughter is a . . . friend. If you can send a message there by a trusted hand I will carry it south before the day is out. All the arrangements are in place.'

'It seems I am even more in debt than I knew. The Bridge Tavern?'

'Yes, sir.' His eyes drifted over Valerius's shoulder. 'Take care on your journey. It seems you are not the only one around here who is interested in his surroundings.'

Valerius followed his gaze to where two men watched them from one of the towers by the gate. From their beards and saturnine complexions Valerius had no doubt they were Parthians.

XIII

The road from Legio took him first south, then west. He set a fast pace, only stopping to water the mare and the pack horse, and to change the animals at a government way station beside the road. It was a substantial place, as was to be expected on such a busy route, with several paddocks and a shaded terrace for weary travellers to rest and eat. He ate bread and olives there, and drank from a flask of watered wine, relaxed, but his eyes never leaving the road back to Legio. The plain all around was blessed with few distinguishing features and by the time he remounted he was certain enough he wasn't being followed.

As he rode, he considered what Marius had told him. Not much on the face of it, but the fact he felt the need to draw attention to what Valerius might expect in Asturica was message enough. *Trust no one until they've proved themselves worthy of your trust.* Naturally, for a man of Valerius's experience, that led to the question of whether he could trust Marius. The courier had made no attempt to show the supposed letter from Pliny, which left open the possibility of a trick. Yet . . . there was something about the young man that made Valerius inclined to believe him. For one thing, behind the boyish naivety lay a core of something much harder: you didn't become an Imperial courier if you balked at the first obstacle. In some ways, Marius reminded Valerius of Tiberius Crescens, the tribune who'd accompanied him on his journey to join General Gnaeus Domitius Corbulo in Syria. Tiberius had betrayed him in the end, but that wasn't the point. It had been nothing personal.

He retrieved the scroll case the courier had given him from a sack tied to the saddle. Using his left hand and his teeth he pulled a roll of parchment clear and sat back with his leg hooked over one of the front pommels, allowing the horse to make his own pace. The contents both surprised and intrigued him. He'd expected one of Marius's charcoal drawings, but it turned out to be something much more valuable. What he had in his hands was a detailed map of Asturia, with Legio and Asturica Augusta towards the east and the Lusitanian border in the south. Roads and rivers, mountains and bridges, but most significantly the sites of the region's gold mines all defined in ochre. He studied it closely, taking in the changes in terrain and the little clusters of brownish dots. Where on this poorly cured piece of hide would he find what he was looking for? What was it he was looking for?

He was wondering whether he'd have to stop for the night after all when the dipping sun created a blood-red sky that silhouetted a low chain of mountains on the horizon. Thanks to Marius's map he realized he must be close to Asturica Augusta.

An hour later he approached the walls of a city that lay squat and secure on a low mound overlooking a river. Like Legio, Asturica had most likely begun life as a military camp, but had evolved into a civilian settlement at the end of the Cantabrian wars. Its location made it the gateway to the mountains and the goldfields they contained. A position like this, dominating major trading routes, had made the city of Emesa in Syria rich, and Valerius didn't doubt he would find something similar in Asturica. Unlike Emesa, though, the riches Asturica gathered didn't stay in the city's treasure houses. They were transported to the treasury in Rome. At least they were meant to be.

He pondered his next move as he rode slowly towards the gate. Logically, it would depend on the reaction to his arrival. He had an introduction to the leader of Asturica's council, and another to the man Pliny had suggested might be able to help him find Petronius. On the other hand he was hungry, tired and travel-stained. If he wanted to reach the *mansio* before they shut down the fires for the baths and the kitchens he'd have to leave the introductions till tomorrow. On reflection he decided there was no hurry. The delay would give him the opportunity to check out the lie of the land. He slapped his horse on the shoulder and laughed. 'It never does any harm to have a bolt hole in mind.'

Proculus's warrant ensured there was no trouble with the watch and a gate guard directed him towards the south wall and a stable not far from the *mansio*. He paid a groom to look after the beasts and carried the packs with his belongings to the guest house as darkness fell.

Tired or not, he quickly became aware of his shadow. A single man, if his instincts were to be believed. Only time would tell whether he posed a threat. For the moment he was keeping his distance, content to dog Valerius's footsteps. Still, from what he'd heard of the depth of corruption, and presumably suspicion, in

Asturica it wouldn't be a surprise to find a stranger being followed when he entered the city. For the moment there was nothing he could do about it. He checked in, took a bath – ensuring he always had company in waters well polluted by the previous occupants – and had a simple meal in the communal dining room.

Returning to the private bedchamber he'd paid for, he paused for a few moments listening for any follower. When he was satisfied he hauled the bed across the inside of the curtained doorway. He lifted the thin mattress and placed it on the floor in the corner of the room and lay down with his sword within easy reach of his left hand and the wooden fist securely strapped to the right.

No point in taking any chances.

The next morning he rose early and broke his fast with a bowl of thin gruel sweetened with honey, followed by flat bread and olives. He already wore his sword belt beneath his cloak, but in a *mansio* frequented by soldiers loath to be parted from their weapons it excited no comment. He finished his meal and left a coin on the wooden table. The kitchen lay at the rear of the room behind a curtained doorway and he walked quickly across and stepped through.

A slave tending flat breads in a shimmering oven looked up as he stepped into the kitchen. Valerius met his puzzled frown with a stare and nodded imperiously as if he were here to inspect the place. Three strides took him out of the back door, which opened on to a noisome yard filled with reeking buckets of slops, empty amphorae and the gutted remains of soiled mattresses. On the far side a wooden door led to the alley beyond.

He followed the alley until he reached a cobbled roadway that hugged the inside of the walls. This would once have been the *intervallum*, the road that separated the barrack buildings from the walls. Now it was home to stalls already filled with produce from the fields outside the fort, and workshops where entire families wove cloth, cobblers hammered new nails into the soles of worn sandals, and carpenters worked to smooth timber baulks. Turning north, he passed a factory where thousands of bricks were drying in the sun, and another where two small twin boys in ragged tunics watched wary-eyed for any cats that threatened to walk across the ochre roof tiles laid out ready for the kiln. Clearly this was a place that encouraged enterprise.

The reason became clear as he walked the increasingly busy streets. Every one seemed to have at least one ostentatious villa and often more, the homes of rich men who could afford the finest of everything. The complacent, stony faces of those same men stared at him from each corner. Uniformly firm-jawed, their expressions were designed to convey honesty, intelligence and toil, the painted marble smoothing away the unpleasant realities of the human existence and creating something close to a god.

Valerius studied one statue that dominated the square in front of a large ornate building complex. Dressed in a formal toga, the man had narrow, patrician features and stared across towards the columned frontage. A dedication identified the building and its benefactor 'The Guild of Pipemakers set this up in thanks for the kindness, generosity and devotion of Cornelius Aurelius Saco, *architectus*, who financed and dedicated these baths in the first consulship of the Emperor Aulus Vitellius Germanicus Augustus.'

Someone had chiselled a line through Vitellius's name to indicate he was now in *damnatio* and deserved no honour, but it wasn't that which drew Valerius's attention. It struck him that Aurelius Saco must be a very successful builder to pay for something on this scale. Then again, perhaps Marius's warning had made him overly suspicious and the man merely came from a wealthy family.

Another turn brought him to an enormous building site covering an area fully a hundred and thirty paces square. On the far side dozens of slaves and craftsmen worked on a columned portico that took up the entire length of the square. Closer to Valerius, others manhandled sections of fluted pillar towards a partially built but already impressive basilica. A line of statues lay waiting like a row of dead bodies to be raised to positions at the top of eighteen – no twenty – marble columns. He recognized one of them as the official image of Vespasian the Emperor had approved for the provinces, and he had a feeling a figure in a sculpted breastplate might be Titus.

The sound of a minor altercation on a street off the square drew his attention. A master was beating his slave with a stubby block of wood from the building works. At first it was of little interest. In Rome it wasn't becoming to be seen beating your servants on the street, but this seemed proof that Asturica's sophisticated veneer was only wafer thin. A moment's study confirmed that the man being beaten was the same who had followed Valerius the previous night. Presumably the slave's job had been to follow him this morning and he was now reaping the reward for his failure.

Valerius stepped into the shadows of a shop awning and observed the scene with greater interest. The person doing the beating was tall, thin, and sharp-featured, a stork in human form, probably in early middle age, while his victim was little more than a boy.

A man in a toga was passing by with a pile of scrolls in his arms. Valerius stepped out to meet him with a smile and a gesture with the fingers of his left hand that signalled a fellow lawyer. 'Excuse me, sir, but I am new to Asturica Augusta. Am I to understand you are renewing the entire forum?'

The lawyer sniffed, not best pleased to have been prevented from going about his business, but constrained by good manners from ignoring another professional. 'That is the case, sir, but I beg you not to include me in the project. The old one suited me well enough and I do not much like pleading cases in the temple precinct during the construction.'

Valerius nodded his understanding. 'It seems that at least one person believes it is too slow.' He gestured in the direction of the slave, who was now on his knees and bleeding from a scalp wound as the other man stood over him. 'Is it usual for masters to beat their slaves in the streets of Augusta?'

'Why, no, sir, it is not,' the lawyer said stiffly, 'but in this case it would not be technically accurate. Though I do not know his identity, I am acquainted with the fact that the person chastising the slave – I'm sure for the best of reasons – is in fact the secretary to one of our leading citizens.'

'May I enquire the name of the citizen?'

The other man frowned. This was close to impertinence. Still, at least one of them had to show manners. 'If you wish. The gentleman in question is a member of the *ordo* and *magister* of the guild of builders, Cornelius Aurelius Saco.'

The *ordo*, the council of one hundred, was the administrative heart of any provincial Roman town. Its members were elders of the property-owning classes and usually had substantial personal wealth. They acted as magistrates, set taxes, officiated over planning disputes and decided on water rights, but their authority was illusory. Real power lay with the *duoviri iuri dicundo*, the two senior members of the council. No decision could be ratified without their presence and they decided who was appointed to which court, and even which cases they tried. As Pliny had explained it, the system was ripe for exploitation in a place like Asturica. A plaintiff might bribe a certain friendly member of the *ordo* to take his case, but before that could happen part of the bribe would first have to travel upwards to ensure the *duoviri* appointed the correct person. It was one of the *duoviri* whom Proculus had suggested Valerius meet.

Normally the council would conduct business from a large room at the centre of the basilica, but Valerius discovered that because of the construction work Aulus Severus ran his little empire from his home in the east of the town. He changed his tunic for a toga and left his sword and other valuables in the *mansio*'s strongroom. His shadow stood hunched in a doorway down the street, more conspicuous now with his bandaged head and swollen eyes. Valerius felt a little sorry for him.

The slave was still some way behind when they reached Severus's splendid house. A doorkeeper stood between the twin pillars to repel unwanted guests, but the seal on Proculus's letter and a short exchange persuaded him to allow Valerius through the atrium and into a waiting area. The room had a polished mosaic floor depicting an alarmingly lifelike brown bear standing on its hind legs with its bloodied mouth open. Birds of different species pecking at grapes and nuts in a leafy canopy surrounded the central image. The workmanship wasn't particularly fine, but whoever had designed the mosaic had done the subject justice. Valerius studied it until the waft of a particular scent told him he had company.

He turned to look into the eyes of one of the most striking women he'd ever seen. Her eyes, the aquatic green of a sunlit Aegean bay, seemed to strip him bare. Tall enough that she topped his shoulder, her dark hair fell in waves of tight curls and tendrils to a slim neck the colour of ivory. He barely registered the dress of bright red silk, cut low to show off the swell of her breasts. In Rome, she might have been mistaken on the streets for a courtesan, but this was not Rome and Valerius knew he was looking at the lady of the house. They studied each other for what seemed a long time before she smiled.

'My husband is indisposed.' She had a soft voice with a hint of affected sibilance. 'I am here to entertain you till he is free.'

Valerius ignored the unmistakable hint of suggestion and returned her smile. 'Then I fear I am going to be very poor company. I'm here on a business matter and I hope your husband can help me. I'm sure you are not interested in business.'

'No,' she admitted, her eyes still holding his. 'But I would be happy to hear about Rome.'

The smile froze on Valerius's face. 'What makes you think I have come from Rome?'

'Your courtly manners and the way you deal with a lady's impudent suggestion.' The full, reddened lips twitched. 'But mainly the rather fine cut of your clothing. We are ardent followers of the latest fashions in Asturica. My dress, for instance, what do you think of it?'

Valerius knew a trap when he saw it and under

those knowing eyes he decided he'd never faced a more dangerous one. The truth would never do. A lie would be instantly detected. Faced with no other choice he was forced into the soldier's last resort, an orderly retreat.

'I'm afraid I know nothing of fashion, my lady; all I can say is that such a dress has never graced a finer form.'

He thought he'd gone too far, but after a moment's puzzled hesitation she laughed. 'So I was right about your courtly manners. Let us see what else I can get right. You have been a soldier, I would guess.' His left hand went up to touch the line of puckered flesh on his cheek. The right had been part-hidden in the folds of his toga, but he guessed she'd seen it, so he drew the wooden fist clear.

'A memento of Britannia,' he said wryly. 'It happened when I was very young and I barely notice it now.'

'Do not apologize for it.' She took a step closer and the scent of her perfumed oil threatened to overpower him. 'It makes you . . .' He thought she was going to say interesting, but the word that emerged was '. . . distinctive.'

She took a step away and turned smoothly as a short, balding man enveloped in a toga appeared in the doorway behind her. 'Husband.' She bowed her head in welcome. Aulus Severus might have been her father, rather than her spouse. He had the wizened, irritated face of a newborn kept too long from its mother's tit and a voice that dripped sarcasm.

'My dear, I told you to take our visitor to the receiving room.' His Latin, like his wife's, had an over-quick sing-song quality. He turned to Valerius. 'Sir, if what my *atriensis* tells me is correct, you will be desperate for refreshment.' He nodded at the woman with a tight smile of dismissal. Valerius watched as she walked from the room with a swivel of the hips that would have done an Armenian veil dancer credit.

'I arrived in Asturica last night, but I'm well rested. A little wine would be welcome, though.'

Severus gestured for Valerius to follow him through to another sumptuously decorated room with a pair of couches facing each other over a low table. He waved a hand to one and took the other as Valerius settled himself on his side.

'My *atriensis* spoke of a letter of introduction from Tribune Proculus at Legio?'

'That's correct, sir.'

'May I see it?'

It would have been good manners for Severus to formally introduce himself, but Valerius ignored the slight and pulled the scroll from the folds of his toga. The doorman appeared at his shoulder with his hand out for the document. Valerius handed the scroll over and the man passed it to his master.

Severus peered at the document through narrowed eyes as the *atriensis* held an oil lamp behind his head to improve the light. 'If I read this correctly, Proculus informs me that you are a Hero of Rome,' he frowned. 'I apologize, sir. Aulus Aemilianus Severus welcomes you to his house. If only I had been informed of your status – the Corona Aurea, after all – I would have received you in a suitable style, rather than in this wretched fashion. We do things in the proper style in Asturica Augusta, you know.'

'I apologize, sir.' Valerius bowed his head. 'In the circumstances modesty forbade me from making an issue of my position.'

'But the protocol . . . ? Zeno, bring us some wine.' He returned to the letter. 'He says you seek my help in some

123

matter.' A sniff and a little groan to let Valerius know what it was costing him. 'Perhaps I should explain. My fellow *duovir*, Regulus, has been indisposed for several months and I carry the burden of running Asturica alone. Of course, we will do everything in our powers to bring your visit to a satisfactory conclusion, but . . .'

'I would be very grateful, sir.' Zeno placed a cup in front of Valerius and filled it. Then did the same for his master. Valerius took a sip and only just managed to suppress a cough. Experienced as he was in the rawest tavern piss, this made his eyes water. It tasted as if someone had marinaded a legionary's foot wrap in vinegar.

'And the matter is?'

'I have a friend.' Valerius cleared his throat. 'An old army comrade. He saved my life in Armenia. I received a letter from Asturica Augusta asking for my help. Unfortunately, by the time I could reply it appears he wasn't in a position to answer.'

Severus frowned. 'His name?'

'Marcus Florus Petronius. He was an engineer. I believe he was interested in your celebrated mining techniques.'

'Of course,' Severus preened. 'We lead the world.'

'But you have had problems?' Valerius accompanied the suggestion with a puzzled frown.

'What makes you say that?' Suspicion and alarm combined to give the older man's face an almost comical expression.

'There was a suggestion in his letters.'

'No, no,' Severus assured him. 'We have the same problems every mining area does. Collapses, mass asphyxiations, flooding, but nothing to be concerned about.' He stood up and walked to the door. 'I can assure you I will do all I can to find this fellow Petronius if he is in this city. As *duovir* it will be strange if I cannot track down his whereabouts. It may take a few days, but . . .'

'I am happy to wait upon you whenever is suitable.' Valerius took the hint and rose from his couch. 'I've heard Asturica is a region of natural wonders and as a student of such things I am keen to witness them.'

'Then I will send you a note. But wait, we cannot have a Hero of Rome staying in the *mansio*. The *ordo* keeps houses for honoured guests. Zeno will call on you and arrange your transfer.'

Valerius knew there was no refusing this offer of hospitality if he wanted Severus's cooperation. 'You have my thanks, sir.'

Zeno escorted Valerius to the door. Severus waited a suitable interval then summoned back the slave. 'Now get me some proper wine.'

A familiar scent tickled his nostrils. 'He seemed to impress you, Calpurnia. What did you think?'

'I think he was lying.'

XIV

The light of a full moon turned the river into a ribbon of molten silver and confirmed Serpentius was on course. Fourteen men had escaped the tunnel; now they were only nine. They'd barely travelled three miles before the weakest had pleaded to stop and rest. Serpentius ignored them and carried on without a backward glance, his loping leopard's stride covering the ground with relentless stamina. The others had hesitated, but they knew their pursuers couldn't be far behind and soon the desperate cries faded.

Nine, but the best of them. Clitus and Thaumasto, a grinning thief called Placido, and five others who were just names to him: Elius, Floro, Felix, Gentilis and Celer. They wasted precious moments before they found a crossing point a little way upstream from a triple-arched Roman bridge. Serpentius knew they'd have made faster progress using the road, but three times already they'd been forced into cover as single riders passed at the gallop. Without hesitation he plunged into the water and forced his way thigh deep through the powerful flow. The others followed readily enough, but as they climbed the far bank Serpentius winced at a sharp cry.

He looked back to see Thaumasto bent over and holding his ankle, teeth gritted against the pain.

Clitus went back to check on his friend. 'It's just a sprain,' he said after a moment. 'I'll help him until it eases.'

'No you won't. He can manage on his own.' Serpentius met Thaumasto's eyes and hardened his heart against the plea he saw there. 'We're wasting time.'

Serpentius carried on, but Clitus stood his ground. 'We wouldn't have got out of the mine without him,' he persisted. 'He fought while others lay there and did nothing. Have you no compassion?'

Serpentius stopped and let out a long breath. He turned and strode back to where Clitus stood by the injured man. 'Do you hear that?' He put his face to Clitus's. At first the only sound Clitus could hear was the rush of the river, but gradually he made out a faint baying that froze his blood. 'They'll be here soon,' Serpentius continued. 'If we cross the river two or three more times we can delay them long enough to give ourselves a chance. What do you think will happen if we carry Thaumasto?' He drew the dagger from his belt and placed it in Thaumasto's hand. 'You were brave at the mine,' he said quietly. 'Now you must be braver still.'

He turned and led the men through the scrub that lined the river bank. After a few moments he sensed Clitus by his side. The river snaked its way through the valley, sometimes hemmed in close by the hills on one bank, and sometimes the other. Twice more in the next hour they crossed. The dogs would lose the scent where they entered, but the hunters would carry on in case they were being tricked before they finally decided to cross. The ruse cost precious time, but for what Serpentius had in mind it was vital to put confusion in the minds of his pursuers.

The sight of the Roman bridge had brought back a memory. He knew exactly where they were. And that meant they still had a chance.

A mile ahead he recognized the place he was looking for. 'We cross here,' he said. 'But we only go a hundred paces before we cross back.' The others looked at him in puzzlement. 'You must trust me.'

They crossed and recrossed. At the point where they returned to the bank a large rock jutted out from the hillside.

'Wait here,' Serpentius ordered, as the men gathered in the shadow of the boulder.

They watched bemused as he continued north for forty or fifty paces before retracing his steps.

'Now . . .' He chewed his lip and stared at the flat rock face that rose ten feet above them before it angled to meet the near sheer hillside. 'Clitus? Placido? Stand here and join hands, like this.' He made his fingers into a cradle and the two men did as he asked despite their bewilderment. They stood facing each other about two feet from the rock. Serpentius took three steps back. 'When I shout, you heave upwards with all your strength. Do you understand? Wait for my shout.'

Clitus and Placido nodded. The other men stood watching, their faces a mask of suspicion. Serpentius knew what they were thinking. Was he going to abandon them? But that wasn't his problem. He launched himself forward. One, two. On the third stride he lifted his right foot into the cradle created by the four hands and pushed himself upwards. 'Now!' He used the lift to propel him high enough so his hands hooked over the edge of the boulder, hung for a moment with bolts of fire shooting down his arms, then, with an acrobatic flip, twisted his whole body on to the top surface. He lay with his back to the cold stone breathing heavily for a few seconds. The sound of barking could be heard clearly now. It would be so easy just to get up and leave them to their fate.

Shrugging off the thought, he raised himself on one knee and untied the leather sword belt he'd taken from the dead guard. The scabbard was attached by two loops and he pulled the belt from them and lay on his stomach on the lip of the boulder. 'Clitus? Get someone to lift you and grab hold of this.'

Placido was the last man and they retrieved him by tying three sword belts together and lowering them down to him. Ten minutes later they were two hundred feet up an almost invisible track that zig-zagged its way across the mountainside. Serpentius would never have found it, but for the fact he'd passed this way once on the return from a plunder raid on one of the valley settlements. The 'path' was a mere inches-wide ledge of dust and pebbles that sometimes disappeared completely, and even the Spaniard was forced to watch where he put his feet. His companions clung to the rock wall and edged their way forward as best they could, always conscious of the long slope below. It wasn't a sheer drop, but anyone who slipped wouldn't stop tumbling until they hit the river bank.

As he climbed, Serpentius was constantly aware of the rising volume of the hounds' cries. He knew the type of dogs the mine overseers used to hunt down escapers: big rangy beasts, long of leg and deep of chest, bred to bring down deer and boar and see off wolves. They'd been trained to hate men in rags and to follow the scent of fear. If their handlers were slow to reach them they

129

could tear a man apart. He registered the moment they lost the scent downstream, soon confirmed by the shouts of the hunters.

'Stay,' he hissed to Placido, the man behind him. He dropped to a crouch and the others followed suit. The moment the hunters recrossed the river would be the most dangerous, when they were looking directly towards the mountain and had time to allow their eyes to drift upwards. Better to stay still and avoid the chance of making a noise that would attract attention. A single rolling pebble would be the death of them all.

They waited, frozen in place while the hunters and their dogs climbed the near bank in the shadow of the big boulder, followed by a half century of what looked like auxiliary infantry. The dogs found the scent again almost instantly and set off on the false trail Serpentius had created, only to lose it just as quickly. He heard the hunters curse and risked a glance as they huddled together to discuss whether to carry on or cross the river again. The officer in charge of the soldiers harangued the men for a decision and soon they were climbing down the bank and recrossing the rushing waters. Serpentius could almost feel the relief in the men around him, but he knew this was only a temporary reprieve. Eventually the hunters would work out what they'd done and they'd soon discover the path. He waited until the sound of the hounds faded before rising and setting off again, shoulders hunched against the slope.

Serpentius allowed them a short rest when they reached the top and shared out the food they'd found on the bodies of the guards. As he chewed on the hard bread he felt a rare moment of uncertainty. He knew where he wanted to go but not what he'd do when he arrived.

The other problem was getting there.

The full moon provided a certain amount of visibility and confirmed his memories of the place. From here the mountain rose in a series of boulder- and scree-strewn slopes and false crests, broken ground carpeted in scrubby trees. Treacherous terrain even in daylight. These were Serpentius's mountains, but he knew the dangers of travelling by night.

Should he risk waiting for dawn and the certainty of reaching his destination, or forge ahead and risk losing more men?

He let his eyes drift over them. Clitus he could depend on up to a point, and Placido and possibly one or two others. The rest were too weak or too beaten by their captivity to be of help in a fight. He could survive alone in these hills, so it was obvious: wait till they fell asleep then slip away and let them live or die on their wits. Wasn't that the way it had always been? The strong survived and the weak perished.

The old Serpentius would have abandoned them without a thought and with a sneer at their weakness. But he wasn't the old Serpentius. When he'd whispered his plans in the eternal darkness of the deep mine they'd placed their faith in him. True, some hadn't acted when they should have, but in battle it was always that way. Valerius would never have considered leaving them. Responsibility, that was it. Valerius had always taken responsibility for the men under his command, whether they deserved it or not. It had been like that at Bedriacum, where he could have left the First Adiutrix to their fate, and at Cremona the year after when he'd led the suicidal charge that had saved the Seventh Galbiana.

'We'll rest here for the night and continue at dawn,' he whispered to Clitus. He saw the exhausted man's eyes roll in relief. 'I'll take the first watch, you take the second. I'll wake you when the moon is above the highest tree.'

'Yes, lord,' the other man whispered, his eyes already closing.

In the moonlit gloom Serpentius smiled. Slave, freedman and now lord. If he lived it couldn't be too long before he became Emperor. If he lived.

As he sat with his back to a stunted tree his nostrils detected a scent of pine that took him back to his youth. A girl. What had her name been? His hand went to the depression on the back of his skull. He'd had difficulty remembering things since it happened, but at least the ghost moments when he wasn't certain whether he was dead or alive had stopped. A girl. With hair the colour of a raven's wing and eyes that flashed like fire. Hard breasts that pressed into him when he kissed her under the pines and that glistened with droplets when they swam naked in the river. She'd been a year older and she'd taken him as her own, flaunting him like a trophy of her womanhood. It couldn't last, of course. They'd been too strong-willed. Like iron and flint striking together they'd created sparks. She'd come at him with a knife one day and that had been that. He grinned, but the grin quickly faded at the sound of the dogs returning below.

He shook Clitus by the shoulder. 'Change of plan. Wake the others.'

One of them wouldn't wake. Celer, an older man who'd been in the mine longer than most. Serpentius had been surprised he'd lasted this long. Clitus shook the sleeping man, but he didn't move. 'I think he's dead.'

Closer inspection proved Clitus was right. Celer hadn't been ill or any more exhausted than the rest of them. He'd just given up. The life force that sustained him had faded and died. There was no way to bury him in the rocky ground. And no time.

Because they were coming.

Serpentius struggled to maintain a straight course as they stumbled through the darkness, but it was near impossible among the rocks and the brush and the scrub pine. The best he could do was work his way in the general direction with low branches whipping his face and viciously hooked brambles tearing at his bare legs. His injured feet burned like balls of fire and had started bleeding again. The moonlight created random patches of dark and light beneath the trees that made it difficult to read the ground. He stepped into one dark area and felt himself pitch forward, nothing but air beneath his foot. A bolt of terror shot through him as he realized what it was. Careless fool. One mistake and it is your last. He was already greeting the gods when a hand grabbed the rear of his tunic and hauled him back to the brink, where he stood for a long moment on shaking legs.

'Vertical mine,' Clitus said. 'Probably worked out before the Romans came, or maybe it was just a test pit.'

'Either way it was almost my tomb,' Serpentius said breathlessly. 'You have my thanks, Clitus, and some day I will repay this debt if I can.'

'There is no debt,' the other man said solemnly. 'But for you we would still have been down the mine. At least if we die here, we do so in the clean air and not lying in our own filth in that choking pit. Wherever you lead I will follow. The others feel the same.'

Serpentius felt a moment of shame that he'd considered abandoning these men. 'Warn the rest about the pit,' he said gruffly. 'And tell them to watch their feet. It may not be the only one.'

Dawn found them on a ridge line and when he studied the shapes of the mountains around them Serpentius discovered to his relief he was less than a mile off course. As he pushed on through the dense scrub a flare of excitement rose in him. They were going to do it.

As he pulled aside a branch to enter a sunlit clearing he became instantly aware of another presence. A bearded soldier leaned on his spear less than four feet away. An auxiliary caught half asleep, but already bringing his spear up to meet the unexpected threat. Serpentius, the former gladiator, drew his sword in a single lightning movement and swung it backhanded across the man's throat, cutting through beard, flesh and sinew until the edge grated off the bone of his spine. A spray of blood misted the air and the auxiliary's head flopped forward as he dropped like a stone.

Serpentius spun at the sound of a new threat from behind, the bloody sword raised and ready to strike. The blade froze an inch from Clitus's neck. 'Get back,' Serpentius hissed. 'He was a sentry and his friends will find him soon enough.'

How had they managed to work their way in front of him? How many were there? Whatever the answers he cursed himself for allowing his companions to stop and rest. The soldiers must have found another track into the hills. That didn't matter now. All that mattered was that they were here. He led his ragged comrades in a wide arc away from the auxiliary encampment. When they were well clear he increased his pace to a trot and called Clitus up beside him.

'We'll soon reach a narrow gorge with a single bridge.

It's a rickety thing, just planks and rope, but it'll get us across. Once we're over we'll cut the ropes.'

'What if they're already across?'

'Always the cheerful one, Clitus,' Serpentius grinned. 'In that case the gods have forsaken us and we're already dead.'

'Back there,' Clitus wheezed. 'I've never seen anything like it. He saw you and he was dead. I wasn't even certain you'd moved until I saw the blood. How . . . ?'

'I've spent a lifetime killing people, my friend. I know a thousand different ways and if we get out of this alive I might even teach you a few.'

Soon they broke out of the trees into the open and a barren area of flat, dusty ground. Serpentius could see the dark line of the gorge a quarter of a mile ahead. A pair of upright posts marked the position of the bridge. The Spaniard angled his run towards them with the others staggering behind, their weakened frames already blown by the short run.

Something wasn't right. He could see the posts on the near side of the gorge, but not on the far one. His blood went cold as they reached the ravine and he understood why.

The bridge was gone.

XV

Or, as it turned out, not gone. What remained hung by the anchor ropes from their side of the gorge. Serpentius looked over the edge and his head spun at the sight of the sheer drop to a foaming stream far below where the jagged rocks stood out like fangs. No question of climbing down. They could keep running east, but he could already hear the spine-chilling howl of the dogs. It was only a matter of time before their pursuers hunted them down.

His companions slumped on the ground in despair, but Serpentius continued to study the chasm. The far side and safety were so tantalizingly close. He tried to imagine a horse leaping the void, but each time it ended up smashed to red ruin on the rocks below. Serpentius reckoned the gap at something like seven paces, maybe a little more. Say twenty-one or -two feet as the Romans measured it. He'd seen acrobats in the arena make some prodigious leaps, but this far? Yet the more he considered it, the more it became the only option. And if, given wings by the gods, he made the jump, what then? Clitus might be persuaded to try, but none of the others had a hope. Look at them, already beaten. Dead men, but for the formalities and the pain that would precede it.

He looked down past the shattered remnant of the bridge. Did he even have the courage in the first place? A strand of fluttering rope caught his attention and new hope flared within his breast. 'Clitus?' he barked. 'Get Felix and Gentilis and haul the bridge up here. I'll need as much rope as you can salvage from it.'

Clitus just looked at him. Serpentius stamped across to where he lay and hauled him to his feet by the front of his tunic. 'Do you want to die?' he snarled into the other man's face. 'You and you, help him.'

They did as he ordered and Serpentius untied his sword belt and stripped off his tunic to leave himself naked.

'You're mad,' Placido whispered as he realized what Serpentius intended. 'No man can jump that.'

'It can be done,' Serpentius assured him, studying the chasm again and thinking Placido was probably right. 'The alternative is to sit here until the dogs find us and then cut each other's throats.'

'But even if you get across, what then?'

'You'll see.' The sound of snapping wood signalled that Clitus and his helpers were breaking up the bridge. 'Get me enough sound rope to cross the gap and back,' he called. A sudden increase in the dogs' howling made them all stare at the trees. 'Quickly!'

Within moments Clitus approached with a coil of rope. It looked old and frayed, but it seemed strong enough. Serpentius tested the strands and nodded. He tied one end round his waist, knotted it firmly and tossed the other end to Clitus. 'Put three good men on that and for Fortuna's sake don't let go. If I end up on those rocks I'll make a special trip back from Hades to strangle you with your own guts. The rest of you bastards,' he spat at the men still lying on the ground, 'get off your arses and pick up a sword. If the dogs get here before the auxiliaries you'll have a chance of fighting them off.'

Serpentius turned and walked to the edge of the gorge counting his paces and testing the ground with every step. His last pace brought him perhaps a foot short of the edge. With infinite care he retraced his steps and repeated the exercise, trying to still the pounding of his heart and deafen his ears to the increasingly loud barking from not so very far away.

He retreated for the last time and stared at the yawning gap that seemed to get wider every time he looked at it. His whole being concentrated on the far edge of the narrowest point. It was only seven paces wide. Surely a man could leap that far? He took a deep breath. Only one way to find out.

With a roar of defiance Serpentius threw himself towards the gorge, arms pumping and his pace increasing with every stride. The drag effect of the rope surprised him, but it was too late to worry about that now. He willed every ounce of strength into his legs, bounding towards the precipice at a furious, breakneck speed. Three paces. Two. One. The Spaniard used the last step to catapult himself up and out, soaring across the gap. He kept his eyes fixed on the far edge where a low bush marked his landing point, but already he could feel the drop pulling at him. His heart froze at the knowledge he'd miscalculated. The roar of defiance turned into a scream of frustration. He'd hoped to touch down with a foot to spare. Instead, he was a foot short. His knees, braced for the landing, crashed into the crumbling rock and his chest slammed against the lip of the gorge. At the very last second he'd pushed his arms forward and as his weight began to pull him down he scrabbled for a hold. He clawed with his fingers at the rock-hard ground. A sear of agony as a nail tore away. Then his left hand felt something solid beneath it. A tree root. Slim and narrow, but strong enough to arrest his momentum for a heartbeat. It was all Serpentius needed. He managed to get both hands to it and used the purchase to flip himself sideways, throwing one knee on to solid ground. A moment of agony as he hung there between this world and the next, before, by sheer strength of will, he managed to transfer his weight on to the welcoming earth.

He lay with his back on the ground and stared at the cloudless blue sky. He was alive. His legs shook like winter reeds as he forced himself to his feet, but there was not a second to spare.

'Tie your end of the rope to the strongest of the posts,' he called across to Clitus, unknotting the loop from his waist. 'And throw me my tunic and weapons.' He'd hoped to find the remains of similar anchor posts on this side, but the only evidence of their existence was two holes in the ground. Fortunately, a clump of thorn bushes grew nearby and proved strong enough to hold the rope.

'What now?' Clitus's voice shook with fear. The others gathered around him on the far side of the chasm, staring at the sagging single strand of thin rope.

'Now you cross one at a time.' Serpentius tried to sound confident. 'It's simple. But you have to be quick. They're coming.'

'On that?'

'It held the bridge, it can hold you.'

Clitus shook his head.

'It's this or die,' Serpentius urged him. Still the other man didn't move.

The Spaniard closed his eyes. Logic said he should leave them, but logic hadn't made a promise to himself. He dropped to the ground at the cliff edge by the rope and took it between two hands, testing the anchor point on the far side. It looked feeble, but he was certain it was strong enough. Gritting his teeth he lowered himself so he was hanging by two hands and then swiftly pulled himself hand over hand to the far side where Clitus helped pull him up.

'See?' He met the men's eyes one by one. 'It's easy. Just get into a rhythm and whatever you do, don't stop.'

He dropped on to the rope again and made his way back. 'You first, Clitus. I'll be here to help you up.'

Clitus glanced at the thin line to safety, then at the trees. He dropped to sit by the rope then tentatively lowered himself. Serpentius saw a line of blood dribble down his chin where he'd bitten through his lip. A momentary hesitation before Clitus's face set in a scowl and he launched himself forward like a swimmer hauling himself through a heavy sea. By the time he reached Serpentius sweat was pouring from him and when the Spaniard took his hand it shook uncontrollably.

Serpentius looked up. On the far side the rest were staring at each other in consternation. At first he thought nobody would move, but Floro, a thin balding man, dropped to take his place on the rope and hauled himself across with smooth, easy movements.

'That's the way,' Serpentius encouraged. 'Who's next?'

A dog howled not too far away, and suddenly there was a rush for the rope.

'One at a time,' the Spaniard warned. 'Or you'll all end up down there.'

Placido fought his way to the front and quickly hauled

himself across, but the next man, Elius, was slower and the two remaining escapees, Gentilis and Felix, screamed at him to speed up. They were among the weakest of the former prisoners and Serpentius belatedly realized he should have seen them over first. His eyes scanned the tree line and his heart fell as a group of men emerged into the open. They halted for a moment and he saw them crouch down before two grey blurs streaked across the flat earth.

Wolf hounds. Big and rangy with lithe sinuous bodies and long legs that covered the ground in great bounds. Gentilis let out a scream of fear and fled along the lip of the ravine. Felix leapt for the rope and it bowed alarmingly as he began to cross in a faltering hand over hand movement.

'Hurry,' Clitus shouted at Elius, but Elius had felt the lurch as Felix's weight fell on the rope. Now he looked over his shoulder and howled in terror, losing his rhythm and finally stopping to hang in the air just out of reach of the companions.

The dogs had swerved to follow Gentilis and Serpentius winced as he saw him bowled over and heard the shrieks as the savage beasts tore at him with their fangs, mercifully silenced when one closed its jaws over his windpipe. By now the hunters had been joined by a squad of auxiliaries who emerged from the trees led by a single horseman and trotted towards the makeshift crossing with their spears at the trail.

'Get back.' Serpentius ordered his men out of range, while he crouched by the clump of bushes that anchored the rope. 'Just two more holds, Elius,' he encouraged. But fear had frozen Elius in place. He hung, sobbing, with his eyes closed as Felix gained on him, screaming for him to move.

Serpentius heard a shout and looked up to find the auxiliaries on the lip of the gorge. There were around a dozen, with more on the way, and they studied the two men on the rope as if they were flies wriggling in a puddle of honey. Felix tried to work his way past Elius, but Elius found one last burst of strength to fight him off. The horseman dismounted and stood for a moment with his hands on his hips before calling out an order. One of the auxiliaries hefted his spear, took a second to judge the distance, and hurled it at the two struggling men. The point took Felix in the spine and he let out a piercing shriek of agony. At the same time his arms closed in a death grip around Elius's neck. For a moment they hung, swaying gently in the silence, before the extra weight of Felix's body broke the grip of first Elius's left hand, and then, an agonizing moment later, the right. Dead and living dropped away accompanied by a wail that seemed to last for ever.

The auxiliary commander stared at the little group of men standing just out of range of his spears and knelt to test the rope. Serpentius, still partially hidden by the bush, knew the calculations that would be going through his mind. Could he cover the far bank with his spearmen long enough to get a small party across? The men he could see weren't soldiers, they were the filth of the mines. Yet all it would take was one or two determined defenders and he'd suffer casualties. He'd already lost one man to these vermin and he didn't want to lose more.

He was still tugging at the rope when one of his men caught a glimpse of Serpentius and called out a warning. The officer stood up and Serpentius rose out of hiding to face him. A spear fell in a swooping arc towards the Spaniard. In the space of a heartbeat Serpentius transferred his sword from right hand to left, stepped out of the spear's flight and flicked out his right hand to catch the shaft in mid-air. It was a simple arena trick, the fruit of many hours of patient exercise in hand and eye coordination, but it never failed to impress. He spun the spear and made as if to return it towards the officer. The man took a step back, but Serpentius halted the movement in mid-throw and grinned at him.

Another auxiliary raised his spear, but his leader shouted an order and he lowered the weapon. The commander advanced to the very edge of the gorge and stared at Serpentius with pitiless basilisk eyes filled with hatred.

'I have heard of you, the one they call the Snake. Well, Snake, be assured you cannot run for ever. The First Parthorum will hunt you down, and when we've finished with you the mine overseers have something special waiting for you. A black hole has been dug in the deepest part of the mine, where you will be walled in and left to starve to death or drown in other men's shit, whichever comes first. You will die screaming, Snake, and I will visit you every day to listen to your descent into madness.'

'A mouse's fart holds more threat than you do,' Serpentius laughed. He pointed to the rope. 'Why don't you cross and we'll see who dies screaming.' He flicked his sword into the air, so it spun five times before the hilt settled back into his hand and his eyes never left the Parthian. 'I've killed Parthians and it gave me almost as much pleasure as slaughtering Romans. Bring any four men you like.'

The auxiliary officer spat into the gorge. Serpentius took a step to his right and drew his sword edge down to sever the rope so it flopped to fall down the wall of the Parthian side. He backed away to join Clitus and the others.

'My name is Claudius Harpocration, prefect of the First Parthorum, remember it. We will meet again,' the officer shouted.

'I will count on it,' Serpentius assured him.

XVI

The accommodation provided by Severus was part of the upper portion of a flat-roofed town house, all fine mosaic floors and walls painted with lifelike hunting scenes and mountain vistas. It was close to the main baths Valerius had passed the previous day and he quickly discovered it had the disadvantage of being very difficult to enter or leave without being seen. Severus had also ensured the house was well supplied with his own staff. Clearly the identity of anyone Valerius brought here would be reported to their master, or his oddly disturbing wife.

Still, he had to find a way to meet Pliny's contact, and preferably without being seen. During his tour of the city he'd taken particular note of the alleys and smaller side streets where a man could lose a follower if he knew what he was doing. It didn't take him long to identify his latest shadow. Saco had replaced the young slave with an older man who had a shock of grey hair and a limp. In fact he was so obvious that Valerius took even greater care in case his presence was designed to draw attention away from the real thing.

He purposely timed his excursion for the hottest

part of the day when the Asturian sun seared the eye-balls and the furnace heat bounced from the walls of the more exposed streets. Heat multiplied the stench from the underground sewers, particularly noxious if you walked close to a drain cover. Competing with the sewer reek were the smells from butcher shops and tanners: blood and offal and the shit evacuated by terrified beasts awaiting slaughter, the contents of the piss pots where the leather workers collected the urine necessary for their trade, boiling tubs of fat and the rotting carcasses of dead cats and dogs in the cess pits, occasionally offset by the welcome aroma of a perfume stall.

Valerius took his shadow on an entire circuit of the city. He managed to lose the old man when he began to wilt in the heat, by darting up the alley behind the *mansio*. The house he'd been told to look for was at the other end of the city, a modest affair located between the Temple of Jupiter and the eastern wall. A servant answered the door and said he would carry Pliny's introduction to his master. Valerius waited for him to return. Instead, it was a large cheerful-looking man who appeared calling out a welcome.

'I am pleased to call any friend of Pliny a friend of Marcus Atilius Melanius,' the big man growled. 'Please, come inside, that dolt of a servant of mine should never have left you standing out here. How is the old devil? I haven't seen him for five years. Still up to his knees in bones and tusks and decaying manuscripts?'

Tall and broad with a vast belly, Melanius had a round face topped by a shining bald dome of a head, but any hint of threat from his scale was more than offset by the mischievous glint in his pale blue eyes. Valerius felt he was in danger of being washed away by his host's exuberance, but he grinned in return. 'I believe it has reached as far as his waist and it's growing every day, sir.'

'A glutton for knowledge and a mind that forgets nothing, unless of course you count dinner when he has his nose in a book.' Melanius led the way, talking as he went. They passed through a room decked out with shelves filled with leather scroll cases that seemed to indicate he was as well read as his friend the proconsul.

'I fear he isn't as active as you'd remember him,' Valerius said. 'When I last saw him he was laid up with an attack of gout. I think he would have come himself if he hadn't been indisposed.'

'A pity then.' Melanius's wide brow puckered in a frown where his eyebrows would have met. 'It would have been good to see him. I don't travel so much myself these days, so I doubt I'll be visiting Tarraco. I was surprised when I heard he'd been appointed proconsul – pleased, of course – but not your natural authoritarian bureaucrat. Mind you, he was as good an officer as I ever served with. You have been a soldier yourself unless I miss my guess?'

'I served in Britannia, Armenia, and most recently in Judaea.'

'You were with Titus.' Melanius's tone took on a measure of awed respect. 'I'd be pleased to hear about Jerusalem if you feel disposed to tell the tale. In fact, I insist you stay for dinner. Judging by Pliny's letter there's a fair amount I have to tell you.'

Valerius bowed his agreement.

'Good,' Melanius grinned. 'I never got any further than Germania during my service. All swamps and murderous savages. Pliny and I had to listen to tales of Vespasian's triumphs at the head of the Second, who'd been based just down the Rhenus from us.' They took their seats in the main room and he called for wine, which came in clay cups, but was of excellent quality. 'How do you find Asturica?'

'A little claustrophobic.' Valerius smiled as he told him about the men who'd followed him.

'Yes.' Melanius nodded solemnly. 'That would make sense. You have to understand, Valerius, that this is a place of secrets where everyone has a position to defend. I decided to settle here for my health when I retired as camp prefect of the Tenth. Did you know this was originally their camp?' He smiled at Valerius's evident surprise. 'Yes, this is why I chose this house. It stands exactly where the *principia* of the first camp would have been. I once saw the original plans. Double ditches filled with water, would you believe. They'd never countenance that now. But to get back to the subject in hand, I retired here. Although I have taken no part in local politics or business, I considered it wise to make myself acquainted with what went on. On the surface, Asturica is just another Roman provincial city, but beneath there are many different currents at play. Have you met anyone of significance?'

'Proculus, who commands the contingent of the Sixth at Legio, suggested I call on Aulus Severus, *duovir* of Asturica's *ordo*.'

'Quite right,' Melanius nodded. 'An opportunity to present your credentials as someone not to be ignored, but with a reason to be in Asturica not associated with Pliny's main objective. Severus is enormously rich and his position on the council gives him a certain power, but he is regarded as something of a figure of fun. He's in thrall to his new wife the way only an older man can be with a much younger woman. Not a fool by any

148

means, and certainly worth cultivating, but not a man to be feared.'

'The name Aurelius Saco was mentioned in connection with one of my followers.'

'Now there is a dangerous man.' Melanius frowned again. 'Rich as old Croesus and with an iron in every forge. There have been murmurings for years about how he came to make his money.' A pause of significant silence. 'Sometimes the people who did the murmuring ended up with their heads broken. You must be doubly careful, young man, if Saco is taking an interest in you.' The frown melted into a smile. 'Now, I am a man of regular habit and, as you can see from my fine figure, one of large appetite. This is the time I normally dine.'

Later, they lay back on couches and picked at plates of flaky white carp and succulent pork brought by Melanius's servants, and drank cups of a fragrant, light wine – 'Falernian, no less,' Melanius announced – and then he devoured two whole chickens in a short sitting, reminding Valerius of the gargantuan appetites of Aulus Vitellius. When he was finished, Melanius released a delicate belch.

'Pliny asks me to assist you in any way I can, but he doesn't give any detail?'

'I'm looking for a man called Petronius.' Valerius studied his host carefully for any reaction. 'An engineer who was carrying out an investigation into certain irregularities in the gold mining operations around Asturica. Have you heard the name?' Melanius shook his great head and Valerius continued. 'Pliny suggested Petronius might call on you for help if he encountered any difficulties.'

'If he had I would have certainly done all I could for him, but unfortunately he did not.'

'Unfortunately?'

Melanius gave him a shrewd look. 'You would not be here, Valerius Verrens, if Pliny didn't think something unfortunate had happened to Petronius.'

Valerius held his gaze. This, he decided, was not a man to be trifled with. Clearly Marcus Melanius was far from the jovial buffoon he liked to portray. Pliny had left it up to Valerius how much of his mission he revealed to his old friend. During the journey his inclination had been to keep most of the information to himself. Now he was in Asturica with enemies on every hand he could see the situation from a different perspective. If Melanius didn't know the detail of what he was trying to achieve, how could he help him achieve it? And who else could he trust in this snake pit?

'My first task is to find Petronius,' he said. 'Or discover what happened to him. Once that is completed, or it becomes clear I can do neither, I am to continue his investigations.'

Melanius leaned back on his couch. 'Perhaps if you were to enlighten me a little further I could advise you what kind of assistance I might be able to provide?'

'The Emperor believes that someone in Asturica is stealing his gold.'

A snort of disbelief burst from Melanius. 'Surely no one would be so foolish? A lingering death would be the best of it.'

'Nevertheless,' Valerius continued, 'that is what he believes. It is undeniable that the flow of gold from Asturica has dropped dramatically since the civil war. Pliny estimates by half.'

Melanius's features twisted into an almost painful grimace at the astonishing extent of the losses. 'I'd heard rumours that the yields from the mines were down, even that the seams were close to being worked out. There's no doubt the war caused difficulties.' He toyed absently with a gold charm at his neck. 'There were loud complaints about Galba's decision to strip the province of its finest young men for his new legion and Asturica suffered proportionately. As I understand it, those were the very men who carried out the most important tasks in the mines. And leaving the country so poorly defended encouraged a new and more dangerous breed of bandit to flourish. If it is out and out thievery you suspect, then perhaps that should be your first avenue of investigation?'

'Perhaps,' Valerius admitted. 'But for the moment Petronius must be my priority.' He hesitated. 'There is one other thing you should know. I will be acting in an unofficial capacity in order not to attract attention, or worse, to scare the people behind this into covering their tracks. But when the time comes to act the Emperor has conferred on me the full powers of a *legatus iuridicus metallorum*. No mining area will be closed to me and no document remain sealed.'

Melanius struggled to hide his astonishment. 'But this gives you the power to decide who runs the mining operations and every contractor who provides the supplies for them. You can make or break any man in Asturica.'

'That's true,' Valerius acknowledged with a wry smile. 'But only a fool would try to wield such power without knowing what he was doing with it. I'm no mining expert, Melanius. I'm a soldier who happens to be a lawyer and that's why I was chosen. I need to understand what is happening here before I present Severus with my warrant. Even then all I will use it for is to bring the guilty to Pliny's justice.'

'Wise words, my young friend.' Melanius stood and clapped Valerius on the shoulder as if he were an old comrade. 'One that surely shows why Pliny and the Emperor selected you. Another man might have been so intoxicated with his new authority that he wielded it regardless of the result. But you do understand it could also place you in great danger were it to become known you possess the Emperor's warrant?' His voice dropped and he looked over his shoulder towards the kitchens. 'Rich and powerful men like Saco and Severus have their spies. There may even be some amongst my own household.'

'You're right,' Valerius said. 'I was careless. But I can't take the words back. All I ask is that you keep the information to yourself.'

'Of course, but you haven't said how else I can help. When next you visit, come by the kitchen door. It will always be left open for you. I can put out subtle enquiries about Petronius. I can supply you with a reliable man to act as a guide . . .'

'Can you get me down a mine?'

XVII

When Valerius returned to his lodgings he found Zeno, Severus's *atriensis*, awaiting him.

'My master wished you to know we have discovered where your friend Petronius was staying,' the doorkeeper said. 'It is in a district favoured by lawyers and the like in the north of the city. I am to take you to the house if that is your wish, or we could wait until morning?'

There was still more than an hour till dusk so Valerius said he'd accompany the man immediately.

As they walked through the streets shopkeepers were closing their shutters and clearing their stalls. Valerius would have expected Zeno, servant to an important man in the city, to be well known to the tradespeople. Instead, men and women turned away as he passed, as if to make eye contact was to become tainted. He tried to make conversation, but the *atriensis* wouldn't be drawn either on his opinion of Asturica, or how long he'd worked for his master.

'This is it,' he said, when they came to a green door in an impressive block of town houses. 'According to his servant he rode from the city with another man on the kalends of August and never returned.'

'May I speak to the servant?'

Zeno's face froze in a tight smile. 'I am afraid he has left the area.'

Whatever else you are good at, my friend, Valerius mused silently, you are a very poor liar. 'Do you have a key?' he said. 'I won't learn much staring at the door.'

'Of course.' The servant reached inside his tunic to retrieve a large key on a leather cord and used it to open the door. They stepped into the entrance hall and walked through to the atrium, with the usual opening in the roof and a rain pool in the centre of the tiled floor. Small bedrooms opened out from the atrium, the interiors hidden behind curtained doorways. Valerius checked both. They were empty of any signs of occupation.

'As you can see the new occupant has yet to take up residence,' Zeno explained.

'What happened to his belongings?'

'The servant,' the *atriensis* shrugged. 'He was owed wages.'

They moved through to a room split to create a dining area and an office. Oddly, it contained no writing desk though the far wall was lined with niches for scroll cases.

'His papers? He had an office. He must have had papers.'

'I . . . I don't know, sir.'

The unnatural level of cleanliness struck Valerius as odd in the heat of summer with the wind bringing in dust through every open window, but somehow it had been achieved. The room was so clean even the slightest blemish caught his eye. He bent to look closely at something in the crack between two tiles.

'Sir?'

Valerius took out his knife and scraped a little of the

substance away with the point. 'What do you think this is?'

Zeno looked utterly bewildered. 'Dirt, perhaps ink or some kind of pigment?'

Valerius studied the dark smudge. 'Perhaps.'

They went from the kitchen via a rear door out into the garden, where a blackened patch of earth answered Valerius's question about the fate of Petronius's papers. He walked around the perimeter and stopped beside a patch of slightly disturbed soil by the wall.

'I've seen enough, thank you, Zeno.'

He could almost feel the other man's relief as he locked the door of the house behind them.

'I'm sorry, sir, but it is my master's belief that your friend has been killed by bandits and his body hidden.'

Valerius shook his head sadly. 'You're probably right. I'll make my own way back to the house.' Zeno was about to protest, but the Roman forestalled him. 'Leave me, Zeno, I wish to remember Marcus as he was.'

Zeno left with a tight nod. Valerius waited till he disappeared from sight then walked towards the darkened entrance of the alley that adjoined the town house. Once in the shade he counted his steps till he guessed he was opposite the disturbed patch of earth on the far side of the wall. A few cracks and areas of missing mortar would make it simple enough for a man to scale the wall. And the tell-tale scratches from the hobnails on a *caliga* sandal told him someone had done so quite recently.

Marcus Petronius was dead all right. But he hadn't been killed by bandits. Gaius Valerius Verrens knew what dried blood looked like. Marcus had been murdered in the house, or injured there before being taken elsewhere and killed.

* * *

Abilio, the *decurio* in charge of the Vardulli contingent, put a finger to his right nostril and snorted out a glob of grit and snot from the left, then repeated the exercise in reverse. Naturally the commander of the Parthian convoy escort had stationed the strangers at the rear, where they ate the dust of everyone ahead. Worse, they had to curb their spirited cavalry horses to the plodding pace of the oxen, continuously hauling at the bridle and trying to stay awake in the saddle. If Abilio had been in charge, he'd have had his men ranging the flanks where they could do some good, checking any potential ambush places. But he wasn't, so he had to grit his teeth and take it like the rest.

He licked his cracked lips and spat. He supposed it didn't matter too much. The terrain was as flat as a table top with only an occasional tree or farmstead to break the monotony. Not much chance of being ambushed when you could see a rider approaching from ten miles away. He supposed it accounted for the relaxed manner of the Parthians, who laughed and called to each other in their outlandish language. Abilio could see that it made his men uneasy, and he understood why. There'd been times when he'd caught the bearded troopers staring with their hooded, dark eyes and he'd swear they were laughing at him.

He was surprised when the prefect of the auxiliaries dropped back and reined in beside him.

'Escort duty can be deadly dull, can it not,' Claudius Harpocration smiled. 'Especially out here where there is nothing to see and a man has so much time to think he could drive himself mad.'

'Your men seem to be cheerful enough,' Abilio pointed out.

'Those troopers are excited because they've been given

leave in Tarraco until the next supply train. After a year in a dusty hellhole like Legio, Tarraco is a paradise on earth for them. Perhaps your men will show them some of the better places to visit?' Abilio smiled politely but said nothing. 'The civilian who arrived at Legio with you. I wasn't certain at first, but I think I recognized him from somewhere. Perhaps I was wrong. The man I'm thinking of would have been an officer.'

'No,' Abilio decided it would do no harm to show a little cooperation, 'you may be right. It would depend on where you served. His name is Verrens, Gaius Valerius Verrens. He won the Corona Aurea in Britannia with the Twentieth, was with Corbulo in Armenia, fought with the First Adiutrix at Bedriacum and commanded the Seventh Galbiana at Cremona . . .'

'Yes, that might be it,' Harpocration nodded. 'We accompanied the Seventh to Rome with Emperor Galba, of blessed memory . . .'

'Blessed memory,' Abilio muttered the automatic reply. 'Our man is a proper hero. You'd certainly remember him if you'd seen the wooden hand.' He was staring straight ahead so he missed the flash of consternation that crossed the Parthian's face. 'The right hand. He seems to be a little wary of showing it, because he kept it under his cloak a lot of the time.'

'Now I have him.' Harpocration quickly recovered his false smile. 'I remember the wooden hand. When we return I will introduce myself and we can talk about old campaigns. We will reach the river soon,' he nodded ahead. 'No point in going further when there's fresh water and reasonable grazing at hand. I will send a squadron ahead to prepare a campsite.'

'The Vardulli will be happy to take the first watch,' Abilio offered.

'Not at all, my friend,' Harpocration said. 'Your men have been eating dust all day. In any case, you are our guests,' he said over his shoulder as he rode ahead. 'You should let them bathe and wash their clothes, have some food and get a decent night's rest. There will be plenty of opportunity to stand guard before we reach Tarraco.'

That night Abilio unrolled his blanket among his men and slept the sleep of the truly exhausted. Much later his mind registered a soft shuffling sound and his eyes snapped open. As his hand sought the hilt of his sword he became aware of shadowy silhouettes against the stars. He opened his mouth to cry a warning, but before he could make a sound a horny palm clamped itself over his mouth and his sword hand was pinned. A glint of light gave him warning of what was to come and he tried to scream as he felt the sting of the blade across his throat. The last thing he saw before he drowned in his own blood were Claudius Harpocration's pitiless obsidian eyes staring down at him.

XVIII

Rome

'In some ways the greatest tragedy in the destruction of the Temple of Jupiter was not the death of my poor brother Sabinus, may the god succour him, but the loss of the Senate records,' the Emperor lamented. 'Much of our current law is based on the statutes they contained. Now they are nothing but meaningless puddles of melted bronze. Anyone with an opinion – and our colleagues in the Senate are not short of those – can impede the new legislation I'm bringing forward. How is the search for the copies progressing?'

'We've recovered a few hundred out of an estimated three thousand,' Titus, lounging on the right of his father beside the gold banqueting table, admitted. 'We know of several hundred more, but they have a symbolic and emotional value for the families who own them and they won't give them up lightly.'

'I don't suppose we could confiscate them as documents of the state?' Vespasian saw the look of alarm on the face of another of the people lying on their sides around the heavily laden table. He was notorious for the simplicity of

159

his regular fare, but he liked to indulge those he valued, and he valued this guest highly. 'No, my dear,' he smiled. 'You're quite right. I'm unpopular enough already.'

Domitia Longina, wife of Vespasian's son Domitian and daughter of the celebrated General Gnaeus Domitius Corbulo, returned his smile. He thought her a melancholy creature compared to Antonia Caenis, but she was both intelligent and highly attractive and the Emperor liked to surround himself with attractive women.

'Perhaps some show of Imperial favour could be made to the families involved, Caesar? An assurance that the tablets, which no doubt contain the names of revered ancestors, will be displayed with suitable prominence and honour?'

'An excellent notion.' The Emperor turned to his younger son who was in charge of the final stages of the temple's restoration. 'What do you think, Domitian, could a room be set aside for their display?'

'I think they'd part with their heirlooms quickly enough if we offered them gold.' Domitian's voice was slurred by the wine he'd consumed. 'But then we don't have any.'

Vespasian's smile tightened. He glanced up to see if there was any reaction from the slaves stationed just out of earshot in the huge room. If any of them displayed signs of having enhanced hearing they'd be on an auction block before the day was out.

'As you know,' he told his son, 'we have taken steps to alter that situation and we have high hopes of their success.' Domitian snorted derisively, but his father ignored him, more interested in the fleeting shadow that fell over Domitia Longina's face. He was aware that Domitia had played a part in saving the life of Gaius Valerius Verrens, but did not know the detail. There were undercurrents here he didn't understand. 'Is something wrong, my dear? You're not eating. Please try another honeyed quail.'

Domitia accepted his offer of one of the tiny birds and Vespasian turned back to Titus. 'What is our latest news from Plinius Secundus?'

'A message arrived today by way of Portus.' Titus let his eyes drift to Domitian. 'One of our cryptographers decoded it just before I came here. Pliny tells us that our agent arrived safely, but that during their discussions there was a determined attempt to take his life.' Vespasian's face darkened and Domitian's jaw dropped as the implications hit him.

'No, I—'

'The attempt was on Pliny's life,' Titus continued smoothly, gracing his brother with a cold smile. 'Fortunately our agent was on hand to ensure it was not successful. He is, as we know, a man well-versed in the art of survival. They captured one of the assassins and put him to the question, which led them to one of Pliny's clerks, now unfortunately dead. However, further investigation has produced evidence that places the origin of the attack in the north.'

'Asturica? What does that mean for our agent?' Vespasian said, almost to himself.

'Pliny doesn't believe our agent has been compromised,' Titus assured him. 'But he can't be certain. It was always a risk, but he's overcome these difficulties in the past. Who else could have tricked their way into Vitellius's palace at the height of the late war?'

'Who else but a traitor.' The sneer came from the other side of the table. 'And I'll lay odds he'll betray you again,' Domitian continued. 'Better that he'd died under the executioner's sword.'

Domitia Longina rose abruptly from her couch with an apologetic smile, but the effect was spoiled by the white line of her compressed lips. 'I am sorry, Caesar, but you were right: I am indisposed. I ask your leave to return to my rooms.'

'Of course, my dear,' Vespasian said solicitously.

Domitian watched his wife walk from the room, every step a picture of suppressed fury.

'My wife is always indisposed when that man is mentioned,' Domitian sniffed. 'His continued survival is a stain on my honour, Father.'

'You may yet have reason to be grateful to *that man*,' Titus spat.

'Enough,' Vespasian intervened. 'Domitian, you may feel you wish to follow Domitia Longina and offer her comfort.' It was phrased as a suggestion, but the words had a touch of steel and Domitian hesitated only fractionally before obeying them.

When he was gone his father sighed. 'Poor Domitian. I do believe he has no worse enemy than himself.'

'Poor Domitia Longina.' Titus shook his head. 'I don't know why she ever married him.'

'Oh, I think any daughter of Gnaeus Domitius Corbulo is well equipped to cope with your brother. I was more concerned with his reaction to your announcement about the attack.'

'I agree.'

'Then perhaps you should do something about it.'

'I already have.'

XIX

Of them all Floro impressed Serpentius most, ignoring the hunger pangs gnawing his guts and scampering up the steep inclines at the Spaniard's back like a mountain hare. Clitus and Placido stumbled along far behind, the sound of their harsh, rasping breaths carrying twenty paces in the clear mountain air. Serpentius wouldn't slow for them. He'd vowed not to make the mistake of slackening the pace again. Being soft had killed Felix, Elius and Gentilis. Or perhaps he was wrong and they'd been killed by their own fear? He shook his head. What did it matter? They were dead and in Serpentius's world dead men had never existed. What mattered was that the Parthian auxiliaries would eventually find their way round the gorge and back on to the trail.

But these were Serpentius's mountains and he was confident he'd find a way to escape. He reached the spine of one of the endless ridges and stared down at the familiar glittering expanse of a large reed-fringed lake. It must be a day and a half's march round the bank, all clinging mud, endless bog and ancient, rotting trees.

Floro appeared beside him, sucking in deep breaths.

His eyes lit up when he saw the lake. 'If we can cross that they'll never find us.' He shook his head as reality struck. 'But how?'

Serpentius waited till the others caught up. 'Follow me.'

He'd been prepared for it not to be there after twenty years, but his tribesfolk had always been people of habit, using the traditional places. This was the bay where fishermen had moored their boats for generations. It took him time to work out the right tree, but he found the rope – a surprisingly new rope – carefully camouflaged at the base of a stunted willow. He followed the rope into the water and his groping hands discovered the canoe in the fringe of reeds. It had been loaded with stones and submerged in three feet of water. A primitive thing, carved from a single trunk and four paces in length, but it had an oar and it would carry them all. With difficulty they managed to refloat it and bail it out. Serpentius, the only one among them with any experience of these unwieldy craft, steadied it as the others clambered nervously aboard.

'Sit in the centre and stay still,' the Spaniard ordered. He took his seat in the rear.

'What do we do if it overturns?' Placido asked nervously.

Floro turned his head to study him. 'Can you swim?'

'No.'

'Then you drown,' the bald man grinned.

No one drowned. When they reached the far side Serpentius ran them into a mud bank. Clitus and Floro slipped over the bow and started dragging the canoe further into the shore, but Serpentius shook his head. 'No. Leave it to me.' Placido tried to step over the side and fell face first into the stinking, black mud, which had the others howling with laughter.

Serpentius ignored them and pushed the little craft out into clear water. When he was waist deep he tossed the paddle over the side into the bottom of the canoe and thrust it out towards the centre of the lake. He saw the puzzled glances as he waded to the shore, but didn't bother to explain. The prevailing wind would push it down to the western shore and his people – if it was his people – would find it again. If the auxiliaries happened to stumble on it they'd think that was where the escaped prisoners had disembarked and waste hours searching for them.

'How far, lord?' Clitus asked.

'There,' Serpentius pointed towards a great wall of mountains at the eastern end of the lake. The men groaned. 'We will be safe when we reach the summit,' he assured them. But did he believe his own words?

More effort. More climbing. Serpentius considered stopping for the night, but they had one last push in them and he doubted Clitus, who'd begun to cough up blood, would survive another night in the open. They found themselves on a height above a steep gully, filled with rock falls and cascades, where the stream fed the lake from the east. Serpentius's heart quickened as he hurried the final four hundred paces to the head of a long slope that swept down to a valley filled with cultivated fields and lush meadows. The men and women who worked the fields were making their way home after the day's labour. At the far end he could see a huddle of grey houses.

Avala.

A winding path led them down to the fields and they followed the stream towards the village, a walled settlement of twenty close-packed round houses built of local grey rock and thatched with reeds from the lake. Serpentius felt his throat tighten as they approached the little group of buildings. He knew every moss-covered stone. The house he'd built with his own hands for Lyda lay near the wall on the north side. To his eye it would always be fairer than the others. It was as far from the great opulent palaces he had seen in Rome as a man could be without living in a hole in the ground, but he had been as proud of it as Nero of his great Golden House. He felt a lightning bolt of anger and sorrow as he remembered that final day. Fighting the Romans to his last breath as the torches rained down on the thatch and in the doorway. The flames leaping up like a great red and gold curtain trapping them inside. Lyda's screams as she burned alive. With his son. He only realized he'd bitten through his lip when the blood ran down his chin and into the hollow at his throat.

They were thirty paces from the settlement when a group of men emerged. Savage, uncompromising eyes stared at them from bearded faces hardened by wind and weather and bitter experience. A few of them held spears, but most carried axes and scythes and held them as if they were ready to use them. They wore familiar striped tunics and *braccae* leggings to below the knee. Serpentius watched them, gauging the threat they posed, and smiled as ten more appeared to the right, and others to the left.

The smile only made them angrier. Hands tightened on the shafts of spear and axe. 'Lay down your weapons.' He placed his spear on the ground and unhooked the sword belt at his waist.

Placido hesitated. 'They'll just slaughter us anyway.'

'Just do it.' Serpentius's eyes never left the men in

front of him. Placido's sword clattered to the ground to join the rest. The Spaniard singled out a grey-bearded elder in the front rank of the men at the gate. 'This is Castro Avala and you are of the Reburi clan of the tribe Zoela?' The old language sounded unnatural on his lips, but he saw their puzzlement at hearing their own tongue from the mouth of a stranger. The men opposite handled their weapons uneasily and looked to the grey-beard for leadership. He glared at Serpentius for a long moment before he spoke.

'And how would a foreigner know these things about us?'

'What makes you think I am a foreigner?' Serpentius drew himself to his full height and stepped forward. A rustle ran through the ranks facing him as they began to understand the manner of man who had appeared among them.

'Because you wear Roman tunics and carry Roman swords.' Serpentius was surprised that the voice came from the group to his right. 'Yet you have the ragged appearance and pallor of escaped slaves and the Romans pay well for escaped slaves, even from the likes of us.'

Serpentius searched the men for the source of the words.

'Whatever the pay, you will discover the price of earning it is too high,' he assured whoever had spoken. He fixed on a pair of intense feral eyes in a face that might have been carved by an axe. A flick of long dark hair hung over a narrow brow and the man had a thin-lipped mouth that reminded Serpentius of a cobra he'd once encountered. Young, perhaps not much more than twenty, but a thrill of anticipation ran through him as he understood where the true danger lay. And the leadership. One thing was certain: if it came to a fight, this one would be the first to die.

'Brave words from a ragged outcast,' the young man said. 'But we are thirty and you are four.'

'You may be thirty now.' Serpentius grinned and allowed his fierce gaze to travel over the men opposite. 'But ask yourselves how many you will number when it is over. I see farmers and fullers and potters, able enough to see off a wolf or a bear, but who have never faced warriors.'

'And I see a worn-out old man,' the voice sneered. 'They had a bear once, in Asturica, chained to a pole to be baited by dogs. It was old and scarred and beaten. You remind me of it.'

Serpentius sighed. 'Who is this who makes a noise like a warrior, but isn't prepared to show himself?'

The young man Serpentius had been staring at stepped out from the huddle. Tall and spare, he held a long spear in both hands and his dark eyes glowed with an arrogant, contemptuous certainty. The sudden realization was like being drenched in ice water. Those eyes . . . It couldn't be? But the more he studied the face behind the beard, the more certain he became.

'I am called Tito, stranger; look upon me and see your death. Pick up your spear.'

'I don't need a spear to kill you, puppy.' Serpentius marched unarmed towards his enemy. A murmur went through the Reburi.

The young man frowned. 'This is not right.'

'You want to kill me?' The Spaniard continued his advance. 'I'm making it easy for you. So kill me.'

Tito moved to meet him, the spear balanced and the leaf-shaped iron tip aimed at Serpentius's chest. The Spaniard didn't flinch at the sight of the polished metal and when he came within range Tito rammed the needle point at his heart. It was a perfect thrust, fast and well-aimed. Tito was already experiencing an odd mix of exultation and regret when he realized his victim was no longer where he'd aimed. Serpentius had slipped past the point in a blur of movement and now he danced round his attacker so Tito had to spin to face him.

Anger clouded the younger man's face. He'd felt almost sorry for the interloper, but now the man had humiliated him. With a snarl he rammed the spear at Serpentius's throat. This time the Spaniard simply swayed aside and allowed the point to slide past his neck, flicking the shaft away with his right hand and dancing clear. It looked so easy that Placido laughed, and he was joined by a few of the men standing in front of the *castro*.

Serpentius wasn't so cheerful. He'd made it appear easy, but Mars' hairy arse the boy was quick. He had to end this soon.

Tito attacked again, with the same result, and now confusion replaced the anger on his savage features.

'If you're going to kill someone,' Serpentius kept on the move so the spear point had to follow him, 'don't jab at them as if you only want to scratch them. Ram it in and twist, so their guts spill out on the ground when you withdraw. Of course,' he kept his tone conversational, 'some people don't have it in them to kill another man. The thought of splitting another human being open makes them puke. They're the men who die screaming in the arena and on the battlefield. Are you one of those, Tito?'

The jibe lit a fire in Tito's head and he charged. This time there would be no mistake.

'That's better,' Serpentius encouraged him. He let the spearhead almost touch him before he twisted clear and grabbed the shaft in both hands so he could rip it from Tito's grasp. In the same movement he spun so the length of ash caught the younger man behind the knees and whipped the legs from under him. Before he knew what was happening Tito was on his back staring at the sky with the point of the spear at his throat.

Serpentius's gaunt face appeared in his vision. 'That's how you kill a man,' the Spaniard's voice dripped ice-melt. 'You know how to kill a man, but do you know how to die?'

Tito closed his eyes.

'Does any among you remember a man called Barbaros,' Serpentius continued, 'who once lived in this *castro*?'

Tito opened his eyes and stared at the man above him. What was this? A moment passed before he heard the voice of Valuta, the grey-beard. 'I know of Barbaros. He brought the Romans down upon this place and then left its people to their fate. He had a wife, called Lyda.'

'Yes,' said Serpentius. 'And a son called Tito.'

XX

Melanius's 'bodyguard' Aurelio turned out to be an unassuming fellow of medium build, with mousy hair chopped short across the brow and at the neck. Eyes a little too close together, nose a little too long and a mouthful of crooked teeth. To Valerius's eye, the face of a rogue, but the type who could blend in with any crowd and never be noticed.

Aurelio bowed and introduced himself before pulling a piece of parchment from the folds of his tunic. 'This is a warrant from the *praefectus metallorum* for the district of Asturica. Julius Licinius Ferox instructs his officers to give you every assistance and allow you access to any site or process, providing there is no danger to your person.' He shrugged. 'It covers mines, dams, aqueducts, canals, crushing and smelting houses, but not storehouses.'

Valerius didn't hide his astonishment. 'I thought I'd be fortunate to get within five feet of a disused shaft,' he laughed. 'How did Melanius arrange this kind of access?'

'My master doesn't tell me these things, lord.' Aurelio shrugged. 'He says go there and do that and that's what I do.'

'When can we start?'

'With your permission I thought we could begin this morning, lord. We can be at the Red Hills by dusk and you'd be able to see the mines in the morning. With respect, though, I wouldn't be wearing your best finery. It's a dirty business.'

'I'll bear that in mind,' Valerius said, wondering if the man was mocking him.

'There is one other thing. Because of the hostility against Rome from some of the hill tribes the *praefectus metallorum* insists on providing you with an escort.'

'I thought you were my escort?'

'I don't count, lord,' Aurelio said with a tight smile. 'I'm only here to make sure you get what you're looking for. It'll be three or four men, and the prefect is right. We've had word of attacks by bandits and ruffians and the like. Six men is better than two, especially if four of them are likely lads carrying spears.'

Valerius packed his travel clothes in a leather bag while Aurelio fetched his horse from the stables. They rode together to the city gate where the escort waited. Valerius felt his gut tighten when he recognized the four heavily bearded men who studied him from the saddle of their ponies.

'Parthians?'

'The prefect has the use of a squadron of cavalry and a century of infantry from the auxiliary unit at Legio to supplement the security provided for the mines. My master believes Councillor Severus mentioned your name, and the great honour awarded you by the Emperor, at a meeting of the *ordo* last night. The prefect decided he couldn't risk losing someone of your rank and fame.'

Valerius looked the men over. They wore the same pot

helmets and fish scale armour as the troopers he'd seen exercising outside the fort. Valerius had faced Parthians in the battle of the Cepha gap and had reason to be wary. They were as sly as the desert fox and as unpredictable as snakes. 'So we can't send them back?'

'That would be seen as an insult to the Prefect of Mines,' the guide advised, 'and,' he dropped his voice, 'my master's ability to influence his decisions in future.'

It was full dark by the time they saw the lanterns of the mining camp that served the Red Hills. The four Parthians had proved as taciturn during the ride as they had been on first meeting. Barely a word passed between them, and none with the men they were escorting. Nothing had occurred to justify Valerius's initial wariness and he'd finally relaxed. He allowed himself to enjoy the magnificence of his surroundings, which were extraordinary even for a man so far travelled: glorious mountain vistas to left and right, the slopes patchworks of emerald meadow and olive forest, and deep gorges with clear fast-flowing rivers. On arrival, Aurelio showed the mining prefect's warrant to the commander of the gate guard. He led Valerius to a crude guest house while the Parthians laid their blankets in the nearby barracks. The Roman fell asleep almost instantly, with the sweat stink of the bed's previous occupant in his nostrils, and a curious bittersweet scent that for some reason reminded him of a fresh-dug grave.

The grave smell was still with him when he woke the following day. Valerius washed in a stone basin while Aurelio went to see the officer in charge of the camp. He returned a little later with a basket of bread and ham and a stone jug filled with small beer.

'Fortuna is with you,' the guide announced. 'I spoke to a *praefectus cuniculi*,' he saw Valerius's blank look, 'a

173

tunnel manager – of one of the mines a little way from here. He believes it will be ready for the final stage of the mining process later today, or tomorrow morning at the latest. I took the liberty of telling him you would be interested in inspecting the interior of the mine and then watching the process happen.'

'Thank you, Aurelio,' Valerius smiled. 'I don't know what I would have done without your help and that of your master.'

'Then we will leave as soon as you are prepared,' Aurelio said. 'There is no need of the escort in the mining area.'

They loaded their horses and set off with the sun on their backs. Valerius had expected the tunnel manager to be a big man, of the type he had often seen overseeing slave gangs on building sites in Rome. Instead, Hostilius Nepos was small and fat, with a twitchy, nervous manner and a tic in his left eye. He clearly enjoyed the sound of his own voice and would have given Valerius the entire history of the mining industry and every stage of the process. 'You will be astonished, I assure you—'

'Please, sir,' Valerius stopped him in full flow. 'I beg you to wait until I can actually see what you are describing in such technical terms.'

Nepos reluctantly agreed and immediately launched into a description of his workers' failings.

'We feed, clothe and house them and they repay us by failing to turn up for work and barely doing any when they do appear. If it wasn't for my supervisors nothing would get done on time. And there are few enough of them, these days, since the war, when Emperor Galba, of blessed memory . . .'

'Blessed memory,' Valerius and Aurelio mumbled together.

'. . . took the very best of them to serve in his legion and never to return to their native land where they could do something productive . . .'

'Are the workers well paid for their labours?'

'Why no, sir.' Nepos shot Valerius a look of outraged innocence. 'They are not paid at all. The heads of their villages pledge their services to offset the tax burden imposed upon them. A magistrate with responsibility for, say, ten *castros*, that is settlements, will set the tax at a certain amount and it is up to the headmen of the clans to decide whether to pay in cash or in kind. Since they seldom have any gold, and are loath to part with what they have, they send their menfolk to work in the mines and their surplus food to the granaries.'

Valerius didn't hide his bewilderment. 'But surely the reason they do not have gold to pay their taxes is that we don't pay them?'

'But that is the joy of the system.' Nepos smiled complacently. 'A bonded man will produce more gold in a single month down the mine than he will pay in taxes in his entire lifetime.'

It seemed a very one-sided system to Valerius, but he supposed it was better than slavery.

Nepos shook his head dolefully. 'From my own point of view slaves would be an advantage. At least you can always get work out of a slave.'

They passed a group of grey stone buildings in a walled enclosure and Valerius asked if this was where the workers lived. Belatedly, he realized the houses had no roofs.

'No, these are the hovels their ancestors lived in. Since Tiberius's time we have provided them with houses on good Roman lines sited close to the mines where they are needed.'

They came upon one of the settlements less than a mile later. Built of the same grey stone, the windowless houses were laid out like barrack blocks and surrounded by a high wall. As they passed the entrance Valerius saw women listlessly washing clothes and sewing on the doorsteps of their homes.

'Look.' Nepos drew his attention to the hillside above them. 'There is one of the canals that supply my mine.' He pointed to what looked like a score across the broken landscape and Valerius followed it upwards to an improbable height where the linked arches of an aqueduct hung as if suspended in mid-air between two peaks. 'It runs for twenty miles, fed by a mountain stream, and goes through mountains or round them. Every foot of it has to be monitored, maintained and repaired. And that is only one of seven.'

'It sounds like an enormous task.'

'The Red Hills mines are an enormous project. Possibly the largest in the Empire.' The tunnel manager couldn't hide his pride.

'Yet I hear there have been problems,' Valerius ventured. 'Poor yields. Bandits.'

He sensed Aurelio stiffen in the saddle, and wondered why. Nepos looked at him warily.

'I take interest only in my own problems,' Nepos said defensively. 'Lazy men and lack of manpower, and rock too stubborn to be shifted. My yields have never faltered, let no man say that. As for bandits, I have heard the stories, but there are always stories.'

Valerius would have liked to ask him why, if his yields were unaltered, others' had fallen. Why else would the flow of gold to Rome have slowed to a trickle? But this wasn't the time. A proper talk with Nepos could wait for another day.

They approached a rise in the ground where the road forked. Aurelio took the path to the right, reining in at the top of the ridge, and beckoned Valerius forward. Valerius rode up to where he sat. When he saw what lay below, the breath caught in his throat. 'Mars save us.'

'I said you would be impressed,' Nepos cried.

The scene that greeted Valerius was another world from the mountains and valleys they'd traversed on the way from the camp. It was as if a giant hand had reached down and clawed the earth with huge nails, or an enormous beast of legend had savaged the very hills with its terrible fangs. The landscape had been quite literally torn apart, its entrails glowing blood red in the sun and strewn in great heaps for miles around.

'*Ruina montium*,' Valerius whispered.

'Precisely,' Nepos said proudly. 'This area has been worked out using the hydraulic method,' he explained. 'We use the immense potential of water to expose and extract the gold from the ground, but it is not just a question of brute force, as you will discover.'

'It's astonishing.' Valerius turned to find Aurelio studying him as if gauging his reaction. The guide's face twisted into a sardonic smile.

'It comes as a shock when you first see it. Now let us continue and Nepos will show you how it is done, and why.'

A shock indeed, and Valerius's heart was still fluttering as they rode down into the chaos of disturbed red earth that gave these hills their name. He was familiar enough with destruction perpetrated in the name of Rome. He'd watched as the blackened shell of the Great Temple of Jerusalem was torn down and that once beautiful city taken apart stone by stone. And he'd walked the streets of Cremona as the houses and apartments burned around him, and their occupants with them. Yet somehow this tearing asunder of the very earth he stood upon felt worse. An abomination against the gods.

He remembered Serpentius speaking about the hidden glories of his bleak Spanish homeland, the soaring mountains and the fertile valleys. He wondered how he would have reacted had he looked upon what Valerius had just seen. It gave him some satisfaction to imagine the Spaniard ripping out Nepos's guts and strangling him with the coils.

That thought sustained him as they travelled east through a tortured landscape riven with great chasms and cut by streams of vile liquid that looked like the run-off from an abattoir. Eventually they came to a hillside and a shelf of land scattered with odd-shaped mounds that, on closer inspection, turned out to be spoil heaps. A line of men staggered towards one of the mounds bowed beneath the weight of the large baskets they carried, before returning more lightly burdened to what looked like the mouth of a cave. Meanwhile other workers wielded picks to extend some kind of rock-cut channel towards the entrance.

'The mine,' Nepos confirmed. He craned his neck to study the mountainside. Valerius followed his gaze to a sluice gate several hundred paces above them. 'Yes, they are making the final preparations for the release,' the tunnel manager said. 'Wait here and I will ensure we are given time enough for you to be shown round the workings.' He turned his horse and urged it towards a track that wound up the steep slope.

'How did you explain to Nepos why I want to inspect the mine?' Valerius asked Aurelio.

'I didn't. All I did was show him the warrant from the

prefect of mines and that was it. Believe me, you don't cross Licinius Ferox, not if you're fond of life.'

'There seem to be a lot of people in Asturica Augusta a man shouldn't cross,' Valerius said wryly.

'It's that kind of place— Stand still, you bastard.' The other man curbed his fidgeting horse. 'A frontier town like those settlements that grow up outside our forts on the Danuvius. A man can get rich if he's not too scrupulous and prepared to get his hands dirty, but tread on the wrong toes and there's always someone who's willing to stick a knife in your ribs for a bent *denarius*.'

'That sounds reassuring.'

Aurelio grinned, but his face quickly turned sombre and he nodded towards the mine entrance. 'Do you know what you're in for down there?'

'I've been in a few black holes.' Valerius remembered with a shiver the damp, slippery foulness of Hezekiah's Conduit beneath Jerusalem.

'Not like this one.' Aurelio's pale features twisted with distaste, but Nepos's return silenced anything else he was going to say.

'We have two hours.' The mine manager pushed his horse past Valerius and set it on the path to the entrance. 'So we must hurry. There is much to see.'

They dismounted by the entrance where four workers laboured at a massive bellows attached to a leather pipe a foot in diameter. Nepos picked up a short pole resembling a centurion's vine stick. He called to one of the men carrying an empty basket to hold the horses, and another to fetch an oil lamp. When it was lit the man led the way inside, with Nepos following. Valerius waited for Aurelio, but the guide shook his head and glanced at the black portal. It was perhaps two and a half paces wide and just high enough to allow a tall man

179

to pass without bending his neck. 'You're not getting me down there. I'll wait for you here.'

He walked off and Valerius hurried after Nepos into the ill-lit tunnel. He noticed the engineer took care to keep close to the right-hand wall, allowing room for the filthy, grunting creatures who passed them going the other way. The leather pipe twitched like a living thing every time the bellows were pumped and Valerius guessed it carried fresh air to the lower reaches of the mine. It was certainly needed. The smell of damp and sweat mixed with the smoke of the oil lamps that occupied niches in the wall every ten paces was thick enough to choke a man in the confined space. Even this was overwhelmed by the sewer stink of freshly evacuated human shit. Clearly the workers were expected to defecate where they stood when the need came upon them. Valerius had to stifle the urge to add his vomit to the vile mix.

'This is a diagonal shaft.' The echo from the streaming rock walls gave Nepos's voice a metallic ring. 'But other mines have vertical shafts which you have to negotiate by ladder. The conditions there are much worse.'

Worse? Twenty paces in and Valerius could feel the sweat running down his back beneath his tunic. The ragged miners who passed him with their enormous baskets of stone were so sunk in their own eternal misery that none would meet his eyes. They had a habit of coughing, hawking and spitting and he grimaced at the dampness he could feel seeping its way through the iron-shod soles of his sandals.

'Faster, you dog.' Nepos lashed out with his stick at a man who was struggling to put one foot in front of the other. 'See,' he looked over his shoulder at Valerius. 'Did I not tell you they were lazy?'

They passed a side chamber where a group of workers were chipping away at the walls with picks.

'They are extracting what they can from a seam before we release the flood.' Nepos stopped for a moment to allow Valerius to see what was happening. 'All the gold that can be dug by hand is removed by traditional methods and the ore carried away for smelting. It is only when we reach this stage we begin the preparations for *ruina montium*. We call it honeycombing. Many tons of soil and rock are excavated in a way that creates thin-walled chambers and weakens the interior of the hill. It is a very precise business. Take away too little and the operation will fail. Take away too much and the tunnels will collapse, crushing everyone inside.'

Valerius glanced at the roof above his head, expecting to see cracks. Did he see cracks? 'Has there ever been an accidental release from the sluices?' he asked.

'Oh, yes,' Nepos admitted. 'But fortunately it doesn't happen often.'

'What happened to the people inside the mine?' He had a feeling he knew the answer, but Nepos surprised him.

'All we found of a hundred men were a few scraps of flesh and slivers of bone.' Despite the admission Nepos looked supremely untroubled. The tunnel manager turned off into another side chamber, with further smaller chambers off it, in a fan shape. 'The chambers here have been completed,' he said. 'We are doing the last of the work on the lower levels, close to the face of the hill.'

They continued until they came to a vertical shaft with a pair of ladders, one for descent and the other for ascent. Nepos turned to Valerius. 'This is where we go down.' He looked at Valerius's wooden fist as if seeing it for the first time. 'Will you . . . ?'

'I can do it,' Valerius assured him. Reaching for the ladder with his good hand, he swung himself on to the upper rungs and hooked his right arm around the upright. It took no time to reach the floor. He noticed that the basket bearers had thinned out and guessed the work must be almost completed.

'Nothing to see on this level.' The rotund tunnel manager descended the next ladder with surprising agility and beckoned Valerius to follow. 'We have completed the chambers, as you can see. Unless . . . Yes. If you'll follow me.' Nepos led the way through a long tunnel until the oil lamp showed a flat wall covered in pick marks that stood out stark and white against a blackened surface. 'This is what delayed us,' Nepos said in a voice tinged with frustration and regret. 'A block of solid quartzite, unbreakable despite being subject to fire quenched by vinegar. The method is normally good for the hardest of rocks. We lost three men to the fumes before we decided on *ruina*.'

They descended another ladder and Valerius followed the engineer's retreating back along a tunnel that sloped gently downwards for about fifty paces. Halfway along he heard the sound of picks. He was bemused to feel a draught on the back of his neck and he looked up to see a circular shaft perhaps the length of his arm in diameter.

Nepos saw his puzzlement. 'This far from the entrance the air is virtually unbreathable even with the help of the air pipe, as I'm sure you've noticed. Yet because of the shape of the hill we are not too far from the surface. We bored a narrow conduit down to meet this pipe cut by the workers.'

'But how . . . ?'

The mine manager's face took on a look of smug

complacency. 'For a man who can trisect an angle it is nothing to work out how to make two straight lines meet at a single point. Now, we haven't much time.' He led the way towards the end of the tunnel. 'The final decision is mine, but I have been assured the work is almost complete.'

Five chambers, each containing four or five men wielding picks. Nepos entered the nearest.

'Enough,' he ordered. The men stopped working and slumped to the floor. Valerius noticed something different about them. Apart from their heavy beards and haunted, exhausted features, what made them stand out was their truly foul and ragged appearance and the fetters fixed to their ankles and wrists.

'I thought you told me there were no slaves in the mines.'

'These men are not slaves,' Nepos corrected. 'They are the Lost. Condemned prisoners who work at the lowest level and never leave the mine until it is worked out. If I am correct these men will soon see the light of day for the first time in six months.' He studied the far wall of the chamber for a few moments before putting his ear to the rock and tapping the wall with his knuckle. Valerius watched in puzzlement as he repeated the exercise in each of the chambers, muttering to himself and nodding his head. Suddenly he turned with a beaming smile. 'We are ready.'

XXI

Serpentius had been assigned the place of honour to the right of Valuta, the clan chief, as they shared meat from the great bronze cauldron in the traditional fashion. They were surrounded by the *castro*'s elders, and Tito, who seemed to have some kind of special status in the clan. He sat directly opposite Serpentius and the dark eyes smouldered with hatred as he listened to the words of the man who claimed to be his father.

'Look beyond my years,' Serpentius urged the elders. 'See the man who was, not the man who sits before you. How can he be other than my seed? He is swifter in thought and action than anyone in these mountains, as his father Barbaros was. His skill with weapons is bettered by none. His greatest weakness is that he allows his anger to rule him,' he lowered his eyes, 'like his father before him.'

A long pause as he stared into the flames of the fire.

'That day lives in my memory more than any I suffered in Roman chains. That hour more than any hour I spent waiting to enter the arena knowing my life could be forfeit before it ended.' He looked up and turned to the man next to him. 'You were right, Valuta, I brought the Romans down upon Avala. In my pride I believed we were untouchable; that our remoteness was protection enough. I did not understand what they were capable of. That they believe themselves invincible. No cliff is too difficult to traverse, no river too wide to cross, or mountain too high to climb. Even if they came I believed I could protect us with my strength and my skills. I was a fool and I acknowledge my responsibility.' He shook his head. 'But I did not abandon you.'

Tito snorted his contempt for the words and leaned across the fire, but the elder on his left placed a hand on his arm and the young man withdrew.

'You are angry.' Serpentius spoke directly to the man who was his son. 'I too would have been angry. I too would want to kill the father who made an orphan of me, even though I was not an orphan. But I did not abandon you, Tito.'

Tito turned away, but Serpentius was driven by an urge to unburden himself in a way he'd never felt before. He spoke in a detached, emotionless tone that placed a barrier between the man and the events he related.

'The first we knew was the cry of a nightjar. I knew instantly that something was wrong, for it was not the nightjar of these mountains. Then came another cry. The cry of a man who knows he is dying. It was Pedrito, one of our bravest, and the sentry who stood watch at the valley entrance. I rose naked, armed only with a spear, and my wife Lyda begged me not to leave her alone with our son' – again Tito let out a snort of rage but Serpentius ignored him – 'but I did not listen. My responsibility was to the *castro*. I told Lyda to take Tito north to the hidden place where our clan always find sanctuary. So I went to meet them, calling out a warning and taking with me what men emerged from the

185

huts as I went. The Romans had torches. I had never seen so many torches. They were like fireflies in the night, to the right, to the left and in front. It was here they were concentrated and here I counted on taking out their heart even if it cost my life. I screamed the war cry of my people and charged them.' For a moment the barrier was breached and a groan escaped him at the memory. 'How we fought them. Our warriors died one by one, their souls sent to the gods by sword and spear. Again and again we charged.' Serpentius's hand twitched on his sword as he fought the battle once more. 'But they would not give a single pace. Instead, they pushed us back to the *castro*. In the end I was alone and surrounded. I fended off blade after blade, but a man's arm must tire and his strength must fade. By now the *castro* was burning and the heat of the flames seared my skin.' He felt a tear roll down his grizzled cheek and knew that his tone was a lie and the barrier an illusion. 'I believed Lyda had fled to safety with my son. My last wish was to go to the gods with the blood of one more Roman on my spear point. Then I heard her scream. I looked round and the house was on fire. The doorway a curtain of flame. She screamed again and I forgot the fight and the Romans. My only thought was to save my family. Before I could move the world turned red, then black, and I believed I was dead.'

'Yes, that is how it was,' Valuta nodded. 'And you are Barbaros the Proud. I see it now through the years and the suffering. I was guarding sheep with my son on the high pasture when they came,' he continued in a flat voice. 'We saw the torches streaming up the valley and the village burning. By the time we reached here it was already too late. All we could do was help those left alive to the Cave of Echoes. There we stayed for many days until the Romans left. When we returned, the Romans had stolen our animals, destroyed the crops and mutilated our dead.'

'They placed me in a cage so small I could barely crouch,' Serpentius continued his story. 'When I regained consciousness I was covered in blood and filth. I couldn't understand why they didn't kill me. On the first day they laughed as they brought me the heads of my comrades, saying they thought I might enjoy their company. On the second two officers came to look at me. They didn't know I understood their language and spoke quite freely. One wanted to have me crucified at the head of the pass as an example to anyone tempted to defy the Empire. The man in the red cloak said no. He planned to give a great games as a celebration of his victory and I would be part of the entertainment. A great champion had been summoned from Rome and on this day he would earn the *rudis*, the wooden sword that symbolized his freedom. I have never seen a colder smile as the officer detailed my end. The champion enjoyed cutting a man apart, one piece at a time, for the pleasure of the crowd, before castrating his bleeding torso, opening the chest and tearing out his heart so it was the last thing his dying eyes saw.'

'A true Zoelan would have chewed through his own veins on the first day and bled to death,' Tito spat his disdain.

Serpentius shook his head. 'A true Zoelan would suffer any humiliation and bide his time, waiting for the moment he could have his revenge on the man in the red cloak, my son.'

'Do not call me that.'

'Do you deny the evidence of your own eyes?'

'I have no father.'

187

Serpentius speared him with a look that made the young warrior shiver. 'They kept the man who was your father in the cage for sixty days and treated him like a wild beast. By the time he reached Tarraco, where the great games were to be held, he looked like an animal, and after his long, cramped confinement he could barely walk. It was fortunate the great champion had been delayed and that being part of the planned entertainment meant being kept in conditions where I was able to recover my strength. Still, every day of my captivity I imagined the end the man in the red cloak had decided for me. I resolved to take my own life, but only if I could take his first.'

'Yet you lived. So you did neither.'

Serpentius met his son's eyes. 'I lived. The champion's exhibition was to be the main event of the games. I was the last of three prisoners he would kill. They held me beneath the arena at Tarraco and I could hear the ecstasy of the mob as the other two men died. When the time came they handed me a sword and men in armour shepherded me out with the points of their spears. I remember understanding that these were my last moments and the smell of the sea and the warmth of the sun on my face almost unmanned me. They marched me through a blood-spattered avenue strewn with the arms and legs of my predecessors. The arena wall was too high to climb and the man in the red cloak beyond my reach. This was the moment I should plunge the point of the sword into my own body. But I hesitated.' He turned to Valuta. 'You called me Barbaros the Proud. It is a name I had long forgotten, but it fitted the man well enough. My opponent waited for me at the end of the avenue. A huge man, his face hidden by a masked helmet and his body protected in armour. A god of war. He held an axe in his right hand and a long sword in his left and both dripped with the blood of his previous victims. I looked upon him and my pride would not let me die before I had tested myself against him. Yes, Barbaros the Proud. Death is death, but for a proud man the manner of it counts more than the pain . . .'

As he told his story, Serpentius refought the battle that saved his life. Naked but for a loin cloth, they'd given him a sword because the legate whose soldiers captured him had heard of his prowess with a spear. He'd killed six legionaries and wounded a dozen more before they managed to bring him down. The sword should have been unfamiliar and put him at a disadvantage, but Barbaros – how strange the name sounded – had been chosen for warrior training at the age of twelve. This sword, a heavy type the Roman auxiliary cavalry carried, was similar in style to the one he exercised with and it felt comfortable in his hand.

The great champion, Asiaticus, wore the full-face helmet of a Thracian, with mesh eyeholes, a broad brim and a griffon crest. Of course, Serpentius had known nothing of these things then. Later he would discover that a Thraex, as this type of gladiator was known, normally wore only light armour protecting the shoulder. Asiaticus preferred a decorated metal breastplate and wore greaves to protect his lower legs.

Was his younger self truly as calm as he remembered? Did he truly consider sacrificing an arm to make the opening for a killer blow? Ten years later it would have been the work of a moment to slaughter this colossus. Then, they had studied each other for a moment that seemed to last a lifetime. Asiaticus ostentatiously swung his axe to draw his victim's attention, but Serpentius's eyes never left that iron mask. Finally, the giant danced forward with the axe raised, but when it came it was the sword that swept in for the killer blow.

Serpentius parried the thrust . . . just as Asiaticus intended. As the Spaniard's blade swept along the gladiator's sword the axe came down in an overhand blow that would have taken Serpentius's arm off at the elbow. Instead, he somehow managed to spin clear and the axe blade hissed through fresh air.

Serpentius had believed speed would be his greatest weapon, but now Asiaticus had seen what his enemy was capable of he matched it and his skill with weapons was far greater. Time after time the Spaniard would escape serious injury by the breadth of a sword edge. Twice he felt the sting as the razor edge sliced his skin. Blood dripped from his right forearm and left wrist.

Only the fact that Asiaticus had a reputation to defend saved Serpentius. The veteran gladiator was an entertainer who killed in a certain, very precise fashion. He'd chopped his previous opponents to bloody rags and his audience expected more of the same. When it didn't happen quickly they hooted and booed. Always the axe sought out the right arm or the left and Serpentius discovered he could more or less ignore the sword point. It was a distraction, nothing more, to open the way for the axe. Not once in the early moments did he come close to touching his opponent, but he danced and wove, pirouetted and jinked, making Asiaticus follow every move. Not speed, then. Endurance. If he could stay alive long enough he had a chance.

Serpentius began to use every inch of the arena floor, always managing to stay just out of range of the great axe, and he sensed the bigger man's growing bewilderment.

Asiaticus had always killed quickly. A combination of skill, strength and speed had made him the greatest gladiator of his age. He was on the threshold of receiving the *rudis* and his freedom. His opponents knew they were going to die and either cowered before him or did their best to meet their end with honour. He'd never faced anyone like this lean, lightning quick, bearded savage. It felt like fighting a wisp of smoke. He tried to concentrate and ignore the growing jeers of the crowd, but anger and frustration grew inside him like a wildfire.

The more Serpentius dodged, the harder Asiaticus chased, and the Spaniard ensured he always held out the tantalizing prospect of a killing blow. He couldn't afford to be careless, Asiaticus was much too good for that, but neither could he allow his opponent to realize he was being toyed with. Another feinted attack and the axe sliced past his right side almost taking the hairs off his arm. Was it his imagination, or was the gladiator showing signs of slowing? Yes! And his breathing was becoming ragged. Soon.

But Asiaticus too had his tricks. From somewhere he found a new burst of energy and forced Serpentius to back away from the scything sweep of the axe. The champion had forgotten his carefully laid plans for dismemberment. He would settle for Serpentius's death. The crowd sensed it and roared for blood, the crescendo of sound rising in waves over the arena. As Serpentius backed away he felt something soft under his foot and stumbled over the remains of one of the gladiator's previous victims. Suddenly he was down and the axe was plunging towards his face. He twisted his head and felt the blade shear through his tangle of dark hair, the sharp sting as it nicked his ear.

The crowd gasped, but even as the axe fell Serpentius's sword hand had been moving almost of its own volition. This was the risk he'd needed to take to create an opening. Asiaticus had to stand over his victim to make the strike. Now Serpentius rammed the sword point up and into the giant gladiator's unprotected groin. A savage cry of exultation erupted from him as he felt the moment it pierced flesh and muscle, the momentary resistance as it grated on bone. With a twist of the wrist he ripped the edge upwards tearing a great gaping wound in Asiaticus's flesh and almost emasculating him. Warm blood sheeted his sword arm and his victory cry mingled with his opponent's shriek of mortal agony and the crowd's howl of consternation. The weapons fell from Asiaticus's nerveless hands and he stood shuddering for a moment before he toppled face down in the sand.

Serpentius pushed himself to his feet. He turned to stare at the soldier in the red cloak who sat with other notables beneath a silken canopy. The man's face was a mask of fury.

With great deliberation Serpentius laid down his sword and picked up the axe. He kicked the Thracian helmet from the dying gladiator's head and with a single blow severed the neck. He picked up the bloody token by the hair and as the crowd roared their acclamation he hurled it high over the wall towards the soldier.

He was smiling.

The elders muttered their approval at the gladiator's fitting end. 'I would gladly have died then,' Serpentius remembered. 'A troop of legionaries surrounded me with their spears. But one of the men who watched the fight was a senator with an interest in a gladiator school in Rome. He bought me from the legate and I began my journey to the city in chains.'

Tito had listened spellbound with the rest, but now

his expression changed to anger. 'You should have killed yourself rather than serve the Romans.'

'But I did not,' Serpentius rasped. 'Instead, I nursed my anger and waited for my opportunity.'

'And did you take it, Barbaros?' Valuta asked.

'The Roman who ordered our village burned was the legate of the Sixth legion, a man called Julius Pompeius Gracilis.' He'd been given the name by the guards who'd taunted him during the terrible, agonizing journey from Asturica to Tarraco and had never forgotten it. 'I cut his throat and burned his house as he lay dying.'

It was the first time he'd revealed the truth to anyone. Gracilis had been an old man by the time Serpentius tracked him down to a villa on the Quirinal Hill. It had been when Valerius had first hired him, along with Marcus, the *lanista* of the gladiator school. They'd been tasked with hunting a man called Petrus and his Christus followers. Serpentius had simply slipped away one night to the house he'd been told about. It was long before he called Valerius friend, and he had no regrets about deceiving him, or killing Gracilis. The old man had destroyed his life. Only now after twenty years did he have an opportunity to resume it. The only question was, would the Romans let him?

'Why have you come here?' Tito, of course.

'This is my home. I have dreamed of these mountains for twenty years. And because the Romans will not leave you alone.'

It had been one of the things Petronius discovered before his untimely death. The mines had an insatiable greed for labour. A great sweep was planned using every available auxiliary and legionary. They would round up the impudent pockets of isolated tribespeople who still believed themselves beyond Roman rule.

'You are on one of their lists, but you do not work and you do not pay taxes. That is unacceptable to an Empire whose wealth is based on taxing every egg and bushel of corn. They will come for you and they will come soon. If you want to avoid that fate you must flee or you must fight. I am here to help you do either.'

'Then we'll fight,' Tito said.

The elders looked at him with dismay, but Serpentius smiled at his son. 'It occurs to me that there may be another option. One way to stop them coming here is to cause them problems somewhere else.'

'And how do we do that?'

'I will think on it.'

XXII

When Valerius walked from the mine into the glare of the late morning sunlight it felt as if he was emerging from a tomb. He could only imagine the torment of the filthy, shackled men who staggered from the shaft in his wake, hampered by their ankle chains and whipped by overseers for the slightest stumble. When they reached the entrance the prisoners cried out at the searing brightness of the longed for sun and threw up their hands to protect eyes that had seen nothing more brilliant for six months than the flame of an oil lamp. They sucked in the air as if it was the sweetest nectar and some fell to their knees to kiss the earth. Whatever evils they'd committed Valerius felt only pity for these men. Before the day was out they would be consigned to the deepest levels of the next mine up the valley.

He looked around for Aurelio, but despite his promise neither the guide nor his mount was anywhere to be seen. But Valerius was given no opportunity to search for him.

'Please, we must hurry.' Nepos ushered him towards the horses. 'There is not a moment to lose.' As they wound their way up the mountainside, the tunnel manager explained that the prefect in charge of the mine didn't want to waste another minute of daylight. 'We still have many hours of daylight left and the men standing around idle. It will not do.'

Up and up, until the mine entrance was just a speck on the landscape below, identifiable only by the spoil heaps dotting the ground nearby, and the deep channel that led arrow straight down the slope towards it. When they reached the sluice gates Valerius discovered they held back an astonishing volume of water in a reservoir cut from the rock. A dozen slaves stood by the winding mechanism waiting for word to release the deluge.

Even though he'd witnessed the results of *ruina montium*, Valerius couldn't quite bring himself to believe this innocuous pool of inert liquid was capable of creating such incredible destruction.

Nepos dismounted and approached a tall, thin man with a long nose. He stood beside a priest holding a young goat that bleated and struggled in his arms. They had set up a small, portable stone altar nearby. After a short discussion the thin man nodded. The priest began a long chanted appeal to Pluto, god of the underworld, to accept this sacrifice and yield up the wealth of his realm to Titus Flavius Caesar Vespasianus Augustus, through the medium of Gaius Ulpius Frontinus, district procurator. When he'd completed the call he drew a razor-edged knife across the goat's throat, allowing the blood to pour over the altar. Gradually the animal's struggles ceased and he placed the carcass on the ground and opened its belly. Nodding to himself, he prodded among its entrails until he found some piece of offal that pleased him immensely.

'The omens are good,' he announced with a look of satisfaction.

The thin man, presumably Frontinus, rapped out an order to a worker and the man waved a red flag twice above his head. Far below the flag was answered in similar fashion from the centre of a large group of workers who had gathered a distance to the west of the mine entrance.

'Now!' Frontinus cried.

Urged on by an overseer the men at the sluice launched themselves at the winding mechanism, a large circular block with wooden staves protruding from it. Within moments the gate creaked as pressure was brought to bear by a system of ropes and pulleys. At first it seemed even the efforts of twelve strong men couldn't shift the massive gate, which consisted of seven or eight tree trunks, roughly shaped and covered in pitch. But they persevered, barking out a rhythmic chant as they heaved at the staves. Valerius noticed a tiny spray of water at the base, which multiplied until it formed a trickle, then a stream. As the gate slowly rose the stream turned into a torrent that tumbled down the channel, bubbling and frothing and picking up speed with every passing moment. Still higher and the torrent became a raging force of nature emerging in a single enormous fountain a dozen paces long that rumbled and thundered and was barely contained by the channel. By now the first of the waters had reached the entrance of the mine and Valerius could hear a muted roar above the rush of the flood.

'Observe how the waters enter the mine shaft to be absorbed by the chambers.' Valerius found Nepos at his side, his eyes bright with anticipation. 'A certain amount will already be filtering into the lower levels, but the majority will fill the upper tunnels, sealing the air inside the mine. We call this method hydraulic, because of the

197

canals and reservoirs, but in truth the air itself is our greatest weapon. As more and more water is forced into the shaft and fills the second level the pressure builds and the air is compressed. May I ask what you think will happen then?'

'If I had not seen what I have seen, I would say that the waters would reach a point where the mine could accept no more,' Valerius admitted.

'Then you will certainly be surprised,' Nepos smiled.

They waited. And waited. Nothing happened, but Valerius could almost feel the sense of anticipation growing. Nepos leaned forward, craning his neck.

'What—?'

The climax was so unexpected Valerius was almost knocked off his feet. His eyes were fixed on the cave mouth when the hillside beyond it seemed to bulge outwards and upwards. The bulge grew like a goatskin filling with water and cracks began to appear on the surface like giant knife wounds to reveal the terracotta earth beneath the surface. The cataclysm was all the more surprising because it happened in silence. Yet in the next instant the quiet was broken by an unearthly roar that made the horses rear. Within a heartbeat of the terrible sound the ground below tore itself apart and leapt high into the air. Valerius felt the earth jump beneath his feet as if someone had kicked him on the soles of his sandals. The impact made him stagger, but his eyes remained fixed on the hill where water pulsed in a great red wave from the broken slope beyond the mine entrance, sweeping rocks and trees and the very ground with it. Without warning the roar took on a new ferocity and some part of Valerius's stunned mind found time to marvel that a sound could be as terrifying as facing a Parthian battle line. He watched in awe as the entire lower portion of the hill crumbled and dis-integrated, to leave the shattered unearthly landscape he had witnessed on the way to the mine. Gradually the roar faded and Valerius turned to find Nepos grinning at him like a young boy.

'Are you impressed?' Valerius could barely hear him for the ringing in his ears.

It took a few moments before he was able to find his voice. 'Astonished.'

The workers below swarmed over the broken ground even before the waters fully subsided.

'Some of them will search the site for visible pieces of gold,' Nepos explained. 'Or other elements on the surface. Most will carry the disturbed earth to be sifted through what we call leads, a set of conduit steps floored with gorse branches. Since the gold is heavier than the silt, it is caught in the gorse and drops to the bottom of the lead. And any gold-bearing rock that has been revealed will be mined and sent for smelting.'

'Your entire operation seems remarkably efficient,' Valerius congratulated him. 'So much so that it makes it difficult to understand the rumours I've heard about the amount of gold reaching Rome.'

Nepos's face instantly went blank. 'Sir, I do not know why you are here, or who sent you, but I am a lowly tunnel manager who knows nothing of these things. Perhaps the *praefectus metallorum* . . . ? No.' His voice quivered and he darted a frightened glance towards Frontinus. 'I did not mean that. Please say nothing.'

'Very well,' Valerius assured him. 'If that is your wish. But tell me, Nepos, have you ever been approached by a man called Marcus Florus Petronius? An engineer like yourself, who would be most interested in the workings of the mines. He is a friend and I'm concerned for his welfare.'

'Petronius?' Valerius hadn't heard Frontinus approaching. 'A man of that name came here a few weeks ago.' The long nose twitched disdainfully. 'An inquisitive fellow who asked all sorts of impertinent questions. Are you one of the same stamp?'

'As I was telling Hostilius, he is a friend. He hasn't been seen at his lodgings for some days. I'm concerned for his welfare.'

'Well I sent him on his way. The workings of this mine are my affair and mine alone. As I would have done with you, but for the warrant you carry from the prefect. For some reason your friend took a great interest in the water supply. The last time I saw him he was following the line of the canal on that hill yonder,' he pointed to a structure high up on a neighbouring mountain. 'It is dangerous country, and not just because of the terrain. He would not be the first fool to fall from a height or walk into an ambush up there.'

Valerius studied Frontinus. Frontinus stared back at him, aloof and full of his own importance. This is my domain, he was saying, and no scrap of parchment with Ferox's name on it is going to change that. Valerius realized he would get no more out of the procurator.

'I thank you for your kindness.' A thin smile flickered on Frontinus's lips at the obvious sarcasm. 'And for Nepos's tour of your mine.' He bowed to the plump tunnel manager. 'It was most illuminating. A marvel of engineering skill and the effect was truly awe-inspiring. When I return to Rome I will be able to tell my friends that I quite literally saw man move a mountain.'

Frontinus's expression softened at the unexpected compliment.

'In that case I wish you a safe and speedy home-coming. Now, forgive me, but I must return to work.'

Valerius and Nepos reclaimed their horses and rode back down the hill. There was still no sign of Aurelio and Nepos could find no one who had seen him since they'd entered the mine. 'It is most unusual,' he frowned. 'I will find a man to guide you back to the camp. Perhaps there will be news of your friend there.'

No news, as such, but a stolid Parthian who handed Valerius a note etched with a stylus on a birchwood shaving. If Valerius read it correctly, Aurelio had received an urgent summons from his master to return to Asturica Augusta. He hoped Valerius had a successful visit to the mine and would call on him on his return.

The Parthian escort had gathered at the stables and Valerius felt a twinge of concern under the gaze of the dispassionate bearded faces. With Aurelio by his side he'd felt secure enough in their presence. Now that he faced seventy miles in the saddle alone with them he saw the matter differently. They wouldn't make Asturica by nightfall, which meant a night camp by the road-side unless they could find a *mansio*. His travels with Serpentius had given Valerius ample experience of what could happen on a dark night by a lonely road.

'You will return to Asturica Augusta immediately,' he told the leader, a man with a scar running from his forehead to his cheek. 'I have further business that will keep me here for another day, possibly two.'

'Our orders are to escort you to the Red Hills and back to Asturica,' the man growled.

'It is not a request, soldier,' Valerius snapped back. The Parthian's dark eyes glittered rebellion and Valerius decided to make the order more palatable. 'I will return with the next gold train. I'll be perfectly safe. I'll also be happy to put the order in writing and explain to your master that you protested against its contents. Will that suffice?'

The Parthian glowered for a moment, but eventually nodded his consent and held out his hand. Valerius rummaged in his pack until he found stylus and waxed pad on which to scribble out the order. He handed it to the Parthian. With a last glare the man snapped a command to his comrades. They vaulted into the saddle and Valerius watched them ride out of the camp gates. When they were out of sight he ordered the stable hand to ready a fresh horse. He had work to do.

XXIII

When Valerius mounted half an hour later his cloak covered the worn and patched mail vest he'd kept since it had saved his life in Antioch. A *gladius* hung in its scabbard on his right hip, ready to be cross drawn. It wasn't that he felt any imminent sense of danger. What he planned carried an element of risk, a risk that must be accepted, but which he would take every care to offset.

The question had plagued him since Frontinus revealed Petronius's interest in the canals and aqueducts that supplied the Red Hills mines. What was it that drew the engineer to those fearsome heights? The only answer was to go and discover for himself. He knew how dangerous it could be to travel alone, but what choice did he have? Aurelio wasn't available. Allowing the Parthians to escort him would be worse than having no escort at all. One nudge in the wrong place and an unhappy accident would rid whoever controlled what was happening in Asturica of a niggling problem.

Valerius left the camp and took a route west that made it appear he was retracing his journey of earlier in the day. After an hour, and when he was sure no one trailed him, he turned on to a stony track leading into the mountains. Out of sight of the road he reined in and studied the map Marius had given him. It wasn't detailed enough to show the track Valerius had followed, but it gave him an approximate idea of his position. He traced his finger northwards along the line of a stream until he reached a valley a few miles ahead. From what he could tell it rose to bring him close to a canal that fed the Red Hills mines. He had no idea of the terrain he'd face, but if he could get to the canal it would allow him to explore the area that had interested Petronius.

He let the mare pick her way upwards as the track wound through scree and boulders and stunted bushes into the mountains. The only sound was the even clip of the horse's hooves on the stones and the buzz of insects that filled the air. Sweat ran down his back and the fiery sun roasted the top of his head. He stopped and drank from his waterskin and wished he'd thought to bring the broad-brimmed straw hat Aurelio had suggested he buy in Asturica. Was he being too cautious by wearing the chain armour that felt as if it was slowly cooking him? Turning in the saddle he studied the ground around him. Better cooked than dead. You could lose an army among the thicker patches of scrub.

The country was too steep and rocky for farming and he suspected the track must lead to some isolated spring pasture or popular hunting ground. A sharp cry split the silence and he looked up to see a pair of vultures spiralling above. The birds were a common enough sight in Hispania, but for some reason he was reminded of the aftermath of the siege of Jerusalem. Thousands of carrion birds – vultures, buzzards, eagles and crows – had turned the sky black as they waited patiently to feast on the countless dead.

He forced the image from his head and nudged the mare on, his thoughts turning again to Serpentius. The Spaniard had been Valerius's trusty right arm for so long that losing him had felt like a new disfigurement. Not long after Valerius and Tabitha arrived in Rome word had come of the Spaniard's decision to return to his native land. More worryingly the news was accompanied by hints of a man broken in spirit if not in body. Valerius had a vision of the quivering figure who could not make himself enter the Conduit of Hezekiah. No. Remember the man who stood by your side at First Bedriacum as a tidal wave of vengeful legionaries were advanced to engulf the little knot of survivors. The Serpentius who had risen wraith-like from the charnel pit after the night of confused terror on the Cremona road.

He studied the high peaks surrounding him. These were Serpentius's mountains. If ever he had need of his old friend it was now. He froze as the little mare whinnied and danced beneath him. No imminent threat in sight, but his left hand instinctively dropped to the hilt of the *gladius*. Still wary, he allowed her to have her head, wandering off the track and sniffing the air. Her route took them around a shoulder of the hill they had been climbing and soon the ground began to drop away. Valerius looked to the north and saw daylight appear where there had been none. She'd led him to the valley.

He discovered what had attracted her when the trees thickened and they broke through to a shimmering stream of clear, bright water that tumbled and frothed over the rocks. Patting her on the shoulder he let her drop her head to drink and slid from the saddle. He dipped a cupped hand in the water a little upstream from the mare and drank the cool, clear liquid.

When the mare had drunk her fill he pushed on,

205

staying as close to the line of the stream as he could in the broken ground. By now he was familiar enough with the terrain to know there was little chance of the horse being able to make the ascent. Eventually the narrow, rocky divide became so constricted he decided there was no point in pushing her any further.

He turned the mare and rode back to a shaded glade they'd passed earlier. Even in the thin soil a stand of oaks thrived on the moisture from the stream and the grass grew thick and lush along the banks. He dismounted, removed her saddle and tethered her to a nearby branch with enough freedom of movement to drink when she chose. She'd be safe enough here while he made the climb and he'd be back well before nightfall. If they had to spend the night in the open it was no hardship with good grazing and water and firewood in plentiful supply.

Before he set out he contemplated the slope again. Steeper than he'd bargained for, with some tricky scrambles and a few out and out climbs close to the top. A difficult proposition for a man with one hand, but doubly so for one burdened by a mail shirt. Reluctantly, he unbuckled his sword belt and undid the hooks on the shoulders and chest of the mail. Using his left hand he hauled the heavy metal armour over his head with an awkward wriggle of his upper body. He replaced the sword belt over the padded leather jerkin he wore to make the mail more comfortable and concealed the saddle and mail beneath a gorse bush.

He started through the trees towards the slope.

The rocks glowed a bright ochre in the afternoon sun and when he used them as handholds they were almost too hot to touch. Fortunately there were also firmly rooted bushes and scrubby, head-high pines he could use for support and he made good time on the lower part of the hill. Above him loomed a great red cliff, but his objective was a lower ridge to the right, which should hide the line of the Red Hills canal. Valerius crabbed in that direction, sometimes forced to retreat as the broken ground crumbled beneath his feet or he slid back on the loose scree. Within minutes his legs felt as if they were on fire, sweat poured from his hairline and a cloud of black flies circled waiting to sip the salty liquid. As the discomfort increased he cursed the whim that led him this way. Why hadn't he just gone back to the mine where he could have ridden most of the way to the canal?

The answer lay in the fear he'd seen in Nepos's eyes when Valerius had asked about the decline in gold production, and the way the tunnel manager looked at Frontinus. That, and something indefinable about the procurator's manner, had placed him on a list of suspects growing longer by the day. Severus, head of the *ordo*, and his voluptuous and much too inquisitive wife. Ferox, the *praefectus metallorum*, either involved in the conspiracy or the most incompetent bureaucrat in the Empire. And the mysterious Cornelius Aurelius Saco, avaricious and ruthless, and much too interested in Valerius's movements. It occurred to him that another he couldn't discount was Proculus, camp prefect at Legio. In Valerius's experience very little happened in a legion's area of operations of which the commander's spies weren't aware. And if the conspiracy involved Proculus, why not his faithful prefect of the First ala Parthorum, Claudius Harpocration?

Yet, apart from Petronius's disappearance and his own instinct he didn't have a shred of evidence they'd stolen one single talent of gold. If he was right, the thieves included army officers, bureaucrats and the local aristocracy. Vespasian would not be gentle with the guilty. Their lives, and possibly those of their families, were at stake. They would do anything in their power to avoid the plot being uncovered.

He stopped to rest his legs and looked down. The glade where he'd left the mare seemed very far below. Movement off to the west caught his eye and he noticed a faint dust cloud. Hunters on the track? A herd of the big-horned mountain sheep they stalked? Or something more sinister? No matter, he was committed now. He set his shoulders, gritted his teeth and attacked the slope once more.

Another hundred paces brought him to a little plateau where he rested again. Here the foliage of the scrubby trees hid his direct line of sight down the slope. Something about the dust cloud made him uneasy. He crouched by a narrow pine and pulled back a branch. The gap allowed him to scan the base of the hill and the valley where he'd left the mare. A flash of turquoise and white zipped through the trees and his mind rather than his eyes registered it as a jay. He waited. And allowed himself to breathe as two fallow deer skipped effortlessly across the scrubby ground before disappearing into the trees lining the little stream. Smiling at his own foolishness, he was turning away to resume his climb when he saw him.

Stealthy, oh so stealthy. Spear held in two hands at the ready. No tell-tale glint from the needle-tipped iron point. The man who wielded the weapon had deliberately dulled the tip to lessen the risk of detection. A second man came into view, similarly armed. Every footstep deliberately planted to ensure silence as he advanced towards his prey. Yes, prey. For these were certainly the hunters whose dust he had seen. But they weren't hunting deer. They were hunting a man. And Valerius had no doubt who that man was.

The pot helmets and green tunics identified them, but even without their uniforms Valerius would have recognized these hard-eyed, bearded men for what they were. Parthians. His eyes caught movement beyond them and two more moved into view, separated like the first by about ten paces. One of them bent and studied something on the ground and Valerius saw him signal with his hand. An order must have been given because they changed direction, angling towards the point where he'd joined the stream. He shivered as he realized they were tracking him over that impossible broken ground. Soon they'd find the mare. Then their attention would be drawn upwards. He'd made no attempt to conceal his progress up the hillside even if it had been possible. It was only a matter of time.

Valerius looked desperately around the hillside seeking some avenue of escape. Plenty of concealment at this level, but the higher he went the more patchy the cover became. He turned to his left and for a moment his brain refused to believe what his eyes were telling him. Less than twenty paces away in the shadow of another pine tree a savage, bearded face was staring at him. He blinked and the image vanished. Had he imagined it? No. He'd seen what he'd seen. But what to do? He swept his surroundings. The way the man had disappeared, so suddenly and without the slightest sound, meant he could be anywhere. Valerius felt an imaginary knife point pricking his spine. Another Parthian? Surely he would have been calling to his comrades to join him for the slaughter. But if not, who? And were his targets the Parthians or Valerius?

He risked another look at the men below. They were

approaching the stream bed. It had to be now. Keeping low he moved through the trees to his right, away from the man who'd been watching him. There were gaps in the trees and bushes, but he gambled the Parthians would be blinded by the oaks that thrived by the stream and he made good progress over the rough ground. If he could push far enough ahead they wouldn't be able to get close to him before nightfall. Sunrise would bring its own problems, but he'd worry about that when it came.

When he crossed the shoulder of the hill he was beyond the view of his hunters, but now he faced a decision. Should he climb to the level of the canal and continue his quest to discover what had attracted Petronius? Or find his way back to the road and look for somewhere to go to ground until nightfall? Hunger wasn't a factor; he'd packed a day's rations of bread and olives in his pouch. The stream or the canal would provide him with enough water to reach either the mining camp or the mine itself.

The canal then? But Valerius had been plagued by a growing certainty that this potentially deadly encounter with the Parthians was no coincidence. Frontinus had presented him with Petronius's interest in the canals like a gift. Valerius doubted the mine prefect was a man who offered gifts lightly. Where better for someone to disappear than in these remote heights? And he'd leapt at the bait like a trout at a dragonfly.

He began making his way carefully downwards using the bushes as anchor points. When he was halfway, the roots of one of the plants gave beneath his grip. He teetered for a moment before losing his balance and tumbling down the hillside. It wasn't a long fall and he only suffered a few scratches, but when Valerius regained his balance he saw to his horror that he'd created a small dust cloud. He pushed himself to his feet and resumed his descent more swiftly now. And with good reason.

A shout rang out from somewhere to his left.

Valerius's heart stuttered at the confirmation someone had seen the dust, but he sent up a prayer of thanks to the gods. Whoever had called out had saved his life – at least for the moment. If they'd stayed silent they could have surrounded him and pinned him with their spears. At least now he had a chance.

Keeping low, he drew his sword and trotted in the opposite direction. He hadn't gone twenty paces when a bearded figure rose out of the ground in front of him. The sword came up – and froze.

The bearded tribesman from the mountain stared at Valerius and, with a quick sweeping motion of his hand, encouraged the Roman to follow him. A dozen questions ran through Valerius's head, but this was no time for hesitation. Instinctively, he followed the retreating back through the bushes. Younger than Valerius had first thought, the stranger wore a striped tunic, cloth *braccae* and leather sandals. He set a diagonal course to take them across the front of the advancing Parthians. Already Valerius could hear his pursuers charging through the undergrowth. He was becoming convinced his 'saviour' was going to get him killed when the man disappeared.

When he reached the same spot he saw his mysterious companion had dropped on to his belly in a barely perceptible piece of dead ground. Without hesitation he followed the tribesman's example. They squirmed for perhaps thirty paces along what must have been some kind of ancient water course before the stranger raised a hand to halt. The sound of the advancing Parthians came closer. Valerius sensed the hunters' progress was more painstaking now. A search rather than a chase.

He froze with his left hand clutching the hilt of his *gladius*. Ten paces separated him from his companion and their hiding place was cloaked by the low scrub. Without warning a pair of legs appeared before Valerius, hesitated, then moved stealthily onwards to vanish in the foliage. Behind him he heard a shuffling as another of the Parthians crossed the depression where he hid.

He tensed for the moment the spear pierced his back and pinned him to the earth, but he hadn't been seen. The man in the striped tunic waited for the count of ten before moving off again and Valerius followed in his wake. When he reached the cover of the trees Valerius's saviour rose to his feet and disappeared silently downstream. By the time Valerius reached the same point the man was almost out of sight, trotting over the stream bed as easily as if he were walking down a cobbled street.

Within a few minutes they reached the glade where Valerius had left the mare. He heaved a sigh of relief when he saw she was still where he'd tethered her. The bearded man went to the mare and scratched her head, nodding appreciatively as he ran a hand over her shoulder and chest.

'A fine horse.' It was the first time he'd spoken and Valerius struggled with the curious sing-song Latin. Valerius went to the bush where he'd hidden the saddle and mail as the other man continued, 'Just follow the line of the stream and you'll eventually reach the road. There's a deer track. You'll have to walk in places, but the cover is good. Eh?' He stared with astonishment at Valerius's wooden right hand.

212

'What about you?'

'I'll be taking care of the hook-noses.'

'But they are four and you are just one.'

The saturnine face broke into a savage grin that sent a shiver through Valerius. 'They are the sheep to my wolf. The mountain hare to my lynx. Their horses are close to the road. I will cut their tethers and scatter them.' Valerius threw the saddle over the mare's back and worked at the girth with his left hand until the other man appeared to help. 'Here, let me.'

'They would have killed me. Why did you save me from them? I mean nothing to you.'

The native frowned, as if he wasn't certain himself. Eventually, he said: 'The hook-noses are my enemy. Their enemy is my ally.'

'Then I thank you.' Valerius tried to think of some way to show his gratitude, but there was nothing, unless . . . He picked up the mail shirt and offered it. 'Would this be of value to you?'

The tribesman took the mail and weighed it in his hands. That unnerving grin again. 'Good iron. Yes, I can make use of it. It will turn a hook-nose spear and that is all that matters.'

Valerius had his doubts about that, but he didn't voice them.

'What do they call you?'

The young man stared at him. 'What they call me does not matter, Roman. Just because you are my ally today does not mean you won't be my enemy tomorrow. Best we leave it at that. Be on your way.' He offered his cupped hands and Valerius accepted a boost into the saddle. 'Remember. Stay by the stream.'

'Again, you have my thanks.' Valerius nudged the horse into motion. 'If ever I can repay you.'

When he reached the edge of the trees he looked over his shoulder, but the glade was empty.

That face. What was it about that face?'

214

XXIV

'They were planning to kill me.'

'I would be surprised if that were the case.' Melanius looked doubtful. 'Aurelio spoke to Orodes, who commanded the escort. He said they were concerned for you. As they left the fort they had word of a new sighting of the bandit responsible for attacking the gold shipments. They decided to keep to their original orders, but by the time they returned you were gone. That was unwise, by the way. These hills can be very dangerous for a man on his own.'

'So I keep hearing,' Valerius said. He'd made his way to Melanius's house as soon as he returned to Asturica, using the kitchen entrance as he'd been advised. Pliny's friend had shown no surprise at his appearance. He immediately ordered his servants to provide refreshments, fresh fruit, honeyed nuts, and another jug of vintage Falernian, of which he seemed to have an endless supply. 'But when I was told Petronius had taken an interest in the canals and aqueducts it seemed worth investigating.'

'They followed until you turned off on a track that led into the hills,' Melanius continued his explanation.

215

'Fortunately, they are expert trackers and picked up your trail. They also found signs of the bandits, so they were on the alert against the threat. They tethered their horses while they searched for you and when they returned these bandit scum had scattered them.'

It was a plausible enough explanation. Valerius might have accepted it without question, but he knew when a Parthian was in a killing mood. Orodes and his friends had had blood in their eyes. Still, that was nothing to do with Melanius.

'I must thank you for making it possible for me to visit the mine. It has given me a notion about how to proceed. I'm certain in my own mind poor Petronius discovered something significant—'

'Poor Petronius?'

'I should have told you.' Valerius took a sip from his cup. 'Severus sent a servant to show me the house where Petronius lodged. The place had been thoroughly cleaned, but I discovered what I believe is blood in one of the rooms. I think Petronius was killed there, his body disposed of and his papers either burned or stolen.'

'Killed? Here?' Melanius looked shocked. 'In my city?'

'I can't be certain,' Valerius admitted. 'But I believe so.'

'Then the killers must be found.' Melanius was a picture of outraged determination. 'My contacts extend to certain less-than-honest individuals – a man cannot always be fastidious where he gets his information. I will make enquiries. If the man or men responsible were from Asturica someone will know.'

'Please don't put yourself at risk,' Valerius urged him. 'If the killers are still here we'll find them soon enough.'

'How would that be?' Melanius asked, picking at a tray of pomegranate seeds.

'Because they will come after me.'

The older man studied Valerius for a long time. 'Perhaps . . .' He hesitated, clearly uncertain whether to continue. 'Perhaps it would be safer if you returned to Tarraco. You will forgive me for making the suggestion, but I don't believe Pliny would have sent you here had he understood the danger you would face. I am in a far more secure position to carry out this investigation. If you would only let me know how you make secret contact with Pliny I would place all my resources at his disposal and pass on any information I can discover.'

It was a good offer, and, with the local knowledge and contacts Melanius possessed, even a sensible solution. Valerius understood he was meddling in matters of which he had little or no experience, in a place and among a people he didn't know. Melanius was right, it might get him killed or drive the conspirators underground. Neither would be of any help to Pliny. Yet he'd made his promise.

'I am sorry, Melanius, I appreciate your offer, but I cannot accept.'

Melanius smiled. 'I thought that would be your answer, Valerius, but it was an offer I had to make. What will you do now?'

'The more I learn of this matter, the more certain I am it can't be the work of one man.' Valerius reached up to touch the scar on his cheek, but quickly withdrew his hand. It had become a habit since he arrived in Asturica and habits were a weakness. 'I keep being told the gold yields are down, but a tunnel manager at the Red Hills took great pride in informing me the amount generated from his mines has never varied. If the gold is being stolen it is being taken either from the storehouses or while it's being transported. Who provides the wagons for the convoys?'

'There are various suppliers, but the main contractor is Aurelius Saco.'

'Saco again, but he can't be doing it alone. If the figures being sent to Rome are wrong, someone must be falsifying them. What do you know of Ferox, the *praefectus metallorum*?'

'Officious and arrogant,' Melanius shrugged. 'A born bureaucrat from the tips of his toes to the topmost lock of his perfectly groomed hair. He knows his job, though, and is utterly rigorous and merciless towards anyone incapable of doing theirs.'

'Then surely if there is a conspiracy such a man must be at the very heart?'

'We are not friends,' Melanius held his gaze, 'but in my experience he is also faultlessly honest. A man of the utmost probity. Why would he be so quick to give you access to the mines if he was doing something dishonest?'

It was something Valerius hadn't considered. In his eyes Ferox had always been suspect because of his position. 'You are probably right, but I still think I need to speak to him.'

'I will do what I can to arrange it, but I'm not certain what pretext we can use this time. He has already donated time and resources to you at my request. He may feel he has done enough.'

'Then perhaps it's time I used my warrant from the Emperor as *legatus iuridicus metallorum*?'

He saw Melanius grimace. 'That would certainly ensure you are granted a meeting, but will it gain you his cooperation, a cooperation you have already identified as vital? Think on it, Valerius. Firstly, he will know that you – and I – deceived him. As a man of faultless honesty he would be outraged. Secondly, you would be usurping his position and authority as *praefectus metallorum*. As a man of honour he may well feel unable to continue in his role. I beg you to reconsider. The time will come for such a step, but I fear it is not now.'

'Very well, but if not Ferox, who?'

'Perhaps one of my people could find one of his staff. Someone who is amenable to talking with you in confidence in return for some trifling gift?'

Once again Valerius marvelled at Melanius's seeming ability to conjure up a source at will. Clearly Pliny had underestimated his friend's capabilities or he'd have had him investigating this nest of vipers in the first place.

'If that was possible . . .'

'Only time will tell, but come, you have not told me of your immediate plans. I would be most happy if you would stay for dinner.'

'It would give me nothing but pleasure to accept your kind offer,' Valerius bowed. 'But I'm concerned that if I stay here any longer my presence might place you in danger.' Melanius puffed out his cheeks in mock exasperation. 'In any case I must begin drafting my preliminary report to Pliny.'

'Very well, I concede, but if there is any help I can give with your report. The use of a scribe . . . ?'

'I will consider it,' Valerius smiled. 'Once more I must thank you for your generosity.'

Valerius caught the familiar scent as he reached the top of the stair. He slowed, checking his surroundings, and his hand reached for his sword as he pushed the door slowly open with his right fist. Flickering oil lamps created ever-changing patterns of light and shade on the walls. She lay back on a couch beside a table laid out for dinner. When he walked into the room she poured a cup of wine and as she offered it to him the front of her dress fell forward to reveal the curve of her breasts.

He allowed his hand to drop away from the sword. 'Shouldn't you be with your husband?'

'How do you know he didn't send me here?'

He shrugged and tried to suppress a smile. 'I confess I hadn't considered the possibility.'

'This is Asturica Augusta,' she smiled back. 'A provincial backwater, not Rome. You would be surprised what people have to do to survive here.'

Valerius unhooked his cloak and handed it to a servant who appeared then disappeared just as quickly. He accepted the cup and lay down on the couch opposite, eyeing the heavily laden table.

'I thought you would be hungry after your exertions of the last few days, Valerius.'

'You have me at a disadvantage, lady.' He allowed his voice to harden, 'I don't believe I've ever been given your name. I'm also curious to hear what you know of my *exertions*.'

'My name is Calpurnia.' She didn't flinch from his gaze. 'And my husband Severus did not become the head of the *ordo* by ignoring what goes on around him.' She waved an elegant, slim-fingered hand towards the painted walls and silver platters. 'You are our honoured guest and a Hero of Rome, of course he would be interested in your activities, particularly after your concerns about this mysterious Petronius.'

'Mysterious? You knew him?'

'Knew of him,' she admitted. 'They say he was like a hunting dog on the scent, always poking his nose where it wasn't appreciated. He kept strange hours.'

'How would you know that?'

'How do you think?'

'Your husband was having him watched?'

She took a sip of wine. 'Of course.'

'Then he may know more about his disappearance than he acknowledged?'

'You would have to ask him.'

Valerius intended to. 'Why have you come here?'

She stared at him and the reflection of the oil lamps turned the dark eyes into pits of fire. Did he really have to ask? 'Because Calpurnia Severa knows what she wants. I find you desirable, Gaius Valerius Verrens.' She stood up and rounded the table until she was standing over him. He didn't move as she bent to take his face in her hands and brought his lips to hers. A slight shadow of confusion crossed the beautiful features at his lack of reaction. 'And in Asturica Augusta she gets what she wants.' Still Valerius didn't respond and she took his head again and pulled his face to hers, lips pressing almost painfully hard against his. Eventually she pulled away, cheeks pink with indignation. 'Are you made of stone?'

Valerius laughed and rose to his feet. 'By no means.' He shook his head. 'You are a very attractive woman, but I am a married man.'

'A married man who has not seen his wife for many weeks . . .' Her eyes narrowed. 'And who I sense has lacked female company.'

Valerius felt the blood rise to his face. 'There is also the question of your husband. The servants . . .'

'My husband questions neither my movements nor my actions.'

'Nevertheless, I cannot afford to alienate him.'

The fire in her eyes subsided but when she stepped closer he could smell the desire on her. 'Why are you here, Valerius? Why are you in Asturica?'

'To find Petronius.'

'No,' she shook her head so the mane of dark curls danced in the lamplight. 'Petronius's disappearance may be the excuse, but not the reason. There is more to it.' Her eyes widened. 'I see it now. The visit to the mine. All these questions. You haven't come to find Petronius, you have come to replace him. But what is it you seek? And what if I could help you discover it? What then, Gaius Valerius Verrens? Would you accede to a lady's whim if she helped you to achieve your mission?' She reached out to place a finger on his chest, testing the hard muscle there. 'An inconsequential night of freedom. Two fine bodies taking pleasure from each other.' She drew in a breath at the image she created. 'And such pleasure, Valerius. Pleasure as you have never experienced it before or will ever again.'

Her hunger was so powerful Valerius had to take a step back. 'You flatter me, Calpurnia.' He knew there was no point in denying her instinct about Petronius and his mission. 'But I have nothing to offer you.'

Her nostrils flared, but she made no move towards him. 'Very well, Gaius Valerius Verrens, but remember this. One day you will need a friend in this city and you may discover I am not a forgiving woman.'

XXV

'Well?'

'It was as you said,' Tito told his father as he dismounted from his pony. 'They have weakened the guard on the convoys from the mines to Asturica Augusta.'

'To draw us in and destroy us.'

The younger man nodded. 'The hook-noses had left their tracks all over the hills north and south of the road. There are hundreds of them. A half-cohort of legionaries too, camped in a gully, but on the alert.' Serpentius noticed he had something bundled behind his saddle. Tito untied it and hefted it from the horse's back. It was obviously of great weight and he dropped it at Serpentius's feet. 'A gift,' he said solemnly, 'from one warrior to another.'

'Where did you get this?' Serpentius studied the tight-knit mail shirt, noting the brighter patches where it had been repaired and the places where the rings had been forced together by the impact of a blow. Men had fought and died in this relic. Still, it was of good quality. But what was this? Tito was watching him as he inspected it. 'I said, where did you get this?' Serpentius demanded with more urgency.

'There was a man. He was being hunted by the hook-noses. A Roman . . . I wasn't sure what to do, but there was something about him.' He shrugged, unable to fully explain his actions. 'I decided to help. He gave me the mail in thanks. Did I do wrong?'

Serpentius ignored the question and fingered one of the mail's leather straps where it had been repaired. 'What was he like, this Roman?'

'Tall, lean and dark, with a scar on his cheek, here,' he ran a finger down the left side of his face from eye to lip.

'No, what was he *like*?'

Tito searched for the correct words. 'Not frightened. Angry. Fierce. He looked down upon his enemies like a hawk waiting to strike, but they were too many and well armed.' The young man stared at his father as his thoughts converged on a conclusion. 'Menacing. He reminded me of you.'

Serpentius shook his head and his expression took on a faraway look. 'And was there some mark – other than the scar – that would identify him?'

'His right hand was made of wood.'

Tito watched his father's face for a reaction, but Serpentius had long ago learned to keep his emotions to himself. Inside, his mind was racing. Valerius here? But how? And more important, why? Their last meeting had been in Jerusalem with Serpentius lying face down on a bed with an open sword wound in his back, delirious from pain and fever. He had only the vaguest memory of their parting, but he was certain there had been a mention of Rome and Tabitha, the Judaean princess who had stolen Valerius's heart. A marriage? Why then would he leave his new bride to come to the seething snake pit of Asturica?

Gaius Valerius Verrens was a dangerous man, almost as dangerous as Serpentius himself. Yes, they had been friends, but time and circumstance could erode the strongest of friendships. Valerius was a Roman and in Serpentius's experience most Romans were the most pragmatic of creatures, willing to sacrifice whatever it took as a means to an end.

Someone had been stealing gold the Romans claimed as their own, though it came from the earth Asturians had hunted, ploughed and lived upon for a thousand generations. Someone had decided Serpentius made a convenient scapegoat for the banditry and murder. He'd been meant to die deep in the mine at the hands of Cyclops. And there his crimes would have died with him, leaving the true perpetrators to find new, more subtle avenues to satisfy their avarice. Now he was on the loose, a hunted beast in the mountains he had once called home. That same someone knew exactly how dangerous he was, both as a warrior and as a threat to the conspiracy. The Parthian auxiliaries were scouring the hills for him, but how much more appropriate to send a friend, equally dangerous – a sword masked by a smile – to draw him out?

Yet the Serpentius who had ridden at Valerius's side struggled with this logic. Honour and loyalty were Gaius Valerius Verrens' code. A code not just to live by, but to die for. Serpentius had been his slave, his tentmate and his friend. He couldn't believe a man like Valerius would betray that friendship.

Unless it was in the greater interests of Rome.

It came to him in a tumble of half-formed memories. At one of their meetings Petronius had let slip that the man he reported to was the most important official in Hispania Tarraconensis. Just after he arrived in

Asturica, Serpentius had heard a whisper that a man called Gaius Plinius Secundus had been appointed proconsul of the province. Plinius Secundus had been one of the few men prepared to speak for Valerius at his trial for treason after the death of Vitellius. Serpentius remembered him as a man of patent honesty and intelligence. When Pliny's eyes and ears in the north ceased to function what would be more natural than that he call on the man most capable of replacing them: Valerius.

'You did the right thing,' Serpentius told his son.

His father's praise seemed to make Tito grow a little taller, but he was still wary. 'Is this man's presence enough to make you change your plans?'

'It's possible,' the Spaniard said thoughtfully. 'But it depends *why* he's here in Asturica. Perhaps the Parthians were trying to kill him, but there is always the possibility they only wanted us to think that. Whatever we decide, he must be watched. I want to know his movements, who he meets, where and when. You were right. He is a dangerous man, probably the most dangerous I have ever known.'

'So you do know him?' Tito's voice held a hint of irritation: why not just say it?

'I was his slave—'

Tito gave a snort of disgust. 'Then I should have killed him—'

'—but he gave me my freedom and I became his friend.'

'There is no friendship between us and them.'

'Nevertheless, it is true. He saved my life, more than once, and I his.'

'Then you owe him nothing.'

Serpentius laughed at his son's certainty. 'There are no debts between friends,' he corrected.

'I still think I should have killed him.'

The Spaniard smiled. 'You couldn't kill me. What makes you think you could kill a man who won the Gold Crown of Valour. A Hero of Rome who fought his way from the northern fastness of Britannia to the desert wastes of Africa and Armenia. A man who broke a legionary battle line and opened the way for his men to take their eagle?'

For a moment Tito looked almost impressed. He understood that to take a legion's eagle, the standard placed in its care by the Emperor himself, was to take its soul and bring dishonour to every man who allowed it to happen. The look vanished as quickly as it appeared. 'Just stories,' he said. 'Campfire tales that turn men into giants.'

'Not stories,' Serpentius shook his head. 'I was with him every step of the way when he broke that line.'

'You sound as if you admire him.'

'He is a certain kind of Roman.' The older man seemed to look inside himself. 'I learned to hate the Romans. Oh, how I learned to hate them, as they howled at me to take the next life or spill the next blood. I hated them as they laughed at the agonies of a man crawling through the sand with his guts trailing behind him. Or a gladiator staring at the stumps of his wrists and his life pouring out of his veins. Let us be entertained, they would cry, and I would lust to be among them with a sword in my hand, hunting them like chickens and sending their heads flying.' He sighed, a deep, aching sigh as if it pained him to admit what followed. 'Yet there is another type of Roman, rare as a phoenix egg. Stern and unyielding, but brave to the point of foolishness. A Roman prepared to purchase the burned-out shell of a gladiator to save him from certain death in the arena.

To treat him like a man. To give him his freedom and to offer an Asturian outcast his friendship. Valerius is that kind of Roman, Tito, the kind that allows you to understand how they could conquer the world and then rule it when they were done. Titus, the Emperor's son, is another. But with a harder edge. Fail him and you will end up hanging from a cross. There is no hatred or malice in Valerius. He thinks he can kill without conscience, but the shades of the men who die by his sword weigh heavily on his mind.'

'Then he is a fool.'

'No, just a man. Leave me now, I must think. He is to be watched, but make sure our friends in Asturica keep their distance. I want names,' he repeated. 'I want to know who he meets. Only then will I know why he is here.'

'What if—?'

Serpentius's voice hardened. 'If he cannot keep himself alive he is not the Valerius I knew. Now go.'

Left alone in the home he had shared with his wife Serpentius's shoulders slumped. He studied the walls of grey stone with their niches and shelves, the hearth in the centre of the floor with the smoke swirling up into the roof space, and the bed – not their bed, but similar to the one they'd once shared. Once this house had been vibrant and alive, filled with the sound of a woman's laughter, a child's hungry cries, and the contented silence of a man who wanted nothing more than what he had. Now it was sterile and soulless. Just an empty space. The very thought of it had sustained him through the long years of exile. So why did he feel a stranger here? A tear ran down his grizzled cheek, the first suggestion of weakness in many months.

Was he still the Serpentius Valerius had known?

He lifted his hand to his shaved head and his fingers explored the depression the width of his thumb just behind his right ear. Explored, but did not probe. Titus's *medicus* had warned him against interfering with the wound, suffered as he'd tried to save the Emperor Vitellius's son during the sack of Rome. He no longer experienced what Alexandros had called his *absences*. The *medicus* had drilled into his skull to release the fluid that had gathered there. Serpentius had been under the influence of distilled poppy during the operation, but Alexandros took great pleasure in describing every detail of the procedure. The *medicus* had laughed as he'd explained how even a slight blow near the wound would certainly result in the Spaniard's death.

Then there was the panic that had unmanned him in those early moments after he'd regained consciousness in the mine. If Valerius had come to Asturica Augusta for the reason he hoped, was he even capable of providing the help he would need?

And was the Roman truly aware of the danger he faced?

XXVI

When the invitation to dine with Aulus Severus was delivered by a servant, Valerius's first reaction was suspicion. This was certainly no social invitation. Severus had been complicit in wiping clean Petronius's lodgings and destroying his papers, if he hadn't actually ordered it. He must be aware by now that Valerius was a threat to his position, possibly even his life. The only explanation could be that he wanted to know how much progress Valerius had made. Calpurnia Severa could have told him that, and more. Had she arranged the invitation? The thought sent a guilty thrill through him. For all his good intentions and fine words she was a remarkably attractive and persuasive woman.

That conviction returned when he was shown into the dining room and he was met with an amused smile from where she lay among the reclining figures on the cushioned divans around the low table. She wore a dress of aquamarine blue and her neighbour was the only other female in the company: a slim, dark-haired girl who barely glanced at the newcomer.

One or two of the other faces were familiar. Severus, of course, the host, and head of Asturica's *ordo*, lying back with a dreamy smile on his lined features and a silver cup held loosely in his right hand. The man to his left couldn't have provided a greater contrast. If his scowl and the twitch in his right cheek were anything to judge by, Tiberius Claudius Proculus would rather have been anywhere else. As the dishes came and went, the camp prefect of the Sixth barely touched the sumptuous food. When he raised his cup Valerius noted that it seldom made contact with the thin lips. A man on edge. A man for whom a banquet was an unwelcome distraction from the other cares in his life.

In the background, a male slave played a simple melody on a lyre. The music meant voices were necessarily raised to make themselves heard over the music. Valerius did his best to ignore Calpurnia and found himself in conversation with two other guests, both of them long-serving members of the *ordo* and therefore potentially members of the conspiracy. Atilius Rufus owned a brickworks and the tile factory Valerius had noticed on his first day in the city. The other man, Lucius Octavius Fronton, bought and sold grain, which was milled and turned into bread to supply the mines. He also had a wagon business that transported both supplies and gold. The girl beside Calpurnia Severa was Fronton's daughter. Valerius attempted to draw him into conversation about his mining activities, but he was a nervous, taciturn man, tall and spare as a spear shaft. After ten minutes of evasion and forced silences the Roman decided to look more closely into Fronton's background on another day.

Atilius was much more prepared to talk, but the mining industry was of little interest to him apart from providing his clients with the wherewithal to add to their properties. A former soldier, he was interested in

Valerius's military achievements. Where had he served? Did he know this tribune or that? It turned out Atilius had been with Corbulo in Armenia and they had acquaintances in common from Valerius's time in Syria. Eventually the talk drifted back to the local situation.

'I hear the Sixth may soon be replaced by the full-strength Seventh,' Atilius said. 'That will quickly put these bandits in their place. No more poorly guarded convoys.'

'Excuse me.' Fronton abruptly rose from his couch and dashed from the room. His daughter looked up in alarm and, whispering her excuses to Calpurnia, followed him out.

'A minor indisposition I hope.' Atilius frowned. 'You were about to speak, prefect?'

'I guard the convoys with as many men as I can afford.' Proculus had only caught the last part of the conversation, but he was visibly incensed at any slight against his soldiers. 'What did you say about the Sixth?'

'That the Emperor will soon be replacing your detachment with a full legion. Our lads from the Seventh Galbiana, though now we must call them Gemina. My apologies if it is supposed to be secret.' Atilius bowed his head. 'I learned of it from a trader recently arrived from Tarraco. Perhaps you heard something too, Verrens?'

Valerius shook his head, but he saw the look of consternation on Proculus's face and the glance he shared with Severus. Clearly if there was any truth in it this wasn't welcome news. Which raised the question why?

Gradually, Valerius became aware of intense scrutiny from the other two men at the table, as if they were assessing him in some way. One was Proculus's aide, Calpurnius Piso, an aristocratic young tribune of the Sixth who seemed to believe a conversation wasn't a conversation unless it included the sound of his own voice. The other was a man of great interest to Valerius, but one he'd spent the evening studiously ignoring: Julius Licinius Ferox.

He barely noticed Fronton return to the table with his daughter holding his arm, his thin face the colour of a time-worn sheet of papyrus. Instead, he let his gaze drift to the other end of the table. Ferox and Piso continued to stare at him. Piso's puffy features were twisted into a sneer and he was whispering into the other man's ear. Ferox was tall with dark hair styled in ringlets that fell to his neck, protruding front teeth and an elongated horsy face that matched Piso's for arrogance. The *praefectus metallorum* had provided the escort of Parthians Valerius strongly suspected had intended to kill him. He held overall authority for the gold output from Asturica and his responsibilities included its safe transport to Tarraco. He was also the source of the excuses that bandit attacks and lack of manpower, of which Valerius had yet to see any evidence, were to blame for the shortage. Despite Melanius's assurances, Valerius was certain of one thing. If a conspiracy did indeed exist to steal Vespasian's gold, Ferox was up to his elongated neck in it.

Valerius met the other man's gaze and smiled, but the smile froze on his face as Piso's overloud whisper reached his ears.

'Of course, a man with only one hand is only half a man.' He'd heard the opinion often enough, although seldom quite so blatantly, and learned to ignore it. Yet for some reason this irritated him beyond measure. Perhaps it was the young tribune's dismissive tone or the mocking look in his eyes as he said it, but Valerius felt a heat burning at the centre of him that threatened

233

to explode into outright violence. 'And good officers do not lose their hands. Good officers direct their soldiers like true equestrians. It is our birthright to command,' Piso finished with condescending certainty.

Valerius studied the young officer for a dozen heart-beats. A stillness seemed to settle over the room and he knew without having to look that Calpurnia Severa's eyes were fixed on him. 'Not to fight?' he asked eventually.

Piso blinked, unaware he'd been overheard. Valerius's voice betrayed no emotion but some instinct made the young aristocrat shift on his couch. 'To fight?'

'Soldiers fight,' Valerius persisted. 'The equestrian class was Rome's fighting force long before Marius formed his legions, is that not so, Atilius?'

'True, true,' Atilius muttered into his wine. 'Only class that could afford horses, weapons and armour.'

'So equestrians and patricians have to fight.' Valerius smiled as he remembered the terrible day the First Adiutrix captured the eagle of the Twenty-first Rapax before being swept away in a maelstrom of blood and horror. The smile was so cold it could have frozen a jug of Setinian at twenty paces and Piso seemed to shrink into himself. 'At First Bedriacum,' Valerius continued, 'Orfidius Benignus, the legate of the First Adiutrix, and every tribune on his staff, fought and died to the last man. So officers have to fight. Sometimes they have to fight and sometimes they have to die. Have you fought, tribune? Have you tasted another man's blood on your lips? Felt the point of your *gladius* grind into his spine? Smelled the bitterness of his last breath? Looked into his eyes as he died?' As he spoke he kept his own eyes fixed on Piso's as if he was imagining that very moment.

Piso's cheeks turned a flaming red. 'Of course I've

fought,' he bristled. 'I've led search operations against the bandits.'

'I said fight.' Valerius laughed. 'Not chase a few terrified peasants through the hills as if you were hunting wild dogs. When did you last stand shield to shield in a battle line?' Piso didn't answer and Valerius hadn't expected him to. He knew the detachment of the Sixth had been at Legio throughout the civil war. He doubted Piso was the type to volunteer for active service. He had the pampered look of the fashionable young tribunes for whom six months with a legion was merely the next step on the *cursus honorum*. A period of tedium and overly close contact with the sweaty lower classes which must be endured if one was to advance. 'So you don't know what it's like. Maybe you'd like to fight me?' Valerius accompanied the challenge with a smile. Everyone else around the table thought it a joke, but Piso was looking into his eyes and he saw the lethal intent there. They stared at each other for a few moments before the younger man looked away.

Calpurnia's laugh broke the embarrassed silence and Valerius glanced across to find her staring at him and whispering to her companion. Severus saw the look they exchanged and sobered suspiciously quickly to enquire how Valerius's search for Petronius progressed. The way the question was posed told Valerius the other man already knew the answer, but also that Calpurnia had kept her thoughts about his true mission to herself. Which was intriguing.

'I've had little success, but I'm still hopeful,' he said.

'Then you will be with us for a while longer?' Calpurnia enquired artlessly.

'It seems so,' Valerius admitted. 'I think there's still more to discover.'

'Indeed.' Her smile and the tilt of her head sent a shiver down his spine.

Severus's only reaction was a tight smile. Valerius turned away to where Atilius and his neighbour were talking about some local dispute. Valerius heard the name Saco mentioned.

'My apologies for interrupting,' he said. 'I keep hearing the name Saco in conversation. I seem to have come across almost every other leading member of the *ordo*. Who is this mystery man?'

'There is no mystery.' Surprisingly, it was Severus who answered. 'If there is a dispute in this city then you may be sure that Cornelius Aurelius Saco is at the heart of it. He plays one man against the other to the detriment of both. He says one thing and then does another. He builds a house on a foundation of sand, uses half the materials he claims and sells it for twice what it is worth. If something goes missing, look for it in one of Saco's yards. If some*one* goes missing—'

'Surely you would not accuse him of murder?' Atilius's look of consternation turned to shock.

'You are one of his suppliers so he cannot afford to alienate you, Atilius. You do not know him as I do.'

'Yet he is immortalized in stone for dedicating the city baths,' Valerius pointed out.

'That was before people knew him for what he was . . .'

While they'd been speaking Piso's slurred bray had increased in volume. Calpurnia was staring at the young officer. Severus shot him a look of alarm as he realized the subject of his discourse.

He was talking treason.

'Vespasian is a new man,' the young tribune lectured Ferox, who stared at him like a mouse beneath the gaze of a cat. Clearly there had already been more in the same vein. 'He has neither the status, the social standing, nor the legitimacy to be Emperor. It was a mistake to give the purple to an uncultured nobody. Galba made my cousin Lucius his heir because he knew that bloodline and manners were as important in a ruler as mere ability.'

'I think I must bring this gathering to a close . . .' Severus got to his feet.

'The Senate have already realized their mistake and they will—'

'Tribune,' Proculus said sharply. 'You have said enough.'

'Do not presume to lecture me, old man.' Piso pushed himself to his feet. 'You are a mere plebeian. Soon,' he stood swaying and his gaze turned to Valerius, 'the patrician class will take its rightful place at the head of the Empire.' Ferox tugged at his toga trying to get him back on to the couch, but Piso brushed his hand away. 'Soon, I will have true power, and you,' he pointed a finger at the one-handed Roman, 'will pay the price for your insults.'

Before Valerius could react a blue blur streaked across his vision and a sharp crack echoed from the walls. Calpurnia Severa withdrew her hand and stood, chest heaving, before Piso. 'You dishonour my husband and you dishonour this house,' she hissed.

Piso's hand went to his inflamed cheek and he stared at her with a mix of shock and hatred. His hand dropped to his belt, but Ferox stepped in to take him by the arm and drag him snarling from the room.

A long moment of disbelieving silence before Severus gathered his wits and went to his wife's side.

'I must apologize,' he said. 'A young man addled

by drink. My wife was correct to remind him of his responsibilities, though he meant nothing of it, I am sure. Nevertheless, I must ask you to keep what was said between those who are in this room. It would do none of us any good to be associated with such sentiments.'

'I too beg your pardon.' Calpurnia met her companions' eyes one by one. 'The insult to our guest was more than I could bear.'

Did Valerius imagine it, or did the dark eyes linger on him for a moment longer than necessary? And if they did, there had been no sign of contrition in them. Perhaps not quite a challenge, but . . .

And what did the altercation reveal? Piso had treated his legionary commander like a subordinate and Proculus had done nothing to stop him. Yet Piso had barely reacted to Calpurnia's blow, and her husband had done nothing to censure her.

Just who was in charge in Asturica Augusta?

238

XXVII

Valerius could almost feel the eyes on him as he made his way from Severus's house to his lodgings. The wine he'd drunk at Severus's dinner party had dulled his senses, but not so much that he wasn't aware when he was being followed. Fortunately, the streets were busy with traders and their customers so the threat was slight as long as he kept to the main thoroughfares. He passed through the Forum, where work on the basilica continued, and drew a glance of irritation from the sniffy lawyer he'd met on the first day. As he approached the city gates he recognized a familiar, but surprising face among the customers sitting drinking beneath the awning outside a bar.

Petro, the loquacious trader he'd befriended aboard ship, looked up and gaped in surprise as Valerius's shadow fell over him. 'Gaius Valerius Verrens!' His features split into an enormous grin. 'This rustic backwater is the last place I would have expected to find you. What brings you to Asturica?'

'A social call.' Valerius returned the infectious grin. 'I'm here visiting a friend.' It was close enough to the truth that he didn't feel guilty deceiving the other man. 'And I could ask the same of you.'

'Oh, I must go wherever a man may turn a profit,' Petro chuckled. 'For all its lack of refinement Asturica Augusta has wealth in abundance and, strictly between us, trading with these country bumpkins is not so different from fleecing a new-born lamb.' Valerius laughed and the other man moved to make a place beside him. 'But come, old friends should not talk business. Slave,' he called back over his shoulder, 'bring me a new jug of that horse piss you call wine and another cup.' Valerius protested that he'd had enough, but Petro winked. 'It's not too bad really, but I intend negotiating a discount.'

Valerius took a seat overlooking the street. Behind them four pots set into the top of a stone wall bubbled over a glowing fire, filling the air with the scent of herbs and cooking meat. A surly plump girl appeared and placed a jug of wine and a cup on the bench between them. As she turned, Petro gave her wide rump a slap. She swung round with a look of fury, but when she saw the broad grin on his face the look faded and she shook her head.

'It will be the highlight of her day,' the trader assured Valerius, 'but we'll make this the last one just in case. *Salus*.'

'Health,' Valerius returned the greeting. 'How long have you been here?'

The merchant shifted his bulk to a more comfortable position. 'I arrived two days ago. Fortunately, I picked up some bolts of fine cloth in Clunia for a bargain price from the wife of a recently deceased dressmaker. I've already made a decent return on my investment.'

'And how do you find Asturica, apart from its rustic nature?'

Petro took his time before answering. 'Much like any

240

other frontier town. Full of possibilities, but keep your eyes open because when they smile into your face like as not they'll be picking your purse. And tense.' He gave Valerius a shrewd look. 'Take those two auxiliaries in the shadow of the awning about twenty paces up the street.'

'Yes?'

'When they turned the corner they looked terribly concerned. Their eyes searched the street and when they fell on this bar they suddenly relaxed.' He shrugged. 'A trader learns to keep his wits about him and to read a man's face or he won't be a trader for long. They've been sitting there ever since, watching us. Tell me, is it me they're interested in, or you?'

'Does it matter?'

Petro grinned. 'No, I suppose it doesn't.' He drained his cup and picked up the jug. 'A pity to waste this.' He stood up. 'Wait a few moments before joining me inside.' He disappeared through the doorway. Valerius took two more sips of wine and followed without a glance at the hovering auxiliaries.

Petro was waiting by an opening at the rear of the bar, where the slave girl stood to one side rubbing a silver coin between her fingers. 'This way,' the merchant said. They emerged into a living area. From there Petro led the way to a doorway out on to a street that ran parallel to the one where they'd been sitting. 'I will not ask you why someone would be following you,' he continued. 'For me, it is natural. A man who travels for a living picks up news and gossip and will trade it for other pieces of news and gossip. It is not long before he has the word "spy" dogging his footsteps.'

Valerius nodded in understanding 'A friend once told me: *From Antioch to Alexandria every man is a spy and today's friend is tomorrow's deadly enemy.'*

'Wise words, lord,' Petro said. 'And you would do well to keep them in mind while you're in Asturica. How long do you intend to stay?'

'I'm not certain,' Valerius admitted. 'My time here hasn't been as productive as I'd hoped.'

'A pity to be away from your new wife for any longer than necessary.' Petro smiled at his reaction before Valerius remembered he'd let slip the news of his recent marriage during the voyage. 'And perhaps the pain of your long parting might be eased if you returned with a suitable gift.'

Valerius frowned. 'What do you have in mind?'

'As it happens part of my haul in Clunia was a bolt of the finest Indian silk. I will sell you enough to manufacture a dress that will make your lady the envy of every other woman in Rome . . .'

'I don't . . .'

'And at the same price I paid for it.'

They'd returned to a square near the city's main gate and Valerius stopped to consider. Perhaps Petro was right? He remembered Tabitha glowing with pleasure as she'd studied lengths of cloth outside a dress shop in Apamea. 'Which is your stall?' He looked around for a likely candidate.

'Not in the city.' Petro looked at him as if he were mad. 'These thieves would squeeze me until I didn't make a sesterce of profit. Taxes? Only a fool pays taxes. No, my wares are outside the walls. Come, I will show you.'

Valerius followed him out of the gate past the disapproving glares of the tax officials. Petro flicked his fingers in an obscene gesture and laughed.

The merchant crossed the ground surprisingly swiftly

for such a bulky man. He led the way through the avenue of tombs that lined the road into Asturica, before turning off into a wooded area. They followed a path through the trees to a clearing by a stream where Petro had set up his tent. An assistant, who must have been recruited since the trader arrived in Hispania, watched over wares set out on a portable table. Nearby a tethered horse and a string of mules stood nibbling at the long grass.

'The silk is too valuable to leave on display in the sun.' Petro ducked into the tent. 'See,' he held out a bolt of shimmering turquoise cloth, inviting Valerius to run his fingers across it.

A flicker in Petro's eyes should have warned him. As Valerius bent to touch the cloth a rope whipped round his neck and a knee smashed into his back knocking the breath from him. Only the act of bowing his head saved him from being choked to death in those first few seconds. Instead of tightening on his throat the cord caught on his chin, pinning it back against his neck. As he struggled against the terrible force his assailant sawed the rope into his flesh and tried to find a position where he could get a killing grip.

Valerius ignored the burning pain and clawed at the rope with his left hand, flailing behind him with the wooden fist of his right. The blood roared in his ears, and he heard the sound of Petro's mocking laughter. Something smashed into the back of his head and the assassin used the stunned heartbeat that followed to shift the position of the rope. Valerius cried out as he felt it tighten round his windpipe in a grip of iron. He couldn't breathe. His vision began to go.

'Remember to let him know he's dying, Lucius,' Petro ordered. 'Our employer was most insistent about that.'

A momentary slackening allowed Valerius to gasp in

a mouthful of air before the rope tightened again. No matter how he struggled it was impossible to reach the man behind him. He was going to die.

Without warning the rope slackened again. This time it was accompanied by a flood of something warm on the back of Valerius's neck. He waited for a renewal of pressure, but it never came. Instead the cord fell away and he slumped forward clutching his throat and cawing like an angry crow. He looked up to see Petro standing with a look of horror on his face. The fat merchant turned to run, but before he'd gone two paces a knife hilt materialized in the centre of his back and he collapsed on his face with a cry of mortal agony.

A tall, dark-haired man strode past Valerius and plucked the knife from Petro's spine, wiping the blade on the trader's tunic. He nudged the body on to its back with his foot and ran the knife across his victim's throat just to make sure. When he was satisfied, he returned to where Valerius lay still stunned. Without a word he lifted the Roman's chin. Valerius waited for the sting of the knife, but eyes the colour of a gathering storm only studied him thoughtfully.

'You'll live,' the man said eventually. 'It'll burn for a few days, but you should find someone in Asturica who can give you balm for it.' He nodded over Valerius's shoulder. 'You were lucky he was told to make it slow or they'd have been burying you along with them.'

Valerius turned to see Petro's servant lying on the ground with a pool of dark blood around his head and a ragged gash across his throat.

'Who are you?' He winced as he massaged his throat.

The tall man ignored the question. 'For reasons I haven't been told, it would have been inconvenient if you died today, but my employer says to tell you the reprieve is purely temporary.' A cold smile flickered across the craggy features. 'Who knows, it might be me who comes for you next time.'

'Your employer?' Valerius was utterly bemused.

'If you want my advice,' his rescuer continued as if Valerius hadn't spoken, 'you'll get out of Asturica tonight. I saw two auxiliaries following you, but there was another, more dangerous by far. I knew he was there, but I could never mark him. I'm sure he'll be watching us now, which means my work in Asturica is done.'

'I can't leave . . .'

'Then you will surely die here.'

XXVIII

The tall man departed without a backward glance leaving Valerius sitting with two lifeless bodies. Valerius knew he should move, but somehow he couldn't get the message to his legs. He'd seen this kind of behaviour before in the aftermath of a battle. Soldiers utterly paralysed by the recent terror of a brush with death. If he was found with Petro and his servant in their present state, awkward questions would be asked, at the very least. His powerful enemies in Asturica would certainly use it as a pretext to have him arrested or expelled from the city.

He forced himself to his hands and knees. His mind spun and a fiery jet of bile burned his throat as he spewed up the contents of his stomach. He wiped the back of his hand across his lips and tried to keep the folds of his toga out of the spreading pool of sick. The vomit seemed to clear his head and he managed to stagger to his feet with the help of the tent pole. He stood for a moment, swaying, before he headed back to the city on shaking legs.

Nobody took any notice as Valerius staggered through the gate against the flow of traders leaving for the night.

He made his way east towards his lodgings. The rope burns on his chin and neck throbbed terribly. He should buy some kind of ointment, but most of the shops were closed.

He flinched as someone appeared at his side without warning. 'Are you all right, lord?' Aurelio asked. 'I saw you stumble a while back and your face is very pale.'

'I . . .' Valerius couldn't get the words out and his vision blurred. Aurelio took him by the arm and led him towards a nearby bar, coincidentally the one he'd sat at earlier with the now deceased Petro.

'A cup of wine will help,' Aurelio said. Valerius reached for his purse, but the other man shook his head. 'Elia?' he called. 'Two cups of well-watered wine and put it on the master's account.'

The slave girl emerged and placed the order on the bench beside them. Aurelio handed Valerius one and he tentatively lifted it to his mouth. The action exposed his neck and Aurelio sucked in a breath.

'What happened to your throat?' Valerius shook his head mutely, still unable to speak. 'You look as if you've tried to hang yourself. Or,' he'd said it with a smile, but the smile transformed into a frown, 'someone tried to do it for you?'

Valerius took another drink, swallowed tentatively and at last found his voice.

'Two men,' he croaked. 'They tried to kill me.'

'Two men? Here?'

'Outside the walls. There's a wood. They lured me there and one tried to strangle me.'

'But why?' Aurelio demanded. 'Why would anyone want to kill you, unless . . . Could it be something to do with your search for your friend?'

Valerius shook his head and took another drink.

247

'Thank you.' He lifted the clay cup. 'No. One of them was on the ship that brought me from Rome to Tarraco. He befriended me during the voyage and must have tracked me to Asturica. Like a fool I followed him.'

'Yet you survived.' Aurelio's eyes drifted back towards the main gate. 'And they?'

'Are dead.'

Aurelio considered this for a few moments before making his decision. 'You must wait here.' He got to his feet. 'If you need another drink just ask Elia. Melanius needs to know about this. The odd murder isn't unusual in Asturica, but two in one afternoon might draw attention where it's not needed. It'll be dark soon so they probably won't be found until morning. If we act quickly, maybe we can do something about it by then.'

He stalked off leaving Valerius with his drink. Though his mind still reeled from what had happened it had begun to recover its logical powers. He noted, for instance, that Aurelio hadn't asked how the two men died, assuming that Valerius had somehow over-powered them. It meant either he had a surprising faith in Valerius's physical capabilities – of which the Roman was certain he'd given no evidence – or Melanius had revealed more of Valerius's background than he was comfortable with. Likewise the sudden, violent deaths of two men had elicited no visible reaction. That was unusual in a civilian, even one employed by the very capable Melanius. One thing was certain. The Aurelio who'd accompanied him to the Red Hills mine differed greatly from the man who'd reacted so calmly tonight. And that bore thinking about.

As did the man who'd saved him. Only now, when the turmoil in his mind had settled, could he properly consider what had occurred and what had been said.

*It would have been inconvenient if you died today,
but my employer says to tell you the reprieve is purely
temporary.*

There were plenty of reasons in Valerius's past that
could have brought Petro to Asturica. He was not a man
who made friends easily, but he'd made enemies from
Britannia to Syria, some of them at the highest levels of
Roman society. Yet when he recalled Petro's last words
only one face came to mind.

Remember to let him know he's dying, Petro had
said. That spoke of a long-nursed hatred and a deadly
enmity. Titus Flavius Domitianus had sent assassins to
dog his footsteps from Rome to Antioch and beyond.
Valerius had killed at least two and seen off several
more. Domitian was now a prince of Rome. Valerius had
believed his own new status as a valued adviser to the
Emperor gave him immunity from his enemy's wrath.
Yet Petro had undoubtedly been sent by Domitian.

So who had sent his saviour?

*My employer says to tell you the reprieve is purely
temporary. Who knows, it might be me who comes for
you next time.*

It seemed so bizarre and unlikely as to be impossible,
yet there could be no other explanation. Domitian
had sent the first assassin, Petro, and for some reason
experienced an unlikely change of heart. In typically
ruthless fashion he'd then dispatched a second assassin
to assassinate the first. What had caused this change
that saved his life? Valerius could only speculate, but
he guessed it must have involved pressure from the
Emperor, or Domitian's brother Titus. There was also
a third, tantalizing, possibility. That somehow Domitia
Longina Corbulo was involved.

Whatever the reason, he was alive. The only question

was whether he could stay that way. Elia emerged from the bar, lit two lamps and hung them from the awning. Soon Valerius would need a torch to see him home and there was no sign of Aurelio. He made his decision.

'If Aurelio comes back tell him I decided to leave,' he told the girl.

Few carts used the streets at this time of the night and he kept to the centre of the cobbles, his way lit by the glow of lamps from the adjoining houses and workshops. Every shadow and darkened alleyway felt like a threat. The scent of woodsmoke from a thousand cooking fires competed with the daytime reek from gutters that were little more than open sewers, and the warm, soft air created an almost physical barrier. He touched his left hand to his neck where the rope had bitten into his throat and winced at the fiery bolt that made his eyes water. Two more seconds. If the tall man . . . The thought made him shudder. One more try. He would give it one more try and if it failed he would return to Tabitha, forget Asturica ever existed and make a life in Fidenae. For the first time in a long while he felt alone and vulnerable. Vespasian and Titus thought him hard and ruthless – he almost laughed aloud – but, in truth, war had worn him thin. Not physically. He retained the physical attributes that had kept him alive against all the odds. Inside his head, in a way that made him a shadow of the man he had once been. He hated this solitary existence in a place where he could trust no man and call none friend. He remembered Petro's companionable laughter and the moment his face had changed. The old Valerius would have been ready with a blade in his hand. Would never have turned his back on the servant. He longed for the comradeship of Serpentius and the brotherhood of the legions. A companion to share his worries and act as his faithful right hand.

The distant mountains created a jagged silhouette against the faint glow of the dying sun. Where was Serpentius now? Was he truly the bandit they called the Ghost? Or had he set up home with some dark-eyed beauty, drinking his own wine and making a fortune growing olives? The hills drew Valerius's eyes again. He snorted with self-disgust. He wouldn't know where to start looking and without an escort he'd be as vulnerable as a newly hatched chick.

The faint sound of stealthy footsteps behind him. His left hand slipped towards the wooden fist and anyone listening carefully would have heard a soft metallic click. He turned the next corner and in a single fluid movement slipped into the nearest shadow.

A hooded figure appeared with its right hand raised. Valerius stepped forward and placed the tip of the wooden fist's four-inch blade against the pulsing artery in his pursuer's neck.

'You have many enemies in Asturica, Gaius Valerius Verrens, but I am not one.' The hood slipped back of its own accord and Aurelio opened his fist to reveal a small wooden tub. 'A balm for your burns. It is made from aloe and spirits of wine and the man who mixed it assures me it will ease your pain.'

Valerius took a step back, but he didn't lower the blade.

The Asturian's eyes widened imperceptibly when he saw the hidden weapon and his voice was full of admiration. 'Clever. Very clever. Now I understand how you were able to survive the attentions of a pair of hired assassins. Don't worry, your trader friend and his assistant won't trouble you any further. They will vanish like the fog on a summer morning and I'm pleased to

251

say their wares will pay for it.' He grinned at his own ingenuity. 'That was what kept me, but you shouldn't have left the bar. These streets can be dangerous.'

Valerius turned and pressed the point of the knife against a wooden doorpost so it retracted into the fist.

'Before I was attacked tonight I attended a dinner at the house of Severus, the *duovir*. There was a young man, a tribune from the Sixth at Legio, Calpurnius Piso. What can you tell me about him?'

Aurelio laughed. 'A preening peacock with an over-loud screech. If you are looking for new enemies I would look elsewhere.'

'His relationship with his commander, Proculus, interested me.'

'Proculus is an old man out of his depth.' The Asturian shrugged. 'It's common knowledge he counts the days to his retirement and marks them off on a board in the *principia* at the fort. The real power in Legio lies with the Parthians.'

'Harpocration? An auxiliary? It would be an unusual legionary centurion willing to take orders from an auxiliary prefect.'

'Nevertheless, it is true. He is a formidable man.'

Valerius had a thought. 'And he hires out his men to Severus?'

'So?'

'I have a feeling Severus had something to do with Petronius's disappearance. If that's the case, who better than Harpocration or his men to make it happen?'

Aurelio considered this for a moment. 'It's possible, but I don't know what difference it makes. They are many and you are one.'

'Still, it has given me an idea.'

XXIX

The men were mere shadows in the darkness. Only the whites of their eyes showed in the blackened faces. Twenty of them lay on the crest of a hill looking down towards the twinkling lights of a substantial villa. Daylight would have shown the villa surrounded by olive trees and vines, but at night the complex was identified only by the oil lamps now being extinguished one by one in sequence from left to right.

'Remember,' Serpentius whispered. 'There is to be no killing. We subdue any guards, round up the servants and the slaves and search the place.'

'Burrus, the overseer, beat me every day when I worked there during the harvest last summer.' Serpentius recognized the voice of Allius. Short, sturdy and with the face of a startled shrew, he'd fled to Avala to avoid the increasing legionary and auxiliary presence in the mountains north of the mining areas.

'If he resists, you may pay him back in kind, but I doubt he will,' Serpentius predicted. 'With his master staying the night in Asturica it's unlikely Burrus will risk his neck to protect Fronton's property. Tonight Lucius Octavius Fronton will learn that the gold he receives from the Romans is only being held in trust. We will take all we find, along with such arms and provisions as we can carry. Any scrolls or documents are to be brought to me.'

'What if the slaves want to come away with us?' Tito asked. 'Fronton has a reputation as a hard taskmaster.'

'They're welcome if they are prepared to fight, but remind them there's a long, hard winter ahead. They know the fate that awaits them if they are recaptured.'

The last lamp in the building flickered out, leaving only the two torches marking the main gate to show their objective.

'Follow me.' They knew what to do, there was no point reminding them further. Serpentius led the way, skipping down a steep deer track he'd marked earlier. Tito stayed close on his heels but the others struggled to keep pace. Most wielded spears, but a few carried ancient, rust-pocked swords their ancestors had hidden after the conquest a hundred years earlier. As he ran, Serpentius's senses tested the darkness for any potential threat. He'd had the place watched throughout the day and he doubted any patrol could have approached without being noticed, but you could never be too careful. When he reached the bottom of the hill he halted to allow his men to catch up. In front of them stood a broad grove of olives, with grape vines strung between. He dropped to his front and slithered along a tunnel formed where the vines clung to the lower branches of the olive trees.

Moving through the foliage with the ease of the reptile that gave him his name, he reached the far end within minutes. Here he was confronted by the wall that surrounded the villa complex. Beyond it lay a strip of vegetable garden and the north face of the building. The house formed three sides of a square, with the accommodation for the slaves and servants to the rear, and stables on the far side. Serpentius sprang upwards and pulled himself to the top of the wall. With his legs straddling the stonework he reached down and helped the others over, one by one, to drop silently into the garden.

By the time the last man crossed, Tito was already leading three quarters of the group to round up the slaves and servants. They'd be kept under guard until Serpentius and the others had had a chance to search the villa. But first he had to deal with the two night watchmen Fronton employed to guard the gate.

'Allius? Placido? With me. Bring the ropes. The rest stay here.'

He trotted through the furrowed earth of the vegetable garden until he reached the wall of the villa. With the others behind him he slipped along the white stucco, careful to stay below window height, until he reached the corner. The gatehouse was visible in the light of the torches at the end of a cobbled driveway about a hundred paces away. From what Serpentius could see both men remained inside, but he couldn't be certain.

He stepped out of the shadows. Placido would have followed him, but Serpentius put a hand on his chest. 'Stay here and wait for my shout.'

He ran silently over the hard-packed earth beside the driveway. When he reached the gatehouse he drew a short wooden club from his belt. The entrance faced the roadway and he could see no sign of the gatekeepers. Somehow he had to draw them out.

He stooped and searched the ground until he found a decent-sized stone which he tossed beyond the gate so it rattled on the surface of the road. With a muffled oath a big man stepped out of the gatehouse doorway to check the noise. Serpentius hit him with the club on the base of his skull and he dropped without a sound. The former gladiator was moving even before his victim hit the ground, ramming the club into the stomach of a second guard as he sprang to his feet. The blow bent the man double and Serpentius whipped the club up and brought it down on the back of his head with a distinct *thwack*.

He called softly to Allius and Placido.

'Tie them up and follow me,' he ordered.

The villa's main entrance was barred from the inside, but Serpentius simply forced a nearby ground-floor window with the blade of his sword and Allius, the nimblest of his companions, slipped inside. Moments later came the sound of the bar being withdrawn and the door was open.

Tito appeared from the darkness. 'The slaves and servants are all in one room under guard,' he said. 'We had a little trouble from a couple of them who wanted to tear the overseer limb from limb. I persuaded them to let him live, but he's a little battered.'

'Good,' Serpentius whispered. 'That should just leave the family servants.'

They stepped inside. Serpentius found an oil lamp and lit it. Tito gasped at the opulence of the interior. The entrance hall opened on to a large atrium, with an opening in the ceiling to provide light in daytime and a pool to collect rainwater. A bronze statue of a small boy stood in the centre. Various curtained rooms opened off the atrium and Serpentius's men searched them one by one, rousting out four or five astonished house slaves. Scenes of rural activities covered the walls: men and women planting cereals, tending vines, picking grapes and olives and pressing them with their feet. Intricately decorated vases and pots stood on pedestals alongside painted marble busts of what Serpentius guessed must be Fronton's ancestors. But the most astonishing sight was the mosaic.

Serpentius had been in enough Roman houses to know when he was looking at something special. Laid out around the pool was a beautifully lifelike hunting scene with a pack of hounds chasing a pair of deer. The deer leapt over fallen branches while the hounds bounded behind, their jaws open so you could almost hear them baying.

The whole effect was very Roman in style, yet the man who owned this villa was an Asturian just like the men who'd taken over his house. The difference was that Fronton's family had collaborated with the invaders from the beginning, bending the knee to Augustus and offering their help in enslaving their countrymen. Serpentius had chosen the villa because Fronton was one of the richest men in Asturia and one of those suspected by Petronius of being implicated in the gold thefts. Fronton supplied men for the mines from the district he controlled, then he supplied the bread to feed them, part of a network of providers without whom the system would collapse. Nothing could change in the mines without it affecting them. Yet as the gold yields had fallen during the civil war Fronton had become richer, not poorer. Serpentius hoped to find out why when he searched the house.

'Take anything portable that's of value to us, but I want all documents brought to the *tablinum*.' He pointed to a room at the end of the atrium.

Everything was going well. Too well. Scrolls and sheets of papyrus came, along with waxed slivers of wood filled with numbers, but all were to do with the running of the house, not Fronton's business. Midway through a long list of purchases Serpentius was interrupted by the sound of galloping hooves from the direction of the roadway.

'What in the name of Mars' hairy scrotum is that?' He leaped to his feet and ran to the door.

Placido met him in the doorway, breathing hard and with a look of horror on his moon face. 'One of the overseers was in the stables fucking a slave girl. We missed him during the search. Forgive me, lord.'

The calculations raced through Serpentius's head. An hour to reach Asturica and raise the alarm, perhaps another to gather a force large enough to overwhelm the raiders without incurring too many casualties. Time enough. Unless the overseer met a patrol on the way.

'Put a lookout with a torch in the trees overlooking the road and detail a man to watch for his signal. He's to let us know the moment there's any sign of riders.'

Placido nodded and ran out into the night.

'Father. You should see this.' Serpentius followed Tito through to a small storeroom. 'It was hidden under a rug.'

A heavy iron door was set into the stone floor. To one side of the polished metal was an odd-shaped hole, presumably for some kind of key. Serpentius studied the iron and shook his head. 'This explains why we've found no treasure or private papers.'

'I've sent Allius to find some tools. A crowbar . . .'

'It's a strongbox set directly into the floor when the house was built. It would take us a month to get it out of there, if we ever did. We don't have—'

'Nathair?'

'What now?' Serpentius snapped. Everything was

falling apart. He turned to find Allius with a crowbar in one hand and holding a young girl by the arm with the other.

'She was hiding in the garden. The *atriensis* says she's Julia, Fronton's daughter.'

The Spaniard studied her with more interest. Slim and dark, she barely came up to his shoulder and her only covering was the thin cotton shift she'd been sleeping in.

'Where is the key for this strongbox?'

He took a step closer so she was treated to the full effect of his savage features, but that diminutive figure contained a hidden strength and her eyes showed no fear.

'I don't know.' Serpentius felt Tito stiffen beside him at the fierce passion in her voice. 'But even if I did I would not tell the likes of you. My father will have every last one of you flogged and crucified for this.' She turned to look Allius in the eye. 'And I will think of something special for this filth with his wandering hands.'

Allius growled and raised a hand to strike her, but Tito snarled at him: 'Put her with the others.'

'Wait,' Serpentius ordered. 'She may come in useful. Whatever we are looking for is behind the iron door. The only way to get it is for Fronton to open it for us.'

'He will never—'

'We'll see how much he values his daughter, though judging by her manners he may be happy to be rid of her.'

Allius laughed and Julia spat at him.

'Tito? You look after her and make sure she has everything she needs for the journey.'

Allius reluctantly parted with the girl and Tito took her away.

'We should burn this place,' Allius said as they walked back through the house.

'No,' Serpentius insisted. 'It would serve no purpose. We have already made our point. Fronton will never sleep easy in this house again. And we have his daughter. And Allius?'

'Yes, Nathair?'

'As long as the girl is with us she's our guest. If any harm comes to her you will answer to me.'

XXX

What had he missed? The question nagged at Valerius in sleep and in waking. Apart from a few details he believed he could picture the overall form of the conspiracy, perhaps even the faces of the main conspirators. But where was the proof? Julius Licinius Ferox had been confident enough of his invulnerability to encourage Valerius to visit the Red Hills mine, but he would never allow him to get near the documents and the figures. They undoubtedly existed. Yet without that physical evidence what did he have? Theory and conjecture and a gut feeling that he was going in the right direction. Perhaps Ferox was unaware of just how much information Valerius had been able to glean from Nepos, but little good it did the Roman.

Petronius had known where the proof lay; perhaps he even acquired it. But Petronius was dead and, if it existed, the proof died with him. Any evidence had been completely destroyed when Severus's servants cleaned the house. But had it? A blackened patch of earth in the garden, but what did that mean? Just how thoroughly did the arsonists carry out their work? The key to the conspiracy could have been lying there a finger length beneath the surface all the time. In fact, he'd had little opportunity to check the garden area at all. There must be a dozen places where Petronius could have hidden copies of the documents he'd obtained. The engineer had been a careful man. It was just the sort of thing he would do.

Valerius made his decision. He would go back to the house.

Market day and Asturica Augusta was on the move early. The lodgings Severus had provided made it difficult to enter or leave without being seen, but not impossible. Valerius dressed in his worn travelling tunic and stole a sack from the kitchen. He filled it with anything portable he could find until it looked like something he might be taking to the market. With the sack over his shoulder so it hid his face he stepped confidently into the street.

The direct route would take him past Severus's villa so he took a detour through one of Asturica's many alleys. It brought him out into a street that ran inside the eastern wall of the city. He'd only been walking for a few moments before he realized someone was close behind him. He tried changing his pace, now slow, now faster, but the follower simply matched him. In desperation he darted into the next opening.

His last memory was of a hand poised over him before an explosion of light and the world faded to black.

When he regained consciousness he thought he was blind, but gradually he realized he wasn't the only person in Asturica capable of stealing an old sack. It smelled of dead birds and something tickled his nose. He struggled to breathe against the stifling heat. And not just inside the sack. He could feel it on his legs and arms. Legs and arms that were tied brutally tight to whatever he was sitting on. An unnatural heat. The heat of glowing coals. Valerius had to still a swift surge of panic, returned for a moment to Pliny's stable and the gruesome fate of the would-be assassin. Would he even get the opportunity to speak? And all those other questions. The who? The why? Had this been brought on by his pursuit of Petronius? Or did the attack have its origins in Rome? One thing was certain, this time there would be no tall, bearded saviour to the rescue.

'He's moving.' The sound of an unfamiliar voice muffled by the sack.

'Good.' More authority in this man's tone. 'I feared you might have hit him too hard. Remove the hood.'

Someone grasped the sack from behind and hauled it over Valerius's head. He flinched at the blast of heat that hit his face and the red glow that seared his eyes and blurred his vision. When his sight cleared he was facing a tall, dark-haired man on the far side of an iron basket filled with shimmering coals. Not the grim-visaged torturer he'd expected. A narrow face with chiselled, handsome features and a long, thin nose that had been broken at some point. Solemn grey eyes and full lips pursed in an expression of extreme distaste. He wore a white tunic belted at the waist with a rich gold chain. Valerius had never seen him in his life.

He was in a cellar of some sort, with the instruments designed to instil terror artfully displayed in the glow of the coals. Smoke swirled around the ceiling despite the vents that served to dissipate the suffocating heat. Yet something about the frightful display puzzled him. These tools could be used to inflict pain, but that was not the purpose they'd been designed for. They were functional implements borrowed from a blacksmith or a foundry – hammers, chisels, pincers and a pair of fearsome looking shears. Frightening, in this context, but not the specialist torturer's tools he had seen used on the man who had tried to kill Pliny. This was a carefully prepared setting, like the backdrops at the rear of the stage he'd seen during performances at the Theatre of Marcellus in Rome. They could hurt him, of that there was no doubt, but their priority was to get him to talk and Valerius was happy to talk.

Then there was the question of just who *they* were. If they formed part of the conspiracy why not simply cut his throat? It was just possible Valerius had more to gain here than to lose.

'Let us begin,' said the man he could see.

'This is how it works.' A hand gripped Valerius's hair and a fiery streak of pain shot through his scalp. A reminder, if he needed one, of why he was here. The pain faded as the grip relaxed and a hand reached out for a poker that glowed red and dangerous in the heart of the coals. The hand wore a leather glove and when its owner turned with the poker and came into view, Valerius had a moment of utter confusion. It was the man he'd seen beating the slave who'd followed him on his first day in Asturica. 'When my master speaks you answer. If you don't answer I will hurt you. If we think you are lying I will hurt you. Just bear in mind we know more about your activities than you think.'

'It would help if I knew who I was talking to.' Valerius flinched as the gloved fist moved the poker closer, but the man in the chair held up a hand. 'You will notice that I do not demand to be released or protest that I shouldn't be here,' he continued. 'I am perfectly happy to speak, but surely there is a more civilized way to have our discussion?'

'That is not possible, for the moment. I do not wish to torture you, but I will if I must. Who are you?'

264

'My name is Gaius Valerius Verrens, but I assume you already know that since I have done nothing to hide the fact. Do I have the pleasure of addressing Cornelius Aurelius Saco?'

The glowing poker shifted to fill his vision and Valerius jerked his head back. 'You do not ask. You only answer,' the torturer snarled. But Valerius had seen a flash of consternation cross the tall man's features and he knew he was correct. It gave him the confidence to risk everything to retain the initiative.

'You had a slave follow me when I arrived in the city – I make no judgement, I assume you had your reasons – unfortunately he wasn't cut out for subterfuge and I managed to elude him. Later I witnessed him being . . . chastised . . . for his failings and a gentleman in the street identified your secretary.'

'I see . . .' Saco said thoughtfully. 'Yet that changes nothing.'

'Perhaps, but it raises the question why you felt the need to have me followed. Everything I've been told since coming to Asturica Augusta points to you being the man I've been looking for. Yet if you are, I wonder why I'm not already dead?'

Saco stared at Valerius with a hint of puzzlement in the grey eyes. Clearly the moment of decision had arrived. Valerius held his breath and waited. Either the torture would begin or Saco would decide he'd get more information from Valerius by less painful means. Eventually, Saco waved the poker away. Valerius realized he'd been straining against his bonds and slumped back in the chair. He waited for Saco to cut the ropes, but apparently his captor still hadn't reached that stage of trust. Instead, he asked: 'What are these things you have been told?'

Valerius held his gaze. 'That you are an important man in Asturica. Rich. You endow buildings and put on regular entertainments. A man of power, unless I miss my guess.' Saco shook his head, but Valerius continued. 'It has also been suggested in certain quarters that you are ruthless, avaricious, unscrupulous and not averse to using violence to further your business interests.'

Saco winced. 'Some of this may have been true in the past, but whatever I have done I hope that my more recent acts have atoned for any pain I caused.'

'I suppose that would depend on just what you've done and how much pain,' Valerius said. 'What interests me more is just how you came by the riches that allowed you to endow the city baths and the other buildings that bear the name of Cornelius Aurelius Saco.'

'What are you suggesting?' Saco bridled.

'That you may be involved in criminal activity which threatens the good government of the Empire.'

Now Saco was out of his seat and his bulk seemed to fill the room. For a moment Valerius thought he'd provoked him beyond control, but the builder only glared at him. 'You dare to accuse me of disloyalty to the Empire?' he hissed.

'You asked me what I had heard. I answered honestly.'

'Then you have been speaking to the wrong people. Yes,' Saco sighed and sat back in the chair, 'I was all of those things. But a man can become so rich that the next success has little value to him. He has time to look back on his life and wish that certain things could be undone.' He leaned forward with his shoulders hunched and the fingers of his hands entwined, a frown creasing the narrow brow. 'Of course, that is not possible. But when my wife died I decided to make an effort to repay what I had taken. To give back to the community that which I owed. The enemies I made are still enemies. No amount of public goodwill will change that, but the people appreciate what I have done and I am content.' He picked up the heavy shears and for a moment Valerius had a vision of the point plunging into his body. Instead, Saco stepped behind him and used the twin blades to cut the ropes holding him. 'Now, the question is, who are you? – Oh, I know your identity and a certain amount about your background – but why are you in Asturica Augusta? A former soldier. A man who is forever seeking information. Who consorts with the worst elements in our society. People who have undoubtedly been pilfering the Empire's gold . . .'

'You have proof?'

'Not proof,' Saco shook his head. 'I sent word of my suspicions to Tarraco three years ago, but for his own reasons the then governor chose not to, or could not act. He was replaced. Since his successor also did nothing I fear his loyalties had been bought and my report was never passed on.'

'Suspicions?'

Saco turned to his secretary. 'Leave us, Claudius.' When the man was gone he poured water into a cup and handed it to Valerius. 'In a way your accusation was correct, at least partially. There was a time when I profited more than was right from the mines. I convinced myself it was only business, but of course, it was more than that.'

'Corruption?'

A nerve twitched in Saco's cheek at the word, but he nodded. 'It was part of the system and we treated it like a game, making jokes as we passed over the bribes that would win business, or make twice as much profit as a job was actually worth. Yet the sums involved then were relatively small. Gradually, I realized I was prostituting myself and putting my family at risk. I resolved to get out. To become a simple honest businessman.' He gave a bitter little laugh as if he didn't quite believe it himself and Valerius realized that behind the confident exterior Cornelius Saco was a frightened man. 'I'd only just started the process when, around the start of the civil war, it was suggested to me that I could be part of something that would make me immensely rich. Nothing specific was mentioned, but it was clear to me that whoever was behind it was deadly serious.'

'Who made the offer?'

'A lawyer from Tarraco. He said he was acting as an intermediary for the principal parties.'

Valerius grunted in frustration. Always another layer of shadow. 'And what was your answer?'

'I said I wanted nothing to do with it.' He must have seen the doubt in Valerius's eyes, because he insisted: 'You must believe me.'

'Did the lawyer have a name?'

Saco nodded. 'I made enquiries. Marcus Tulius Veranius was found drowned in his bath shortly after his visit to me. An accident.'

Valerius froze. A coincidence? No, there were no coincidences where the Emperor's gold was concerned. The same men who had tried to kill Pliny had murdered Veranius. 'Did you include this when you reported your suspicions?'

'Yes,' Saco said. 'But as I said, nothing was done.'

'Gaius Plinius Secundus never received your report,' Valerius said firmly. 'But even so he needs more than suspicions. I was sent here to investigate the disappearance of a man called Petronius.'

'I knew Petronius,' Saco said guardedly. 'I did what I could to help him.'

'My mission is identical to his. Will you help me?'

Saco hesitated. 'I have a position to maintain in this city. If there were prosecutions, accusations would be made. That position might be threatened.' He gave Valerius a shrewd look. 'Petronius promised me immunity against prosecution for *any* previous misdemeanours I committed. Can you do the same?'

The lawyer in Valerius noted the choice of words. He had a feeling Saco wasn't talking about a few business sweeteners, but what choice did he have? 'I have the governor's authority . . . and the Emperor's. You will have your immunity.'

At the mention of the Emperor Saco licked his lips. 'You can prove this?'

'If I must,' Valerius assured him. He could produce Vespasian's warrant if necessary, but first he needed to know just how far he could trust the builder. Thankfully, Saco appeared willing to accept his good faith.

'Then I will do what I can.'

'Good. When you say I consort with the worst elements in the city, I take it you mean Severus? It was he who damned you in much the same terms.'

Saco nodded. 'Severus, yes, along with Ferox, the *praefectus metallorum*, Fronton. I am certain of them. I have my suspicions about two of the military men at Legio. Petronius felt that too many gold shipments were being attacked where one or two wagons would go missing, but the escort suffered only a few light casualties and often none at all. He said you should look for patterns.'

Valerius remembered his interview with Pliny. 'He told Plinius Secundus he believed he was on the verge of exposing a conspiracy much wider than the mere theft of gold. Do you have any idea how he would have come to that conclusion?'

Saco's face took on a guarded look. 'Just before his death Petronius told me he had uncovered a new and potentially decisive source of information. Someone inside the conspiracy, though he would reveal neither the identity or whether it was one of the major figures. The possibilities clearly excited him. If this source fulfilled the potential he hoped for, it is possible he could have achieved a vital breakthrough. Perhaps even laid hands on the direct proof you say the governor needs.'

Valerius stared into the glowing coals. 'When your men took me I was on the way to Petronius's house to search the garden. Severus's people burned documents there and buried the ashes. I hoped—'

Saco shook his head gloomily. 'I too hoped, but I personally checked the burned area and crumbled ashes is all that remains. Not a single charred piece that might provide a clue.'

'Then I don't see what more we can do. Whatever Petronius knew died with him.'

'There was one other man who helped him,' Saco said. 'A most capable character who was Petronius's eyes and ears on the road.'

'Then we must find him.'

'It is not so simple.' The builder shook his head. 'He disappeared at the same time as Petronius. I learned a few weeks later that he had been taken and condemned to work in the mines. He is probably dead by now.'

'Then it is finished.' Valerius struggled to disguise his despair. 'Unless we can track down Petronius's source the conspirators have won. Whoever they are they must have had some contact. Is there any way of building a picture of Petronius's movements in the days before he disappeared?'

'I can try, but it will be difficult to ask the right questions without the risk of discovery. If they believed we were on the scent of something important they would close every avenue.' He sent Valerius a glance full of meaning. 'Permanently.'

'Have they threatened or tried to attack you personally?'

'No, not yet,' Saco admitted. 'I don't believe I have given them reason to fear me. All they've done is blacken my name, but I know what they are capable of. That's why . . .' He gestured to the coals and the smith's tools.

'You are not like them,' Valerius said. 'I knew that the instant your man removed the hood and I looked into your face.'

'There is one other thing.' Saco's voice mirrored his uncertainty. 'The men I spoke of *must* be part of the conspiracy. Each of them is a link in the chain of gold production and supply. Yet I do not believe any one of them has the intellect, the nerve or the ingenuity to achieve what they have done.'

'What do you mean?'

'I believe there is another, unseen hand guiding them.'

'Do you have any suspicions who it might be?'

'No,' Saco said regretfully. 'But I know he is utterly ruthless, wields great influence in Asturica Augusta, yet is able to operate from the shadows. A very dangerous man. It seems to me from what Petronius hinted it is not just the theft of Vespasian's gold that is at stake here, it is the very future of the province of Hispania Tarraconensis.'

XXXI

Valerius said his farewells in the gateway of Saco's brick-works where he'd been held, reflecting that his departure might have been very different had the 'interview' taken a less cordial turn. They arranged to meet again in a week unless either came up with new information of value. Most of Saco's contacts with Petronius had been through the secretary, Claudius. Saco promised to have Claudius make subtle enquiries to try to discover the engineer's movements during the final week of his life.

When Valerius stepped into the open he realized it must be close to mid afternoon, yet he could swear he'd been in the cellar for no more than an hour. A wave of fatigue, more mental than physical, swept over him and his throat felt as dry as the dusty street under his feet. He stepped beneath the awning of a pavement bar to order a cup of wine. He forced himself to concentrate. It had all happened too quickly. The threat of a painful death and relief at his survival had made him stupid. He should have asked a dozen more questions. Probed deeper into Saco's business relationships with the men who were now his enemies. Discovered more detail about his relationship with Petronius and enquired

272

further about the mysterious helper who'd disappeared soon after the engineer's death.

Saco's sudden change of heart still puzzled him. From potential torturer to prospective ally in less time than it took to down a cup of wine. Yes, Valerius had been able to supply the answers the builder wanted to hear, but there had been an element of desperation in his desire to accept them as truth. To the experienced inquisitor it was clear Saco had all but determined the outcome from the start, and the tools and the brazier were little more than theatre.

A familiar figure appeared at the end of the street. Valerius watched Saco's aide, Claudius, march down the cobbled thoroughfare with the purposeful air and intense focus of a man late for an important meeting. On the face of it a lowly secretary, yet, in the glow of the coals, Valerius had seen something more visceral. Something more familiar in a soldier than a man who wielded a stylus. Claudius had *wanted* to see blood spill and smell the stink of burning flesh. If Saco had decided to inflict pain he couldn't have found a better instrument. And what did that information add to the portrait of his new ally forming in Valerius's mind?

It was clear he could disregard what Severus had said about Saco. If the man was a known threat to the conspiracy it was in the *duovir*'s interest to tarnish the name of his enemy. So, Saco the benefactor. Saco, the successful businessman. Yet Saco claimed the sums involved in his bribery were relatively small, which, if true, gave at least a hint that the scale of the contracts he was bidding for were of similar nature. So where did the vast sums come from that had funded the baths and the city library? The obvious answer was that Saco had been lying. Rather than being peripheral to

273

Asturica's corruption he was up to his neck in it, right up till the point when he'd felt the noose begin to tighten. That would explain why he was so ready to accept Valerius as Petronius's replacement. If – when – the conspiracy was finally uncovered, Severus, Fronton and the rest would implicate him in what had gone before. Without the Emperor's protection Saco would face the same bloody retribution. Saco needed Valerius, just as much – perhaps more – than Valerius needed him.

Yet an ally driven by self-interest was just as valuable as one driven by principle.

Valerius paid for his wine and continued back to his lodgings. His route took him past the Severus villa. By chance his arrival coincided with the *duovir*'s exit at the heart of a swarm of clients on the way to preside over some tribunal or case. On impulse Valerius slowed and changed direction. By the time Severus and his entourage moved out of sight the one-handed Roman was approaching the villa entrance.

He knocked on the great wooden door and waited, uncertain of his reception, or even why he was taking this chance. All he knew was that he couldn't wait a week for Saco or Melanius to make progress. His lawyer's training counselled patience, but sometimes a case needed a touch of the whip. Sometimes you just had to shake the bushes and see what came out.

Zeno, Severus's *atriensis*, answered the knock and greeted Valerius with a look that was far from welcoming.

'My master is out.' He made to close the door, but Valerius put his left hand to it.

'I am here to see the lady Calpurnia.'

He saw a flare of consternation in the other man's eyes that confirmed his mistress was at home.

'What is your business with her?'

'No business of a servant with ideas above his station.' Zeno flinched as if he'd been slapped. 'All you have to do is announce me.' Valerius pushed harder and stepped inside.

Zeno gave him a look of hatred, but led the way through to the room with the bear mosaic. Valerius waited while the servant went to fetch his mistress. His absence was followed a few moments later by the sound of raised voices from the interior of the house before Calpurnia appeared, eyes glittering dangerously and with a look on her face Valerius hadn't seen before.

'What are you doing here?' she demanded without preamble.

Valerius smiled. Even in a simple white *stola* Calpurnia Severa was striking, and the pink flush of anger in her cheeks made her more so. 'I confess you gave the impression I had a standing invitation to visit you.'

'Do not patronize me, Gaius Valerius Verrens,' she snapped. 'That would be a great mistake. If you wish to speak to my husband he is not here.'

'No,' Valerius assured her. 'It is you I came to see, and not just for the obvious pleasure of your company. When we last met you asked certain questions and made certain observations. Since then I've had time to consider their implications and I wonder if you are truly aware of the situation in which you find yourself . . .'

'I should have Zeno throw you out on the street.'

'You could have him try,' Valerius agreed.

'Yes,' a wry smile flickered momentarily across her lips. 'But we have more than one servant.'

Valerius allowed his voice to harden a little. 'I came here because I decided I could be of some service to you after all. It's possible I may be able to save you much pain. Possibly even save your life.'

A snort of derision, but she didn't storm from the room or fly at him with her long nails. 'You think you know me, Gaius Valerius Verrens. Because I am a woman you have the presumption to treat me as if I am weak and powerless. Yet you are much mistaken.' Her tone changed and her words emerged like lashes of the whip, each stinging more than the one that had gone before. 'My family owned a small cloth-making enterprise in Carthago Nova, but my father was a drunkard and we would have been destitute if my mother and I hadn't taken control. By the time I was fifteen I was running the business. Five years later I had expanded it tenfold. Severus didn't marry me for my beauty, or even the promise of this body. He married me because of my ability, my intelligence and my strength of will. It was I who encouraged him to join the *ordo*, and who gave him the ambition to become a *duovir* and made him a power in Asturica Augusta.'

'Then you know, or at least suspect, what Severus is involved in.' Valerius waved his wooden fist to encompass the room, with its sumptuous wall hangings and marble statuary. 'You undoubtedly benefit from the proceeds. Perhaps you approve. I like to think that you do not, but maybe it excites you to be part of something illicit?' He waited for her to interrupt, or deny, but she just stared at him. 'But have you considered what it means to even share a house with Severus? Innocent or guilty, your silence and proximity implicates you in what he has been doing. If Severus and his friends are arrested, the first thing the governor will do is confiscate their property. At best, you will be left destitute, at worst, you will lose your liberty or your life.'

276

In the long silence that followed, the only sound was the whistle of the light breeze through a gap in the outer door. Calpurnia's face betrayed nothing, but he noticed the fingers of her right hand were twisted in the folds of her *stola*. To stop them shaking? But with anger or from fear? After what seemed an eternity, she said: 'Your words are like the ravings of a deranged soothsayer, but I'm curious. If there was any truth in them what would you have me do?'

Valerius knew the question held a trap, but he had no alternative but to plunge on. 'There must be things you know that would help someone charged with investigating this matter. You will have seen who comes and goes from this house. Overheard conversations. You know the names of the men he has power over, and perhaps those who have power over him.'

'You would have me betray my husband?'

Her voice held a contemptuous edge that irritated him beyond constraint. The words were out before he could stop them. 'You seemed happy enough to betray him when you visited me the other day.'

The look on her face told him instantly that he'd gone too far. Fury seemed to make her grow and he could see she was only just holding herself in check. 'I think you should leave,' she hissed.

He opened his mouth to urge her to consider what he'd said, but the slightest shake of her head silenced him. He turned to go.

'Of course,' the words that followed him were perfectly composed, 'there is another, much simpler solution. If my husband is the dangerous criminal you suggest, all I have to do is ask him to bring me your head on a silver plate.'

* * *

Six fruitless and frustrating days later, Valerius slipped out of his lodgings to meet Cornelius Aurelius Saco at a house in the north of the city, in the Street of the Engravers. 'It is the home of one of my managers,' the builder had explained. 'You will recognize it when you see where the *signatores* have been at work urging voters to elect honest Lucius Octavius Fronton as *aedile* instead of the less-deserving Cornelius Aurelius Saco.'

Saco's man Claudius slipped in behind him as he approached the house and whispered confirmation that he hadn't been followed. The builder was waiting just inside the door.

'I wish I had better news for you,' Saco said as they shook hands. 'I fear I am no closer to finding Petronius's source or identifying the guiding force behind this nest of thieves. Claudius made enquiries among the neighbours about Petronius's movements, but either he seldom left the house or he covered his tracks well. No one had noticed any visitors.'

'Petronius would have been careful,' Valerius acknowledged. 'Though much good it did him in the end.'

'I will keep looking, but I do not hold out much hope.' The builder sounded disheartened.

'There may be another way,' Valerius said. It was something he'd been considering since the confrontation with Calpurnia. 'If we can't find Petronius's source, perhaps we can create one of our own. Severus, Ferox and Fronton can't be working alone. To siphon off that much gold and cover up its existence would require any number of well-placed people.'

'True,' Saco agreed. 'But how many of them would be in a position to supply the kind of evidence the governor requires?'

'All it needs is one.' Valerius understood the shortcomings of his plan, but they had to start somewhere. 'You know how things work in Asturica Augusta. Think about how *you* would go about stealing the gold. Who would you have to corrupt to make it happen? Make a list and together we'll identify their strengths and weaknesses, starting with the main conspirators.'

'Severus is an opportunist.' Saco's lip twisted with contempt. 'He is driven entirely by greed and he won't give up what he's stolen lightly. Ferox knows the fate of an Imperial official who is caught with his hands on Vespasian's gold. It would be difficult – I think impossible – to turn him against the others.'

'Fronton?'

Saco nodded slowly. 'It's possible. A man frightened of his own shadow. He won't even look me in the face if we meet on the street. It would depend,' his eyes drifted to Valerius's wooden hand, 'whether he was more frightened of you than he is of Severus and the others. By approaching him you'd risk forcing them to take direct action against you. Let me put together the list you asked for. You know,' he said, with a rueful smile, 'in a way it's a pity. All those people on the thieves' payroll have contributed to making Asturica Augusta the fine city it is. They buy jewellery for their wives. Horses for their children. They buy the houses I build and rent the apartments I own. Even the lowliest clerk massaging Ferox's figures. If you – we – succeed, this city will never be the same again.'

They agreed to another meeting and Valerius returned to his lodgings. As soon as he entered the main room he sensed something had changed. He'd always been a tidy man, even a creature of habit. Tabitha laughed at the way the oil for his stump must always be in the same place. His shaving gear placed precisely so in reach of the bed. The bag containing his spare clothing had been in a certain position, but it had been moved ever so slightly. It was the same with everything else in the room. Servants cleaning? But it had been done only yesterday. The writing materials he'd laid out to record his lack of progress in finding Petronius were also out of place. The scroll case containing Marius's map. Valerius picked it up and opened the flap. The rolled-up map was still there.

But the Emperor's warrant that had been hidden inside it was gone.

XXXII

The sound of thunder woke Valerius from a troubled sleep. It took a moment before his stunned mind worked out someone was hammering at the outer door. He'd slept with his wooden fist attached to his wrist and he tightened the laces before pulling a tunic over his head. A new round of frantic knocking reverberated through the house. Where were the servants? At least one of them should have been awake.

He stepped out of the room. The house was in darkness apart from a single oil lamp illuminating the stairs. There was still no sign of the household staff Severus had allocated him. He ran down the stairs as the hammering continued, but by the time he was able to unbar the door it had stopped. He hesitated for a heartbeat waiting for it to begin again, but all he could hear was the sound of hoarse breathing.

When he pulled the door inwards a shadowy figure in a hooded cloak slumped towards him and he stepped forward to take the weight of the falling body in his arms. The hood fell back to reveal the twisted, blood-drained features of Cornelius Aurelius Saco. Saco's right hand clamped convulsively on Valerius's arm and a soft groan escaped his lips. Valerius looked into the dying man's eyes and saw a moment of recognition there. Saco tried to say something, and Valerius bowed his head so his ear was close to Saco's mouth. All that emerged was a long sigh and he felt the all-too-familiar sensation of life fading from a body. The moment when a living, breathing human being became nothing more than an inert piece of meat. One look at the sightless eyes confirmed his fear and he lowered Saco to the marble tiles.

The sound of urgent voices echoed in the street and Valerius saw the flicker of torches in the distance. His mind spun. He looked down at what had been a white tunic to see it stained with Saco's blood that also covered his left hand. A running figure carrying a torch appeared from a cobbled alleyway opposite, quickly followed by another. With relief Valerius recognized the first man as Aurelio, Marcus Atilius Melanius's servant. Aurelio stared at him and Valerius was about to step into the street to explain what had happened when the grim resolve on the other man's face transformed into a broad smile.

'Murderer!'

The cry came from the second man, Saco's secretary Claudius. A chill ran down Valerius's spine as it was taken up first by Aurelio then a dozen others who appeared and began to run towards the house. He snatched up the bar with his good hand and kicked the door shut, ramming the wooden crosspiece into place.

Fists hammered at the door and he could hear Aurelio urging the crowd to action and Claudius extolling the virtues of his late master. Valerius closed his eyes and tried to think. Reason with them? He remembered the look on Aurelio's face and dismissed the thought. With a last glance at Saco's body he dashed upstairs to his quarters, blocking the door with a couch and a bed frame. He pulled his sword from its scabbard and waited, heart pounding, knowing this siege could have only one outcome. Better for the orchestrators if the mob tore him limb from limb, but, whatever the outcome, Aurelio would ensure he never appeared before any magistrate.

Aurelio! Suddenly everything became clear. Saco's guiding hand belonged to that fat goat's turd Melanius. Working together it would only have been a matter of time before Valerius and Saco came up with the answer. Melanius couldn't risk that. Claudius must have been spying on Saco from the start. No wonder they'd been able to act when Petronius was about to make his breakthrough. Valerius remembered the fawning welcome and sumptuous hospitality, the brotherly pats on the shoulder, and prayed that one day he'd have the chance to ram his sword down Melanius's throat.

Not that it seemed likely, with the muffled roar of a growing crowd audible on all sides. He checked the windows on to the adjoining street and they must have seen his shadow because he was greeted with a hail of stones for his trouble. Go down fighting then. But could he kill innocents who'd been duped into arresting him by Aurelio and Claudius? He whipped round at a sound from the inner room. Mars' arse, they'd found a way in already. He ran to the door and hauled it open. And froze.

'You?'

'Don't just stand there like an idiot.' A tall, whip-thin figure threw a satchel and Valerius dropped his sword and caught it with his left hand. 'Put together whatever you think you'll need to get by in the mountains.'

'The mountains?'

'Would you rather stay here? What started all this?'

'They think I killed someone.' Valerius found his cloak and stuffed it into the leather satchel.

'Did you?'

'Not this time. How did you know I was—'

'There's no time for that now.' Serpentius sniffed the air. 'I think I smell smoke.'

'So do I.'

'Jupiter's wrinkled balls, they're in a hurry to kill you. What have you done, apart from killing . . . ?'

'Cornelius Saco.'

'A pity, he was a good man.'

'This will have to do.' Valerius hitched the bag over his shoulder and picked up his sword. 'What now?' White smoke billowed from beneath the door and they could see the red glow of fire in the gap. He looked to Serpentius. His old friend had aged in the years since they'd last seen each other. The short stubble that covered his skull was a dull silver and the lines in his ravaged face had deepened, giving him the sunken, decaying look of a week-old corpse. But he was as decisive as he'd ever been.

'The roof,' Serpentius answered Valerius's question. 'Help me with this.' He pushed a bust from a high table to smash on the marble floor tiles. Valerius sheathed his sword and took an end and they carried the table to the garden room at the rear of the house. It was edged with plant pots and had an opening in the roof to allow rainwater to gather in a small *impluvium*. 'This is the way I got in.'

They positioned the table below the opening and the Spaniard leapt on to it. Balancing as easily as a cat, he bent his knees and sprang high enough to allow his claw-like fingers to grasp the edge of the opening. With a swing of the legs and an acrobatic flip of the hips, he used his own weight to help drag himself out on to the roof. 'You now,' he said to Valerius. 'What happened to your neck?' he asked when he saw the raw red line.

Valerius clambered on to the table with a little more difficulty and stood swaying beneath the opening. 'Someone tried to kill me. Here, take this.' He threw the satchel up and Serpentius caught it and pushed it out of sight.

'On three,' the Spaniard muttered, allowing his arms to dangle as low as possible. Valerius threw himself upwards and Serpentius's iron grip closed on his wrists. The Spaniard grunted in pain and shifted his grip. Valerius looked up into the agonized rictus of Serpentius's face as he tensed, and with a convulsive heave pulled Valerius on to the roof.

'I think you've put on weight,' Serpentius said as they lay gasping side by side. They heard a crash from below and a billow of smoke poured into the garden room and out of the opening. Serpentius grunted. 'That was quick!'

'They want me badly.' Valerius pushed himself to his feet and picked up the satchel. 'But not badly enough to let one of Severus's houses burn down. Time to go.' He helped Serpentius up. 'Which way?'

'This will take us to a place where we can get down to the street.' Serpentius led the way northwards across the roof. 'Then there's a little gate in the wall. I have a pair of horses waiting.'

'I should thank you,' Valerius said formally.

'We're not clear yet,' Serpentius spat.

'What in the name of all the gods are you doing here?'

'I could ask you the same thing.'

'When we get to the horses,' the Roman gasped.

They heard a furious shouting from behind and leapt down to a lower level just as a head popped out of the opening from which they'd escaped. Eventually they reached a point where they were able to lower themselves to ground level. Serpentius led the way unerringly to an iron gate cut low in the wall, accessed by a set of stairs hidden among scrubby bushes. It opened without a sound and Valerius realized his friend had prepared for just such a situation. He remembered Saco's talk of the capable character who was Petronius's eyes and ears and wondered what else Serpentius had prepared for. But that was for later.

'Won't they follow us?' he asked as they reached the grove where a big man waited already mounted and holding two horses.

'This is Placido,' Serpentius informed Valerius. 'He's a good man. They'll send the hook-noses.'

'The Parthians?' Valerius remembered the bearded native's name for the auxiliaries.

'That's right, but it will take them time to gather them. After that,' Serpentius shrugged as if outdistancing his enemies was an everyday event, 'we know ways they don't.'

'And these are very good horses.' Valerius patted his impressive mount's shoulder.

'They should be,' the Spaniard grinned. 'The day before yesterday they were owned by Lucius Octavius Fronton and he reckons himself the best judge of horse-flesh in the whole of Asturica.'

They headed north, staying off the roads and moving through gullies and along remote paths barely worthy of the name, bypassing settlements and never seeing another human being. Once or twice Serpentius reacted to some inner sense and drew them into shelter and they listened as a column of horse moved past at a fast clip. When the pursuers were gone the Spaniard would look thoughtful before leading Valerius and Placido off in a different direction.

As they rode, they swapped stories.

'Vespasian sent me,' Valerius began. 'Vespasian and Pliny. The gold yields from the Asturian mines have dwindled since the civil war, as I suspect you know . . .' He grunted as his mount lurched across a dried-up stream bed and up the other side. 'You are this Ghost they all talk about?'

'Someone created a bandit,' Serpentius said contemptuously. 'They gave the name to me, but it is all smoke.' He grinned at Valerius. 'I wouldn't have left them with a single bar of gold. No one except the Parthians has ever seen him. The wagon drivers will say nothing because they're frightened of losing their jobs, or worse. All the wagons are supplied by the same small circle of men, just as all the miners are supplied by the same circle of men, and the bread to feed them, and the timber for pit props and to build the storehouses and the smelting rooms . . .'

'I was sent here to look for our old friend Marcus Florus Petronius.' Valerius was watching Serpentius's face and saw the Spaniard's bony jaw harden.

'Petronius is dead.' Serpentius's voice was as cold as a year-old grave. 'They accused you of killing Saco. With me it was Petronius.'

'You're certain?'

'I saw him dead. I'd been watching a convoy for him. He suspected the wagons which were supposedly taken in these raids had already been stripped of their gold and he was right. When I went to his house to confirm

287

it he was lying across his desk with his throat cut. He was a good man, and clever, but he was too trusting. Someone betrayed him.'

'Saco's man Claudius was working for them.'

Serpentius turned to meet his eyes and Valerius saw a flicker of the former gladiator he'd first met, kept alive by his hatred and a burning need for revenge. 'Another debt to pay. They were waiting for me, and a fat man in a Roman officer's helmet and armour sentenced me to be worked to death in the mines.'

'I've seen the mines,' Valerius said bleakly, remembering Serpentius's terror in the Conduit of Hezekiah beneath Jerusalem.

'It was like being buried alive. Another week and I'd have gone mad.'

Valerius reached across to touch his arm. 'But you escaped, old friend, because you are still Serpentius of Avala.'

Serpentius brightened at the sound of his name. 'Serpentius of Avala.' He smiled as he savoured the words on his tongue. 'Barbaros the Proud.'

'Barbaros?'

'My name before I was taken.'

'A good name,' Valerius conceded. 'A small circle of men, you said. Severus, the *duovir* of the *ordo*. Ferox, who runs the mines and without whom nothing is possible . . .'

'Fronton, one of the main suppliers,' Serpentius supplied the next name. 'Harpocration, the prefect of Parthian auxiliaries, who provided the military threat and carried out any killings that were required.'

'He killed Petronius?'

'You may be certain of it. Petronius had marked them all, but he could never find the proof, not till right at the end. The night he died he had arranged a meeting with a man he believed would supply him with that proof. Names. Numbers on papers. Figures that would show each and every one of them was involved. He had long puzzled over Saco's insistence that none of the names they uncovered was capable of carrying the others with him on such a perilous road. A mysterious figure stood in the shadows directing and uniting, threatening and cajoling. At one point he even suspected Severus's wife, but if she is a conspirator she hides it well.'

'He was wrong to suspect Calpurnia,' Valerius confirmed. 'Though she may well be part of her husband's schemes. No, the man behind this is a man who appears to have no power, no ambition and no position. A man who will never have his statue in the Forum, but who realizes the value of information and knows how to use it. He is the puppet master who controls all the others. For a time he even controlled me.' Serpentius darted his friend a look of surprise. 'It's true, Serpentius. He sent me to my death with a smile and I even thanked him for his kindness. But his greed led him to overstretch himself and now the forces of justice are closing in on him. His name is Marcus Atilius Melanius.'

'I've never heard of him.'

'Because that is the way he wants it. His greatest strength is his invisibility. Did Petronius ever mention the name Piso?'

'No. Who is he, another invisible man?'

Valerius smiled. 'Just the opposite. A young tribune of the Sixth legion who thinks he's the next Caesar. When I had dinner with Severus and the others a few days ago he boasted as much. I think his ambitions are being encouraged by Melanius.'

Serpentius thought about *that* for a while. 'So maybe

Petronius was right and it's not just about the gold?'

'If Pliny is ever given proof they're guilty every one of them will go under the axe, if they're fortunate. They can kill us, but they know Rome will keep sending people until they get an answer. In Germania, the Batavians who followed Civilis are spent, their cohorts scattered across the Empire. It can't be long before Vespasian is able to disengage a legion from Germania. When that happens Pliny will march north and take this place apart until he finds the truth. From their point of view it makes sense to act before that happens.'

'Then they're fools. Vespasian will crush them like a grape in a walnut press.'

'It's possible, but think about what would have happened if Galba had supported the Vindex revolt in Gaul a few years back.' Gaius Julius Vindex, a tribal leader in Aquitania, had risen up against Nero, claiming to be acting in the name of freedom. 'The legions of Germania were on the brink of mutiny. If all three had combined, they'd have brought down Nero a year earlier and the civil war might never have happened.'

A dry laugh escaped the Spaniard. 'You've obviously forgotten how lovable Galba was.'

Valerius returned his grin. Servius Sulpicius Galba had been a bitter, parsimonious dry stick of a man whose penny-pinching had cost him the purple. The Praetorian Guard had killed him because he refused to pay them the money he'd promised . . . and because he chose the wrong heir. 'Galba's heir was another Calpurnius Piso.'

Serpentius gave him a certain look. 'That bears thinking about.'

'But first we have to track down Petronius's informant.'

'All I know is his name. A man called Nepos.'

XXXIII

'Welcome to Avala.' Serpentius's voice dripped irony, but Valerius understood he was as proud as any senator opening the door to his twenty-million sesterce mansion. 'It's not much, but we call it home.'

Valerius studied the little huddle of stone huts set into the hillside and the sprawling fields that clung to the sides of the stream. How appropriate that this desolate place should spawn a man like Serpentius. A hard life in a hard land had created a warrior forged from iron and stone and imbued him with a fierce loyalty to his people and his friends. The Roman could see it in the way the men and women deferred to his friend: a mixture of pride, wariness and respect. As they rode closer the ragged farmers, tradesmen and their families crowded round for a closer view of the stranger.

Valerius and Serpentius dismounted and the Spaniard began to speak. At first it was as if he'd been reading Valerius's mind, but slowly the one-handed Roman began to realize he was being treated to the tribe's traditional ritual of guest welcome.

'These are my people, the Reburi,' Serpentius said in a solemn voice. 'They are of the Zoelan tribe of the

Astures.' He waved a hand to the surrounding mountains. 'And these are our lands which once reached from the Red Hills to the wave-battered shores of Vizcaium.'

They growled at this reminder of what the Romans had taken from them, but Valerius understood Serpentius was not rallying them against an enemy. Instead, he was doing them and his guest honour by initiating him into the history of his people, the people of the high peaks, born into a blizzard and weaned on ice water. He turned to face Valerius.

'You know me as Serpentius, but I was born Barbaros. The moment they cut the cord linking me to my mother, my father laid me out naked in the snow to harden or die as the god decreed. In the mountains a weak child is a burden and to grow to love such a child a greater burden still. Better for it to die never knowing what it is to live. For the tribe to survive, the weak must always make way for the strong.' The harsh sentiment was greeted with a growl of approval because each one of them had suffered a similar ordeal. 'When I was older, perhaps five years, we would drive the sheep to the high pastures in summer and stay with them while they fattened. We had a little food, but gathered what we could to make it last: berries, wild garlic, fish we caught by hand from the streams. Maybe a mountain hare or a partridge, if we were quick and it was unlucky. I had a dog, a big dog, brown and black and hairy, with a head the size of a bull's, like the Alanos the Romans use to watch over their houses. It kept me warm at night, that dog. I still remember the smell, sweet as fresh-picked mushrooms, but bitter too, and the sound of dog dreams. The dog watched for the bear by day and the wolf by night but, more importantly, for man by either.'

'The Vaccei,' a small boy shouted, as if Serpentius

might have forgotten. His grinning father cuffed him lightly on the ear and their neighbours laughed.

'Yes,' Serpentius laughed along with them, 'the Vaccei. They moved through the rocks like snakes, those Vaccei, sliding from one piece of cover to the next until they were on you. They knew to stay downwind of the dog, but the dog had an inner eye; a sense beyond sense. The dog frightened them, because he had a bite that could tear a man's leg off and was as silent as they. Every boy carried a sling. They were usually enough to see off the wolf, even the bear if you shouted loud enough, but never the man. Of all the predators of the mountains, man was the most dangerous, and he is even more dangerous now.'

Valerius understood Serpentius was talking about the men who had taken him, and the men who would undoubtedly come looking for them both.

'You look at the mountains and you see majesty and grandeur,' Serpentius continued. 'We look at them and see only hardship and death. Perhaps soon we will all have to seek sanctuary there and there are things you must know.'

He allowed his gaze to take in the men, women and children, for this message was for them as much as for Valerius.

'Shelter and fire. It will be winter soon. If it comes to it, we can use our horses and our livestock for shelter. But to survive in the mountains you must learn to make fire in rain so thick you can catch fish in it, and in a wind fit to carry you to the ends of the earth. Without fire you will freeze. If you do not have fire and shelter the snow gods will come for you. First they take away your mind, so you are helpless against them. Then they take away all your feeling so that your body does not know what is happening to it. Then they remove it from you one piece at a time.' He allowed his eyes to range over them and his voice filled with authority, so each sentence became an order to be obeyed. 'We will collect wood for kindling, and logs, and moss to dry for our fire strikers. Thick blankets and all the food we can spare. Go now, because we may not have as much time as you think.' They began to disperse and his voice dropped so he was speaking only to Valerius. 'I have seen men wandering blind in a snowstorm with every finger and every toe missing and their arms and legs turned black and frozen solid as that walnut fist of yours. I do not say it will be like that, my friend, but take the mountains lightly for but a moment and they will destroy you.'

A young warrior approached. Valerius recognized him as the tribesman who had helped him escape the Parthians. Yet there was something different about him. This was an oddly polished version of the tattered stranger who'd moved so easily through the rocks. A thick copper torc adorned his neck, he wore a brightly coloured tunic, and his beard was trimmed tight to his lean, hatchet features.

Their eyes met and Valerius looked in astonishment from the younger man to Serpentius. It was impossible. Yet there could be no doubt.

'My son, Tito,' Serpentius confirmed with stony gravity. 'Though how he comes to be dressed like a peacock I do not know. Perhaps when the hook-noses arrive he intends to dazzle them with his finery while we escape to the mountains.'

'Gaius Valerius Verrens at your service,' Valerius bowed. 'I thank you again for guiding me away from the Parthians. I'm sure your father is only speaking in jest.'

'My father never speaks in jest,' Tito said. 'He thinks smiling is a sign of weakness.'

Serpentius was about to reply when he saw the direction of Valerius's eyes and the ravaged features took on a lugubrious cast. A slim, dark-haired girl stood watching them. Her face was sombre, but her expression didn't detract from a luminous beauty that would have made her stand out from the other Zoelans even without the fine clothes. Valerius was astonished to recognize the girl who'd sat with Calpurnia at Severus's dinner.

'I do not suppose it will do any harm to introduce you to the lady Julia Octavia Fronton. Perhaps you will get more out of her than I can.' He explained about the raid and his failure to secure Fronton's records. 'I had some notion she would know of her father's involvement, or, failing that, we could ransom her for the information. But she declares outrage even at the suggestion Fronton might be disloyal to Rome, and an exchange with snakes like Fronton entails too much risk for my liking. If I wasn't certain she'd lead them back here, I'd send her straight home.'

'I still say she has value to us,' Tito burst in. 'She may not know directly of her father's involvement, but she knows of his movements and who he met where and when. If they do come for us she would make a valuable hostage at the end.'

'Of course,' Serpentius didn't hide his sarcasm, 'it will be the industrious Tito who spends many tedious hours in her company questioning the lady Julia. And at the end will it be you who holds the knife against her throat?' He smiled, and Tito's anger turned into consternation. 'No, I thought not. Still, you may be right and she will be of use to us yet. We will need every weapon at our disposal to survive this.'

'So you are prepared to fight them if it comes to it?' Valerius said.

'No,' Serpentius spoke with the force of utter certainty. 'I will not risk one of my people to further Rome's aims. It is nothing to them if Hispania, Gaul and Germania separate from the Empire. If Vespasian has not the wit to keep his provinces, he doesn't deserve them. Perhaps it will mean the gold is kept in Hispania and helps to improve the lives of the people who dig it. Those whose ancestral lands it is torn from. Better the mining stops altogether and that vile metal remains in the earth where the gods willed it. We cannot undo the destruction and the ruin brought upon us by the Roman lust for gold, but at least we could end it.'

'That will not happen and you know it,' Valerius said just as forcibly. 'The men pillaging the goldfields for their own ends are as greedy as any in Rome. At least before there was Roman order, and there will be Roman order again, and more.' He took Serpentius aside. 'Pliny told me Vespasian plans to bring about an extension of *civitas* in Hispania. That means more citizenship and more legal protection for those who hold it. Your people will own this land with their rights of ownership enshrined in Roman law. You can create larger settlements and more employment. Expand your fields and grow more crops.'

'You don't understand, Valerius. This,' he swung a hand that took in the houses and the fields and the mountains and the trees, 'is all we want. For my people citizenship is just another form of slavery. This is already their land and as long as they are prepared to fight for it they will own it. That is the way it has always been and the way it will always be.' Valerius bit back a retort and the Spaniard shook his head. 'I know you mean well, and perhaps Vespasian too, but it is not for us. Do not mistake me, brother, though I will not risk my people, you are my friend and I will help you in any way I can.'

Tito had half followed them and picked up at least part of the conversation. Valerius sensed a confusion in him. Clearly, he was as complex a character as his father, and just as volatile.

'You do not take decisions for me, Nathair.' The young man confirmed Valerius's suspicions. 'And too much lies on this to leave it to a Roman who crashes through the countryside with the stealth of a runaway buffalo. I think you will need eyes and ears in the city, Roman?'

Valerius looked to Serpentius, who acquiesced with an almost imperceptible nod.

'My escape will have thrown the conspirators into a certain level of confusion. The fact I received help from a previously unknown source will likely provoke some kind of meeting to decide what to do next. My concern is that their reaction might be to lash out against those they fear. If we can have the movements of Ferox, Severus and Melanius watched, the very fact of an assembly will give us time to prepare.'

Tito nodded and turned to go, but Valerius called him back.

'There is one other possibility, which may help or may not.'

'Yes?'

'If you can spare a man or two with the right qualities, men who have the subtlety to drop a suggestion into another man's ear without appearing to do so, have them seek out the soldiers' haunts in Legio.' He hesitated, stroking the scar on his cheek with the fingers of his left hand, trying to find the right form of words. Finally he had it. 'There is talk of rebellion, but everyone knows it will only benefit the officers and the rich. A trader from Nemausus told a merchant in Clunia that the First, or maybe the Seventh, is already on the march from Germania. Only a fool would risk his neck for one man's doomed ambition. You see, Tito? Anything that might make a soldier think twice before he acts. If it reaches enough ears it may make them hesitate when the time comes. Even a single century standing its ground would make a difference.'

'It will be done as you say.' Tito's face creased into a savage smile at the prospect. 'I have just the man, and woman, who can do such a thing.'

When he was gone, Valerius turned to Serpentius.

'There is one thing I didn't tell you.'

But Serpentius's eyes were on the south-west and he put up a hand. Valerius felt a flicker of unease as he followed the Spaniard's gaze. At first it was just a hazy shimmer on the horizon, but gradually it evolved into a white cloud that turned into a thin pillar as they watched.

A lookout on the hill behind the village shouted out and a murmur of dismay went up as every eye locked on the smoke.

'It has already begun,' Valerius whispered.

'No,' Serpentius corrected him. 'That is the Castro of the Wild Goats, they can have no reason to link it with us. This is something different. Petronius warned me of a plan to bring the tribes of the high peaks under their control. It was only a question of the timing. If their ambition is as great as we believe they cannot let remain a potential threat to exploit what they leave behind.' Another pillar of smoke appeared a little closer and further east. 'As I thought, this is just the start. Valuta!' An elderly grey-beard shuffled towards them.

'They will come for us eventually, but not for a few days yet. Before we leave, the survivors from the other *castros* will flee here seeking aid. Is the sanctuary prepared?'

'The caves were stocked with provisions even before your orders, but if there are many more mouths to feed . . .' He shrugged.

'It will have to suffice.' Serpentius looked thoughtful. 'While we have time you will send all our most vulnerable people ahead. The old and the sick, mothers with young children. They must carry what they can, but only essentials, and bury their valuables in the usual places. When the others start to arrive, do the same. Any man able to wield a sword or a spear must stay, ready to fight. We can muster a hundred, but we'll need more to defend the pass.'

Valuta croaked an acknowledgement and stumbled off, calling to the members of the village council.

Tito reappeared, with the girl Julia half a pace behind him. 'Does this change what we spoke of earlier?'

Valerius chewed his lip. 'No, I think we must carry on with our plans.'

The young man turned away, but Julia hesitated for a moment, her puzzled green eyes locked on Valerius.

'You will be safe with the others,' Serpentius assured her, as gently as a man of his disposition could. 'Tito will look after you.'

'I know,' she said, and turned away.

'You said there was something you hadn't told me,' Serpentius reminded Valerius.

'I have met the man Nepos.'

XXXIV

Hostilius Nepos released a long contented sigh as he ascended the steps of the house he rented in Asturica after an hour sharing gossip at the baths. Such a relief to be back in civilization after the noisome, grubby and relentlessly vulgar existence of the mining camp. The house had once come with a woman and he wished she were still here. If ever he needed someone to share his troubles with, it was now. One moment his mind soared with exhilaration that he'd survived, the next he was almost collapsing from the terror of what might have been, and might yet be. How had he got himself into this?

Greed, he acknowledged, was part of it. And yes, weakness. He had always been a weak man, easily influenced by others. When Ferox had asked him to alter a few figures, first in return for the odd favour or a hint of promotion, and later for money, it had seemed a relatively small thing. A favour for a respected superior, or so he'd told himself. But it had grown so quickly it had felt like standing in front of the reservoir sluice gates when they were opened. Before he realized it he was drowning in a sea of corruption.

And, despite his every effort to wriggle free, he'd been drawn ever deeper into the plot. Eventually the day came when he woke up aware that unless he did *something* it would end with a visit from that dreadful Harpocration and a shallow grave in the forest.

At first, when the mystery man approached him, it felt like salvation. He promised immunity, rewards and Nepos's sandalled feet under Licinius Ferox's desk. Nepos had almost gone on his knees in relief. Yes, yes, he'd cried, take me away from here and I will tell you everything you need to know. Of course, that wasn't enough. The mystery man promised to spirit him away, but first he must know everything. Hour after hour Nepos sat with him repeating over and over the little Ferox allowed him to know, answering questions about answers he'd given weeks earlier to questions he didn't even remember. The one thing he'd kept to himself was the involvement of Marcus Atilius Melanius. Melanius would be his last throw of the dice, the bargaining chip he would use when the time came that the mystery man no longer needed him. More, always more. 'I need evidence,' the mystery man insisted. 'Not just names, but numbers. This conspiracy is like an octopus, with tentacles everywhere. Severus, Ferox and the others cannot control it on their own. You are Ferox's man. Who does Severus use to falsify the licences? Fronton sends bread for four hundred men to the Red Hills mine, yet he's paid for six hundred. Someone must sign it off. This is a bureaucracy. Nothing can be done without a piece of papyrus or a scroll. I need those pieces of papyrus and copies of the scrolls.'

Oh, he'd tried, standing for minutes outside an office willing himself to go inside. Hovering with his hand over a pile of papyrus scraps, unable to will his fingers

301

to close on one. Just as he'd not been cut out for conspiracy, he didn't have the disposition for spying. He'd managed to steal a few minor documents, passing them over with shaking hands, the papyrus damp with the bearer's sweat. But minor documents weren't enough. The mystery man knew Nepos had access to the information he wanted. That's why he'd been recruited by Ferox in the first place.

So he'd reverted to forgery. Now that he could do. Nepos knew more or less what should be on the papers the mystery man was interested in, so he created what he believed was wanted. Simple enough to take a pile of blank papyrus and he had his own copy of the departmental seal. What could be better?

It all went so well ... until the night the mystery man pulled out another document and placed it next to the one Nepos had just delivered. 'You see, Hostilius,' he'd said gently, 'they do not tally. Why is this? Could it be that you have been deceiving me? If that is the case, I will grieve for you, because it's the axe for you, my boy. No immunity, or reward, or promotion. Just the cold edge against your neck. The pause for one last breath. Then . . .'

Naturally he'd wept and pleaded and raved as if his life depended on it, because it did. He'd given up Melanius, but to no avail. He'd accused the mystery man's other informant of forging his own documents. But no. The mystery man had watched as the papyrus was taken, there was no doubt of its authenticity. But if you have an informant who has access to this, why do you need me? Because you are important, Hostilius. You have attended their meetings; my other little spy is a minor player in this drama, while you have shared centre stage. Besides, if I didn't need you I would have to give you up. It wouldn't be the nice, quick, friendly axe for Hostilius Nepos if Claudius Harpocration thought you'd been betraying his friends, would it? It would be the hot coals and the gelding knife and the pliers and the leaded whip. No, Hostilius, you have one last chance to bring me what I need. We will meet again two days from now and you will bring me the papers or your name will be on Harpocration's desk by morning.

He spent the next day in the depths of a Red Hills mine praying to the god of the underworld to bring the tunnel down on his head rather than end up under the knife of Claudius Harpocration. Eventually, he came to understand that the mystery man had left him no choice. He could draw a razor across his own throat or do as he was ordered. Oddly, it turned out it wasn't so difficult after all, once you'd steeled yourself to do it.

The following night he'd gone to the meeting place with a satchel of papers and waited. And waited. And waited. The mystery man had never turned up and Nepos returned to the house, confused and disappointed, but not frightened. The next day he looked for the sign that would initiate a new meeting, but he found nothing.

Days passed without contact from the mystery man and disappointment had given way to elation. He was gone for good. Hostilius Nepos was free. His life would continue, without threats of hot irons and axes. He had a choice now. Continue to do what Ferox asked of him, which was simple enough, but . . . Or he could disappear. Leave Asturica Augusta by night and make a new life somewhere they appreciated engineers and weren't stealing the gold from the Emperor's fingertips.

But was he truly free?

If the mystery man had vanished, it was unlikely he'd done it intentionally. That meant someone had made him disappear. And if he was dead, what had he blurted out before he breathed his last? If he'd uttered the name Nepos there would be only one outcome.

Hostilius had woken up sweating in the night knowing that without the mystery man he'd never feel safe again. If he stayed in Asturica death was the only way out, either when the conspiracy was discovered, or when Ferox decided he was no longer needed. If he fled, they would find a way to place the blame for the entire scheme on him. He would be wanted throughout the Empire. A man who had stolen the Emperor's gold. A reward on his head and the prey of every bounty hunter or mercenary.

His days passed in a bemused, fear-filled trance and he dulled his nights with wine.

He reached the top of the stairs, opened the door and stepped inside. For a moment he felt like weeping and he had to use the wall as support. What will become of me, a small child asked inside his head. Yet at a deeper level he gradually became aware that something was different. A scent tickled his nostrils he didn't associate with this time or this place. A mix of hard-ridden horse and unwashed clothing.

The sound of flint on iron and an oil lamp flared. Nepos bit back a scream as a terrible face appeared before him, the merciless eyes of a wild beast glaring in the flickering yellow light, nostrils flared wide above a sneering thin-lipped mouth. The face of a demon, all deep shadow and stark planes and lines that looked as if they'd been carved out by a knife point. He'd believed nothing was more terrifying than the thought of being in the hands of Claudius Harpocration, but the owner of this terrible countenance must be capable of inflicting agonies from a man's worst nightmares.

'Good evening, Hostilius.'

He started at the voice from behind. A voice he recognized? A tone that promised a possible reprieve from the awful creature who had paralysed him with a single look. He felt faint with relief, but still he couldn't break the hold of those feral, predator's eyes.

The scrape of a couch being dragged across the floor. 'Sit, please.' He backed up until he could feel a padded surface and almost collapsed on to the seat. A shadowy figure appeared at the edge of his vision and advanced to take up position on a second couch opposite the first. 'Do you recognize me, Hostilius?'

'Of course.' Tension made Nepos's voice sound brittle and cracked. 'You are the man who visited the mine.'

'Then you know you have nothing to fear from me.' Nepos glanced at Serpentius, who had broken off from staring at him to light a second lamp. Valerius saw the look. 'My friend is here to ensure my safety – and yours.'

From somewhere Nepos dredged up the courage to demand: 'Why should I need protection?'

'We will come to that, but first I want to ask you a few questions.'

'You claim you mean me no harm, yet you have broken into my home with this . . . and they say you killed a man.'

'A misunderstanding,' Valerius said. 'But one that meant I could not contact you in the normal fashion. Though, of course, if I'd done so *they* would have known, and I doubt you would want that.'

'I don't know what you mean.' Nepos seemed to have trouble breathing.

'Do not be coy with me, Hostilius.' The tone didn't change, but the words held a clear warning. 'In this matter

I represent the Emperor Titus Flavius Vespasianus Augustus. You were not aware of that fact during our previous discussion, but now you are, you should reflect on what it means for you.' At the mention of the Emperor sweat broke out on his scalp and the beads ran unchecked down the tunnel manager's deathly pale features. 'Do you know why we are here?' Nepos hesitated and Valerius got to his feet, so that he loomed over the smaller man. 'I would consider your answer very carefully.'

Hostilius Nepos's emotions had swung from terror to relief when the threat of immediate execution faded, and back again. Mention of the Emperor instantly brought his mystery man to mind. Of course, when he'd vanished they'd send a replacement. And this oh-so-capable, scarred, one-handed veteran was just the man they'd choose, with his pet wolf tagging along for security and any dirty work that needed to be done. But how much did the one-handed man – belatedly he remembered the name Verrens – know? His identity, clearly, but what else? He must discover the answer to that question before he placed his neck back on the block.

'It is about the gold.'

'That's right, Hostilius,' Valerius encouraged him. 'And the work you were doing for Marcus Florus Petronius.'

The name came as a complete surprise. It was on the tip of Nepos's tongue to deny all knowledge of him, but he felt the heat of the wolf's gaze and blurted out the truth. 'I never knew his name.'

'Do you know what happened to him?'

Nepos shook his head. 'We were supposed to meet, but he never turned up.'

'And just when you had something big for him.' The

rasping voice came from the wolf and sounded like an accusation. It sent a shudder through Nepos. Did they think he had betrayed this Petronius?

'I—'

'The first thing we will require,' Valerius cut in on the defensive whine, 'is the evidence you were to hand him that night.'

Nepos was aghast. 'But I do not have it. When – Petronius – disappeared, I feared they would come for me next. Naturally, I returned the papers before they could be reported missing.'

Valerius suppressed his disappointment, but Serpentius wasn't so sanguine. The unmistakable metallic whisper of a blade being drawn cut the silence.

'You must believe me,' Nepos stuttered. 'I do not have them.'

Valerius nodded to Serpentius and he replaced the sword.

'That is a pity, Hostilius, because it means you will have to steal them again, No,' he silenced the inevitable protest, 'there is no other way. Your life depends on it. I know how Petronius worked. He chose you because you were at the heart of the plotters' bureaucracy. A reluctant part, I have no doubt, but an active one. When the governor arrives to destroy this nest of snakes, as he will, you will be condemned along with the rest,' Nepos emitted a groan at the dread word, 'unless you do as I say. Now, what was in the papers?'

Nepos twitched as Serpentius slammed a chest lid somewhere in the house. 'I believe it was lists of disbursements and the dates they were handed over.'

'You believe?'

'These documents were protected by some kind of cypher, but Petronius said it didn't matter because he had the key.' He looked up apologetically. 'I was not his only informant.'

Valerius had been concentrating on the tone of the engineer's answers, listening for any hint of deceit. Nepos had gone from denial to reluctance, but the Roman sensed he'd now reached the stage of resigned capitulation. 'Tell me how it worked and how you became involved.'

First Nepos confirmed the identities of the conspirators. 'I believe the original idea came from Severus, but Melanius was the true architect. He had names for his fellow conspirators. Severus was the Facilitator; Julius Licinius Ferox the Sceptic; Harpocration the Enforcer; Fronton the Weakling.'

'Did Ferox mention Proculus, the *praefectus castrorum* at Legio? Or a man called Calpurnius Piso?'

'To my knowledge, Proculus is not an active member of the group, but it is certain Melanius holds some sort of sway over him. He was persuaded to give Severus almost sole use of the Parthian auxiliaries under Harpocration. When it comes out he either knew of the thefts and turned a blind eye or actively cooperated he will die with the rest. Even if he is guilty of simple incompetence his career is over. I think he believes it in his best interests to work with them. The name Piso has never been mentioned in my hearing.'

'Very well, continue.'

'It was just after Sulpicius Galba, who was governor then, marched for Rome, that Ferox came to me. He brought a bundle of scrolls and placed them on my desk. He said he had found a mistake, indeed several mistakes. The output figures are wrong, he said, I am sure they were much lower. I checked them and found they were correct. But he insisted, most strenuously. When I didn't cooperate he mentioned a name. There was a lady. A husband. Such a pity if he were to find out. He was my superior, so I had the documents replaced. A few days later a purse of gold arrived and a letter thanking me for my strenuous efforts on behalf of the Empire. When he returned and suggested I report the yields one-fifth lower than the actuality,' a shrug of resignation, 'what could I do?'

'How does the actual theft happen?'

'At first it was very simple. Ferox diverted a fifth of the yield and shared it out with the others. Severus used his influence to make sure the *ordo* didn't interfere. Harpocration and his men dealt with any dissent from those in the chain. Fronton had to be bought off because he suspected what was happening. The demand for his wagons was reduced, but the amount of men he supplied remained the same. As well as gold he is paid for supplying and feeding six hundred miners when he only supplies four hundred.'

'You said "at first"?' Valerius looked up as Serpentius appeared in the doorway and shook his head. There was nothing incriminating in the house.

'Yes, Melanius was certain Galba would be too busy with matters in Rome to concern himself with Hispania. The then governor was a fool who could barely count to ten. But when Galba was killed he realized someone might be suspicious at the sudden and oddly consistent drop in the yields. That was when they decided to raise the yields again, but have bandits steal the gold from the convoys.'

'The Ghost?'

'It also allowed them to carry out raids on the hill settlements and bring the people under control, depriving them of their lands and forcing the men to work as miners.'

'You seem to know a great deal for someone who is not a central member of this pack of thieves,' Serpentius growled.

'Oh, sirs, I am certainly not that. I am a victim as much as that poor man Saco who has been a thorn in their flesh once too often. The truth is that Ferox is at heart a lonely man who can be very indiscreet in wine. Once I understood that, it seemed sensible to cultivate him as a drinking partner. A man in my situation can never have too much knowledge.'

Valerius acknowledged the sentiment with a nod, but reflected that if any of the other conspirators learned of this arrangement it might well be the death of Hostilius Nepos.

'One thing puzzles me,' he said. 'Surely they realized this couldn't last for ever? At some point the Emperor, whether it was Otho, Vitellius or Vespasian, would have sent an auditor to check the books. With the amount of gold being stolen they must have all become rich men in a very short time. Why not just stop, gradually allow the yields to return to their former level and cover their tracks?' Probably by incriminating some minor player like Nepos and perhaps one or two others. Naturally, by the time of any investigation the scapegoats would be conveniently dead and in no position to argue their innocence.

'The simple answer is greed,' Nepos said glumly. 'By the time Melanius persuaded them to stop it would have been too late. But he'd already insisted they stockpile a fifth of what they'd stolen for contingencies and in case of emergency.'

'Stockpile where?' Serpentius growled.

'That I never discovered,' the engineer insisted. 'But I suspect Ferox would have allocated him a storehouse in one of the mine complexes for his own use. Where better to hide a hoard of stolen gold than in a place you'd expect to find the metal legitimately?'

'How did you arrange your meetings with Petronius?'

Nepos's face fell as he realized that nothing he'd said had changed anything. Valerius still wanted him to steal the documents.

'Sometimes we arranged them in advance, otherwise I would place a message behind a loose brick in the wall behind this house. Petronius had it checked every day.'

'Then we will do the same. We will meet at a time and in a place of your choosing. Somewhere you feel secure. Do you understand, Hostilius?'

'Yes, lord,' the mining engineer bowed his head.

'You have a week,' Valerius smiled.

XXXV

'I was wondering . . . ?'

'Yes?'

'Why would you be getting our fat little friend to risk his neck for some pieces of papyrus we won't even be able to read?'

They were heading north from Asturica through a maze of deep valleys and Valerius took his time before he answered. 'You mean apart from the fact that he's a dishonest little weasel who'd sell his sister if he thought it would save his neck?'

'Apart from that.'

'Because even if *we* can't read the cypher I'm gambling that a man as clever as Pliny will be able to find a way. We might only have one chance. Besides, who knows what else he might bring us?'

'You're harder than I remember, Valerius.'

Valerius reined in his mount and sighed. 'I just want to finish this and go home, Serpentius. Get back to Tabitha. Complete the villa and settle down to a normal life. I seem to have been fighting battles or chasing shadows most of my life. I'm sick of it.'

'I know what you mean.' Serpentius sounded almost

wistful. 'Sometimes a man just wants to sit back and watch the crops he's planted grow and ripen. When you're younger you think you'll live for ever, but since Jerusalem I've felt as if death was riding on my shoulder and counting down the days.'

Valerius contemplated his friend. 'That's just the hole in your head talking.'

'Makes a change from talking out of the hole in my arse.' The Spaniard urged his horse into movement and Valerius followed. Moments later Serpentius returned at the trot and grabbed Valerius's reins, hauling his horse off the track and up a tree-filled gully. 'Hook-nose cavalry,' he hissed. 'Two sections and heading this way.'

Valerius held his breath and prayed his horse wouldn't make any sudden movement. He drew his sword from its scabbard. Not that it would help much against sixteen or seventeen auxiliaries, but it made him feel better. He saw Serpentius had done the same, clenching and unclenching his fingers on the leather-wrapped hilt as he stared at the road. His teeth were gritted and he was breathing hard. If Valerius hadn't known him better he would have believed he was seeing signs of fear. But this was Serpentius.

The sound of hooves on loose stone and a glimpse of movement between the trees. Valerius's unfamiliar mount began to dance under him and he almost lost his sword as he used the reins to curb the animal's antics. Below, he watched the two sections of Parthians pass at a walk in their familiar green tunics and chain armour, seven-foot spears held upright with the ash shafts rammed down the legs of their leather boots.

It was the Parthian way to carry three days' supplies in bags hung from the saddle, but these men seemed particularly heavily laden. Valerius felt Serpentius tense beside him and he twisted in the saddle to see his friend with a look of impotent fury on the savage features. When he studied the passing riders more closely he understood why. The round bundles tied to the Parthian saddles weren't supplies, they were heads. Bearded males with wide, gaping mouths, women, young and old, bound to the pommel by their long hair, and fair-headed children staring blank-eyed in fours from hay nets.

Valerius had seen severed heads before. Auxiliary units in Britannia took them to prove they'd dealt with bandit gangs or village chiefs who hadn't paid their taxes. But this was different. These were innocents whose only crime was to want to be left alone.

They didn't have to die; the dozens of families who stumbled after the horses in roped bunches were proof of that. Someone, likely Claudius Harpocration, had allowed the Parthians to slake their bloodlust before fulfilling his primary mission of gathering labour for the mines. The rest of the Parthian squadron followed the prisoners with Harpocration at their head, a long whip in his hand to encourage any dawdlers. As he passed the trees where Valerius and Serpentius waited on their horses he seemed to sense something because his head swivelled. For a moment he appeared to be looking directly at them. Valerius's fingers tensed convulsively on his sword hilt, but the moment passed and Harpocration kicked his horse forward and flicked the whip at a limping straggler.

Serpentius waited till the last of the Parthians had disappeared out of sight. 'I will kill that man. I swear it on the head of my son.'

Valerius let out a long breath. 'The only way to return your people to their lands is by stopping Melanius and his gang and bringing this place under direct Roman rule again. I pledge Vespasian's word that they will be sent back to rebuild their communities.'

'Perhaps you are right,' Serpentius conceded. 'But, either way, he's a dead man.'

As they travelled deeper into the mountains they discovered that the Parthians had left a blackened corridor through the Asturian settlements. Stone would not burn, and the individual houses still stood, but their contents and anything flammable that lay to hand had been piled inside and set alight.

'It is as if it is not enough to remove us from the land,' Serpentius said as they watered their horses in a stream outside one burned settlement. 'All evidence of our existence must be destroyed, too.'

Valerius surveyed the headless corpses scattered around them. 'The blood is on Harpocration's blade, but Melanius is responsible for this. It suits his purpose that men should fear the Parthians and know there will be no mercy for their families if they make trouble.'

'If he's going to move, he must act soon.' The Spaniard stared at the blackened stones that had once been someone's home.

Valerius nodded. 'It's getting late in the season.'

'You understand I have no choice in this?' Serpentius said moodily. 'I do not have the authority or the right to ask my people to stand in their way.' He looked up to meet Valerius's eyes. 'They are many. They are well trained and well armed. We have a few true warriors and some farmers. If it comes to a fight there will be only one outcome.'

'I understand, Serpentius. A man can only do so much.'

'I have chewed on the matter like a dog with a bone, but it always comes out the same way.'

'I understand,' Valerius repeated. 'We need Nepos to steal the documents. Afterwards you and I will ride south and hope we reach Pliny in time to pull together some kind of force capable of stopping Melanius.'

'If the Sixth—'

'We've done what we can. Now it is up to the gods. You trust your man in Asturica? He understands the urgency of the situation?'

'Allius is a good man and he is not known in the city. He will check the loose brick before noon and after dusk every day. If he finds a message he will bring it directly to us.'

He looked to Valerius for some response, but the one-handed Roman was staring into the distance.

'I've been a fool. I think we must give Pliny a chance to act even without the evidence from Nepos.' He shook his head. 'Too much the lawyer, Valerius. Too scrupulous about the process.' He turned to Serpentius. 'We have the names, we have their methods and we can provide reasonable grounds for suspicion that Melanius is prepared to act against Rome to save his neck. Once Pliny has the information it will be up to him what to do, but he must have it. Is there any chance of laying our hands on some writing materials?'

'Tito insisted we carry stylus, ink and parchment from Fronton's estate. He had some notion of young Julia writing a plea to her father to give up the information he has in exchange for her life.'

'Her life?'

Serpentius gave him a wry grin. 'He follows her around like a moonstruck calf and she's no better. If anyone goes near her his hand twitches for his sword. He reminds me of me, but,' his tone turned sober once more, 'it is all very well committing the details to parchment.

316

How do we get it to Pliny? I couldn't guarantee any of my men bar Tito would ever find their way to Tarraco, and he won't go unless the girl goes with him.'

'I have a way of getting information to the governor.' Valerius struggled not to sound embarrassed.

Serpentius raised an eyebrow. 'You don't trust me.'

'Of course I trust you.' Valerius tugged on his horse's reins and directed him north. 'It just didn't come up.'

'And what if something happened to you? Not that it is likely, of course, what with all the friends you've made in Asturica.'

Valerius grinned at him and shook his head. 'There's a tavern by the bridge as you enter Legio. A young Imperial courier called Marius is sweet on one of the barmaids . . .'

XXXVI

They sensed something was wrong as soon as they crossed the rise above Avala.

Serpentius studied the cloudless blue sky over the settlement where dark specks wheeled in the upper atmosphere. 'Carrion birds.' He drew his sword and would have put his heels to his mount, but Valerius laid a hand on his shoulder.

'Wait. Remember the field by the Rhodanus. Buzzards and crows and a Batavian ambush.' They'd been fortunate to survive that day by the river when the bloated corpses blackened in the sun and the horsemen burst whooping from the trees. 'It won't do any good getting ourselves killed. If those things scattered by the gate are what I think they are, nothing will ever do them good again.'

'Tito.' Serpentius's voice cracked with emotion.

'Tito is his father's son,' Valerius said harshly. 'He's too clever to be taken by a few dozen lumbering auxiliaries.'

But judging by the signs as they gentled their horses down the slope, there had been many more than a few dozen. 'Two hundred at least,' Serpentius estimated as he looked out across the trampled crops. 'Harpocration brought most of his cavalry. If the infantry were with them . . .'

If the infantry accompanied them they would have been strong enough to fight their way through the passes to the sanctuary. The closer they came to the *castro* the clearer it became that this was no sweep to round up workers for the mines. It was a massacre.

Valerius and Serpentius took their time, eyes searching for any sign of threat, but gradually they relaxed. They were alone except for the dead.

Hundreds of bodies lay scattered across the cultivated ground around the blackened remains of the *castro*. They lay in little mixed clumps where the menfolk had vainly attempted to protect their loved ones, or were scattered around individually, the swiftest cut down as they'd tried to flee. Valerius looked down into the dead eyes of a dark-haired boy of ten whose skull had been cloven from brow to teeth. A halo of blood, brain and bone fragments surrounded his head and the still figure of a girl who might have been his sister stretched out a forlorn hand towards him. Her curly blonde hair fluttered softly in the light breeze.

Valerius directed a questioning glance at Serpentius and the Spaniard shook his head with a frown. Serpentius dismounted and led his horse by the reins from one little group of fallen to the next, searching the faces for one he recognized, or turning over what looked like a familiar form.

Eventually, he stood surveying the field of dead. 'I don't understand it. There's no one from Avala among them.'

'We should check the houses,' Valerius said. 'If nothing else we might find a couple of shovels.'

'You'll bury them?'

'As many of them as we can before dark. They deserve at least that.'

Serpentius hid his surprise. Death was no stranger to them. They'd both left friends to rot in the past when necessity demanded it. Maybe they were getting old.

The puzzle of the lack of familiar faces was partially solved when they approached the settlement. Dark patches of ash and the charred remains of blackened branches showed where scores of fires had been kindled and lit.

'They must have come here for shelter when their own villages were attacked,' Serpentius guessed. 'But why would Tito not have taken them on to the sanctuary?'

'I suspect we'll find out in the morning.'

The light was fading and their muscles ached by the time they bedded down amongst the rocks overlooking Avala's northern flank with not a twentieth of the dead beneath the earth. One way or the other tomorrow would be a long day.

The first hint of dawn was showing as an orange-pink line that silhouetted the peaks on the eastern horizon when Serpentius shook Valerius by the shoulder. The Roman raised himself up and bit his lip to stifle a groan at the pain in his back and hips. A little manual labour and he was scarcely more than a cripple. He must be getting soft. Or old. Serpentius peered through a gap between two rocks at the village below.

'What is it?' Valerius whispered.

'Movement.' The Spaniard summoned him with a jerk of the head and moved to the side. Valerius slithered across to take his place. The ground below was covered by a layer of mist and it took him a few moments before he saw it. The sight sent a shiver through him. Disembodied torsos seeming to float on the haze. Had the dead risen? Don't be a fool. The dead are just the dead, you've killed enough people to know that. He looked to Serpentius.

'I don't know.' The Spaniard spoke so softly Valerius struggled to hear him. 'They came from behind us, in the direction of the sanctuary. Maybe the Parthian commander sent a cohort of infantry to slaughter our people, then told them to wait for our return?'

Valerius thought about it and shook his head. 'No. Harpocration might be a psychopath, but he's no fool. He'd have left half a squadron of horse in case we were able to make a run for it. There's nothing Harpocration would like better than to place our heads at Melanius's feet.'

A terrible scream rent the air and Serpentius leapt to his feet. This time Valerius didn't have the chance to stop him. All he could do was follow as the Spaniard sprang from rock to rock until he reached the fields leading down to the *castro*. No time to contemplate what lay ahead down there in the mist. The bright blades and the spurting blood and the blessed release of the last cut. More screams, but now Valerius recognized them for what they were. Not the scream of someone in pain, but the prolonged cries of unbearable grief. His legs almost gave way with relief. He'd been certain he was charging to his death. Great Jupiter hear my prayer. If I survive this I'll never stray from my hearth again.

By now the sun was over the horizon and the mist cleared to a few stray wisps. Across the fields below Avala hundreds of men and women stood or knelt over the bodies of the slaughtered families. Some plainly knew the dead and their cries were painful to hear, but most just mourned the violent passing of another human being.

A few people recognized him and he heard muttering among the men. Several turned to stare at him and their hands twitched over their daggers, held back only by the sword in his hand. He was a Roman and Romans had brought this upon their people. It would only take one a little braver than the rest and he'd be cut to pieces under a hail of scything blades.

'Gaius Valerius Verrens is a friend of the Zoelan people,' a harsh voice cut the silence. 'And he is under my protection. If any one of you wishes to dispute that I will be pleased to accommodate you. For me, there are enough Asturians who will be under the earth by tonight and we will need every able-bodied man to put them there.'

Serpentius stood with an arm around his son, the first time Valerius had seen him show physical affection to another male. Julia Octavia Fronton was a few paces behind Tito's shoulder, her face a pale ghostly white. Even as Valerius watched, she cried out and crumpled to the ground. Tito wrenched himself from his father and ran to her side.

The young warrior picked her up tenderly and carried her off to where some of the women were raising water from the village well. Nearby lay a number of badly wounded tribespeople who had somehow survived the Parthian attack.

'So they're all safe?' Valerius asked. 'The people of Avala?'

'Not all, but most.' Serpentius's face had a haunted look. 'I must organize the burials. Tito will tell you what happened.'

The Spaniard strode away, leaving Valerius trying to rationalize the pointless slaughter. Did the Parthians think they'd wiped out Serpentius's band, or was this part of some wider plan? He walked to where Tito watched as one woman bathed Julia's brow with a wet cloth while another placed a ladle to her lips. 'I will be all right in a moment,' the girl whispered. She tried to raise herself, but the elder of the women pushed her back.

'I will tell you when you can get up, girl. You may leave her with us, young Tito,' she said with a sly smile. 'This is no place for a man.'

Tito's cheeks turned red and he noticed Valerius for the first time. 'She fainted.' The unnecessary explanation was coupled with a look of baffled innocence that made the bearded warrior appear for a moment like a ten-year-old child. 'So many dead, and killed by her own people – it overcame her.'

'Not her own people,' Valerius said. 'A band of Parthian mercenaries in the pay of a gang of Roman crooks. Your father said you would tell me what happened.'

'Yes.' Tito looked back to where Julia lay. 'Of course. Our scouts reported two hook-nose columns approaching the *castro* from different directions. We were close to being overwhelmed by families fleeing from the other villages and we were too few to face the Parthians. It made sense to retreat to the sanctuary before they were too close.' His face darkened. 'I'd been told that the last of the refugees had come in, but these people must have arrived just as night fell. They had no way of knowing the route to the sanctuary and they must have been exhausted. The hook-noses would have seen their fires and waited to strike at dawn.' He shook his head. 'I should have left a man here to guide them to the caves.'

'Better that you did not,' Valerius assured him. 'All he would have done is lead the Parthians to the sanctuary and you would all be dead by now. What I don't

323

understand is why they killed everyone when your father tells me they are desperate for labour for the mines?'

Tito's dark eyes drifted to where Serpentius was mustering the men into teams to gather the dead and dig pits to bury them. 'Come with me.' He led Valerius back to where they'd left Julia, but they bypassed the girl and instead approached one of the bandaged survivors. He lay on his back staring at the sky and Valerius felt the bile rise in his throat as he noticed the tribesman had no hands.

'They let him live,' Tito explained. 'But they left him like this. The hook-nose commander, the prefect Harpocration, first gave him a message to be passed on to the people of these hills, then made him repeat it. When he was satisfied, he ordered his men to hold out first one arm, then the other, over a wooden barrel, and chopped his hands off.' His eyes drifted to Valerius's wooden fist, but his expression didn't alter and Valerius saw that he was like his father in more than just looks.

'What was the message?' Valerius asked, though he knew he wouldn't like the answer.

'Cadriolo,' Tito bent over the injured man, 'tell the lord what the hook-nose devil told you to say.'

At first Cadriolo didn't seem to hear, but gradually his eyes focused on Valerius. 'He was like a wild beast.' His voice was a hoarse, pain-racked whisper. 'First he killed my wife. Then my children. Why did he not kill me?'

'The message, Cadriolo,' Tito insisted. 'Tell us the message.'

Cadriolo raised himself on his elbows, his neck muscles bulging with the enormous effort. Pink appeared on the bandages over his stumps and quickly turned red. 'Tell them that the Ghost brought this upon them, but . . .' his voice wavered and almost died, 'but they should know they can stop it by delivering his head to the Prefect Harpocration of the First ala Parthorum at Legio.' With his final words the injured man fell back and resumed staring at the sky.

'And that was all?' Valerius asked him. 'That was everything he said?'

'If it is not,' Tito turned away, 'he will never tell us now.'

XXXVII

The Asturians buried their dead in four large pits, but
Valerius was busy elsewhere as they wept over the innocents slaughtered by Claudius Harpocration and his
Parthians. As Serpentius had predicted, Tito was able
to supply stylus, ink and the finest lambskin parchment stolen from Lucius Octavius Fronton's library. The
Roman shut himself in a burned-out house that had
been cleared for the purpose and for three hours
laboured to distil all he'd discovered into a report that
would galvanize Gaius Plinius Secundus to act immediately against the conspiracy.

When he was satisfied with what he'd written, Valerius
tied up the scroll with a strip of leather and emerged into
the sunshine. Tito and Serpentius stood beside the edge
of the last pit as a priest said the rites over the dead.

Valerius had a feeling some of the villagers were
unhappy with the brevity of the ceremony. Tito
explained that the warriors would normally be taken up
the mountain to special burial platforms.

'In our religion it is the tradition that the flesh of the
bravest is devoured by carrion birds who repay us by
carrying their souls to heaven,' he said. 'The bodies of

these people,' he pointed to the grave, 'should be burned and their ashes scattered on the fields. We have no time to make the journey to the high peaks or collect wood to cremate so many dead. Our first priority must be to repair the *castro* and ensure the living have shelter and to replant the fields swiftly so there is food enough for the winter.'

Valerius watched until the pit was filled in, the dirt covering the pale, dead faces. 'I need your most reliable man to carry this to Legio.' He handed the scroll to Serpentius. 'He should go to the tavern by the bridge and ask for Marius. If Marius isn't there he must wait, but without attracting attention.'

'Caeleo can take it,' Tito said to his father. 'He's sold skins at the market in Legio often enough to know his way about the place. If anyone recognizes him he's just another familiar face.'

He called to a small wizened man dressed in a scuffed leather jerkin and striped trews and explained his mission.

Caeleo grinned, showing three blackened teeth. 'A child could do this,' he said gleefully. 'I have a batch of pelts that are ready to go. I might even make a profit.'

'Just make sure the scroll is delivered,' Serpentius warned him. 'You will be well rewarded. But you must stay clear of the hook-noses.'

'Of course,' Caeleo nodded. 'And that bastard tax collector at the fort.'

The goat hunter disappeared and returned a few minutes later with a mule that must have been secreted in some nearby cavern or hidden gully. Valerius handed him a few coins that would make a prolonged stay in the tavern less onerous. They watched as he led the mule up the eastern track from Avala with the scroll hidden in one of the panniers strapped to the animal's back.

'Well, that's it.' Valerius and Serpentius exchanged a glance. 'There's nothing else we can do until we get word from Nepos.'

Serpentius was about to reassure his friend there were fields to dig, crops to plant and houses to clear, but Tito's voice cut him short. 'There may be.'

They turned and saw the diminutive figure of Julia at his side. She stood straight and as tall as she could make herself, with a look of unshakable resolution on her fine features.

'Tito made it clear to me.' She took the bearded Zoelan's hand and he squeezed her fingers. 'They were my people.' She allowed her eyes to slip over the freshly turned earth of the grave pits. 'Roman auxiliaries may have wielded the swords that killed them, but my father and his friends were the cause. If I can do anything to stop it happening again I cannot shirk that duty, for the honour of my family. This is about the gold? The papers he keeps in the strongbox in the storeroom?'

'We believe so.' Valerius's heart quickened. Could this be the moment of Fortuna's favour they had been hoping for? But the feeling quickly passed. In all honour he couldn't send this child where he couldn't go himself. 'But you cannot be responsible for your father's deeds.'

'Perhaps not.' She met his gaze. 'But I have another reason. If they are discovered, his life will be at risk.'

'Either his so-called friends will kill him,' Valerius admitted, 'for we know they regard him as a liability. Or he will find himself kneeling under the executioner's blade when it ends, as it must. They cannot succeed, Julia.'

'Then it is my duty as his daughter to try to save him,' she said purposefully. 'If I succeed in persuading him to give me the documents will you promise to speak for him when the time comes?'

'I give you my word,' Valerius said. 'But you must know he is unlikely to escape punishment entirely. The best he can hope for is exile somewhere on the edge of the Empire.'

She exchanged a glance with Tito and he nodded. 'Then so be it.' She swayed and a visible shudder ran through her, a sign of what this was costing her. Valerius felt a swell of admiration at the enormous fount of courage that existed in that slim form. 'We should go now?' The question was directed at Tito.

Serpentius opened his mouth to deny them his permission, but shut it again like a bear trap. Nothing he could say would make any difference. Julia wouldn't change her mind and Tito was just as capable as his father in this country. He knew the hidden valleys and barely passable heights that would keep him out of reach of Harpocration's patrols.

Valerius reached out to lay his left hand on Tito's arm. 'Look after her.'

'Of course.' The young man nodded and walked away to arrange the horses and an escort.

'I have only met your father once,' Valerius said to the girl. 'But my advice would be not to push him too hard. He is under great pressure and if he feels trapped he may react in a way you don't anticipate. If he refuses, be prepared to walk away.' He hesitated, but it had to be said. 'It is possible that you could be going into danger.'

'My father would never harm me.' She said it with force, but he had a feeling she wasn't so certain.

'I'm sure you're right,' he said gravely. 'But you will think on my words?'

She gave an apologetic nod and turned to her horse.

Like many women aristocrats Julia was perfectly at home in the saddle, though she rode aside, with one leg hooked over the pommel beneath her skirts. Tito helped her into her seat.

Valerius returned to Serpentius's side and they watched the little group of riders pick their way up the hill as they headed south. The Spaniard's lined features looked set in stone.

'It's never easy to watch others ride out to do a task you think you should be doing yourself,' Valerius consoled his friend.

'For twenty years and more I thought I was alone.' Serpentius struggled to control his emotions. 'If my dead wife and child appeared in my dreams I drove them away. I allowed myself to care for no one and nothing. In the arena, I stayed alive to spite the people who placed me there. When you took me from it and gave me hope of freedom I had to choose between life and death. I was forced to remember that I once had a reason for living. I chose life, but hardened my heart against compassion and friendship. Only when our lives became intertwined and the fates brought death so close I could feel the scent of it, did I understand that, even if friendship with a Roman was not possible, perhaps comradeship was. When comradeship develops into brotherhood a man would have to be a fool to refuse it.' He turned and looked directly into Valerius's eyes. 'Yet you are not my son, Valerius. A son is the mirror in which you can see all your triumphs and mistakes. A son is your despair and your hope. A son is everything you wished you could be and an accusation of all you are not. And that son, Valerius, is such a son as any man would pray for. For twenty years I did not know he existed. He was nothing to me. Now I do not know what I would do if anything were to happen to him. Even seeing him ride away is tearing my heart out. To think that he would never return—'

'He will return, Serpentius.' Valerius looked up to where the little group was disappearing over the horizon. 'Tito is as capable as you,' his face split into a grin, 'maybe more capable. It will take more than Claudius Harpocration's hook-noses to bring him low. And he too has something to protect.'

A snort of laughter burst from Serpentius; he wrapped an arm that felt like an iron ring around Valerius's neck. 'You think me old and spent, Roman. Well, we will see about that. There are fields to dig and wood to hew. Anything to take a man's mind off the waiting. By the time we're finished we will see who is old and spent, eh?'

XXXVIII

Tito and his band approached Fronton's estate from an entirely different direction than the night they'd carried out the raid on the villa. Fronton would undoubtedly have discovered where they'd left the horses and his guards would take particular notice. This time a great circular loop brought the Zoelans to an almost imperceptible track that led through the hills from the west. The approach also had the advantage of being covered by a low hogback hill that would give them a vantage point to check out the villa before Tito decided whether Julia could go ahead.

Not, she'd made him aware, that he was likely to have much say in the matter.

During her time in Avala they'd been together often, but neither had shown the inclination for deep conversation. It was as if, Tito thought, they had been gauging the effect of close proximity before taking the next step. They had begun at a discreet distance but the gap gradually closed until they could smell each other's scent. At this point Tito found himself, almost without his own volition, taking a daily visit to the stream that irrigated the settlement's fields. Julia gave no outward sign of approval, but he took the fact that her nostrils no longer twitched at his presence as progress of a sort.

They talked, but not about important things. After the first days she'd come to regard her captivity as an adventure to be savoured rather than an ordeal to be endured. She'd been frightened of his father, of course, who would not be, but from the first she'd sensed something in him – Tito – that made her feel safe. From the first time he'd seen her he'd felt a protective instinct. He would have killed anyone who'd touched her. Even his father? The question had been accompanied by an impish sideways look. His father would never harm anyone innocent or helpless. He hadn't been sure that was true, but he was certain Serpentius would never harm Julia.

The only serious exchange occurred after the massacre when Julia had recovered from her faint. She'd been devastated by what had been done to people who, whatever their circumstances, came from the same lineage as her own.

'What did they do to deserve such a fate?' she'd asked.

With anyone else he'd have been angry. What did she mean by 'deserve'? What could someone do that would justify being hounded from their homes and slaughtered? That was when he'd told her about the gold and her father's part in the plot to steal it. How Claudius Harpocration and his Parthian butchers carried out the bidding of the men involved. At first she'd refused to believe him, but gradually realization replaced disbelief – she'd experienced her father's changing moods and odd absences – and was followed, in that mercurial way she had, by resolve. He must be saved if that were possible, but even if he could not be saved this must stop. Would he help her?

The long ride to her father's estate had provided a different opportunity. As the hours passed and the endless miles flowed by, her thoughts had moved on from what was to come in the hours ahead, to what might become of *them*. It had taken him a number of miles to understand what was happening, but gradually he became aware of what she was saying to him.

They led different lives, yes, but that should not matter to what might happen in the future. She talked of her life, and his, and of Rome, the unifier. He bridled: Rome was no unifier, Rome was the enemy.

'Yes,' she agreed. 'That is the way it has been in the past, but you have to understand, Tito, that Asturica Augusta is not Rome. This is not the way it has to be. My father might be little more than a country gentleman, but he has entertained some of the most important men in the Empire – senators and governors – and I listened to what they had to say. The Empire offers possibilities, it offers opportunity, it offers stability. It is not in the Empire's interest to have this constant enmity and conflict. Of one being the aggressor and one the subdued. I have travelled to Gaul, where the Gauls live their own lives and cling to their old ways and their old gods, and are allowed to do so within reason. Yes, they pay taxes to Rome and their lives are bound by a legal system created by Rome, but Gauls sit in the Senate beside Romans born on the seven hills. They have the power to change the laws they live by. Hispania Tarraconensis could be like that, but not if Melanius and Severus have their way.'

She drew in her horse and stared at him. 'If we can stop them, Tito, the people of this land will have an opportunity to petition Rome for change, but it cannot just be left to the *ordo* of Asturica Augusta. It must be an alliance of *all* Asturians, the people of the hills and the plains, as well as the people of the cities. That means brave men must be prepared to come forward to represent their people. Men like you.'

Tito felt the blood rush to his face at the mix of emotions she ignited within him. Was this what she really thought of him? Some kind of hero? He wanted to be the man she noticed, but he knew he was not. She'd seen the way the others deferred to him and thought he was a leader, like his father. But he was only a leader because he could knock the others down with fighting sticks when they were practising spear craft. Because he could climb faster and jump further than any man in Avala.

'I would not know what to say,' he kept his tone light. 'I have never travelled further than Asturica or Legio. It is my father you should try to persuade, a man who has known emperors and generals and spoken to them as an equal.' She grimaced at him and turned away and he sought to ease her disappointment. 'Only a few days ago his friend, the Roman Valerius, told him of changes the governor in Tarraco had spoken of. Something called *civitas* that would be extended beyond the cities.'

Julia brightened. 'Don't you see, Tito, *civitas* means Roman citizenship for the people of Hispania. Citizenship opens the door to the opportunities I spoke of. Those with the resources, the access and the ability will be able to rise under Rome, and with their rise will come the power to change and improve the lives of those around them. It does not have to be the way it is.'

'I will think on it,' he said, and they rode on in silence.

They reached the top of the rise with an hour of daylight left. The villa complex lay at the centre of a huge bowl laid out before them, ringed with orchards and olive groves strung with grape vines. Below them a track hugged the bottom of the hill before curving away through the fields to the villa. Julia had already decided she would wait till dusk to make her approach. Her arrival at that hour would give her the rest of the evening to persuade her father. If she succeeded, she would slip out in the morning and bring the documents to Tito. It would not be easy to persuade her father that cooperation was in his best interests, but she was sure that given time she could convince him. There must be no interruptions, she insisted, so Tito agreed to stay with the others and wait for her signal.

She remounted as the sun began to set and he watched her ride down the hill towards the villa with a feeling of loss.

Her arrival provoked a flurry of activity. Someone ran from the gatehouse to the main entrance of the villa and Tito saw a little knot of people emerge. He had a sense of great agitation before they disappeared back into the villa and a groom led the grey away in the direction of the stables.

He sat back, but with no sense of relief, and his eyes never left the villa. Soon would come the moment of greatest danger. Julia loved her father with a daughter's sense of fidelity, but he'd gained no sense of that love being returned. Her mother had died four years earlier and since the age of thirteen Julia had acted as her father's housekeeper and hostess. She blamed her mother's death and a series of poor harvests for Fronton allowing himself to be enticed into becoming part of Melanius's conspiracy. There had been dinner parties attended by Melanius, Severus and Ferox, the *praefectus metallorum*, whom she described as 'repulsive'. 'He looked at me as if I was a piece of meat,' she said. They drank far more than in her mother's time and she'd had to be quick on her feet to avoid the prefect's clutching hands. Her father had only laughed. How would he react to this appeal to ally himself with their enemies, from a daughter he appeared to regard with little more affection than a valued house servant?

As the stars made their appearance and the night sky turned from dark blue to inky black, he made his decision. He slithered back to where Placido sat in the darkness holding the horses.

'Stay here with the others,' he ordered. 'I'm going down to keep a watch on the villa.'

'You said you'd wait for her.' Tito detected disapproval in his tone.

'She thinks he'll hear her out and that's it.' Tito tried to justify his decision. 'He'll either agree and hand over the scrolls, or not, in which case he'll let her return to us. Have you ever heard of this kind of thing having such a simple outcome?'

White teeth showed in the darkness. 'No. That's why I ended up down the mine.'

'Give me one of the torches.' A shadowy figure loomed out of the darkness and Tito took the torch, a short length of branch with a bundle of wool wrapped in rags and covered with pitch.

'If there's trouble I'll wave this twice. When you see the signal bring my horse down to that clump of bushes at the bottom of the hill.'

'The girl?'

'If it comes to it he'll have to carry us both.'

'Let us hope it doesn't come to that.'

Placido waited for an answer, but Tito was already gone, in total silence and at disquieting speed.

XXXIX

Julia emerged dripping from the bath with the help of her personal servant and lay face down on a marble table while the girl oiled and massaged her skin. She was glad her father insisted she bathe after the uproar of her return. She'd been overwhelmed by the tearful welcome from the servants, and his veiled hints about any ill treatment she might have suffered. The bath gave her time to think.

The slave girl's hands were smooth and expert as they kneaded the muscles of her back. Julia felt a tingle in her lower stomach as she wondered how Tito's strong, callused spearman's hands would feel on her skin. Eventually she could take no more and asked the girl to remove the oil.

As the curved blade flowed across her body she mustered the courage to make the approach that had seemed so simple when she was with Tito at Avala. Perhaps it was because courage seemed to come so easily to Tito and his father that she'd felt driven to make the offer, but it seemed much more daunting now she was here. She tried to summon up Tito's face, but the only image that appeared in her mind was her father's gaunt

338

features. He seemed to have aged ten years in the past six months and he appeared more nervous than relieved at her return. And she was about to make it worse.

No.

The thought came without prompting. She was not going to make it worse, she was going to save his life. If he continued to be swayed by these people he would either be executed by the Emperor or killed by his fellow conspirators. She had an opportunity to alter his fate and she would be failing in her duty as a daughter if she did not take it. Now Tito appeared to her, the hawkish, bearded features emanating confidence and competence. A man capable of accomplishing anything. The fierce beauty that shone from him had overwhelmed her from the moment he'd first looked into her eyes. The raid and the sack of her father's house had all seemed like a dream involving someone else. He was a man like no other she'd met before.

'Mistress?'

The servant girl had finished with the strigil and Julia stood to be wrapped in a sheet and dried. When she'd dressed, the girl escorted her to the *triclinium*. She took her place on a couch opposite her father, but Fronton barely registered her presence. The dishes came and went but neither did more than barely touch the food. She hadn't realized how thin he'd become. His wrists below the folds of his toga were just bony projections and his neck looked barely strong enough to hold his domed head upright. Whereas she drank sparingly of well-watered wine, the slaves were kept busy filling the cup in front of Lucius Octavius Fronton.

The fear came in waves and her hands shook as she picked at her food, but she steeled herself to act. She made to speak, but he rebuffed her attempt at conversation with a raised hand. In the Fronton household meals had always been for eating, not talk, but when the last of the food had been cleared away, he dismissed the slaves and at last gave her his attention.

'It must have been a terrible ordeal for you, daughter,' he said with what passed for a smile. 'I am glad to see you well, but frankly astonished these creatures allowed you to escape.'

'I must have expressed myself badly earlier, Father.' Julia kept her eyes on the table. 'I did not escape. They allowed me to go free.'

She sensed his surprise – perhaps the better word was unease – at this unlikely behaviour. 'Did they say why?'

It was the moment she'd been bracing herself for, but it had come more quickly in the conversation than she'd expected. The words seemed to stick in her throat.

'They . . . They wished me to . . . They know about the gold, Father,' she blurted out. 'They know what you have been doing. But I can save you.'

'Save me, daughter?' The blood had drained from his face, but the death's-head smile remained in place. 'Why would I require to be saved? And what is this gold you refer to? I fear your captivity has made you delirious. Perhaps you should go and lie down.'

This last was expressed as an order and she rose automatically to obey, hesitated and retook her place. 'No, Father,' she shook her head. 'You must listen. They took me because of what you have been doing. A man came to the village where I was being held, a Roman. The man with the wooden hand at Severus's banquet.' The description made her father flinch as if he'd been struck, but she couldn't stop now. 'He told me of a great conspiracy to steal the Emperor's gold. It involves a man called Melanius, Severus, that revolting Ferox . . . and

340

you, Father. He said to tell you that you will either face execution for your crimes or your fellow conspirators will kill you because they regard you as a weakness.' Fronton stood up as if he was having a seizure and Julia feared he would strike her, but the words kept tumbling from her mouth. 'He says it is finished and that word of the conspiracy will soon reach the Emperor.' Tears flowed unchecked over her cheeks. 'The only way to save yourself is to cooperate with them. Please, Father, you must hand over the papers you have. He promised he will speak for you.'

'And you believe all this of me?'

At first she was mute, but a great anger welled up inside her that he should think her so witless.

'Where did all this come from?' She swept a hand to encompass the fine statues from Greece, the Egyptian vases, and the silken wall hangings brought from the Indus. 'And the stable of thoroughbred horses and the grand house in Asturica? Before Mother died she spoke of selling the slaves and laying off the servants because we could barely feed ourselves after three poor harvests in a row. Four years later we are rich. Where did the money come from? Not from selling loaves of *panis rustica* to the mines, or hiring out wagons. You must believe me, Father,' she pleaded. 'It is not too late to save yourself. I have seen how ruthless these men can be. The Parthians who guard our wagons came to the village where I was kept. They butchered people by the hundreds. Men, women and children, they made no distinction.'

'Bandits,' her father dismissed, but the word held no force.

'Not bandits. Asturian peasants who had done no one any harm. People like your father's father.' She

341

stepped round the table and took his hand. It shook like a frightened animal and suddenly she felt more like a mother than a daughter. 'Tell me you will do it, Father. Take the key and open the strongbox. Give me the papers and I will carry them to the one-handed man.'

'You don't understand—' Whatever he was going to say trailed off in a soft outpouring of breath and he freed his hand and turned away. 'I must think on this. I admit nothing. You defame me without proof. Perhaps I have made mistakes, but . . . Please leave me now. Go to your room and we'll speak again in the morning.'

Julia reluctantly did as he asked and as she left she heard her father calling for his *atriensis*. She hesitated at the doorway of her room and saw the man emerge with a look of profound consternation on his face. What had occurred to make him look so worried? Her mind reeled with doubt and hope. Had she done enough? He had not outrightly denied the accusations.

She'd feared he might throw her out of the house or even attack her, but neither had happened. Yes, she was certain she'd done enough. He was delaying a final decision, but he would do as she suggested. Her head continued to spin, but her body was so exhausted by a long day in the saddle she sank into a deep sleep almost without knowing it. She dreamed of a warm day and a wood fire, but it wasn't until she opened her eyes that she understood what was happening.

Tito was drowsing beneath an olive tree that provided a view of the house when he heard the shrill scream. His eyes snapped open and he was up and running even before his mind registered that it had come from Julia. He was surrounded by vines and as he tore them aside he noticed a soft orange glow above the villa roof.

The gatekeepers had been drawn to the house and the way lay open. Slaves and servants stumbled from their quarters to gather bleary-eyed and still half stunned outside the main entrance. As he ran, Tito saw a figure approach the door and push it open only to dance back immediately as a ball of flame threatened to consume him. Without breaking stride he swerved to the right down the flank of the northern wing of the building, automatically checking each window he passed for the tell-tale glow. At last, one that seemed to be untouched for now.

Tito clawed at the shutters with his fingers, but couldn't get them to budge. Fortunately, a stone rail framed the window and he was able to leap up and grasp it with both hands. He hung suspended for a moment before smashing his feet at the join between the panels. The shutters burst apart with a crack and his momentum took him through to land on his back on the stone floor with an impact that knocked the breath from him. He was in a guest room with a low bed in one corner. It had escaped the flames for now, but enough smoke seeped beneath the curtained doorway to make him cough.

Tito pushed himself to his feet and drew back the curtain leading to the atrium. Choking fumes filled the room, but he found he could breathe if he bent double. To his left the fire ate at the wooden panelling of the main entrance and blackened the roof beams above. To the right the glow of flames shone through the smoke that filled Fronton's *tablinum*. Two separate fires: the words leapt into his mind. Someone had deliberately set two fires, or this room would be burning too.

He took a deep breath and ran to the doorway on the right. Cloth wall hangings and wooden furniture blazed, but the centre was clear. Small pools of liquid flickered with yellow-blue flame and he guessed that someone – Fronton, or one of his co-conspirators bent on his destruction? – had scattered oil around the house before setting it alight. The main source of the flames was another side room and he felt a thrill of fear when he realized it was the storeroom where they had discovered Fronton's strongbox.

'Julia,' he called. 'Where are you?'

The only answer was a choking cough barely audible above the crackle and roar of the fire. Tito fought his way to the storeroom and recoiled at a sudden blast of heat. In the balefire of the flames a shadowy figure stabbed with a long pole in a futile attempt at recovering the burning contents of the strongbox.

'Julia.' He ran to her and attempted to drag her away. 'We have to get out before the whole house goes up.' Her thin cotton shift was holed in a dozen places where sparks had eaten the cloth. She stared at him with red-rimmed eyes and she reeked of the acrid stench of singed hair. He pulled her close, but she fought him with surprising strength.

'My father,' she cried. 'We must help him.'

Tito released her and struggled through the smoke to where she'd pointed. Lucius Octavius Fronton lay on his side at the centre of a spreading pool that shone black in the light of the flames, a dagger clutched in his right hand. A gaping hole in his throat told Tito he was beyond help. He ran back to Julia and took her in his arms. 'There is no hope for him.' He saw the moment the shock hit. Her eyes turned up in her head and Tito caught her as she collapsed.

Fire on every hand, but a breathing space of sorts when he reached the atrium. He searched for the room where he'd entered the building and his heart stuttered at the glow of flames. Yet there was still a chance. He laid Julia on the tiles and picked up a small table. Shielding his face with his free hand he used the table legs to hack down the flaming curtain. A surge of elation shot through him when he saw what he'd hoped: the interior was still untouched and the smashed window shutters clear of the fire.

He returned to Julia and carried her to the window. With difficulty he manhandled her until he had the inert body balanced on the sill. He managed to hold her there until he had lowered himself to the ground, then allowed her to slip down into his arms. Gulping in great lungfuls of fresh air he carried her away from the house unnoticed by the guards, servants and slaves who were fighting a losing battle against the fire.

Julia regained consciousness after he'd staggered a few yards up the track, where Placido was waiting with two spare horses. 'I decided not to wait for your signal when I saw that,' Placido nodded at the inferno they'd left. It was only when Tito pushed her into the saddle that Julia found the presence of mind to turn back and gaze upon the blazing ruin of the villa she had called home. Where Lucius Octavius Fronton's corpse helped feed the flames and the evidence Gaius Valerius Verrens had depended on was nothing but flakes of glowing ash mingling with the giant pillar of smoke.

XL

A shout from one of the lookouts alerted Valerius to the horse picking its way down the rocky slope towards Avala in the soft vermilion light of the new dawn. The animal carried a slumped figure bent forward in the saddle as if the rider was injured or barely conscious. Valerius threw aside the bowl of honeyed oats he'd been eating and ran towards the horse. Before he was half-way he heard a shout and slowed as Serpentius appeared at his side, a sword in his hand.

The Spaniard's wary eyes scanned the horizon. 'Didn't it occur to you it might be a trap, idiot? All it would take was half a dozen Parthians up there waiting until you'd got far enough away from the village and they'd have run you down like a fox taking a rabbit.'

'I was relying on you to cover my back.' Valerius sucked in a breath.

'You'll do that once too often.'

'What do you think?' They slowed as they approached the horse which walked head down and its flanks were lathered with sweat.

'I think that's the beast Allius took to Asturica.'

Their noisy approach provoked no response from the

cloaked and hooded rider. Serpentius reached out to touch his shoulder.

'What!' A hand swooped for the dagger at the rider's belt and he cried in agony as Serpentius's bony fingers closed on his wrist. The hood fell back to reveal a pair of narrow, angry eyes and a long twitching nose. 'Nabia's withered tits, don't you know better than to startle a man when he's having a think?'

'Think?' Serpentius snorted. 'It looked to me as if you were dreaming you were under the blanket with some strumpet. If the hook-noses had caught you they'd have laughed themselves sick before they cut your throat, but at least you'd have died smiling.'

'I only closed my eyes when I saw I was home,' Allius said defensively. He reached under his cloak and brought out a scrap of papyrus. 'This was under the brick when I looked last night. Be grateful that I've been in the saddle ever since. I had to take to the hills to avoid the hook-nose patrols. The bastards are everywhere.'

Serpentius studied the parchment and Valerius could swear his tanned features turned pale. With a shake of his head the Spaniard handed the message to Valerius, and turned to lead Allius's mount down the hill.

'Nepos has the documents and he wants a meeting in two nights' time.' Valerius couldn't keep the excitement from his voice as he trotted to catch the Spaniard.

'Yes.' Serpentius's voice was unexpectedly grave. 'But have you seen *where* he wants to meet?'

Valerius read on and a chill seized his heart. 'In the deepest level of the Red Hills IV mine. He says he'll arrange it so all the guards will have been withdrawn by the time we get there. Do you know it?'

'It's the furthest south they've excavated so far. One

way in and one way out, with half of Hispania waiting to fall on your head.'

Valerius remembered the haunted look in Serpentius's eyes as he'd recounted the horrors he'd suffered in the bowels of the earth after he'd been condemned. The Spaniard had vowed never to go underground again. It made the decision easier.

'It only takes one to pick up the papers from Nepos. If you can get me to the mine I'll go in alone.'

'No.' The Spaniard's voice took on new determination. 'Anything could be waiting down there. You said yourself you need someone to cover your back.'

'My trusty right hand.' Valerius shot him a wry smile, relieved, but not surprised. 'You think this may be a trap?'

'Does it make any difference if it is?' Serpentius shrugged. 'We don't have any choice if we want those papers and that's why you're here. Why Petronius was here. That's another reason why I'll go with you. I owe him a debt.' He looked thoughtful. 'In a way it makes sense for Nepos to choose a mine. You told him to pick somewhere he felt safe. He knows those tunnels the way you know every olive grove on your estate. Even the simplest mine is like the labyrinth that fellow Theseus got himself lost in before he killed his bull. Maybe Nepos has planned in extra galleries and shafts only he and the miners know about? If anything goes wrong he could just disappear and find his way back to the entrance while we're stumbling around in the dark.'

'You make it sound like my worst nightmare.'

The Spaniard studied him seriously. 'If things go wrong down there it'll make that night fight outside Cremona seem like a cosy Saturnalia feast, but if we want to make the meeting we should leave now.'

They took time over their preparations. 'You'll need a thick cloak because it can be cold in the mines at night,' Serpentius warned, 'especially when you're down in the deepest sections. It'll keep the rats off, too. Make sure you don't get bitten. They survive on rotting food and dying men's shit and their bite is as fatal as a cobra's.' Torches, spare flints and iron, food enough for three days and swords concealed in the packs rolled behind their saddles. They would travel as master and servant as they'd done so often before, but they had to accept their identities would have been circulated. Valerius would wear his cloak at all times to conceal his distinctive wooden fist.

They used what was left of the day to make their way out of the mountains along the vertiginous hidden tracks Serpentius knew so well. The Spaniard stayed on the alert for Parthian patrols, but they saw few signs of the auxiliary cavalry Allius said caused him so much trouble. When dusk fell they set up camp overlooking the road that connected Asturica Augusta to the Red Hills mines. Two hours later they were back in the saddle and heading west.

'I know a sheltered gully where we can rest up for the day,' Serpentius told Valerius as they rode through the darkness. 'It's about an hour from the mine. We'll time our arrival for just before dusk. That should allow us to find a place to take a look at the entrance without being seen.'

Valerius heard unease in his voice that matched his own. 'The closer we get, the less I like this. It would have been much easier to set up a meeting closer to Asturica.'

'Not for Nepos, if he is working at the Red Hills mine,' Serpentius pointed out. 'The one thing that puzzles me is how he'll get rid of the guards – the mine where I was held was guarded day and night – and what we're supposed to do if he can't do what he claims.'

Valerius tried to recall the details of his visit to the mine with the rotund engineer. 'They withdraw the tunnellers when the mine is ready for the final stage. If Nepos delays announcing the completion until too late in the day to carry out the flooding, he can justify pulling everyone out overnight.'

'Did it occur to you that all this might be unnecessary if Julia Fronton can persuade her father to betray his friends?'

'Yes,' Valerius said. 'I'd thought of that. But we can't take the chance.'

They crept into position as the light began to fade, leaving their horses in a dried-up river bed concealed by trees. The location, in a tumble of grey rocks, gave them an uninterrupted view down to the mouth of the tunnel. Away to their left lay a huddle of wooden barracks which housed the miners and the guards, but they saw no activity in the area of the mine itself.

'It looks as if Nepos is as good as his word,' Valerius said.

'Do you think he's in there already?'

'I doubt it. He'll have supervised the evacuation and followed his workers to the temporary camp. Probably made arrangements for tomorrow. Everything is in place for the final stage of the *ruina montium*. More likely he'll wait until it's full dark.' Valerius looked to where the crescent moon hung in a sky that had faded from blue to the silver-grey of new ashes. 'We'll give him an hour.'

By the time they set off the sky was black as pitch, but the moon's dull glow allowed Serpentius to follow the route he had marked earlier. Valerius dogged his foot-steps a few paces behind, his eyes scanning the gloom around them and his left hand on the hilt of his sword. They hadn't discussed the possibility of a trap since leaving Avala, but it was never far from his mind. He knew he could rely on Serpentius to provide the vital seconds he needed to be able to react, but experience and speed would count for nothing against overwhelming numbers. The simple truth was that if Nepos had betrayed them they were walking to their deaths. Nothing would change that, but Valerius vowed that he wouldn't be taken alive. If he crossed the Styx tonight he would not be alone.

They reached the mine entrance without incident, negotiating piles of rocky spoil, and timbers that had been stockpiled to be carried away to the next project. Valerius hesitated in front of the stygian void, but Serpentius drew a great breath and plunged inside. What else could Valerius do but follow him? Inside, they lit one of the torches and their eyes met in the flickering light. Valerius saw rivulets of sweat running down Serpentius's face and the Spaniard's gaze held a hint of something close to panic.

'I'll lead,' Valerius said.

'Just this time,' Serpentius said with a sickly smile. 'I'll cover your back.'

Valerius slipped past and started off down the slope with the torch held out in front of him.

Unseen, outside the mine entrance another torch burst into life with a sudden flare of light.

On the hillside above, a stout figure felt an answering glow of satisfaction as he watched the torch make two short arcs. 'Both of them.' Marcus Atilius Melanius smiled. 'So it worked. You were right, Ferox,' he said to a cloaked shadow nearby. 'I was certain Verrens would smell a trap and stay away. But he was too greedy. This time we'll be rid of them for good. Open the sluice.'

'Wait,' Ferox ordered the men around him in the darkness. 'Give them time to reach the deepest level. Less chance of them being identified if they are down there when the mine goes.'

'Very well. You know best.'

Ferox waited for the count of five hundred before he gave the order.

'Now.'

The winding mechanism creaked and soon they could hear water pouring from the gates into the sluice that would carry it with twice the speed of a racing chariot directly into the mouth of the mine.

Where Gaius Valerius Verrens and Serpentius of Avala waited, unaware of the fate Melanius had planned for them.

XLI

They made their way down the long passage, deeper and deeper into the hill. Without the men working the bellows the air was thick enough to cut with a sword and before they'd gone far they struggled to breathe. Valerius turned to Serpentius. 'Nepos must have lost his mind to bring us here,' he gasped.

The Spaniard shook his head. 'Think on it from his point of view, Valerius. This is his world. He is like a mole, more suited to life burrowing beneath the earth than above it. Safer down here than at any house in Asturica.'

Down another level and into a gallery that must have been recently worked judging by the stench of fresh excrement.

'It can't be far,' Valerius muttered. 'We must be almost through to the far side of the hill.' They reached a vertical shaft and Serpentius held the torch as Valerius climbed one-handed down the rickety ladder into the pit of darkness that was the lowest level of the mine. When Valerius reached the bottom the Spaniard threw the torch down to him and made the descent himself.

The one-handed Roman advanced down the tunnel at the centre of a circle of flickering light. Oddly, the air quality had improved and Serpentius pointed to a dark circle in the roof of the tunnel. 'Air shaft, thank the gods. Strange to think we've travelled what seems like a mile underground, but we can't be more than thirty feet from the surface. Not that it makes much difference.'

'Hostilius,' Valerius called softly. 'Show yourself. Light a torch so we know where to find you.'

The only reply was the sound of his own voice echoing in the side chambers that had been dug to honeycomb the surrounding rock.

'He's frightened. Call again, but louder this time.'

Valerius did as Serpentius suggested. Still no reply.

'Maybe he's fallen asleep.'

'Down here? Did you hear that?'

Valerius froze and stood listening. 'What?'

'I heard a scratching sound.'

'I can't hear anything.'

'Listen!'

A sort of fevered scrabbling, accompanied by a low squeal.

'Hostilius?' Valerius shouted again.

'Rats,' Serpentius corrected him. 'From the chamber ahead and to your left.'

The Spaniard sounded weary and resigned, and a shudder of dread ran through Valerius.

They advanced warily, not because they expected an ambush, but because of the implications of what they were about to see. Neither had any doubt of the outcome. Yet it had to be checked, Nepos deserved that. There was always the possibility, however unlikely, that he might have fainted for lack of breath, or had some sort of seizure. The incriminating evidence might be on his person. So many mights, but of course the reality was different.

First, they'd stripped Hostilius Nepos naked, then they'd flogged him with a weighted whip that had left his flesh criss-crossed with glaring red weals. Valerius guessed that alone would have been enough to make Hostilius give up what he knew, but it hadn't been enough for his captors. Once they had their information he must be made to pay.

'You should have run, Hostilius,' Valerius whispered as he looked down on what remained of the mining engineer. 'As soon as Petronius disappeared you should have run away from here and never looked back.'

After the whip had come the heated implements. Fingers removed one by one, the wounds cauterized by the red-hot blade even as they fell. They'd used some kind of clawed tongs to chew great lumps from his flesh, leaving his torso pitted with bloody hollows.

And when they'd inflicted enough pain they'd brought him here still alive, and hacked his arms and legs from his body. The only part of Nepos left unmarked was his plump face, lips drawn back, eyes bulging and teeth bared: a stark portrait of unbearable agony.

All this flashed through Valerius's mind in less than a dozen racing heartbeats, but Serpentius, with the survival instincts of a feral beast, was already moving. 'For all the gods' sake, Valerius. We have to get out of here.'

They raced back along the passage, their legs driven by something not far short of terror, but barely half-way to the ladder Serpentius stumbled to a shaking halt. 'Mars save us,' he whispered.

Valerius stood beside him in the flickering light of the torch, his reeling senses trying to make sense of what was happening. What was about to happen. He didn't have long to wait. They could hear the muffled roar, a kind of muted thunder. The very air around them seemed to change form, accompanied by a sudden pressure on the ears. At the same time the torch flame flared in a way that was beyond natural, something to do with the change in pressure.

Serpentius dropped to his knees, but Valerius hauled him to his feet.

'If you want to live, think,' he snarled. They'd faced death before, but never like this. Never so helpless. Valerius remembered the seething flood surging down the hill into the tunnel mouth with all nature's visceral power behind it. The way the hill had bulged and then erupted as if the very earth was tearing itself to pieces. The gigantic roar and the feeling of being punched. Maybe they should just . . . No! Tabitha's face appeared before him. The moment in the Conduit of Hezekiah when he thought he was drowning and she'd laughed at his fear. There had to be a way. Not forward. Not back. Think! 'This way.' He was already sprinting back down the tunnel and trusting Serpentius to follow. As he ran he kept his eyes on the roof. Where was it? Venus' withered tits, please. There! A black shadow less than a pace across and only a foot above his head.

Think. Think.

He dragged off his cloak. 'Quickly! Wrap the cloaks round my legs.' He saw the bewilderment and defeat in Serpentius's eyes. Had terror driven Valerius mad? Valerius knocked the torch from his hands. 'Just do it if you want to live.'

The Spaniard ripped off his own cloak and bent to do as Valerius ordered. The pressure on their ears was growing now and the thunder almost unbearably loud.

They could actually hear the wall of water hammering down the passages above like a runaway chariot, smashing into the turns and rebounding to rush on. It felt as if the whole hill was shaking, but Valerius knew it was only his legs.

He bent and made a support with his left hand and the wooden fist. Serpentius looked up and at last he understood what Valerius intended. 'Will it work?'

'Have you any better ideas?' Valerius snarled. 'We'll never know unless we try.'

The truth was he had no idea. Probably not. He only knew it was better to die trying than to await their fate in a trance, like sheep. Serpentius and Valerius had never been sheep, and this was no time to start.

'Someone dug that out. They must have had some kind of footholds. Find a support and drop your belt and pull me up after you. But for the gods' sake be quick about it.'

Serpentius nodded convulsively. At the last minute he drew his sword and threw it aside. He used Valerius to boost his way up into the blackened hole. Found a notch that had formed the support for a piece of timber. Squirmed his way further inside, his arms scraping against the crumbling rock.

'Serpentius!'

He had never heard Valerius's voice so close to panic. One foot on either side of the shaft, he unhooked his belt and dropped one end down the shaft, half crouching and stretching his arm to get the maximum extension. His body rebelled against the unnatural position, pains shooting through his back from the site of his old wound.

'Another couple of inches.'

'I'm not made—' Serpentius forced himself down

another inch, his face rammed hard against the rock face.

'I have it.' Valerius roughly tied the belt round the cowhide stock on his right arm. 'Pull me up.'

Serpentius took the strain and with all his wiry strength hauled Valerius up inch by straining inch. His back felt as if it was breaking and something popped in his shoulder, but still he pulled, eventually managing to get a second hand to the leather strap. The torch below flickered and died and they were left in total darkness.

'I'm level with your feet,' came the grating voice from the void below. 'You'll have to move up. I can support myself for a few moments on my elbows.'

Serpentius began to squirm upwards, grunting with the pain of his injured arm. He was just getting settled on a new perch when an enormous blast of air rushed past him. A scream of fear from below as Valerius lost his hold and a jerk on the end of the belt almost pulled the arm from its socket. He braced against the shaft wall, ignoring the pain as he hauled Valerius upwards into the shaft. The rush of air was constant now and accompanied by a massive roar that made communication impossible. Valerius slapped him on the leg and he found a new handhold that allowed him to pull himself up another two or three feet, but the shaft narrowed sharply, the sides already jamming into his shoulders. It was impossible to go any further.

Valerius slapped his foot again, but Serpentius ignored him. There was nothing else they could do, but pray. He tilted his head upwards and saw a single twinkling star in the blackness. Jupiter's wrinkled scrotum, what wouldn't he give to be up there now. From what he knew of the process the miners would normally plug the air hole before they unleashed the flood. At least they could breathe. But would it have a positive or negative effect on their precarious grip on life in this claustrophobic rabbit hole of a sanctuary?

The airflow eased and he guessed the cloaks round Valerius's legs had partially blocked the vent. But the pressure on his ears and from below had increased almost beyond endurance. At times it was so powerful it felt as if Valerius was pushing him upwards and the jagged rocks ground into his shoulders so he gasped with pain.

In the modestly wider gap below, Valerius cursed his friend for refusing to climb any higher. His sandals were two feet at most above the level of the bottom of the shaft, jammed into two tiny crevices. Would it be enough? Already the force of the air from below had almost dislodged him from his position and the roaring filled his mouth, ears and nose and compressed his chest so he found it difficult to breathe. And this was just the beginning. Another incredible noise pushed the roar into the background. A sort of gigantic hiss. It was the sound of the water careening by at enormous speed directly below him. In the time it took to register the fact an enormous crash recorded the moment the inundation reached the barrier of the mine wall. Water forced itself into every cavity of the mine. What had Nepos said about the air being his greatest weapon? *As more and more water is forced into the shaft the pressure builds and the air is compressed.* Valerius felt that compression now. In an instant the pressure increased a hundredfold so he thought his head was being crushed. He opened his mouth to scream and the force eased slightly so he kept doing it.

A moment later a jet of water forced its way past the bundled cloaks. His battered mind fought for some sort

359

of hold on reality. Do something. He moved his feet to try to close the gaps, but it only made it worse. Water surged up to his knees, but the increase in the saturated cloaks' weight made them settle and the flow was stemmed bar a few tiny jets. If it hadn't been for the cloaks they could well have drowned, but within moments Valerius realized drowning might be a mercy. The entire shaft – the entire hill – began to shake like a rat in a terrier's mouth. Pieces of stone crumbled and broke away so he was showered from above and struggled to maintain the position of his feet on the two niches below.

A little voice in his head told him to let go, just drop into the crashing maelstrom and end it all. But Serpentius, whether by accident or design, kicked him in the head with an iron-shod sandal and suddenly his mind cleared.

Endure.

Survive.

The intensity of the shaking increased, accompanied by a new roar. Did he imagine it or was the pressure of the shaft walls on his shoulders increasing? The forces being imposed inside the hill were beginning to change its shape. He remembered the bulging slopes again and the moment the entire hill had erupted like a pullet's egg hit by a sling shot.

He could almost hear the grinding as the stones moved together. So much power was being exerted that soon the shaft must collapse. He and Serpentius would be mere bloody smears and bone fragments lost in the fabric of the earth.

On and on it went until with a clap like thunder his blind world altered fundamentally. The stone support fell away beneath his feet and Valerius's heart stopped as he fell with it. A savage jerk on his wrist halted his plunge. By some miracle Serpentius had retained his hold on the belt. He hung there like a half-drowned rat as water surged up the shaft unconstrained by the cloaks and for a moment he *was* drowning, his nose and mouth filled and struggling for breath. But with a second, much louder thunderous roar the water dropped away as fast as it had risen and his legs were dangling in clear air. Below him the torrent continued to rush by for another few moments before he heard it fade away. They waited in the disbelieving silence until their battered minds convinced them they had truly survived.

'You can drop me now,' Valerius croaked to Serpentius. A moment later his heart was in his mouth as he plunged to land with a splash in the shallow stream below. As Serpentius climbed down after him, Valerius untied the thin strip of leather that had undoubtedly saved his life. They walked slowly in the direction the water was flowing. Fifty paces ahead where there had been a solid wall of rock they could see the far side of a broad valley bathed in soft moonlight and the blur of distant hills. A boulder the height of a tall man and broad as a two-wheeled cart lay where it had been thrown against one wall. Valerius was certain it hadn't been there earlier and marvelled again at the immense power of *ruina montium*. Of Hostilius Nepos there was no sign. He might never have existed.

'Why are we still alive?' Serpentius whispered in awe as they looked down upon the swath of destruction below the opening. The hill had been eviscerated by the hydraulic mining process and now its entrails were scattered in a mile-long trail of mud and boulders that glittered silver and black beneath the moon. By a freak of nature two or three areas of hill survived to stand out as jagged mounds against the night sky behind them.

'I don't know.' Valerius's voice echoed the Spaniard's wonder. 'Maybe the air shaft was designed to be another fracture point. Because we kept the water out, that section of hill survived. Maybe Fortuna was watching over us.'

'Then let's hope she stays with us for a while longer.' Serpentius studied the drop for a few moments before coming to a decision. He levered himself over the ragged edge, grunted as his injured shoulder took his weight and lowered himself on to the mud slope.

He looked up. 'We need to get out of here and back to Avala.'

He waited for Valerius to join him, ankle-deep in the mire. They started off down the incline, their sandalled feet making a loud sucking sound with every step. There were muttered low curses as they stumbled over hidden boulders. Serpentius picked one up. 'If there was any justice one of these would be a great big lump of gold.'

'If there was any justice we'd be dead.'

'The important thing,' Serpentius continued, 'is that they *think* we're dead. They must have had someone watching the entrance, so they know there's no chance we could have survived this. I'd much prefer it stayed that way. With Fortuna's favour the horses will still be where we left them. If we can reach them before daylight I can get us back without meeting any hook-noses.'

'What then?'

'It depends whether Tito and Julia succeeded in persuading her father to change sides. If they did, we need to know what he knows. If not, and we both think that's more likely, you should ride directly for Tarraco, and hand over what little evidence you have to Pliny. Convince him that he's needed here. Melanius is the key. If you can persuade the governor his old friend should be arrested I don't think any of the others will put up much of a fight.'

'You're forgetting about Harpocration and his hooknoses,' Valerius reminded him. 'If he's taken he'll end up hanging from a cross and his men will spend the rest of their lives down the mines. No, the Parthians will either fight or run.'

'I hope they run in our direction,' Serpentius said. 'I have debts to pay.'

XLII

'We march on Tarraco in one week.' In the shocked silence that followed, Marcus Atilius Melanius waited for the inevitable protests. Why should they look surprised? He'd been telling them for months this was the only way to save their skins. Had they really been so deluded as to think it would never happen?

'But you said Verrens and this other man . . .'

'They call him Nathair, dear Severus,' Melanius said patiently. 'A Zoelan troublemaker who previously worked with Petronius.'

'You said they were dead.'

'Obliterated,' the leader confirmed. 'All our searchers found were a few scraps of tattered flesh and splintered bone.'

'I'd still have preferred to see their heads.' A new voice, harsh and heavily accented.

'That is because you are still at heart a barbarian, prefect.' Melanius graced Claudius Harpocration with a smile that took the edge off his words. 'You have seen *ruina montium*. Can you imagine what it must have been like in that mine? I cannot think of a worse or more terrifying death than being torn apart in the bowels of the earth. Quite fitting, I think, and they will certainly never trouble us again.'

'But that is my point,' Severus persisted. 'With Verrens, this Nathair and the traitor Nepos disposed of we have nothing to fear.'

Melanius sighed. For a man with such a high opinion of himself Asturica's *duovir* could be such a fool. It was like herding a flock of sheep with the wolves howling in the distance. Yet he had to admit that, if they were nervous, it was with some justification. Because this was truly the point of no return. He must be patient.

'We are safe,' he agreed, 'for now. But all we are doing is delaying the inevitable.' A stillness fell over the room and he met the gaze of each man in turn. 'What has been done cannot be undone. We are all agreed upon that?' He waited until each man nodded and he saw resistance replaced by equal measures of resignation and resolution. 'And we are all aware of the repercussions if our . . . private arrangements . . . are discovered. The very painful repercussions, both for ourselves and for our families. Let me be entirely frank with you, gentlemen; if we do not act now – agree this very day – then we would be as well going home, taking to our beds and cutting our wrists.'

'Aren't you being overdramatic, Melanius?' Ferox, the other dissenter, flushed with his success at the mine. 'Without Nepos and the information he stole they have nothing. Much can be done in the matter of covering up any evidence.'

'Are we so certain Nepos was the only informant?' Melanius demanded. 'And we have no idea if anything was taken from Fronton's villa before the fire. His daughter is still missing, I understand. What else is still missing? We all know he was our greatest weakness.

A man prone to keeping records. I should have dealt with him earlier. But that is not the point. We have one chance and one chance only. If we do not take it we do not deserve to survive. I have had dispatches from Rome suggesting that Vespasian may be preparing to send a full legion to Hispania Tarraconensis to replace or reinforce the five cohorts of the Sixth stationed at Legio.' An indrawn breath from Ferox, and Melanius saw Severus's fists clench convulsively. They'd heard the rumours, but this was close to confirmation, and they knew what it meant. Melanius used the opportunity to reinforce his point. 'In another month it will be too late. If we do not march now the campaigning season will be over by the time we reach Tarraco. Our wagons will be up to their axles in mud and Pliny will have time to close the gates on us. If we act swiftly, we can take him by surprise. The Sixth are ready, Calpurnius?' He already knew the answer, but it did no harm to allow the Peacock to have his say. Piso had been quivering like a hound who'd sighted a deer since the meeting had started.

'Proculus is being his usual obstructive self,' the young tribune complained. 'But he knows he either does as we say or falls on his sword. He is not of a sacrificial inclination. The tribunes are with me, the palms of the centurions well filled with gold and their heads with promises of advancement. The soldiers will do as they are ordered. They think they are reacting to an insurrection in Tarraco and are looking forward to some action against lightly armed rebels.'

'Good,' Melanius congratulated him. 'And of course,' he bowed to Harpocration, 'we can depend on our faithful auxiliaries of the First Parthorum.'

'They will follow me to Hades,' the bearded prefect assured him.

'But we are so few,' Severus stuttered.

'Enough and more to take the city,' Melanius assured him. 'But you are right: if we are to hold it we will need more soldiers. Calpurnius, perhaps you would like to tell us about your *successful* visit to our friends in Germania?'

'The men of the Tenth have not been paid for two months.' Piso's eyes shone with boyish enthusiasm. 'They feel no loyalty to Vespasian, are sick of the damp and chill winds of the Rhenus frontier and wish to return to Hispania. My cousin has been working on our behalf and I have an assurance from their senior officers that they will join up with us outside Tarraco at the end of July. It will take them a week longer to make the journey so they may already have started their march. The other legions on the Rhenus are still furious at Vespasian for the way he sacrificed them to the Batavians during the civil war and for cashiering their comrades in the First Germanica and Fourth Macedonica when Civilis was defeated.'

'We will take Tarraco and hold it.' Melanius skilfully regathered the reins of the meeting. 'The timing will give Vespasian no opportunity to react before winter sets in. Once the Tenth and the Sixth have hailed Calpurnius Piso, descendant of Divine Caesar, as Emperor, the legions of Germania will do likewise. In the spring, we will combine and march on Rome before Vespasian can summon help from Syria.'

'What about the legions of Pannonia and Illyricum, and those on the Danuvius?'

'The Danuvius was where Marcus Antonius Primus sent the legions he shattered at Cremona,' Melanius said dismissively. 'They have no reason to love the Flavians. He cannot afford to move the others because of the threat from the tribes beyond the river who will take

367

advantage of any weakness. No, we will reach Rome before any force can be gathered to stop us and the Senate will open the gates to us and anoint Lucius Calpurnius Piso to the purple.' He looked each man in the eye with a confident smile. 'And when that happens there will be estates and honours for all those who stood by him.'

He looked to Piso for support. The young man returned the smile, but with a twist to his lips that said that once he took his rightful place he'd rather be dragged through the Cloaca Maxima by his heels than have anything to do with these provincial rustics. But that was for later. Enough for now that he acknowledged Melanius with a nod and that Severus and Ferox were too blind to question his sincerity. Though Melanius did face one further hurdle, which he had expected and was prepared for.

'But surely,' Severus demanded, 'you cannot expect us to fight in the front rank like common soldiers? Naturally, we are happy to ride at our young prince's shoulder when the time comes, but experience tells me that in battle or siege it is much better to leave military matters to the professionals.'

'Of course,' Melanius conceded Severus's point with grace, 'but the officers and men of the Sixth need something to follow. They believe they fight under the orders of the government of Asturica Augusta to help put down an insurrection Plinius Secundus does not have the power to defeat. They will require to see their leaders in the vanguard of the column, and that is where we will ride, you and I.' Melanius smiled at the other man's discomfort. 'Ferox will remain in Asturica to ensure production from the mines continues uninterrupted.'

He turned to the two soldiers. 'We will muster here in Asturica. Gather your men and supplies and be ready in one week from today. All Hispania will be ours in a month.'

XLIII

Valerius and Serpentius made a weary and bedraggled sight as they rode in to Avala with their clothing still stained by the ochre mud of the Red Hills. They'd finally reached the horses after a nightmare trudge through the mud, followed by a two-day semicircular trek across broken country to keep them out of the way of the Parthians. On the second morning Serpentius found a stream where they were able to wash the worst of the clay off their bodies and clean and dry their clothing while they laid up until dark. They travelled in silence, any exhilaration at their unlikely survival long since replaced by a melancholy that both men knew well from the aftermath of battle.

Their demeanour that morning matched their mood. They'd failed and the hangdog attitude of the reception party who awaited them outside the *castro* suggested theirs was not the only failure. Tito stood at the head of a group of elders and young men, his face a picture of misery, but it was Julia who drew Valerius's eyes. She wore bandages on both hands and his heart sank as he recognized the dark *stola* she wore and understood the reason behind it. It was finished. After a meal and a few hours' sleep he'd do what Serpentius advised and ride south in search of Pliny. Caeleo, the hunter who had been sent to Legio to deliver Valerius's report to Marius, the Imperial courier, was among the welcome party and Valerius called him over.

'Were you able to find the young man, Caeleo?'

'Yes, lord.' A smile creased the goat hunter's face. 'It was like you said. He was a-cuddling with this lass in the tavern by the bridge. I took him aside, secret like, and handed him the message. All business he was after that. Lass wasn't pleased to see him go, tears and wailing and trying to keep him from the saddle, but off he went eventually.'

'When was this?'

'The day before yesterday, lord. I came straight back.' He leered. 'That girl didn't want no comforting from the likes of old Caeleo.'

Valerius went over the route from Legio to Tarraco in his head. If Marius used his Imperial warrant to change horses at every government *mansio* he should reach Pliny by tomorrow morning at the latest. Would Pliny see the urgency of the situation and march north immediately? Valerius had done what he could to highlight the dangers, but with little genuine evidence to back it up. Even if Pliny acted immediately he doubted he'd meet the governor of Hispania Tarraconensis till at least Esca, and perhaps further south.

He didn't see Caeleo watching him, or the look of concern that had replaced the smiles. The hunter was a man who lived his life by a certain philosophy. If a shepherd's flock showed signs of disease, but the shepherd was blind to it, Caeleo would allow him a further few days of cheerfulness rather than be the bearer of bad news. Thus he hadn't mentioned that when Marius rode out from Legio, the courier had been followed minutes later by four Parthian cavalrymen. Whatever the outcome of this scene, nothing could be done about it now and Caeleo saw no reason to trouble Valerius with something that could only cause him distress. Suddenly he remembered that there *was* something else he'd been meant to communicate.

'Would your honour be wanting to see your visitor now?'

'Visitor?' Valerius looked to where Tito and Serpentius were deep in conversation.

'No, lord,' the goatherd said. 'He'll be this way.'

Valerius followed him through the newly replaced gate of Avala to a house that had been one of the first to be renovated after the raid by Harpocration's Parthians. His puzzlement grew when he noticed the armed guard outside the entrance. A leather curtain covered the doorway and he pulled it aside and ducked through. The smoke hole in the roof allowed in just enough light to make out a hunched figure sitting on a stone bench in the far corner.

The man looked up and Valerius looked into a face he recognized. 'You,' he said. 'Why would you come here?'

'You're alive.' The man ignored the question. 'They said you were dead. Everyone was certain you were dead. A mine accident.'

'Why are you here?' Valerius persisted.

'I was sent with a message.'

'So?'

The man darted a glance at the doorway. 'A certain person asks for a meeting tomorrow at the crossroads *mansio* south of Legio,' he whispered. 'You should have passed it on the way to Asturica . . . ?'

'I know it,' Valerius said. 'But why should I meet with this . . . person? Why should I trust them? After all, just because I survived one *accident* it doesn't mean I'll survive another.'

'My . . . person understands this. They told me to say that it is in your interest to meet and they sent a token which they said you would recognize.' He held out his hand and Valerius saw something glittering in the centre of his palm. He knew he was expected to pick it up, but he couldn't bring himself to touch it.

'I will think on it.' He turned away.

'And you are to come alone,' the man called. 'My person is very jealous of their privacy.'

Valerius almost smiled at this invitation to place his head once more between the lion's jaws. 'I would have to be mad to do that.'

'Yes.' The man shook his head wryly. 'Almost as mad as someone who agreed to come here with a message and offered to stay as a hostage for your safe return.'

Valerius looked at him with new regard. 'Truly?'

The man nodded glumly. 'I have discovered that loyalty is a dangerous quality.'

'So it is.' Valerius grinned. 'Will your person be alone?'

He shook his head. 'They will be in a carriage pulled by two bays. There is a driver, but he knows nothing of this. The carriage will wait there for two hours after noon.'

'Very well, I will think on it,' Valerius repeated. But they both knew he'd made up his mind.

'Try to stay alive, lord – if only for my sake.'

Valerius laughed. 'You may trust me for that, but I have found it is not so easy in this Asturia of yours.'

* * *

372

Serpentius, naturally, tried to dissuade him. 'Of course it's a trap,' he said with surly relish. 'How could it be anything else after all that's happened? They'll be waiting for you. If it's not the thieves who kill you it'll be someone else. You'd be a fool to go.'

'It's one last chance to do what I came here for. To win some proper justice for Petronius.'

'Then at least let me come with you.'

Valerius shook his head. 'If it's who I think it is they'll just walk away and we'll be back where we started. There's a reason they want to speak to me alone. Just supply me with a guide to take me as far as the Legio road.'

The next day, after a few hours' sleep and another gruelling ride, Valerius approached the crossroads *mansio* an hour after noon. A four-wheeled wagon – more or less a small room on wheels – stood in the dusty courtyard while the driver watered a pair of fine horses at a stone trough by the *mansio* entrance. He looked up as Valerius entered and hurried to the carriage.

A slim hand appeared through the curtained doorway and beckoned Valerius forward. He tied his horse to a rail and approached the wagon, eyes searching the surroundings for any signs of the potential ambush that was so likely. He had no reason to trust the woman who had summoned him here and many reasons not to. His heart thundered in his chest, but it was anticipation as much as fear that drove it. He pulled back the curtain.

'So you did come.' Calpurnia Severa greeted him with a cold smile. 'I feared I had overestimated you.' She reached out and offered her hand to help him into the carriage.

'Did I have any other choice?' Valerius ignored the

373

searching fingers and pushed inside. Calpurnia sat on a cushioned bench to one side. He took the seat opposite, so close they could touch heads if they leaned forward at the same time. 'How did you know I wasn't dead? Everyone else seems to think so.'

'Severus was positively crowing when he announced it,' she said scornfully. 'A little cockerel strutting around on his dungheap. You frightened him, you see.' She shook her head. 'A lot of things frighten him. I told him I was pleased you were dead. The truth is that I couldn't conceive of a pair of crooks like Melanius and Ferox killing a man like Gaius Valerius Verrens. So I sent Zeno on the off-chance I was right. Severus believes he has his loyalty, but the reality is very different. Zeno is devoted to me. He would do anything I ask.'

'He said it would be in my interest to meet you. That suggests you have something to offer.'

'Or,' her eyes hardened, 'I have a dozen of Harpocration's Parthian killers secreted away in the *mansio* in case Ferox and Melanius had failed at the mine. All I have to do is call out.'

Valerius went very still. A certain twist to her lips told him she was enjoying his confusion. On the other hand, that long, slim neck was easily within reach and all he had to do was reach out and the fingers of his left hand would squeeze the life out of her. He could see she knew it, too. 'Why would you do that when you despise the men who want me dead?'

'You men are all alike.' She stared at him, shaking her head. 'So terribly predictable. You refused my . . . attentions. I find that insulting. Why would I not want my revenge?' Valerius considered the question for a long, anxious moment. Had he misjudged her so badly? Before he came up with an answer, she continued. 'But that would be a meagre reason to have a man killed. No.' Her eyes narrowed and she tilted her head in a certain way. 'There would have to be a better motivation. Let us call it power. Yes, I despise Melanius and the rest. But it would be so easy to supplant them. Calpurnius Piso is a young man and not insensible to my charms. A word in his ear and Severus, Melanius and Ferox would be no more. All that gold hidden where they think no one can find it. It would all be mine. And Piso has ambitions . . .'

'Calpurnia Augusta.'

She answered his mockery with a perfectly curved raised eyebrow. 'You do not think I am worthy, Valerius? A clothmaker's daughter from Carthago Nova who rose to become queen of Asturica Augusta in all but name?'

'I think your neck is much too pretty to put under the executioner's axe, where it would certainly end up if you were foolish enough to follow Piso. But then you're not, are you?'

'No,' she agreed. 'I am not.'

'Which brings us back to why you brought me here.'

She reached beneath the seat, drew out a leather satchel and handed it to him. 'This is the information that fat fool Nepos would have provided if he hadn't got himself killed. Everything you need to destroy Melanius and his crew. Names, numbers. How it was carried out. All the people who were paid to look the other way. The key to the cypher is there too.'

Valerius weighed the pouch in his hand, barely able to believe what he'd just been given. 'So you were Petronius's other source?'

'I convinced him to recruit Nepos to protect me. If they suspected they were being betrayed, everything they discovered would have led them to him.' She sounded very

375

pleased with herself. When he remembered the shattered body on the tunnel floor, Valerius reflected that it would be very easy to despise her.

'What I don't understand is why?' he said. 'If I can get this material to Plinius Secundus it won't just destroy Melanius and Ferox, it will destroy your husband too.'

Calpurnia took time to consider before she replied. 'When I first approached Petronius one of the conditions I set was that Severus should be exempted from punishment when the conspirators were taken. I urged him to distance himself from these people, but Severus was too greedy and too frightened of Melanius and that barbarian savage of his. If he had kept faith with me, Severus could have had everything he has now, but without the risk. It all changed when he fell under Melanius's spell. A fool and a coward, and worse, an old fool. He betrayed me as a wife, and worse, he is no longer capable of treating me the way a woman needs to be treated. All I ask now is that after he is executed his wealth passes to his widow. Can you guarantee this?'

Valerius hesitated. Calpurnia had all but confessed that she'd been the driving force behind what went on in Asturica Augusta before Melanius intervened. Clearly, the only reason she agreed to cooperate with Petronius was because she feared Melanius's ambitions would get her killed. What else wasn't she telling him? Still . . . 'If it is within my power.'

A bitter laugh. 'I need more than that. I need assurances. Petronius—'

'I am not Petronius.'

She reached for the case. 'I will not lose all I have worked for. You were sent for this information by the governor. Perhaps if I deliver it myself he will give me what I need.'

'I was sent here by the Emperor.' He saw a flicker of alarm in her eyes and she withdrew her hand. 'I have the Emperor's authority,' he continued. 'And the Emperor rewards those who are loyal to him.'

'Then I must trust you to do what is right.' The words were said lightly enough, but her tone had an edge that told him what she expected.

'What will you do now?'

'Melanius is already suspicious of me. I cannot return to Asturica Augusta unless I want to go the way of Saco and Petronius. My sister has a house in Toletum. I mean to stay there until this is over. Afterwards, Rome, I think, where Severus's money will secure me a place in society. Perhaps we will meet again, Gaius Valerius Verrens? You are an interesting man, I—'

The blast of a trumpet interrupted her. Valerius frowned and pulled back the curtain in the doorway. 'That's the call to close up. Someone's on the move.'

'That is what I was about to tell you,' Calpurnia said. 'Melanius has ordered a move against Tarraco within the week. Elements of the garrison at Legio have been called to Asturica to provide a proper escort for Melanius and the others.'

Soon they heard the sound of metal clinking against metal, shouted orders and hundreds of iron-soled feet on hard-packed earth. Calpurnia craned her head for a better view as the front ranks of a legionary column marched into sight in full armour, four abreast and led by a *signifer* carrying a cohort standard.

Valerius counted them as they went past. 'At least four hundred men.'

'My fool of a husband has been having the servants polish the armour he last wore as a young tribune. He talks as if the battles have already been won. They have all been bewitched by Melanius to believe they cannot fail. Calpurnius Piso? A boy who thinks his bloodline entitles him to command and to rule. And Proculus, a mere caretaker who could have stopped all this three years ago if he'd been man enough to stand up to Melanius.'

'Nepos mentioned that Melanius had some sort of hold over him?'

Her long nose twitched as if something putrid had been placed under it. 'Severus said there were whispers about young girls – very young girls – who went missing wherever Proculus was posted. Nothing of the sort has happened in Legio, or I would have heard. Melanius must have warned him to contain his urges, or he has outgrown them, as old men do.' Her laugh was as bitter as a winter frost. 'Old men, an ambitious boy and a barbarian savage and they think they can take Hispania for their own. Every one will be hanging from a cross before Saturnalia.'

'Only if Pliny can stop them.'

XLIV

'Will Pliny be able to defeat them?' Serpentius sat on a stone bench opposite Valerius in the house in Avala the Spaniard had once shared with his wife.

'That depends.' Valerius continued to pack supplies into a cloth sack. There'd be no mule on this journey. The horse would have to carry the extra weight, because whatever he decided he'd be moving fast. 'The odds are badly against him. Melanius and Piso will lead a force of close to three thousand legionaries, plus Harpocration's Parthian cavalry and the other auxiliaries stationed at Legio, say five thousand men. Even if he reacted instantly to my letter, Pliny will be fortunate to raise five hundred, and most of them will be cavalry from his escort.'

'Ten to one.' Serpentius whistled.

'Even so,' Valerius put his mind to the tactical problems the governor was likely to face, 'he might have a chance if he could choose his own ground. The problem is if Melanius can force battle on him at the time and place of his choosing. Pliny doesn't have any option but to fight, whatever the odds. He can't just give up Hispania to a rabble of garrison troops and auxiliaries. It would put every province in the Empire at risk and probably bring Vespasian down in any case.' He picked up a lock knife, considered discarding it as too heavy then changed his mind. It artfully combined a spoon, a fork and a tool for removing stones from a horse's hoof in a single mechanism, and you never knew when it would come in useful. He placed it in the sack and returned to his subject. 'The big question is whether the Sixth will fight. They don't even know they're rebels. Their officers have convinced them they'll be putting down a rebellion. What will happen if they come up against another regular formation? I've done what I can to sow the seeds of doubt, but who knows if it will work?'

'If we can reach him first at least we can give him a chance to prepare.' Serpentius tried to lift Valerius's mood.

'That's true,' Valerius agreed. 'But even so, is the outcome likely to be any different? If Pliny stayed in Tarraco and defended the walls he might have a chance, but I may have done the rebels' job for them by luring him out into the open.'

'Then what can we do?'

Valerius met his friend's eyes. 'There is one possibility. Melanius has always been the driving force behind this conspiracy. From what Nepos and the others said, without him it would have collapsed long ago.'

'You mean to cut the head off the snake.'

'If I can.'

Serpentius shook his head. 'If *we* can.'

'But we're not committing suicide to do it,' Valerius insisted. 'We can afford to shadow the column for a few days and still be in time to warn Pliny. If the opportunity to kill or capture Melanius presents itself we take it. If not, we'll ride south.'

He hefted the sack and Serpentius followed him out

into the morning sunshine. To his surprise he found Tito outside the gate with close to forty followers, hard-looking men, armed with spears or the vicious, curved *falcata* swords their forefathers had once used. Each stood at the head of a stocky, long-haired pony and their dress ranged from leather jerkins studded with bronze discs to the full set of mail Tito wore, courtesy of Valerius. More men were streaming in on foot through the pass from the mountain. He looked to the Spaniard. What was going on? Serpentius could only shrug and stare at his son.

Tito waved a hand that encompassed his followers. 'We have decided that for our own honour we cannot let you risk your lives alone.' Serpentius let out a snort of bitter laughter at this presumption, but Valerius reached out and laid a hand on his arm. 'If you fail,' the young man continued, 'each of us will suffer the consequences. Better for all if you succeed.' Tito glanced to where Valerius now noticed Julia stood, and she nodded agreement. 'And the greater the force that rides with you the greater the chance of success.'

'I said I would not ask one Zoelan or Asturian to risk his life for Rome,' Serpentius barked. 'You defy me at your peril, boy.'

Tito faced up to his father. 'It is not a question of asking and we are not doing this for Rome, but for ourselves and our families. The old ways are gone and they will never return. The only question is whether we learn to live with Rome or continue to bend the knee to the criminals who have bled Asturica Augusta dry and used the hook-noses to terrorize our people. Everyone here has suffered at the hands of Harpocration and his Parthians. They thirst for revenge. You,' he pointed to Valerius, 'said that the Emperor had promised to extend *civitas* in Hispania. At the time I did not understand what *civitas* meant. I feared we would be exchanging one form of bondage for another. But Julia has explained it to me and it seems to me that we can all benefit. When the time comes will you speak for Avala and the other mountain communities?'

'If it is within my power,' Valerius assured him in a voice strong enough for all to hear. A murmur ran through the growing crowd of men.

'Then we will fight for you.'

Valerius shook his head. 'I will speak out for the people of Avala whatever the outcome, but it must be your father's decision whether you accompany us. These are his mountains and I have learned to trust his judgement with my life.' He saw Tito's angry glance at his father. 'This is no slight on you, Tito, or your comrades, but there are some situations where two men are capable of achieving more than two hundred. This may be one of them. Serpentius?'

Serpentius marched towards his son with a look of grim resolve on his savage features. He stared into Tito's eyes, arms by his sides and his fists clenching and unclenching. Tito tensed and no man could predict the outcome. The silence seemed to last an eternity before Serpentius reached out and clasped Tito by the shoulders. 'You are my son. Your forefathers fought for Hannibal against Rome. Rome killed your mother and condemned me to a living death. But,' now his eyes swept over the warriors who stood watching them, 'discovering your existence has taught me there comes a time when a man must stop looking over his shoulder to the past and strive to create a better future. We can never do that with men like Melanius, Ferox and Severus robbing and enslaving our people. This changes everything.' He looked over his shoulder to where Valerius stood watching. 'We have an opportunity to place Rome in our debt. If you pledge that debt will be paid I will be proud to fight beside my son and my people.'

'Are you certain about this?' Valerius looked over the ragged band of Asturian warriors. Fighters, yes, but not soldiers. What would happen when they came up against the legionaries of the Sixth?

'Your pledge?'

'Of course. But I have the final say in how they're used.'

'You will command, Valerius, as always. You have never been careless with men's lives. But I have some thoughts.'

'Yes?'

The Spaniard nodded solemnly. 'But first we must know exactly what we face.'

Two days later they looked upon their enemies.

Serpentius, Valerius and Tito had left the main portion of their motley force in the charge of a reliable elder after agreeing to meet again midway between Asturica Augusta and Legio. Meanwhile, Serpentius led Valerius and his son to a concealed position among stunted trees overlooking the road. They were plagued by buzzing insects beneath a burning sun that threatened to turn the rocks into glowing coals. This was the day Calpurnia Severa claimed Melanius would begin his march on Tarraco, but as the hours passed Valerius began to doubt. He had just dropped into a weary doze when Serpentius touched his arm.

'Stay down,' the Spaniard hissed. 'Flank guards just below us.'

Valerius crouched behind the bole of a pine tree and looked down towards the road. A half troop of

Parthian auxiliary cavalry rode by in a dusty field just below, their spear points glittering in the sunlight. A hazy cloud marked more horsemen on the far side of the valley. As he watched, the head of the column came into sight. Melanius had called the First and Second cohorts of the Sixth to Asturica to provide a show of strength as he began his bid for power. The legion's involvement would have the twin effect of giving the operation a false legitimacy while simultaneously cowing any potential opposition.

Serpentius, gladiator trained to identify a weakness at a hundred paces, recognized it immediately. His eyes glittered like a hawk marking its prey. 'See how Melanius, Severus, Piso and Harpocration all ride with the vanguard of Parthians,' he pointed out. 'The First cohort is two hundred paces and more behind, and the Second further back still. Then a smaller rearguard of more Parthians. Poor march discipline?' He aimed the question at Valerius.

Valerius nodded. They'd witnessed it often in the early days of a long march. The excitement and hectic discipline natural when setting out was quickly replaced by lethargy, which in turn was magnified by the knowledge the formation was still in secure territory. It was never easy to maintain formation between infantry and cavalry, but doubly so with inexperienced soldiers. Melanius's legionary cohorts, for all their long service, were garrison troops, who'd seldom left the fort for the past three years.

'Proculus likely feels he has nothing to fear until he's beyond Legio,' the one-handed Roman suggested. 'There is no force in Asturia that would pose a threat to two cohorts of legionary infantry. He's allowed the First cohort to drop back so it doesn't have to eat the dust of the vanguard. Melanius is the only one with the wit to see the danger, but I'd guess he doesn't care to get involved in military matters. Piso is sensitive about his status as an officer of the Sixth. Melanius won't do anything that might undermine his position.' He studied the column again, wiping sweat from his eyes. 'But what of it? Proculus is right. Even with the element of surprise our few hundred farmers would be slaughtered before the legionaries were properly warmed up.'

Tito bridled at the insult to his countrymen, but Serpentius cuffed him on the arm. 'Listen to someone who knows what he's talking about and learn from him. Their order of march is a weakness, but we're not strong enough to take advantage of it.'

'Then what's the point of us even being here?' Tito demanded.

'Because,' Valerius suddenly understood what Serpentius envisaged, 'circumstances change and possibilities arise . . .'

'But you have to be in a position to take advantage of those possibilities.'

'And you have an idea?'

Tito looked at them as if they were mad, but his father only grinned.

'I have an idea.'

XLV

'This is where I stopped the gold convoy on the night Petronius died. I don't see why it shouldn't work again.'

They stood where the bank shelved towards the ford across the river. Valerius noted the narrow defile on the far side and the rocks that would protect the defenders. The road cut through a flat plain to reach this point, with two hundred or so paces of dusty earth, tufts of dried yellow grass and prickly shrubs separating the valley walls. They'd coaxed their horses down the rocky slope that formed the north side of the valley. To the south a gradual rise led to a long whaleback hill covered in stunted green pines. Experience told him that with a little effort they might make Melanius pause here – but stop him?

'We don't want to stop him.' Serpentius read his mind. 'Remember? We want to cut off the head of the snake.' He pointed back up the road. 'They come up the track and the Parthian scouts see spears glinting among those rocks. Not enough to frighten them, but sufficient to make them hesitate. Some will have been here with the gold convoy. My men were brave fools who allowed themselves to be lured from their position and were slaughtered. The hook-noses will be confident they can do the same.'

Valerius saw it right away. 'So they won't wait for the legionaries to come up and do the job.'

Serpentius shook his head. 'Harpocration will want any glory for himself.'

'They'll leave men to guard Melanius and the rest.'

'Ten or twenty,' Serpentius said dismissively. 'There's a valley, more of a gully, cut into the north side.' Valerius looked to where the Spaniard was pointing, a barely visible cleft in the rocks. 'If you're coming from the west you can't see it until you're directly opposite. We come out of nowhere and hit them hard and fast. The question is: how quickly can the First cohort react?'

Valerius studied the road and the scrubby ground around it and tried to imagine what he'd do in Proculus's place. 'Proculus will hesitate until he understands exactly what he's up against. Once he's seen how few we are, he'll form line. It will take time.' The surge of elation he felt rang clear in his voice. 'Long enough for us to get to Melanius and Severus and slaughter them like sheep.'

'What about Piso and Harpocration?'

'If you're right, Harpocration will be at the river with his men. Once Melanius is dead Piso is an irrelevance. If Proculus has any sense he'll take back command of his men and march them straight back where they came from.'

'Unless he decides to clean things up properly.' Serpentius frowned.

Valerius had an image of the Asturians being hunted through the hills like rabbits by the legionary veterans. 'If it comes to that Tito and his men need to know they must retreat. They're not here to fight professional infantry.' He hesitated. It wasn't too late. The offer had to be made. 'We can always go back to our original plan and send your farmers home?'

387

The Spaniard stared at him. A moment of uncertainty followed by decision. 'No,' he said. 'It would be a betrayal of their courage and the people they've left behind to risk their lives fighting beside us. They believe if we succeed today their families will be safe from the Parthians and their children will have a better future. I hope they're right, Valerius?'

'I'll make sure Vespasian knows what happened here, if I live. If I don't, you take the papers to Pliny. He'll listen to you. Melanius and his gang will lose in the end, Serpentius, but unless we can win today it will be at the cost of thousands of lives, Roman and Asturian. We've both seen enough blood spilled. Let us end it here.'

'We'll survive.' Serpentius's face broke into a wolf's grin. 'Hit and run. In and out before they know what's happening. Like that day at Bedriacum with Marcus Antonius Primus's cavalry.'

Valerius remembered *that* day with less relish and he hoped this one would turn out better. 'How long before they get here?'

Serpentius glanced at the sun. It was close to mid-morning. 'They don't seem in any hurry, so four hours, maybe five.'

'Then let us finish our preparations in two. The last thing we want is a stray scout stumbling on us. Who will lead the defenders?'

'Tito,' Serpentius said. It had been an awkward conversation. His son had been eager to take a more active role, but he'd seen sense in the end. 'It needs to be an Asturian and Tito knows I'll be more effective on horse-back. I've given him his instructions, but I'll speak to them before we take our positions.'

While Valerius inspected his 'cavalry', Serpentius lined up the two hundred men who had answered Tito's rallying call. Some were driven by loyalty, some saw war as an adventure, but most only wanted the opportunity to avenge loved ones butchered in Parthian raids. They waited on a gravel mound overlooking the river. The water was lower than when Serpentius had last been here, but he hoped he could turn it to their advantage.

'Tito has shown you your positions.' He raised his voice so all would hear. 'And he has told you what you must do. What must you do?'

'We are to pull back across the river when the hook-noses approach, then defend our positions to the last breath.' It was the voice of Placido, and it was accompanied by a murmur of approval.

'Good,' the Spaniard said. 'But what he has not told you is that he has brought you here to die.' Now there was a rumble of consternation and the men looked at each other. 'That's right, every last one of you bastards will die *unless* you do exactly what I say. Some of you will have known Buntalos and Sigilo and the others who once rode with me. This,' he thumped his spear shaft into the gravel, 'is where they died. Are you brave?'

A momentary hesitation before a ragged cry of 'Yes.'

'Well, Buntalos and Sigilo were brave too. Too brave. When their blood was up the hook-noses tricked them into advancing into the river. That river,' he pointed with the spear. 'And when they were in the river they slaughtered them. Those waters ran red with their blood. Once you are in the rocks you will not leave them. Do you understand? Tito,' he called, 'if anyone leaves those rocks who does he have to fear?'

'He has you to fear, Nathair.'

'That's right.' Serpentius ranged along the line of his men, his dark eyes filled with menace. 'He doesn't have to fear the pitiful Parthians. He has to fear me. I will

389

follow any man who leaves cover and gets himself killed beyond the Gates of Hades, rip out his gut and strangle him with it. When the fighting begins and your blood is up you will experience one of two things. If you are fortunate you will feel more alive than at any other time in your life. You will think you're quicker and better than any of your enemies, and maybe you'll be right. If you're unlucky you'll have ice water running down your spine and you'll want to piss yourself. Your spear will feel as heavy as a wagon wheel.' He glared at them. 'Neither of those things matters because you'll stay in those rocks. In a defensive position a man who's pissed himself is just as effective as a man who thinks he is invincible. The Parthians will try to frighten you. They'll try to goad you and they'll try to trick you, but their horses won't be able to reach you. That means they'll have to fight on foot. Cavalry don't like fighting on foot, and it's only the cavalry you'll be fighting.'

'But what about the Sixth, lord?' Placido asked. 'We heard there are two cohorts of legionaries.'

Serpentius's expression turned bleak. 'If the legionaries start to advance across the river you withdraw into the hills where a man in armour will have trouble following. Forget about duty and honour. Your job is to get out alive. You scatter and you go home.' Because if the Sixth advanced while Tito and his men were still in position, it meant they'd reacted more quickly than Valerius expected. It would be all over. They would have failed. And they'd most likely be dead. 'Now,' he said, 'we have work to do.'

While Serpentius was passing his instructions to the foot soldiers, Valerius used Allius as an interpreter to tell the horsemen what he expected of them. Standing beside their horses in an untidy group deep in Serpentius's gully, they were proud, unyielding men, with heavy brows and narrow eyes made for peering into a dust storm. Downturned mouths required just a twitch to transform their disdain for the world into a sneer that would have their neighbour reaching for his knife. They were men of the blood feud and that feud could last generations. Fine horsemen, their Celtiberian forefathers had ridden beside Hannibal two centuries before, but they were not soldiers. The key was to use them to create an opening for Valerius and Serpentius to reach Melanius and Severus.

The thought of what would happen there made Valerius pause. He would take no joy in killing either man. Melanius was a fat crook who Valerius suspected initially became involved only for the pleasure he took in manipulating people. By the time he realized what he'd got himself into there was no going back. Severus was greedy and vain and desperate to impress his beautiful wife. Neither of these was reason to kill someone, but their plotting had led to Petronius's death. They'd unleashed Harpocration and his Parthian butchers on the innocent tribespeople of the mountains. So they would die. They'd stolen Vespasian's gold. The Emperor was not a cruel man, but if he didn't make an example of the men who'd robbed him, they'd spawn a thousand others. As Serpentius always said, a quick death was a good death, no matter how it came. And Serpentius had more experience of death than any man Valerius had ever known. Better for Melanius to die under Valerius's sword than broken on a cross.

But he couldn't do it alone. Whether Melanius died or not would be decided by these men.

'Tell them they should not attack the Parthians directly.' Allius translated the instruction and Valerius saw instant consternation on the horsemen's faces. 'We will certainly outnumber the hook-nose cavalry.' He wasn't certain at all, but they didn't need to know that. 'But the Parthians are expert spearmen and there's no point getting killed for no reason. They are to think of themselves as a swarm of bees. Irritate and threaten, but stay away from their points. Attack only from the flanks, or better still the rear. They must also have one eye for Parthian reinforcements, who could come from either the river or the rear of the column. Hopefully our task will be complete by the time they are alerted. If not they must withdraw. Not run away.' He knew better than to question their courage. 'Withdraw and shield the wounded or help the unhorsed. The same applies if the legionaries of the Sixth move into formation for attack.'

A growl of sullen disapproval followed Allius's translation. 'They do not like this talk of withdrawal.'

'Then they will stay here,' Valerius snapped. 'Or join their friends on the far side of the river. The Romans win because they have discipline. They win because they know how to obey orders.'

A guttural snarl from the rear of the group and Allius grinned. 'They say they are not Romans. They will follow you, but they will only withdraw when you do.'

Valerius saw it was as much as he would get from these hard men of the mountains. It would have to be enough. It would probably be the death of them, but he managed to match Allius's grin.

'When the time comes their horses will have to grow wings to keep up with me.'

That brought a burst of laughter, as he'd intended, and the mood lightened. 'They ask what we do now, lord?'

'Tell them to check their equipment, sharpen their spears – and wait.'

XLVI

Marcus Atilius Melanius bit back a groan and tried to rearrange his vast bulk in the saddle with the least possible discomfort. Every part of him was either scraped, scratched, rubbed raw, aching or on fire. His armour, which had shone so proudly when he'd ridden through the streets of Asturica with the cheers ringing in his ears, was covered in dust and cut into his shoulders and his hips. It was impossible to find a comfortable position for his sword. His splendid helmet with the red horsehair crest seemed to have a mind of its own no matter how tight he strapped it beneath his chins. All his meticulous planning and now this.

Why hadn't he thought of it before? He knew the answer, of course: pride, simple foolish pride. He'd been determined to depart from Asturica a hero, and if a man wanted to be a hero he must look like a hero. At the outset a scarlet cloak had covered his ample form. It was long discarded, but sweat still poured from his brow, stinging his eyes and drenching his tunic. More streamed down his legs. It had been years since he'd done any serious riding. Why hadn't he ordered Severus to provide a carriage? Still, perhaps it wasn't too late.

'You have a carriage, if I remember, Severus,' he hinted. 'A fine, well-sprung affair with a cushioned interior. We have done our preening, but we are sensible men, not peacocks driven by vanity.' His horse tossed its head and he hauled at the reins with a muttered curse, sawing the bit across its delicate mouth. 'We're also not as young as we were. Too old and too senior, certainly, to spend our days eating dust. It would be no shame to take turns in the saddle and for one of us to show himself while the other rested for the rigours which are undoubtedly to come.'

Severus, who'd been sunk in misery contemplating the endless days and weeks ahead, shot him a tight smile. 'I would agree entirely, my dear Melanius, if only Calpurnia hadn't taken the accursed thing a couple of days ago to visit her sister. I'm afraid the saddle it is unless you feel it would not be beneath us to requisition a farmer's cart or some such until we reach Legio. I'm sure Proculus will be able to provide something in the comfort line when we reach the fortress. Shall I send someone to bring him forward?'

Melanius groaned inwardly. 'That won't be necessary.' He doubted very much whether Proculus would go out of the way to find anything that would diminish his agony. In fact, he suspected the prefect would probably revel in it. That was one reason Proculus was at the head of his First cohort instead of in the vanguard with the command party. The other was that, quite frankly, the presence of the veteran soldier made Melanius nervous. His time with the legions in Germania seemed very long ago. A process that had felt relatively simple then now appeared devilishly complex. There were so many things to remember. It was only right that Proculus, as nominal legate of the Sixth, should bear part of the burden, but Marcus Atilius Melanius commanded, and he must be seen to command. He also had to show strength in front of the likes of Severus and Piso, who were already showing signs of strain.

Mars save him, how had it ever come to this? He'd been in Asturica Augusta five years, patiently building a network of suitable contacts and waiting for his opportunity. It had presented itself in the form of Aurelio, who rode, ever watchful, a few paces behind his right shoulder. At the time he'd been working in some vague and shadowy capacity for the department of the *praefectus metallorum*. Melanius suspected he'd been an enforcer who kept the mine workers and their families in their place, some employment that required a potent mix of subtlety and extreme violence. Certainly there had been a hint of menace about the man when he'd appeared unannounced at Melanius's house. Melanius's first instinct had been to have the cocksure peasant thrown out, but something had made him hesitate.

Aurelio had information Melanius might be interested in – it turned out Melanius was not the only person with contacts. Like the fox he was, Aurelio had somehow scented his intent and now he suggested an arrangement. Julius Licinius Ferox, the Emperor Nero's esteemed and trusted *praefectus metallorum* for Asturica, was not just taking bribes for handing out licences, he was also skimming off small amounts of the Emperor's gold. The former was so widespread a practice as to be almost a benefit of office, but the theft? No one had any doubt what the feared and unpredictable Nero's reaction would be. A team of experienced torturers would descend on Asturica. Ferox would die screaming and what was left fed to the feral dogs who patrolled the city walls.

Not surprisingly, Ferox had proved amenable to

suggestion, and a percentage of his profits found its way into an iron-bound chest in Melanius's library. Aurelio now enjoyed a valued place in Melanius's household and, little by little, Ferox had been induced to make small increases in his appropriations.

But the great opportunity came with the civil war. Melanius sensed an opportunity presented by Servius Sulpicius Galba's accession to the purple. Galba had been killed before he could take advantage, but the state of paralysis at Tarraco that followed his death couldn't be ignored. It was now they enlisted the aid of Severus and Fronton. An army of phantom workers doubled the workforce in the mines and the cost to the Imperial treasury. The profits were split equally between the conspirators and Claudius Harpocration, recruited by Aurelio to supply a force which ensured obedience from anyone who had doubts. The figureheads in turn disbursed their own gifts to oil the wheels of the conspiracy, and Aurelio or Harpocration would remind the recipients of their responsibilities from time to time. They had stolen a fortune.

They should have stopped immediately Vitellius's forces defeated Otho at Bedriacum and the Emperor of only a few months committed suicide. In the chaos that followed likely no one would have noticed. If they had, the losses could have been explained away as the fortunes of war.

But somehow the time had never been right. Fronton would have been happy to bring things to a close, but he had little say in the council. Harpocration enjoyed the power of his position – by then Melanius had suborned Proculus and made the auxiliary the true authority at Legio – and saw no reason to change it. Ferox had long been under the thrall of the metal he ripped from the earth. Severus had an insatiable wife and an insatiable greed for the luxuries of life. And he, Melanius? He had been seduced by his ability to control all these disparate elements of a crime on a scale never witnessed before. Blinded by his vanity. By the time he'd realized he'd placed his head in a noose it was too late.

That was when he'd persuaded his fellow conspirators to place a portion of their great wealth in trust with him. If the time came to run, the gold would ease their path. Even then he understood Rome's long reach would find them wherever they fled. They would never be free of the fear of poisoners and backstabbers. It was only gradually that another possibility dawned. A plan so outrageous it might be called insane, but at least it gave them a chance. Gamble all on one final throw of the dice.

Petronius's investigations had supplied the opportunity. Melanius had even provided a little help that allowed him to increase the pressure on the others. He knew they would never act unless they could feel the blade tickling the back of their neck. Now he was able to offer them the possibility of salvation. Win, and advancement and more riches would be theirs. Lose? The end was inevitable in any case. Of course they'd been reluctant; so terrified he'd found it almost amusing. It had taken months of persuasion, but finally he'd won them round. All except Fronton, a man who spent each day frightened of what was going to happen on the next, and who'd preferred death to the chance of making a name for himself that would live through the ages. But Fronton, most opportunely, was gone. Everything was in place and going exactly to plan.

So why did Melanius's gut feel as if it was clenched in the grip of an icy fist?

Calpurnius Piso rode up to his side. The young tribune glanced nervously over his shoulder at Aurelio before he spoke.

'I still think I should have ordered the Tenth to hold their positions east of Emporiae and cover the Pyrenean passes. What happens if Vespasian hears of their defection and sends another legion, perhaps more than one, in pursuit? It would—'

'We have discussed this,' Melanius interrupted curtly. 'We need the Tenth at Tarraco to consolidate our position there. Not everyone will see the benefits of removing Vespasian. The Emperor will still have his supporters among the aristocracy and the civil service. I have the names of those likely to be open to persuasion and of those who may well require to be eliminated. With the Tenth we can place a cordon round the entire city while we weed them out. Only then will they be sent to defend the passes. Do not concern yourself, Calpurnius. If any of the legions on the Rhenus move I will hear of it.' He mitigated any implied criticism with a false smile. 'When we have Tarraco we will send out detachments to demand allegiance of the other cities, gather hostages and recruit young men for a new legion which you will lead. You will be a new Quintus Sertorius. I see much of him in you. He was brave, noble, eloquent and a brilliant soldier. He took and held Hispania.'

Piso looked sceptical. 'But wasn't Sertorius defeated in the end by Pompey?'

'Not defeated, betrayed,' Melanius insisted. 'He believed his position powerful enough to deter any attack from Rome. We will not make the same mistake. This is not about Hispania, it is about seeing you hailed Emperor, by the Senate and people of Rome. When we march on Rome Vespasian is finished. An emperor needs the support of the army, the Senate and the mob. We have the Senate, he does not yet have the mob. We have the Sixth, the Tenth and the majority of the legions of Germania. All it takes is the defection of one or two more legions and we cannot be stopped. Caesar crossed his Rubicon. The moment we cross the Iberus, there is no turning back.'

The sentiment brought a sickly smile from Piso. He'd long dreamed of deposing Vespasian, winning the purple and of reclaiming his illustrious family's destiny. Now he was on the brink of attempting it he'd begun to question whether he was up to the task. His lofty ambitions had provoked scorn from his friends and only Melanius seemed to understand. The older man had encouraged him, pointed out men who could help, and ways the dream might become a reality. Melanius had somehow won the cooperation of Proculus and the support of the Sixth, without which none of this would be happening.

Melanius provided the funds with which he had drawn tribunes from the legions on the Rhenus frontier into the plot. Melanius supplied the fortune that allowed him to win assurances of cooperation from the commander of the Tenth legion.

But what were those assurances truly worth?

He tried to remember the wording of the letters, letters that would destroy him if they ever found their way to the Palatine. But did it really matter? If they failed he would be dead anyway. A shudder ran through him at the thought. No, they could not fail. When ten thousand soldiers appeared at the gates of Tarraco, Gaius Plinius Secundus would have no choice but to surrender or flee. Piso saw himself being magnanimous in victory and his mood lifted. First Tarraco, then Hispania, and before Vespasian had the chance to react, on to Rome. To victory and immortality.

Claudius Harpocration nudged his horse a little closer to Melanius. 'We will reach the river soon. Time to water the horses and allow the legionaries to catch up.'

Melanius nodded his agreement. He looked over his shoulder to where the cohort banner of the Sixth was barely visible. 'I will talk to Proculus and insist the Sixth keep their position.'

Harpocration shrugged. It wasn't for him to say that it would be much more sensible to dismount and walk their horses occasionally. Melanius was neither inclined nor suited to walking.

They'd ridden another half mile and the hills that marked the line of the river were in sight when one of the Parthian scouts rode up at the gallop and snapped out a report to his commander.

'What is he saying?' Melanius demanded.

Harpocration looked thoughtful. 'It seems someone is trying to bar our way to the river.'

'But why?' Melanius shook his head. 'No one can know . . . Could it be bandits?'

The tribune snarled a question at his scout. 'Not bandits,' Harpocration said when he'd listened to the reply. 'Local tribesmen armed with axes and sickles. Perhaps a hundred of them.'

'Should we talk to them?' Severus looked shocked at this unexpected development.

'You don't talk to vermin, you slaughter them.' Harpocration barked an order to the escort. 'The only thing barring your way when you reach the river will be their dead bodies.' He pulled his horse around and took his place at the head of the column of riders who'd formed up in fours at his command. 'I'll leave you half a squadron,' he called to Melanius. 'Wait here for the infantry to come up.'

Melanius watched them trot away. He looked back to the two legionary cohorts. They were still a long way off, but the little knot of Parthians gave him a feeling of security. Harpocration's cavalry would soon deal with a few peasants. But the question of why they were there niggled at him. Finally a face swam into view, a beautiful face that always assumed an expression of contempt when she encountered him. He turned to Severus as a sudden flurry of rage rose in him. 'You fool. You told your wife—'

'No,' Severus spluttered. 'I—'

Melanius would have struck him, but for the warning shout from one of the escorts. 'Look!'

XLVII

Valerius and Serpentius waited in the depths of the gully, their mounts skittish beneath them as they sensed the nervousness of the men in their saddles. Around them, the hawkish bearded faces of the Asturians were set in grim resolution as they waited in the growing tension murmuring quietly to their horses or muttering prayers to whichever god they thought would aid them. Valerius was certain the hillmen would do their tasks to the best of their ability. The only question was whether their best would be good enough. Hidden amongst the rocks above, Allius called out the progress of the column, estimating the narrowing gap at every count of a hundred. Valerius could visualize what he was seeing. The head of the snake. It was just as Serpentius had predicted. Melanius, Severus and their Parthian escort had forged ahead of the legionary infantry.

'They've seen the men at the river.' The hidden informant couldn't conceal his excitement.

Valerius shifted his grip on the leather-wrapped hilt of the unfamiliar, scythe-like Asturian sword. Beside him, Serpentius sat utterly immobile, his lined features a mask of concentration.

'They're talking,' the disembodied voice announced. 'Yes. Now the hook-noses are moving into formation. They've taken the bait.'

'Wait!' Serpentius snarled as one of the riders pushed his mount towards the entrance. 'Another inch and I'll take your head off.'

'How many of the escort have they left?' Valerius demanded.

'Not more than twenty.'

Valerius turned to Serpentius. 'We go the moment Tito retreats across the river.' The Spaniard passed on the instruction to the others in his own language.

'Where are they now?' Valerius's throat was so dry the words emerged as a croak. The timing of their attack was utterly crucial. He couldn't afford to allow Melanius and his Parthian escort to get too far past the entrance to the gully. To do so would take them closer to the main cavalry force at the river and risk bringing the two cohorts of the Sixth within *pilum* range.

'The cavalry or the fat man and his friends?'

'Both.'

'The cavalry are forming line short of the river. The fat man is fifty paces short of the gully.'

A few moments later the distant blare of a cavalry trumpet broke the silence. It was the sound of the charge. If Tito wasn't retreating across the river by now his little force would be cut to pieces.

'Now!' Valerius shouted the order.

The Asturian riders burst from the gully in an untidy bunch, but by the time they'd gone twenty strides they'd formed a ragged version of an attack line. The only sound that accompanied their charge was the rhythm of hooves on the hard-packed earth. Valerius wanted no shouts or screams to alert the enemy. They headed directly for the flank of the little group of riders two hundred paces to their front. Valerius and Serpentius rode a little behind the main line, curbing their mounts to stop their fleeter horses overtaking the smaller Asturian beasts. The plan called for the Asturians to draw the attention of the Parthians and hold it. In the chaos that followed, the Roman and the Spaniard would find a way through to Melanius, Severus and Piso. Valerius glanced to his right where the First cohort of the Sixth were marching down the road four abreast, the long, compact column of legionaries disappearing into the distance. How would Proculus react when he realized what was happening? The best scenario for Valerius was if he perceived a real threat and formed a defensive square. That would keep the legionaries static long enough for his party to do what they'd come to do or die in the attempt.

Still no reaction from the little group of riders. The eyes of Melanius and his Parthian escort must be fixed on what was happening ahead. But even as the thought formed, a shout from Serpentius drew him back to the legionary column. Someone must have seen the riders because the column came to an abrupt halt. Valerius imagined shouted orders as the individual centuries of the cohort began to move smoothly into line. Too quick. It was happening too quickly.

Still no sound but the rush of disturbed air and the thunder of hooves.

At last a shout of warning from ahead. With frightening precision the Parthian escort formed up and moved forward in line to block the attack, clearly undeterred by the odds. As Valerius watched they kicked their horses first into a trot, then a canter.

'Spread out.' Serpentius roared the order to the other riders in their own language and felt a surge of pride as they reacted like veterans. If the Asturians bunched to meet the Parthian charge their small ponies would be smashed back by the cavalry horses and the seven-foot spears would sweep them from the saddle. The only way to survive was to use their greater numbers and agility to confuse and confound the enemy. A ripple ran through the Parthian line as the squadron's commander reacted to the change in formation. Valerius could see gaps between the individual riders and it was to one of these that he set his course, knowing Serpentius would be doing the same.

Two hundred paces rapidly became a hundred. Now the enemy cavalrymen could be identified as individuals, snarling mouths showing pink through the black beards. Dark eyes glaring hatred from beneath heavy brows. A blur of chaotic movement to the left and a shriek as one of the Asturian ponies snapped a leg in an animal burrow and its rider smashed to the ground, rolled three times and lay still. Ahead, Valerius sensed the moment when the Parthian commander noticed the two larger horses and recognized the threat they posed. A shouted order and a pair of spears angled towards him.

Fifty paces.

One of the Asturians veered across his front to engage a particular enemy and he was forced to avoid a collision.

Twenty-five.

He raised his sword to shoulder height. No time to think about the infantry now. One of the Parthians who'd targeted him moved ahead, blocking the other's attack. The flash of a gleaming metal point aimed directly at his eyes. A mistake, because a flick of the sword drove the point over his right shoulder and once Valerius was inside the spear point the other man was dead. Valerius swung his heavy blade in a vicious back cut that caught his enemy across the upper lip. The weight of the blow and the momentum as metal and bone met jarred Valerius's arm and drove the blade upwards in a shearing motion that sliced off the top part of the Parthian's face. He heard a sharp clang as the edge clipped an iron helmet. A muffled shriek and a momentary image of red horror punctured by two disbelieving white eyes and he was past. Around him, screams and anxious shouts, the clash of metal upon metal, but his entire focus was on what lay ahead.

Melanius and Severus and one other were milling in a little confused group, Piso urging his mount back in the direction of the Sixth. Valerius ignored the tribune and kicked his horse on, sword raised and at the ready. He saw stark terror etched on Melanius's bloated red face. Without warning another horse was shoulder to shoulder with his own, blocking the path to his target. He sensed a blur of bright metal at the very edge of his vision and managed to parry the cut aimed at his neck with a frenzied sweep of his blade. Aurelio. How could he have forgotten Aurelio?

Aurelio fought with a mocking grin on his rat's face and his sword edge seemed to come from every angle at once. Mars' arse, but he was fast. But as they tested each other it became clear he'd never fought a left-handed man and that gave Valerius an advantage that outweighed his enemy's speed. The weight and direction of the Roman's parries puzzled Aurelio and soon the mocking grin became a frown of concentration. Valerius sensed the pace of his opponent's attack slacken a little as he tried to work out where his advantage lay.

'You owe Melanius nothing,' Valerius gasped as he

manoeuvred his mount to gain an opening. 'If he dies the conspiracy dies with him.'

'If he dies I *have* nothing,' the other man laughed. 'And you'll come after me in any case. But if I kill you Piso will take the purple and Melanius will make me rich. So you have to die, Gaius Valerius Verrens.'

The jibe was accompanied by a back cut that was so obvious Valerius was able to parry it with a careless sweep of the blade. But he'd seen Aurelio's eyes flicker to his left and he was moving even before Serpentius's warning shout, hauling his horse round and ducking in the saddle. Melanius's flailing sword flashed above his head so close he could feel the disturbed air as it passed. He slashed at the passing figure and missed, but the razor edge of his blade caught the horse across the rump and as it reared Melanius fell from the saddle with a cry of alarm.

Aurelio was on Valerius before he could recover, driving him back with a flurry of attacks and using his horse to protect the fallen Melanius. The fact that he had half an eye for his master killed him. Valerius tried a cut that Aurelio was able to deflect easily. The Roman allowed his sword to fall away giving the other man an opening. He saw the glint in Aurelio's eyes as the bodyguard recognized the opportunity and the blade came up. It was only the slightest flick of the point, yet it would have sliced Valerius's throat open and drowned him in his own blood. But the opening had been deliberate and Valerius was able to divert the thrust with his wooden fist and simultaneously spear the clumsy Asturian sword through Aurelio's exposed body. He felt the moment the point entered flesh, the jolt as spasming muscles clamped on the intruding iron, heard Aurelio scream in mortal agony. He was barely aware of the automatic twist of the wrist that freed the broad, curved blade and ripped Aurelio's bowels from his stomach. Aurelio crouched grey-faced in the saddle clawing at his flopping guts and mewing like an injured child. His horse moved away and Valerius found himself staring down at the face of Marcus Atilius Melanius.

Melanius struggled to his feet, his helmet askew and his armour dented by the fall. Somehow he managed to retain an injured dignity in the circumstances that Valerius found quite brave.

'I surrender my sword and my person.' The words emerged in a stutter, but he drew himself erect with his head held high. 'I throw myself upon your mercy and that of Gaius Plinius Secundus.'

Valerius paused to draw breath. He could hear Calpurnius Piso screaming at the men of the Sixth legion to advance. The sound of clashing metal told him that at least some of the men who'd made the charge with him survived to fight on. He could rely on Serpentius to take care of Severus. Melanius's horse stood nearby, only slightly injured. All he had to do was allow him to get into the saddle and escort him from the field. But what then? He had a vision of the broken creature hanging in chains from the wall of the blood-spattered room in Pliny's palace.

'I grant you mercy,' Valerius agreed. His sword rested on the pommel, level with Melanius's pleading face. With a single movement he rammed the weapon forward and down so the point took Melanius just above his armour. The broad, curved blade pierced the folds of flesh at the base of his throat and lanced diagonally into his body. Melanius's eyes rolled up into his head and a fountain of blood erupted from his gaping mouth. Valerius hauled the sword free and the dying man stood

408

shuddering for a long moment until he dropped as if his legs had been cut from beneath him.

But even as Melanius died Valerius knew it had all taken too long.

XLVIII

Despite Piso's screaming exhortations the two cohorts of the Sixth still hadn't moved and the long lines of legionaries stood motionless as some sort of altercation took place between the young tribune and Proculus. Had Proculus seen Melanius die, or was he just biding his time to discover who emerged victorious from the skirmish?

He would certainly see Aulus Aemilianus Severus die. A hundred paces away Asturica Augusta's *duovir* watched in terror as Serpentius dispatched the last of three Parthians who'd tried to stop him reaching Severus. Now he abandoned his horse and sought refuge among the rocks at the base of the far slope.

Valerius watched as he scurried among the boulders and he could hear his plaintive shouts pleading for help from Proculus and his legionaries. But the ageing Severus was no match for Serpentius. The Spaniard caught up with his prey in seconds as Severus leaned against a rock, head down and chest heaving with the effort. Death came almost unnoticed. Serpentius despatched the *duovir* with the casual ease he would have butchered a rabbit. Valerius saw the sword rise and fall. It was done.

Time to get out.

Little knots of Asturian riders still danced around individual Parthians, but they were far fewer than when they'd ridden out from the gully. Small Asturian ponies dotted the plain, standing with heads bowed over the crumpled bodies of their owners. Beyond them – and between Valerius and the gully he'd marked as their escape route – at least two squadrons of the Parthian vanguard wheeled into position, while two more circled to cut off any escape to the south. With the Sixth legion blocking the road west and the bulk of the Parthian cavalry riding up from the ford they were trapped. Even if Proculus chose not to become involved the Asturians were outnumbered at least ten to one. Serpentius reined in beside Valerius, his face as bleak as a December morning in the Rhenus bog.

'I suppose we could always surrender.'

'This is no time for jokes.' Valerius looked to where Claudius Harpocration had halted his remaining six squadrons. A trumpet call rang out and the Parthians fighting Valerius's Asturian allies disengaged and rode to join their comrades. The Asturians retreated in their turn to form a semicircle of riders behind Valerius and Serpentius. Fully half of them had suffered wounds and two or three were slumped in the saddle, barely conscious. 'In any case I doubt that will be on offer.'

It appeared the surviving officer from Melanius's escort was trying to explain to Harpocration how he'd lost his charge and the cavalry prefect didn't like what he was hearing. Without warning Harpocration and another man broke away and rode to where Valerius waited. They halted ten paces off and Harpocration removed his helmet and pushed dark hair from his eyes.

411

'You will surrender Marcus Atilius Melanius and Aulus Aemilianus Severus to me now and I will spare your lives,' the Parthian said without preamble.

'Even if that were possible I doubt very much you'd keep your part of the bargain.' Valerius kept his tone formal. 'Unfortunately it is not.'

He moved his horse to one side so Harpocration could see the bulky figure in the glittering armour who lay in the dust in a pool of blood. The Parthian growled, but besides anger Valerius saw a fleeting shadow of anguish cross his face. Harpocration knew perfectly well that Melanius's death meant the end of his ambitions.

'You can have Severus,' Serpentius offered with a sneer. Something round and the size of a melon flew past Valerius's right shoulder and landed to roll at the front hooves of Harpocration's mount. The beast skittered and the Parthian looked down into the startled features of the *duovir*.

'You will die slowly and in exquisite agony,' Harpocration promised.

Serpentius watched as the Parthian's hand crept to his sword. 'You're welcome to try.' Serpentius's features twisted into the wolf's grin that never touched his eyes. 'I'd like that. Like it a lot. How about it, hook-nose, just you and me? Then we'll see how brave you are. I noticed you're happy to send other men to fight for you, but you stay away from trouble yourself.'

Valerius laid a hand on his arm. 'It may not come to that.'

The Spaniard glared at him and Harpocration made to circle his horse and return to his men.

'Wait.' Valerius raised his voice to a shout. 'It's over and you know it. Without Melanius and Severus there is no rebellion. Look.' He pointed to where the Sixth were lined up and Piso and Proculus stared at them with the rest. 'Your Roman friends are in no hurry to get killed helping you. Vespasian knows everything, or if he doesn't now, he soon will. There is no hope for you, Claudius Harpocration, but your men were only following your orders. You can save them if you surrender yourself to me.'

'You think to turn them against me, Roman?' The Parthian actually laughed. 'Then think again. These are not just my men. They are of my people and my tribe. They are my brothers.' Harpocration's glittering eyes wandered over the riders gathered behind Valerius. 'Soon your pathetic little band of farmers will feel the point of their spears. But not you.' Now the hate-filled eyes pinned Valerius. 'You and the old man beside you will be taken alive so I may have my pleasure of you. With a sharp knife and hot coals I will make your passing a torment beyond bearing and you will plead for death long before the end.'

'This old man will carve his name on your face with his sword so every man knows who killed you,' Serpentius spat.

'Enough of this time-wasting.' Harpocration spun his horse and trotted back to his men. 'Remember what I said about your end, Roman. I look forward to our next meeting.'

'A fine sentiment, writing your name on his face,' Valerius observed mildly. 'But I'm not sure it helped.'

Serpentius shrugged. 'An angry fighter is a careless fighter and I want the bastard angry when the time comes. In any case it can't make it any worse. Do we make a break for it?'

'That's what I was thinking. At least one or two of us might make it to the slope.'

413

'I'll be at your right hand at the end.'

Valerius felt a lump in his throat. 'A friend by your side and a sword in your hand?'

'Let us make it so. At least . . .' Serpentius's eyes were drawn towards the river. 'Venus' withered tits, what's he doing?'

Tito had done exactly as his father ordered. When the Parthians advanced he withdrew his men through the maze of boulders and cunningly disguised spiked pits he'd created in the bed of the ford. On the far side they'd taken up position among the rocks and behind a rocky barrier they'd created to block the road. A few men stayed on the bank to taunt the enemy and hopefully goad a few into charging to be pinned by a spear or brought down by one of the traps.

But it hadn't worked.

It had been a good plan, but it depended on perfect timing and the cooperation of the hook-noses. In war, as his father had advised often since his return, nothing was predictable. Harpocration had been attracted by the bait, but he was as wary as a fox approaching a farm at night. Tito would swear the Parthian sensed the clash to his rear even before the sound of fighting reached them. His men had lined up along the river bank for no more than a few moments before their commander's head whipped round. With a contemptuous glance at the ford's defenders he turned away and Tito could only watch as close to three hundred riders carried their spears to where his father and Valerius were likely fighting for their lives.

Serpentius's instructions in these circumstances had been clear. The Asturians were to stay in place as long as their presence would draw off any of the Parthian

414

cavalry. If not they must withdraw and disperse, to regroup at Avala, where the others would join them . . . if they were alive.

But Tito was his father's son and his father was out there on that dusty plain. What would Serpentius of Avala, Barbaros the Proud, do in his place? He drew his sword.

'You may take the men and lead them to the hills,' he told Placido, who stood by his side. 'I will go to my father.'

He made to walk towards the river, but Placido followed and grabbed him roughly by the arm. 'I came here to have my revenge on the hook-noses. I will not walk away without a fight.'

'Nor I,' said the nearest man, and his cry was taken by another, then another. Men could see Tito on the river bank with his sword bared. They knew what had happened and they understood his intention, knew also the certain outcome, but soon they were streaming from the rocks by the score. Tito watched them come and his heart stuttered with pride. But this was no time for emotion. He was perfectly aware of the Parthian cavalry's capabilities, but he would not make it easy for them.

'At least he's had the sense to form them into a square,' Valerius said. It wasn't by any means a Roman square, a compact, prickling hedgehog of spears capable of holding off auxiliary cavalry. More a ragged, shambling hedge of men that created a vague representation of that shape.

'They'll still be slaughtered.'

'Like as not.' Valerius watched intently to see how Harpocration would react to this new threat. 'But at least he's given us a chance.'

415

Not much of a chance, it was true, but the Parthian leader felt the need to detach three squadrons – close to a hundred men – to contain Tito's hundred and fifty. A force strong enough to keep the Asturians occupied until they could be destroyed at his leisure. But first he would deal with the men who had thwarted the great conspiracy.

More shouted orders and the blare of the trumpet. The remaining squadrons began to close in at a walk on the twenty or so fighters who now made up Valerius's little group. The Roman risked a glance to where the Sixth remained in place. Surely this would goad Proculus into a decision?

'On my command,' he called, 'we make for the slope; some of us may get through.' Serpentius nodded and relayed the order to his men. They gripped their spears with new strength and acknowledged the order with a throaty growl.

Valerius searched in vain for a weak spot in the ring of Parthian spears. He wrapped the reins tight around his wooden fist and hefted his sword. Whatever happened he would not be taken alive. He scanned the long lines of the Sixth. No way of breaking through and Proculus, whatever his actions so far, would offer no sanctuary. He opened his mouth to give the order.

'Wait, Valerius.' An urgent shout from Serpentius. Something was happening among the Sixth. Valerius could hear Piso shouting and even as he watched a blade flashed in the sunlight and the shouting was replaced by a terrible scream as the young tribune died.

'Look!' Allius, his face a mask of blood, pointed to the southern crest overlooking the valley where a long line of armour glittered in the afternoon sun, soon joined by another and a third. At their centre a group of men on horseback stood beside a standard. Though it was too small to be fully visible Valerius recognized it immediately. An eagle.

'That's a full legion,' Serpentius whispered. 'Where in the gods' name did he find them?'

Valerius was too busy trying to work out the implications of what he was seeing to answer. It felt like a rescue, but even as the thought formed he saw a ripple run through the wall of shields on the ridge line as the long lines of legionaries began to advance. Not towards them. Not against the enemy Valerius had sought out and identified for Gaius Plinius Secundus. But diagonally across the slope in a deliberate, steady march that would bring them against the flank of Tito's ragged band of spearmen. Betrayal? Incompetence? Then it came to him. Pliny had never received his message. This was Vespasian's doing. The Emperor had lost patience and sent a legion to provide Pliny with the military strength to deal with the threat to his gold supplies in Asturica Augusta. But Pliny believed the threat came from Asturian rebels.

'Now!' Valerius kicked his horse into motion. Serpentius took up the cry, urging his riders towards the slope. Both men knew they had only one chance to stop Gaius Plinius Secundus destroying Tito and his men. Someone had to break through to the governor and inform him of his error. And the only person he would listen to was Valerius.

But the same thought had occurred to Claudius Harpocration. He howled at his men to attack.

417

XLIX

Harpocration angled his squadron to cut Valerius off from the hill, but Serpentius called out an order and half Valerius's little force swerved to meet the Parthians head on. Fewer than ten men now accompanied Valerius, but they were brave men and they knew what was required to save their comrades on the plain. They surged ahead to form a protective shield between the one-handed Roman and the Parthian line. Valerius felt a prickle behind his eyes at this conscious act of self-sacrifice. There could only be one outcome in the unequal contest between the Asturians and the professional cavalry. Yet he had no time to mourn them. He sank lower in the saddle, his head between the horse's ears. His only thought must be to make their sacrifice worthwhile. He must stay alive.

A clash of arms and a terrible shriek from behind and to his left. An image of Serpentius, savage, indestructible and indomitable, flitted through his mind before the Parthian line struck the charging Asturians. A long spear spitted the man in front of Valerius like a chicken and plucked him from the saddle. All around, a chaos of screaming ponies and dying men, spurting blood and shattered bone. For a moment he knew he'd failed. He could find no way through and he was surrounded by snarling Parthians and probing spear points. Then he saw it. A dried-up stream bed that split the Parthian line and led to the slope where Gaius Plinius Secundus watched implacably as his legionaries continued their relentless march towards Tito and his doomed Asturian farmers.

Valerius rammed his horse between two milling Parthians. A spear drove at his chest and he parried it upwards, but the shaft clattered against his head, leaving his skull ringing and his senses stunned. Another found its mark and a lightning bolt of agony sliced through his left side, but he was through and urging his mount up the stream bed. The gully twisted and turned, the sides steepening the further he progressed. As he searched desperately for an escape route he could almost feel the Parthian spears reaching out for his back. The clatter of hooves to his rear increased in volume. Soon those below would finish with Allius and the rest and join the pursuit to cut off his flanks.

A cry of triumph from terrifyingly close just as his eyes registered the only possibility of escape, a slope of pink scree slightly shallower than the rest. Valerius swerved the horse without slackening pace, hammering his heels into its ribs and slapping its sweat-foamed flank with his sword. Only a few more paces and he would have made it.

Without warning a huge shadow towered over him and he was thrown from the saddle as a Parthian mount smashed his horse backwards. Valerius landed with bone-cracking force, a bolt of agony in his ribs joining the burning in his side. Jagged stones scraped the side of his face raw as he tumbled head over heels into the stream bed, flailing hooves inches from his face and narrowly missing rocks that would have smashed his brains out. Somehow he clung on to his sword. When he crashed into the stream bed he managed to stagger to his feet, mind reeling and vision blurred. Two Parthians – or was it four? – prodded their spears at his chest. He slashed at the points and backed away. The Parthians laughed and more needle points pricked his back.

A bearded giant in fish scale armour and a green tunic grinned down at him from the saddle. 'Our commander ordered us to take you alive,' he said in a guttural and heavily accented Latin. 'But he did not say you should be undamaged.' To reinforce his words he jabbed his spear point into Valerius's thigh. Valerius cried out and hacked at the shaft with his sword. The wound did no serious damage, but he could feel the blood running down his leg. Another point jabbed into his buttock and he spun to face his laughing attacker. The Parthians could do this until he was bleeding from a dozen wounds and still keep him alive long enough to suffer the torment Claudius Harpocration planned for him. He forced despair from his mind. As long as he could hold his sword they wouldn't take him alive. But the resolution lasted only as long as it took for the ash shaft of an enemy spear to smash down on his wrist. Valerius cried out with frustration as the sword fell from his numbed fingers. His tormentors only laughed all the louder and the ring of spears closed in.

'What is happening here?' The imperious demand came from a tall, mounted figure who appeared at the top of the bank, silhouetted against the sun. Valerius looked up and raised his wooden right hand to shade his eyes. The man cried out in astonishment. 'Valerius? I thought you were dead.'

Valerius had to choke back an outburst of hysterical

laughter. 'I will be unless you can convince these snakes to draw in their fangs, Pliny.'

'Release this man,' Gaius Plinius Secundus snapped. The Parthians looked up in bewilderment at the imposing figure in a legate's armour and scarlet cloak. More mounted figures appeared beside Pliny, the members of his personal guard. 'Put up your spears,' he repeated the command. 'Or you will not live another heartbeat.'

The bearded giant rasped out an order and the ring of leaf-bladed points receded. Valerius scrambled through a gap in the iron and clawed his way up the bank to the governor's side. From here he could see the legionaries continuing their steady march towards Tito's Asturians, who stood in a disorganized huddle by the road. 'Pliny,' he said urgently. 'You must withdraw your men. These are not your enemy. They are.' He pointed to the Parthians on the dusty plain below, and beyond them the two cohorts of the Sixth.

'I don't understand,' Pliny said. 'Those are Roman soldiers.'

'Melanius persuaded them to march on Tarraco. *He* was stealing the Emperor's gold, Pliny. The proof is in the leather sack tied to the saddle of that horse. Melanius is dead and I doubt they'll fight, but you must believe me . . .' His voice failed him for a moment. 'Mars save us. Serpentius!' Only now did he notice that a single conflict still continued among the milling Parthians. Two horses wheeled and circled as their riders fought for position. 'A mount, Pliny. A mount and a sword if you love me as a friend.'

Pliny responded instantly with an order and one of his escort jumped from the saddle and led his horse to where Valerius stood.

'I will call off the attack.' The governor handed

Valerius his own sword. 'Go to Serpentius and stop this bloodshed. Cassito?' he called to the leader of the escort. 'Take ten men and bring me whoever commands the Sixth, by force if necessary.'

Valerius galloped down the slope without waiting for the escort, snarling at any Parthians who blocked his way. A strange listlessness had overcome the bearded cavalrymen as they began to understand the significance of the newly arrived troops and they gave way without protest. Others formed a circle around the battle between the commander who had never lost a fight and the astonishingly swift enemy who had already brought him twice to the brink of defeat. A cry of agony pierced the air as Valerius broke through the Parthian ranks and his heart stopped as he saw Serpentius reel away clutching his stomach. Claudius Harpocration wheeled his horse, sword raised for the death blow. But Valerius's gelding was cavalry-trained and didn't break stride as he drove it chest to shoulder with the Parthian's mount. The impact threw Harpocration clear of the saddle and he scrabbled in the dust to avoid his falling horse.

Valerius dismounted and advanced on his enemy as Harpocration struggled to his feet. A few Parthian spearmen moved to block his way until Cassito and the men of Pliny's escort galloped up and snarled at them to stay clear. Harpocration was clearly suffering from the effects of the contest. His chest heaved beneath the heavy mail of his protective armour and the left arm of his tunic was soaked with blood where Serpentius had cut him at least once. But his eyes glittered with loathing and blood-rage. He moved confidently to meet Valerius's approach.

Any man who wounded Serpentius was a warrior to fear, but Valerius felt the anger growing in him like lava ready to vent. His eyes never leaving his enemy he strode forward with his sword raised and his right side exposed. In battle, Serpentius had always acted as Valerius's shield, or his strong right hand. Now that flank was an invitation to strike.

And Harpocration took it.

The Parthian commander lunged with the speed of a thunderbolt, the point of his sword like a dart aimed at Valerius's unprotected chest. His victory cry rose in his throat, but it remained unfulfilled, because the air rang as Valerius swatted the blade away with a speed and a power that left Harpocration gaping. Before he could react, Valerius hammered his wooden fist at the Parthian's face. Harpocration ducked his head. It was all that saved him because Valerius had deployed the hidden blade and the point would have taken him in the right eye. Instead it was deflected by the iron dome of the Parthian's helmet. Harpocration flailed blindly with the sword, forcing Valerius to step back and winning a moment to recover. But Valerius was back within a heartbeat, the sword in his left hand probing relentlessly at Harpocration's flank and forcing him to parry awkwardly in a move he'd never trained for. Valerius could feel him slow as the strain of the fight with Serpentius continued to take its toll. Claudius Harpocration's muscles were battle honed, but no man could fight for ever.

Harpocration cried out as Valerius's edge added another cut to the one Serpentius had inflicted. Oddly, the shoulder wound seemed to galvanize the Parthian and for a few deadly seconds he hacked at Valerius with renewed strength. For the first time he noticed the blood that streaked Valerius's legs and filled his sandals. A new confidence welled up inside him as he sensed his opponent weakening. Suddenly Valerius's thrusts were less certain and Harpocration knew he had one chance to finish this quickly. He launched a whirlwind attack that tested first right, then left and as his opponent reeled, a final double-handed overhead cut that should have split Valerius from skull to chin. Instead, it met thin air.

Serpentius had taught Valerius that footwork was as important to a swordsman as the blade in his hand. Now Valerius put all the gruelling hours of practice into effect. He spun clear in a pirouette that positioned him for a savage backhand. If it had landed perfectly the blow would have taken the top off Harpocration's skull as if it was an egg. The Parthian managed to sway out of killing range, but the point of the sword scored a bloody line across his eyes.

The Parthian reeled away, shrieking as he realized he was blinded. He clawed at his face with his left hand, but he still had the presence of mind to retain his sword in the right. He staggered backwards, sweeping the blade from side to side in a desperate bid to survive. Valerius disarmed him with an almost casual flick of the sword point and kicked him in the chest so he fell on his back. For a moment he stood over his enemy, breathing hard, staring down at the ruined features of the man who had planned to torture him to death.

In that moment it occurred to him that a life condemned to eternal darkness was what Harpocration deserved. But that was not Gaius Valerius Verrens' way. He lifted the sword and plunged the point into Harpocration's throat with enough force to sever his spine. Blood spurted the length of the blade and the Parthian jerked and flopped like a stranded fish before going still.

Looking down at the dead man, Valerius felt terribly weary, weary unto death. Then he remembered Serpentius.

The Spaniard lay on his back a dozen paces away with Tito kneeling at his side. The younger man had his head bowed as if he was listening. Valerius approached them and Tito looked up, his hatchet face a rictus of anguish and his cheeks wet with tears. Shaking his head, he rose slowly to his feet and walked away.

Valerius took his place, wincing at the dark stain on the Spaniard's tunic; he'd never felt such helplessness and despair. He reached to pull the torn cloth aside but Serpentius's hand came up and his fingers gripped Valerius's wrist so fiercely the Roman thought they would tear the flesh.

'No point.' The former gladiator managed to open his eyes. 'I've killed enough people to know when I'm dead. My sword?'

Valerius reached for the fallen blade and placed it in his friend's hand. 'Hold on,' Valerius whispered. 'Pliny will send his personal *medicus*.' Serpentius closed his eyes and gave a grunt that might have been a laugh. Valerius had always thought of the Spaniard as a big man; now he realized that his size was an illusion created by his strength and his speed and his presence. He bit back the sob that filled his chest and turned it into a cough.

Serpentius's eyes opened again and he stared at Valerius's face as if memorizing it. 'Cold.' The word was so indistinct Valerius almost missed it. The Spaniard let out a long sigh and Valerius had a moment of panic-stricken terror, but the grey eyes brightened a little and the gravel voice rallied. 'You saved me.' A desperate urgency filled Serpentius's words. 'And you freed me. But I was never so free as when I fought by your side.'

His voice faded and he sounded almost puzzled. His final words emerged as one long sigh. 'I'm going home.'

Slowly, the iron grip slackened and the lifeless fingers fell away. When Valerius could bear to look, the Spaniard's grey eyes had already dulled. Gaius Valerius Verrens knelt over the body of Serpentius of Avala, a prince of his tribe, a slave, a gladiator and a friend, and wept.

Historical note

The Valerius books are works of historical fiction,
but I take great pride in ensuring that the historical
foundation for the novels is as sound and accurate
as I can make it. Most are based on recorded events,
such as the Boudiccan rebellion, the Year of the Four
Emperors and the Siege of Jerusalem. *Saviour of Rome*
is different. There's no historical evidence for the large-
scale theft of Roman gold mined in northern Spain in
AD72, or a potential rebellion in the province aimed at
destabilizing and replacing Vespasian. Yet the conditions
existed for just that scenario.

As the historian Suetonius makes clear, the Emperor
Titus Flavius Vespasian faced a financial crisis in
the earliest period of his reign, and this despite the
vast amount of gold booty taken from the Temple of
Jerusalem – the evidence of some of it still visible on
the Arch of Titus in Rome. Partly that will have been
the result of the depredations of the Year of the Four
Emperors – the civil war that raged in the western
part of the Empire in AD69 – when tax revenues would
have been drastically reduced and farming yields
cut. Devastated communities required to be rebuilt;

Vespasian's son Domitian famously handed out money to pay for the rebuilding of Cremona, which had been razed to the ground by his father's troops under Marcus Antonius Primus. There was also the expensive matter of reconstructing the Temple of Jupiter on the Capitoline Hill, burned down, by accident or design, when the Emperor's brother and Flavian loyalists took refuge there from the troops of Aulus Vitellius. Worse, the profligate spending of Emperor Nero, whose death by suicide ignited the civil war, had left the Empire close to bankruptcy. Silver and gold coins minted during the latter years of his rule contained up to fifteen per cent less bullion than their face value suggested. Vespasian needed money to pay his troops and the Praetorian Guard, or he wouldn't be Emperor for long, for regular handouts of bread to keep the mob happy, and to build the great monuments, like the amphitheatre that people would come to know as the Colosseum, without which his reign would be regarded as irrelevant. He needed the Spanish goldfields producing at full capacity.

Yet the war, and the Batavian revolt on the Rhine frontier which paralleled it, had left Hispania denuded of troops. A few cohorts of legionaries were scattered across the country to provide security for the mines, the storehouses, and the convoys that carried the gold on the first leg of its journey to the Treasury in Rome. Vespasian had shown he wasn't impressed by the Rhine legions by disbanding two and refusing to re-establish others that had been wiped out. He couldn't trust those which had followed Vitellius, and the two generals who had won him the Empire were now deadly rivals with ambitions of their own.

One person he did trust was Gaius Plinius Secundus, better known to history as the naturalist, historian and all-round polymath, Pliny the Elder. Pliny's writings show he undoubtedly spent time in Spain, probably during the period Valerius is there, and it's believed he was governor of Hispania Tarraconensis. He amassed an encyclopedic knowledge of the country's plant and animal life, its geology, and the tribes and sub-tribes who inhabited its various regions, including Asturia. More importantly for me, he also left behind a wonderfully detailed treatise on Roman gold-mining techniques in Spain, and the terrible conditions the miners endured, which is well worth reading.

It was more difficult to find the detail that would allow me to paint an accurate picture of Serpentius's people, but they've left enigmatic clues in the wonderful gold work they produced before the Romans came, and the remains of the stone *castros* – small defended settlements – that litter the hills of Asturia. What is clear is that in the aftermath of the Cantabrian Wars, when Augustus was forced to send no less than eight legions against them, the survivors were driven from their homes and forced to live in Roman-ruled settlements where they could provide labour for the mines that would provide the Empire's gold.

The best evidence for what happened next, and the incredible destructive power of *ruina montium*, is provided by the World Heritage Site at Las Medulas. Great swathes of the mountains have been quite literally torn apart in the search for gold, to leave a stunning, almost Martian vista. The effect is awe-inspiring and if you're in the area it shouldn't be missed.

As Pliny says, an emperor's favour is not to be disdained, but being an intimate of the Imperial family seems to have brought Valerius nothing but trouble. Yet Vespasian, pragmatic, self-deprecating, efficient and decisive, was exactly what Rome needed after Nero and the upheaval of civil war. He was ably assisted by his son, Titus, and, possibly, by Titus's brother Domitian, whose reputation I probably do no favours in these books. But every hero needs a nemesis, and I doubt Domitian is finished with Valerius yet.

Britannia awaits, rekindling long-forgotten memories and providing further opportunities for glory with the campaigns of Julius Agricola . . . but the ghosts of the past are stirring.

Glossary

Aedile – a magistrate responsible for the upkeep of public buildings, streets, aqueducts and sewers.

Ala milliaria – A reinforced auxiliary cavalry wing, normally between 700 and 1,000 strong. In Britain and the west the units would be a mix of cavalry and infantry, in the east a mix of spearmen and archers.

Ala quingenaria – Auxiliary cavalry wing normally composed of 500 auxiliary horsemen.

Aquilifer – The standard-bearer who carried the eagle of the legion.

As – A small copper coin worth approx. a fifth of a sestertius.

Asturica Augusta – Modern Astorga, provincial capital of the Roman gold-mining region of Hispana Tarraconensis.

Atriensis – A freed slave who acted as a major-domo with responsibility for running a Roman household.

Aureus (pl. Aurei) – Valuable gold coin worth twenty-five denarii.

Auxiliary – Non-citizen soldiers recruited from the provinces as light infantry or for specialist tasks, e.g. cavalry, slingers, archers.

Batavians – Members of a powerful Germanic tribe which lived in the area of the Rhine delta, now part of the Netherlands. Traditionally provided auxiliary units for the Roman Empire in return for relief from tribute and taxes.

Beneficiarius – A legion's record keeper or scribe.

Braccae – Woollen trousers of Celtic origin favoured by auxiliary units and sometimes worn by legionaries in cold climates.

Caligae – Sturdily constructed, reinforced leather sandals worn by Roman soldiers. Normally with iron-studded sole.

Castro – a small, walled mountain settlement of circular stone buildings in northern Hispania.

Century – Smallest tactical unit of the legion, numbering eighty men.

Cohort – Tactical fighting unit of the legion, normally contained six centuries, apart from the elite First cohort, which had five double-strength centuries (800 men).

Consul – One of two annually elected chief magistrates of Rome, normally appointed by the people and ratified by the Senate.

Contubernium – Unit of eight soldiers who shared a tent or barracks.

Cornicen – Legionary signal trumpeter who used an instrument called a *cornu*.

Decurion – A junior officer in a century, or a troop commander in a cavalry unit.

Denarius (pl. Denarii) – A silver coin.

Domus – The house of a wealthy Roman, e.g. Nero's Domus Aurea (Golden House).

Duovir (pl. Duoviri) – One of two men in charge of the Ordo, the council of a hundred leading citizens responsible for the smooth running of a Roman town.

Duplicarius – Literally 'double pay man'. A senior legionary with a trade or an NCO.

Equestrian – Roman knightly class.

Flammeum – The veil a Roman bride wore at her wedding ceremony.

Fortuna – The goddess of luck and good fortune.

Frumentarii – Messengers who carried out secret duties for the Emperor, possibly including spying and assassination.

Garum – The ubiquitous and pungent Roman condiment made from the fermented blood and intestines of fish, mainly anchovies. Allec was the sediment left after the garum was filtered off. It was sometimes used for medicinal purposes.

Gladius (pl. Gladii) – The short sword of the legionary. A lethal killing weapon at close quarters.

Governor – Citizen of senatorial rank given charge of a province. Would normally have a military background (see **Proconsul**).

Hispania Tarraconensis – Roman province covering a large part of what is now Spain.

Jupiter – Most powerful of the Roman gods, often referred to as Optimus Maximus (greatest and best).

Lanista – owner, manager and trainer of gladiators or operator of a ludus, a gladiator school.

Legate – The general in charge of a legion. A man of senatorial rank.

Legatus iuridicus – The Emperor's legal representative in a Roman province, second in line only to the governor or proconsul.

Legio – Modern Léon, northern Spain, originally a Roman legionary fortress.

Legion – Unit of approximately 5,000 men all of whom would be Roman citizens.

Lictor – Bodyguard of a Roman magistrate. There were strict limits on the numbers of lictors associated with different ranks.

Lituus – Curved trumpet used to transmit cavalry commands.

Lusitania – The Roman province which covered a territory now southern Portugal and part of western Spain.

Manumission – The act of freeing a slave.

Mars – The Roman god of war.

Mithras – An Eastern god popular among Roman soldiers.

Nomentan – A superior variety of Roman wine, mentioned by Martial in his *Epigrams*.

Orbis – Circular defensive position practised by the legions.

Ordo – The council of a hundred leading citizens responsible for the smooth running of a Roman town.

Phalera (pl. Phalerae) – Awards won in battle worn on a legionary's chest harness.

Pilum (pl. Pila) – Heavy spear carried by a Roman legionary.

Praefectus metallorum – The prefect in charge of the mining administration of a Roman province.

Praetorian Guard – Powerful military force stationed in Rome. Accompanied the Emperor on campaign, but could be of dubious loyalty and were responsible for the overthrow of several Roman rulers.

Prefect – Auxiliary cavalry commander.

Primus Pilus – 'First File'. The senior centurion of a legion.

Principia – Legionary headquarters building.

Proconsul – Governor of a Roman province, such as Spain or Syria, and of consular rank.

Procurator – Civilian administrator subordinate to a governor.

Quaestor – Civilian administrator in charge of finance.

Ruina Montium – Highly destructive Roman gold-mining technique documented by Pliny the Elder.

Scutum (pl. Scuta) – The big, richly decorated curved shield carried by a legionary.

Senator – Patrician member of the Senate, the key political institution which administered the Roman Empire. Had to meet strict financial and property rules and be at least thirty years of age.

Sestertius (pl. Sestertii) – Roman brass coin worth a quarter of a **denarius**.

Signifer – Standard bearer who carried the emblem of a cohort or century.

Spatha – The heavy sword used by Roman auxiliary cavalry. Longer than the legionary's gladius.

Stola – Long pleated dress worn by a married Roman woman over her *tunica intima*, or slip.

Testudo – Literally 'tortoise'. A unit of soldiers with shields interlocked for protection.

Tribune – One of six senior officers acting as aides to a Legate. Often, but not always, on short commissions of six months upwards.

Tribunus laticlavius – Literally 'broad stripe tribune'. The most senior of a legion's military tribunes.

Urban cohorts – Force founded by Augustus to combat the power of the Praetorian Guard, used for policing large mobs and riot-control duties.

Vascones – Roman auxiliaries from a tribe inhabiting northern Spain. Gave their name to the Basque region.

Vexillation – A detachment of a legion used as a temporary task force on independent duty.

Victimarius – Servant who delivers and attends to the victim of a sacrifice.

Victory – Roman goddess equivalent to the Greek Nike.
Vigiles – Force responsible for the day-to-day policing of
Rome's streets and fire prevention and fighting.

Acknowledgements

I'm grateful to my editor Simon Taylor and his team at Transworld for helping me make *Saviour of Rome* the book it is, and to my agent Stan, of Jenny Brown Associates in Edinburgh, for all his advice and encouragement. As always, my wife Alison and my children, Kara, Nikki and Gregor, have been the rocks on which this book has been built. And no acknowledgement would be complete without mention of my beautiful new granddaughter Lily who has brought a different and very special kind of joy into my life. Foremost among the many important sources for research which allowed me to recreate life in Roman Spain were a study on *Configuring the landscape: Roman mining in the conventus Asturum* by Guillermo S. Reher, Lourdes López-Merino, Javier Sánchez-Palencia and Antonio López-Sáez, *Roman gold mining in north-west Spain* by P. R. Lewis and G. D. B. Jones, *Mines, territorial organization and social structure in Northern Spain* by Almudena Orejas and Javier Sánchez-Palencia and *Recent archaeological research at Asturica Augusta* by Victorino Garcia Marcos and Julio Encinas.

Douglas Jackson's Rome series, featuring Gaius Valerius Verrens

HERO OF ROME

AD 60 and the warrior Queen Boudicca prepares to lead the tribes to war. Facing them are tribune Gaius Valerius Verrens and the veterans of Colonia.

DEFENDER OF ROME

Tasked with the defence of Nero's Rome, Gaius Valerius Verrens knows the price of failure is high.

AVENGER OF ROME

Given a terrible mission by Nero, Gaius Valerius Verrens must decide whether to obey his orders or risk the emperor's wrath.

SWORD OF ROME

AD 68. In the wake of the death of Nero, Gaius Valerius Verrens is caught in the chaos and bloodshed of civil war.

ENEMY OF ROME

AD 69. Wrongly accused of cowardice and awaiting execution, Gaius Valerius Verrens is suddenly offered a reprieve. But there is a catch . . .

SCOURGE OF ROME

Saved from death but banished from Rome, Gaius Valerius Verrens heads east, into the heart of the savage Judean uprising.

SAVIOUR OF ROME

Vespasian now sits upon the imperial throne and sends Gaius Valerius Verrens to find out who is stealing the Empire's gold. And eliminate them.

All available in paperback and ebook.